by

Daniel D Longdon

To Leane

Best Wishes

Daniel D Longdon

GINGERNUT BOOKS Ltd

www.gingernutbooks.co.uk

First Published in 2011
By GINGERNUT BOOKS LTD

Cataloguing in Publication Data is available from the British Library

ISBN 978-1-907939-07-5

GINGERNUT BOOKS LTD
Head Office
27 Sotheby Ave
Sutton-in-Ashfield NG17 5JU

www.gingernutbooks.co.uk

Special thanks

I would like to thank all the people that have had to put up with constant reminders that I have written a book, I'm sure they've had enough of me by now. Thanks must also go to Steve Wylde for saving the second draft of Devastation from a knackered hard drive, John Henry for his fantastic artwork, Clive Thompson for giving me his printer and all the staff at Gingernut books for their excellent input, especially Trevor and Michelle Gent, without their expertise I would never have gotten this far.

The most thanks however must go to my lady, during the past two years since I started writing my story Emma Fox has been the driving force behind my writing, she has been my proof reader and consultant throughout and I hope she realises how much she is loved.

Prologue

Planet Earth - a shadowed husk of lifeless rock void of air, the atmosphere long gone, blasted out into space.

Earth – a tragedy, a distant star that no longer shone in the night sky, its supernova ending had reshaped the cosmos in a wide area.

Earth's second and artificial moon, Station One was a huge ball of metal that spun in Earth's orbit. Its lights switched off, its power source dead after millennia of abandonment.

A small ship took a turn around the man-made satellite; the box shaped craft fired its thrusters and maintained its position. As he found the docking port, the pilot considered his options, fearing what horrors awaited those who dared to venture aboard.

His fear defeated his avarice and instead he found himself looking towards the Earth, the salvage rights for the potential for scrap not worth the trouble, either imaginary or rumoured.

As the shields on his ship lowered again, sealing the cabin inside their protection from radiation and who knew what else, he lifted the visor of his silver suit and he checked his schedule.

Soon the earth would breathe again, brought back to life by the Planetary Techs. They would use their designer Terraform Technologies as they had on hundreds of worlds before The Great Ending - the cataclysm that destroyed the world and with it hundreds of billions of humans - and brought about the end of mankind's greatest age.

As he sped away from the space station, the pilot smiled.

The salvage craft left the moon's minor gravitational pull and he adjusted his velocity. He took a look at the Earth's natural moon, born out of the same stuff as mother Earth billions of years ago.

Then the banks of blinking lights before him resumed the normal running sequences and everything else was quiet once more and the tiny surveyor blinked only once in thirty seconds to show that it was operational.

Before The Great Ending, many of the designer planets had been created to mirror that of earth, artificially Terraformed worlds adjusted to suit the biology of man. Like Earth, most had been destroyed, only a few beyond the range of annihilation had escaped. And a very few, on the very fringes of the shock wave, had escaped with their life-forms intact, if not their technologies.

Keltica was one such planet and over the centuries of darkness it had clawed its way back from the brink. Its human population no longer travelled to the stars, but they looked skyward and dreamed and they told their stories as myths whilst they created a new history.

The defunct artificial moon was an indistinct smudge in the sky and the salvage craft was invisible from Keltica – even if anyone had been looking for such a sight.

Devastation

The gloom of dusk had quickly become night as Jason de Silva travelled home. As night fell, the eerie glow from Albion, the planet's third moon made the vehicle's headlights obsolete.

'I'm not crazy, I'm not crazy, I'm not', he said over and over inside his own head. He was breathing heavily as he drove his personal vehicle along the dark country road. "I'm not nuts, just ordinary." The words spoken out loud seemed to bring him back to reality.

Jason de Silva often thought of the past and kicked himself for his earlier indiscretions, he knew he should have no regrets but his mind always rode along on a gentle but turbulent wave of madness. It happened most often when he was alone. Desperate to appear normal, he tried to behave how everyone expected him to.

Estendale lay before him, the street lights of his home town were turned off, a non-requirement on the bright night.

Jason crossed the town borderline only yards from his home, he felt fortunate to live only a stone's throw from the countryside.

As Jason pulled onto the driveway, he saw the light from the living room make entrancing silhouettes of his wife's form dance on the wall. As he opened the vehicle's door, the chill breeze gripped at his flesh and he pulled his coat from the passenger seat and wrapped it tight around him, even though the door was just a few steps away.

Jason leaned down and kissed his wife as she met him at the back door, his tall well muscled figure dwarfed her petite frame even as she rose up on her toes to offer her lips for him to kiss.

"Hey babe," Jason smiled as he pulled away from her.

"How was training?" Jacky asked and she watched Jason as he moved around her. By the glow that had risen on her cheeks and the light in her eyes, it was obvious that she was still attracted to him even after all their years of marriage.

"All good, did the kids go to bed okay?" he asked lowering himself into a chair to lean on the kitchen table. He looked at her as she moved around the kitchen and took the opportunity to relax his tired muscles for a moment.

Jason de Silva was a student of the Albion Fighting Arts and for some years he had attended local classes, honing and improving his skills. Jacky never fully understood why Jason insisted on training in something "You are never going to use." "You never know when it'll be needed," was always his reply.

They retired to the living room; she carried the bottle of wine and the glasses. They enjoyed the chance of spending an easy evening in front of the fire, chatting about the day's events. Then, as usual after a heavy training session, they went to bed early.

The following morning was the same as always for the de Silva family.

Jacky left for work in the vehicle, leaving Jason to take care of their two young children Louis and Hector. Louis, aged six, attended school not far from the family home. After Jason and Hector had taken Louis to school, they would return home to housework and the usual stuff. Jason didn't mind pushing Hector's buggy but he did get a little bored with the 'Same old, same old'.

It was a labour of love which Jason didn't mind doing. The love for his family being one of the few things that helped him neutralize a lot of the crazy thought processes which plagued his daily routine.

At around midday Hector was sprawled on the sofa, and fell asleep watching his favourite television show. Jason made himself a cup of coffee, sat down next to the sleeping toddler and changed the channel on the television.

"Yet again the move by the Monarchy has greatly angered the government. The question on everyone's mind is when will the rioters stop their fighting?" The pretty news reporter paused as the screen behind her flashed up images of Skavites being driven back by armed forces wearing the King's 'Five Moons' emblem. "The King's herald was quick to criticise the government and their inability to put down the criminals who take up arms against the state." The woman paused again as the screen flashed to a new image.

The Prime Minister, Peter Dickinson's jowls shook in his fury. The man who had come to be known as 'Fat Power' fumed as he raged on about conflicts of interest and stepping beyond the spheres of legality.

"Doom and gloom," Jason muttered as he turned the television off. "That's enough of that. Things will be better for you my son," he looked down at his youngest child. "The King will see to that."

"Come on young en, time to fetch your brother." Jason said later as he prepared the boy for fetching his older brother at the end of the school day. Jason reached down and scooped the toddler up as Hector's little arms reached out for his father.

Jason strapped Hector into his pushchair and left the house, it was a short walk to Louis' school. Spring was just around the corner, but the air was still fresh and they were wrapped up against the biting winter air.

They were about half way to the school, still within sight of their front door and Jason saw that two Skavs were leaving his neighbours - the Smith's - home by the front door, their hoods up over their heads.

"All right lads?" Jason said, polite enough, but he thought to himself *Tossers.*

They shot Jason dirty looks and left the garden path, walking away from him. Jason didn't really care, all he wanted was to live in peace and be left alone.

They arrived at the school a few minutes before the bell that declared the end of the school day sounded. The day was a bitter one, Jason had underestimated how cold it had dropped. '*It might snow later, make a snow man with the boys, that'll be fun*' he thought as the doors opened.

Louis was the last child out; he was skinny, like most boys his age, but smaller than the average. His little fingers were lost inside the large hands of the teacher that accompanied him. Louis's eyes were puffed up and swollen, his left eye was almost closed and black and purple bruising surrounded his eye socket. His face was wet as the boy was still crying.

"Mr de Silva, I'm so sorry. Would you like to come inside?" Mrs Crawley, Louis's tutor was very concerned; Jason couldn't tell yet if it was concern for Louis or for his own reaction. Louis looked up at her then to his father then back to her.

"What's happened? Look at his face," Jason struggled to find his words. He was fully aware of all the mothers that had paused to listen. He didn't care for their gossip or their politics and didn't care who listened to what had to be said. Jason stood to his full height, as he felt anger at the sight of his little blonde haired boy.

"Tell me, now." Jason felt himself grimace, trying to keep his voice under control.

"Louis got into a fight and this is the result." She waved a hand in the little boy's direction as though she thought that she needed to show Jason where the problem lay. "I can assure you that the matter has been dealt with in-house," Mrs Crawley managed to retain her composure, speaking in that matter of fact fashion that all teachers seemed to inherit with the job.

"What action has been taken?" Jason demanded, he raised his voice so all around could hear. "Who was the other boy? This just isn't acceptable."

"The other boy has been sent home for the day. I can assure you Mr de Silva, the other boy has had a stern talking to." Mrs Crawley raised her voice to match his.

Parent and teacher faced off to each other, the challenge was apparent but unspoken. Jason opened his mouth to speak, and then he clamped his mouth shut. Mrs Crawley folded her arms beneath her chest, her lips thinned as the old lady awaited Jason's next outburst.

The outburst never came. Jason thought of his son and he turned to his injured boy. "You okay son?" he asked.

"No," he wailed and buried his face in his father's coat and sobbed uncontrollably.

"Mr de Silva, I must say I don't like the tone in your voice," Mrs Crawley was annoyed and now looked for confrontation that she had wanted to avoid when she thought that that was what Jason was there for.

"Mrs Crawley, it isn't your child that's been battered," his voice calmed as he stroked his injured child, "I mean look at that bruising," Jason turned the push chair and his back on the teacher and the school. *'Before I say something I'll regret'* he thought.

After leaving the school grounds Jason slowed, turning to his son he tried his best to smile, "Who did this to you son?" Jason's tone was gentle although he did not feel gentle inside.

"It was Charlie Smith, dad," Louis had stopped crying, he looked at the floor as he walked along. Hector looked up at his older brother from his pushchair, he gurgled and cooed and was not at all concerned, he was still at an age where he could not yet understand.

They walked along in silence, looking like any other father and sons wrapped up against the chill of winters end.

Inside though, Jason was a tempest, angry to the core. *'No son of mine is being treated this way, not while I have a hole in my arse.'* he thought as the anger within built even higher.

Turning the corner onto their road, the Smith family home came into full view. Though to Jason it was more like a cesspit than an actual family home, the front yard was beyond unkempt, it was a wreck. Whilst other homes on the street had neat lawns and tidy borders, their front was a scrap yard filled with rusting vehicles and household appliances. Jason could see Old Ma Smith, her huge bulk making the fence bend as she leaned on it. She was talking with her neighbour, their heads close. Old Ma Smith was a huge woman, she defied the laws of nature as she walked, which surprisingly, she did as briskly as someone half her size.

'*Must remain calm, just have a chat about it, sort it out*' he thought as he approached and he tried to keep a calm facade but the anger that welled inside must have shown on Jason's face as he approached the two women.

Old Ma Smith's cheeks were sucked shallow as her impressive and grotesque bulk heaved up off the fence. The old woman folded her arms beneath her huge bosom and faced Jason.

"You got a problem de Silva?" the woman that resembled a fat greasy sow spat the words and she grinned, her one lonesome tooth glinted as her grin made Old Ma Smith even uglier, if that were possible.

"I think we best have a word Mrs Smith, can we keep it cordial? There's no need for any nastiness." Jason tried to tone his voice down, but his trembling body gave his mood away.

"All I see is a tosser and I don't have anything to say to you. I don't care for you de Silva, or your type, thinking ye better than me an' my boys," Old Ma Smith sneered as the front door opened. Standing in the open doorway was a group of thugs. They all wore the unofficial uniform of black tracksuit and peak cap adopted by the rebellious ne'er do wells of late.

"'Nuff said, jog on." The eldest boy jerked his head as

instruction for the direction Jason should follow. The open aggression and heavy disdain in his voice was obvious.

Jason looked down at Louis; fear had brought tears to well up in the little boy's eyes. Jason then looked in the push chair, its occupant had fallen asleep and Hector looked so peaceful in the midst of the animosity. Thoughts invaded his mind, giving him cause to re-think his plan to come to some sort of peaceable arrangement.

'Think of the boy. How many of them are in that house? Don't be a coward.' All manner of conflicting thoughts and advice raced through Jason de Silva's mind but he turned and walked away. '*At least say something!*' His mind screamed Jason's last thought as he pushed the push chair home, the laughter from the Skavites mocking him for a coward.

Storming into his kitchen, Jason slammed the door, shutting off the world from him and his children. He had to take a moment to calm himself before he removed Louis's coat and shoes. Jason forced a smile, he crouched down holding his son by the shoulders, "It don't look so bad, you'll heal in no time at all."

"Dad," Louis looked into his father's eyes, "Why did you let them laugh at you?"

"Go upstairs and play," Jason managed to say gently, at the same time, he felt the shame of a coward. Even his little boy had noticed! "How could I?' he thought, as he watched his young lad walk from the room, his head hung low.

Jason looked at hector, still fast asleep in his push chair. He removed the toddler and placed him on the sofa, "I did the right thing," he muttered aloud.

Jason looked out of the kitchen window and down the lawn; he shook with shame and was close to tears. '*All those years of training'* he thought, '*maybe Jacky was right all along*'.

Two hours passed quickly, Jason slowly calmed and Louis began to act as if nothing had happened, he bravely smiled, trying to please his father.

Then as night fell and with the sky hidden behind a blanket of dark clouds, Jacky pulled onto the driveway. She stepped out of the car and pulled her long, thick winter coat about her. Then she recovered her briefcase from the boot of their family vehicle and headed around the side of the house.

Jason's heart missed a beat as the door opened. *'How do I explain this one away?'* He wondered.

"Darling, are you there?" Jacky called out, as she entered the house.

As she came into his line of sight she smiled, a perfectly formed grin that always melted his heart.

"You had a good day?" he asked.

"Bit hectic, busy with new policies," Jacky put her brief case down, removed her coat and holding onto the chair, she removed her knee high boots.

"You can leave them on," Jason joked.

Jacky smiled again and walked over to him. She put her arms around his waist and snuggled her head to his chest, "You're always so warm," she murmured.

"Darling," he pulled away from her, "I don't want to worry you, but I've got something to say."

Jacky's smile faltered and she gave him a worried look.

"It's Louis, he's fine..." Jason didn't have chance to finish what he wanted to say, Jacky pulled free of Jason and was through the door at a run and onto the stairs before he had time. Jason went into the kitchen and by the time he'd poured two glasses of wine and sat at the kitchen table, Jacky had reappeared.

She looked vacant as she sat down at the kitchen table. Staring across at Jason her face screwed up, her beauty twisted in her distress. "Have you seen our poor boys face?" Jacky sobbed, as Jason reached over and took her hands in his.

"They say they dealt with it! The teachers, I'm not too impressed with their version of dealing with anything. It was that Smith boy, Charlie. I tried to speak with the fat cow, Old Ma Smith but all I got was abuse," Jason explained.

"Well the school is governed by rules, there's not a lot they can do," Jacky wiped her eyes, her makeup smudged by her fingers.

"Political correctness be damned, they should cane the little bastard," Jason slammed a fist into the table, as he bellowed in complaint. "And that bloated bitch, with that pack of thieves, scroungers and idiots. There's no point talking to them, they'll never listen," Jason ended his tirade, his lungs felt emptied as he struggled to finish. Jacky didn't seem to hear him as he ranted.

"My poor little boy," Jacky sighed, after a few minutes of silence, Jason was just glad that her tears were no longer falling, he agreed with her but just nodded.

"So what should we do?" Jason asked, as he sipped at his wine.

"For a start, you can rein your anger in. It'll blow over and they'll be mates next week, I'll bet." Jacky made the observation and Jason knew they were wise words. "I'll get dinner on," she added, forcing a smile as she tried to change the mood.

After their meal, the kids were put to bed. Jason drew the curtains and made the room a little cosier, trying to settle down to relax as usual. Jacky made a cup of tea for them both and Jason sat on the sofa, flicking through the channels on the television.

"Well he doesn't seem too bad now," Jacky called from the kitchen, trying not to raise her voice. She entered the living room, with two steaming cups, "He doesn't appear to be upset at all."

"Yeah, but what's going through the lad's head. I've decided, he can start training with me and learn how to defend himself," Jason looked at Jacky waiting for her protest.

"I still think he's too young," Jacky replied, looking back at him from under her eyebrows. She didn't believe violence could

picking at them. He sat on Jason's wall, his hands together, his elbows resting on his knees as he rocked back and forth, laughing.

There was only one amongst them that bothered Jason; he was the eldest Smith brother. His name was Reggie Smith and unlike the others, he was well built and muscular, he was the only one that looked like he could fight. Reggie stood behind Tommy with his arms crossed and his legs slightly parted. He was nicknamed the Jackal and if the gang had a leader, then he was it. The other gang members were lads that Jason knew from the local area, but didn't know their names.

"What ya doin lads?" Jason strode towards them, his body language important if he was to get out of this without a scuffle.

Curtains twitched along the stretch of street as the neighbours watched. None came to offer Jason any support but Jason didn't expect any.

"What you fakin doin, disrespectin ye betters, ya soz hard bastard?" Tommy grinned.

"Respec'," another youth yelled, offering Tommy his fist as a sign of respect.

Tommy smiled showing his fist in return, which he did with all the pomp of a ritual that perhaps signified some childish rite of passage.

"Listen lads, I've not been disrespectful to anyone, just looking after my child. What would you do if it was Charlie that was battered and bruised?" Jason was surprised they let him say so much; maybe they might listen to reason after all.

"Not going to happen de Silva," Reggie rasped through gritted teeth, puffing out his chest.

"Ya shouldn't let ya boy be pussy!" A skinny youth yelled from the rear and his mates joined in with his laughter.

"Innit," Julian smith smiled.

Jason knew that the language was their own style of slang that they were speaking and he kind of knew what they were saying but he also knew the threats that were held in the words.

Reggie started clenching and unclenching his fists, "You threatening our bro?" he stepped forward and from the corner of his eye, Jason saw Julian heft a half brick.

Jason lifted his arms, his hands outstretched, as if to ward off a blow.

"Pussy man!" Julian shouted, as he threw the brick at the house.

Everything in Jason's mind slowed down, his head seemed to take an age to turn, and he watched the brick fly toward his house. It hit the living room window, the glass exploded in a shower of shards. Jacky had raised her arms too late as the brick and glass hit her face. Jason watched as Jacky disappeared, she fell down behind the window sill. He watched, his mouth agape, as flecks of Jacky's blood, flew from where her face had been.

Sound flooded back into his ears, as time returned to normal speed and he crashed back into real time. The world seemed somehow darker and sharper to his vision and a thousand emotions came together, as the rushing sound of a chaotic gale blasted his senses. The whip cracked, the air went red. An uncontrollable maelstrom of frenzied berserker rage had been released. In a moment his demeanour had transformed, he cracked, his temper exploded and he sprang into action.

Jason charged down his garden path, Reggie and the Smith gang surged toward him. Tommy, who was still in front of his brother, was propelled down the path towards Jason. Tommy's face was a horrified mask of terror as Jason's fist drove into it. Tommy dropped and disappeared beneath the feet of onrushing gang.

The second to receive Jason's fist was a hoodlum that he had exchanged pleasantries with on a number of occasions as they passed in the street. "Bastard," the lad yelled, as he punched Jason on the side of the head. Jason felt his head shake from the blow but felt no pain as his right hook connected with the Skav's nose. The Skav's face was instantly transformed into a bloodied mess and the lad drew back falling past his gang mates.

Hard and fast, a fist hammered into Jason's jaw, Jason didn't feel a thing in his enraged state. There were no thoughts of self preservation; it was all about the next target.

It was Reggie that had landed the blow; Jason smiled as another fist came from the other direction. Jason ducked beneath the flailing arm and pushing his bulk behind the force, he landed a perfect upper cut delivered to the chin of Julian Smith. Julian's head snapped back from the blow and then he went down to twitch in agony on the ground. His mouth was trying to work an almost silent scream, his broken jaw not responding to his brain's commands as it should.

"De Silva, I'm gonna do you proper!" The Jackal leapt forward snarling.

Jason de Silva's reverse punch landed with such power, utilising all of his rage and focussing it in one motion at a single point. Reggie's forward momentum ended there, as the bone crushing blow sent him reeling backwards.

Reggie's gang fled. They abandoned their leader and left him to his fate at the hands of the besieged. Five youths ran off, one nursing a blooded broken nose and all with varying degrees of damage.

Tommy crawled on all fours, Jason watched as he reached the end of the drive.

Julian lay staring at the stars, his injuries causing his body to go into shock. Reggie lay on the lawn, his blood pooled under him from an open wound in the back of his head. His eyes closed and then Reggie was still.

Jacky ran out the house, her face a mask of pain. Blood streaked her blonde hair and ran freely across her face, smeared where she had wiped it from her eyes as she ran.

"Are you all right?" Jacky was hysterical, she almost screamed the question.

Jason began to calm at the sound of Jacky's voice, the temporary psychosis left him feeling strangely calm in the wake of its passing.

"I think so, but what about you?" he asked, looking at his hands. Then up at the starry sky. Cerise, Albion's closest of its five moons glimmered dark red, a shade that paralleled his mood.

"I'll be fine, just a few cuts. That brick hit my arm not my head," Jacky tried to smile as she looked into his eyes. "It was the shards of glass that cut my head, it's not as bad as it seems. I promise."

Howling police sirens came into earshot as Jacky buried her bleeding face in Jason's side. Moments later they came into view, as the local residents began emptying onto the street. Louis ran out the back door, sprinting to his father as fast as he could, tears streaming down his little face.

Tommy got to his feet, taking off in the direction of his home. He passed his mother who was barrelling down the road as fast as she could propel her massive bulk.

"Nice one Jason!" A neighbour shouted.

"I got it all on film!" Another yelled.

Blue flashing lights came into view, pulling up just as Old Ma Smith reached the end of the driveway.

"You bastard!" Old Ma Smith screeched, she cursed like a wild eyed banshee.

The first two police constables on the scene had to subdue the screeching woman. Old Ma Smith tried in vain to get at Jason, who grinned and gave her a cheeky wink. That further infuriated her and she redoubled her efforts to get past the policemen that restrained her.

More Emergency vehicles pulled in, their brakes squealed as they came to a sharp halt. The local police Sergeant, Bernard Willis approached Jason. "Who'd have thought it, the Skavite troubles coming here." he said, as he rolled his heavy shoulders.

Bernard Willis was a massive man, whose bulk and impressive muscular physique, made Jason look small. His long, bushy moustaches twitched as he spoke and he gave the impression that he was one man you didn't want to cross.

"Mr de Silva," Bernard's deep voice sounded from beneath his moustache, "What's happened here then lad?" he stepped over Reggie, who still lay prone on the ground.

"They attacked my house, hurt the Mrs." Jason spoke calmly to the police Sergeant and he nodded towards Jacky to show her injuries. He looked at the Smith boys, who had returned and were getting treated by medics. Then his glance wandered to Old Ma Smith, who still shouted insults. Four policemen were now struggling to contain her flailing arms.

Jacky disappeared inside the house, to check on the baby who'd slept through the whole chaotic episode. Jason looked at two constables; they were busy writing statements from witnesses, who were falling over each other to give their accounts.

One of the neighbours was holding a video camera, "It's all on here." he was saying, he was excited that he'd managed to catch it all.

"Am I in trouble?" Jason asked, as he lifted Louis off the ground.

"I don't know yet lad." Sergeant Bernard walked past Jason. "Shall we go inside? I wouldn't want to air your dirty laundry in public."

Sergeant Bernard walked into Jason's kitchen without waiting for an invite. He had few manners and never smiled. Jacky appeared, took one look at Sergeant Bernard and took Louis from Jason to disappear upstairs without a backwards glance.

"Get the kettle on lad, coffee, black," He sat at the kitchen table and only then did he remove his helmet and placed it in front of him. Another policeman entered the house as Jason turned the kettle on. He was half the size of the giant sat at Jason's table, and looked a little flustered.

"Fuck me Sarge; they had to sedate that fat slag in the end." The constable grinned, secretly happy that the Smith clan had taken a beating.

"Oh no you didn't Mr West," Sergeant Bernard said, shooting the constable a menacing glare.

"Sorry Sarge," the constable had the decency to blush.

"Coffee?" Jason asked.

"White two sugars please." The constable replied.

Jason busied himself making the coffees and the two policemen waited patiently at the kitchen table. After he'd placed the mugs in front of the policemen, he sat opposite Sergeant Bernard.

"I'm Constable West." The man took no time in introducing himself, "I need to take a statement."

Jason took a sip of coffee from his mug, "Do you want to do it here, or down the station?" Jason asked after he'd swallowed.

Constable West produced some papers, from a folder he'd brought with him.

"Shall we start from the beginning then?" West asked, adopting a businesslike manner.

"There's nothing to tell really, my house was attacked by a group of thugs. I defended my home and my family after they started throwing bricks and smashing windows. Jacky, my wife was injured as I tried to reason with them. It was at that point I defended my self and my family. That's all there is to tell." Jason sat back in his chair, happy with the explanation of his version of events.

"You got angry enough to attack a group of teenagers?" Constable West asked.

"If you mean that group of lawless bastards that attacked my house, then yes, I defended my family and my home by attacking them!" Jason began to feel like he was being interrogated, shifting in his chair, he felt a little uncomfortable.

"In your opinion, do you feel that you used reasonable force?"

Sergeant Bernard asked, as Jacky appeared in the doorway.

Jacky had cleaned herself up; she was holding a damp towel to her forehead. "Yes, when your life and the safety of your family is being threatened, you should be able to fight off your attackers." Jacky answered the question, all three men turning to look at her.

"Only reasonable force is allowed in the defence of one's hearth and home." Constable West stated officiously, trying not to make eye contact with Jacky as he shuffled in his chair. The red-headed Constable always struggled around women and on occasion, was even known to stutter.

"Don't quote law to a lawyer, Constable," Jacky replied, and she allowed herself a small smile as the Constable's jaw dropped.

Both the Sergeant and the constable looked at each other, and an uncomfortable few seconds passed between them.

"Hows Louis?" Jason asked.

"In our bed and I've put him a film on," Jacky answered.

"Time to go, Mr de Silva," Sergeant Bernard said, as both he and his constable stood, putting their helmets back on. They didn't wish to interview Jason in the presence of a lawyer, especially one he was married to.

"Can I have a minute?" Jason asked the Sergeant with his usual polite manner.

His moustaches twitched as the Sergeant stared at Jason. The Sergeant was weighing him up, wondering if he would try anything stupid.

"Protocol dictates we can't let you out of our sight, Mr De Silva." Constable West said.

"Oh no you didn't Mr West," Sergeant Bernard gave the constable a stern look and he had no need to even raise his deep voice.

The constable cast his eyes downwards, not daring to look at his superior.

Turning back to Jason, Sergeant Bernard's face resumed its

usual neutrality, "One minute, Mr de Silva and not a second more," he said.

Both policemen went outside through the back door; they stayed within sight of the couple.

"Why is this happening to us?" Jacky was crying, but only a small scattering of tears.

Jason took Jacky in his arms, kissed her on the forehead then held her away from him, "Get your things together, clothes and stuff. Take everything you'll need for awhile. Get the boys and go to your mothers for a few days."

"But," Jacky started to complain.

"No buts, if that gang comes back, who knows what they'll do?" Jason was adamant that Jacky should do as he said.

Jacky hung her head nodding, seeing sense in what he told her.

"It'll be all right sweety; the truth will come out soon enough. Be strong my love." Jason stepped away from her, as the two policemen appeared in the doorway.

"Mr de Silva, I'm arresting you on a charge of attempting to end life, unprovoked." Constable West made sure that he stood straight and pulled back his shoulders as he stated the charge.

"Cuffed or hands free lad?" Sergeant Bernard asked Jason, producing shackles from the inside of his coat as he did so.

"Hands free, if you don't mind." Jason walked from the kitchen, and out of the back door.

Constable West and Sergeant Bernard fell into step, flanking Jason as they all walked to the waiting police vehicle. Jason turned around as they passed the front of the house; Jacky was standing in the living room looking out.

"Love you!" She called.

Only two police vehicles remained, the ambulances had gone and so had Old Ma Smith. The crowd of onlookers lingered, chatting about the nights events. They were all laughing in an almost festive spirit, and they all started to applaud Jason as the door to the police vehicle was opened for him.

"Nice one Jay," one of his neighbours shouted.

"What about the window?" Jason questioned.

"We called the man that deals with that sort of thing for us, he shouldn't be too long, he's a local man." The constable driving the vehicle looked in his mirror as he answered Jason's question.

Constable West sat beside the driver in the front of the vehicle. Sergeant Bernard sat next to Jason, which meant that he didn't have much room because both of them were larger than average men. They drove for twenty minutes in complete silence, bypassing the local station in favour of the headquarters for the district.

Jason realised where he was going before the Sergeant spoke to him.

"That's right lad, you're getting the 'Royal treatment'." Sergeant Bernard nearly smiled at his own jest, nearly but not quite.

They entered Coopers Town, named after the man that had first made a settlement there. The headquarters were at the centre of the town. It took a further ten minutes to get there, driving through the empty streets from the edge of town. The headquarters itself was an impressive building, surrounded by a sturdy defensive wall. It had only been built five years previously and had replaced the antiquated station that had been pulled down in less than a day.

As they approached, automatic gates opened for them, as the sensors inside the vehicle notified the station of their arrival. Minutes after they arrived at the station, Jason was escorted down a pristine corridor and into a small cell.

"Night, night." Constable West mocked, breaking his silence.

Lying down on the uncomfortable bunk was one of the hardest things Jason de Silva had ever done in his entire life. Although it was late already, the night was still going to be a long one. He had to endure his time worrying about his family with a thousand different scenarios running through his mind. Sleep wasn't an option, as the waking nightmares unfolded in his mind. It was all he could do to stop himself crying in the dark.

Eventually, the night came to an end, with the first dim light showing itself on the horizon. Jason yawned as he looked out of his cell window; people were beginning to move about.

By the time the peep hole in his cell door slid open, the soundless void of night had change to the hustle and bustle of the day.

"De Silva, you awake?" the voice was muffled by the metal door. The door opened and revealed a wiry fellow, his creased uniform made him look shabby. He held a tray and he walked into the room to place the food on the bed, "Enjoy," the constable smiled.

"Thank you," Jason replied, genuinely grateful as he felt his stomach complain at being empty.

Jason sat on the edge of his bunk, eating the egg, sausage and bacon. Two flies tried to share his meal with him but Jason wafted them away.

Jason was stuffing the last of his breakfast into his mouth, when the cell door opened again. The constable that had brought the meal, stood there nonchalantly fiddling with the cell door key. Like Sergeant Bernard the copper sported a healthy moustache and a similar attitude.

"Come on then de Silva." The constable ordered with a nod of his head in the direction he wanted Jason to move.

Jason stood and followed the constable down a short corridor. He was led into a room with a table and chairs, '*interview room*', he thought. The door closed behind him and Jason found that he was all alone. He walked around the table, and sat in one of the chairs. There was no other furniture in the room; the only other feature was the large tinted panel of glass. He couldn't see through it, but he knew whoever was on the other side could.

Looking behind him as he ran for the gates, Jason saw the two constables. Paper still fell around the woman, who lay unmoving on the ground.

Jason turned all his attention to his freedom. As he reached the gate, a police vehicle drove slowly through. Jason leaped up on the bonnet, his feet leaving a large dent in the metal. The two constables driving the vehicle looked utterly amazed as Jason launched himself over them. Without stopping, Jason ran over the roof of the vehicle, leaving more dents as he did so.

The air seemed cleaner outside the police compound, somehow sweeter and Jason put that down to a trick of the mind. He looked left and right up the long boulevard. He heard the yells of the constables who gave chase and decided to take off north. As Jason ran up the road the lack of sleep began to tell, his energy levels were at rock bottom and he knew he was tiring. The only thing keeping him on his feet was the adrenalin that coursed through his veins.

Jason glanced back once again; four constables were chasing him on foot. He could hear sirens as the police vehicle fought against the volume of traffic. The constables had gained on him as he flagged and soon he would be caught and he would lose his freedom once again - permanently.

One night in the cells had driven him to despair; a lifetime of incarceration would be unbearable. These thoughts gave him a burst of energy, as fear turned to determination.

Up ahead the traffic had ground to a halt, the fuel cells of an energybike glowed at the rear of the machine. Jason could hear the hum of the bike, as it waited for its power source to be engaged. Jason reached the bike and grabbed the man, pulling him backwards.

"Sorry mate!" Jason yelled as he leaped onto the machine before it fell over.

Foot steps sounded loud, getting closer. Hands of the constables were almost brushing Jason's clothes. Jason engaged the two wheeled energybike, not daring to look behind; he could almost feel the touch of the constables.

He shot off fast.

Jason struggled to keep the machine under control and the police vehicle pulled up alongside him trying to keep pace.

In front of Jason the traffic buzzed in both directions at an intersection. Miraculously the energybike threaded through the gaps in the traffic, narrowly missing a large cargo vehicle. The driver of the cargo vehicle gave a long blast of its horn and refused to stop as Jason passed.

Unfortunately for the police vehicle that had given chase, the gaps in the traffic closed causing them to skid to a stop.

Jason continued as fast as he dared, threading through the traffic. He couldn't hear or see any pursuit, but he knew it was on its way. Jason couldn't help smiling, in spite of his predicament. The excitement he got from riding the ion driven, fuel celled super bike at ridiculous speeds on the busy streets was helping him stay awake.

'*Why is this happening to me? None of this is my fault*' he thought to himself as he neared the edge of town. '*Justice? There is no justice*'.

Jason's eyes narrowed, the wind in his face was almost unbearable. Although this made his eyes water and threatened to blur his vision, it did have the added advantage of helping to keep him awake.

Past the suburbs, Jason entered the countryside with green fields on both sides of the road. Tall hedgerows and deep ditches lined the roads and gave scant cover for the machine he had stolen.

Jason pressed his thumb onto a small button and the energybike accelerated. It was then that Jason heard the sound of his pursuers. Thinking fast, Jason looked around up ahead, he spotted a narrow country lane.

He turned his bike off the road and engaged the accelerator,

voices stopped and the curtain twitched. Then the door opened, just a crack. A narrowed eye questioned his presence, it stared at him for a few seconds then the door opened all the way and the old man that stood in front of Jason wore a broad grin.

The old man was at least eighty, but he stood proud with the energy of a much younger man. He sported a long grey beard and a huge belly, which looked out of place atop the man's skinny legs.

"Don't just stand there, you silly sod come inside, come inside," the old man beckoned. His long grey beard swayed over his belly as he moved out the way, "Margaret, Margaret, its young de Silva."

"Keep ya bloody voice down, ya twaddle headed loud mouthed fool," an old woman stepped into the room behind the old man, her skinny figure moving awkwardly but with determination behind it. Her face was a mask of lines, wrinkling from her forehead to her chin, "Well now boy," she said to Jason.

"Sorry to be so rude," Jason smiled awkwardly, embarrassed for his invasion of the old couple's privacy.

"You might well be, Mr Jason de Silva. Sit down, sit down," the old woman pulled a chair out from under the kitchen table and she gave Jason a stare which invited no argument.

"How do you know my name?" Jason asked, as he sat.

They all sat down together, the elderly couple looked at each other.

"Your name's all over the news lad!" The old man leaned forward, his grey beard twitching ever so slightly as his jaw worked.

"Armed and dangerous, so they say, armed and dangerous," the old woman smiled, showing gaps where her teeth had once been. "You're not are ya?" she asked and the smile left her face.

"Who are you? Why help me, especially if I'm supposed to be armed and dangerous?" Jason leaned back in his chair, puzzled as to why this vulnerable old couple, would risk themselves for a complete stranger.

"I'm Margaret," the old woman said.

"Tom, Tom Robinson, at your service," the old man held out his hand.

Jason and Tom sealed their bond of friendship, with a quick shake of hands.

"You bloody men, with your so called bonds and friendships. Just setting yourselves up to let each other down, all bloody falsehoods," Margaret nagged, not one for mincing her words.

Both men looked at Margaret, Tom then looked down and studied the grain of the wooden surface of the table. Jason opened his mouth to speak, then closed it again, not sure what to say.

"As to your other questions, we're old friends of your grandfather. Armed and dangerous is in your blood lad," Margaret held her chin high and Jason saw that she was proud to have known his grandad.

Tom stood up, the chair's legs scraped on the tiled floor. He moved about the kitchen and for a few moments, no-one spoke.

Margaret broke the silence, "It wouldn't have mattered, the Skavite bastards got what they deserved if you ask me," Margaret said, "We would have helped ya anyway." She smiled that toothless smile.

Tom placed a sugar pot on the table as the kettle behind him began to whistle.

"Tea?" Tom asked.

"Yes please," Jason said, looking from Tom to Margaret, "You say I've been all over the news?"

Tom placed a tray on the table and he sat down and began to pour hot tea into three cups.

"Yes, you were news before it was put on the news," the old man answered, his beard twitching, "word spread like wild fire all about how you saw off the Skavs."

"There's more than just us here applauded what you done,

and you running off from them police. You're an outlaw now lad," Margaret said, "But mark my words, there's plenty that'll help ya. Besides, with all the troubles the Skavites are causing. The coppers'll be too busy to chase you around me lad."

"But I killed Reggie Smith," Jason said.

"Well, I don't know about that me lad, according to the news he's in a coma." Tom said.

"Your real problem was that lady copper, assaulting one of them, well that's serious!" Margaret sipped at her tea before she continued, "King's men will sort it out, you mark my words. They've been out on the streets of Capital City again last night," Margaret smiled, thinking of all the Skavites hiding behind closed doors.

Jason was speechless, thinking of Reggie and Inspector Kingsley.

"If the constables can't manage, why shouldn't the kings guard help?" Tom asked.

"I've been had!" Jason said, as the penny dropped.

Tom and Margaret stopped speaking looking at him.

"Excuse me?" Tom asked, wondering what Jason was talking about.

Jason stopped staring into space and snapped back into the conversation. "That Inspector Kingsley, he lied to me," he said, his anger easily recognised in his tone.

"Ah! That Kingsley, he's a wrong en, mark my words he is." Margaret said.

"You know him?" Jason asked.

"He'd do or say anything for a bust lad," Tom answered. "He used to steal our apples, when he was a youngster."

"Armed and bloody dangerous, we know bloody different." Margaret wagged her finger in the air as she nagged at no one.

"You say you knew my granddad?" Jason asked; he was interested to know what they knew. He didn't know what the old man was like; he had died when Jason was very young.

"Yes we knew him lad," Tom said.

"And a bloody good man he was too," Margaret added.

"I remember him, but I was only nine summers old when he passed on." Jason was solemn, wishing he'd had chance to know his grandfather.

"Well, we're a little older than your grandfather, maybe two summers or more. He would have been proud of you lad." Tom smiled, thinking of the distant past.

"And mark my words, he would have done everything you've done, but with a smile on his face." Margaret stood, "I'll get some food on then," the old lady changed her tone to a happy one, as she busied herself around the old farm kitchen.

Jason looked at the elderly couple, "Thanks for all your help," he said.

They sat in silence as they ate the late supper of cold meats and fruit. After they had finished, they retired to the living room. This room defied the chill night, as a roaring fire blazed in a large open hearth.

Tom pointed to a large leather armchair and Jason sat down first. Margaret sat on the sofa, and Tom went into another room. He reappeared a few minutes later with a tray, upon which sat three tankards.

"I apologise, for leaving you in that hayloft," Tom said as he sat down in the other large arm chair.

"Its fine, I know you could have turned me in, so I'm grateful for everything you've done." Jason said as he took the tankard offered by the old man, "You didn't know how I'd react," he added, looking at the frothy dark liquid.

"No, we'd never turn you in lad." Tom said and then took a long gulp of ale from the tankard.

Jason followed suit, drinking from the pewter tankard he held. The ale was a strong one, an old farmer's special brew. Jason's eyes widened at the taste, the warm spicy flavour warmed his throat like a liqueur would. "It's a bit strong," Jason whistled.

Jason felt and heard his heart pounding as it threatened to blow a hole in his chest, "Well life's certainly not boring any more," he whispered in the darkness and he smiled in spite of all the worries that burdened him.

"No time for messing around, back down the stairs." Margaret grabbed something from out of the darkness, as they turned to make their way down the stairs.

"Can you ride lad?" Tom asked, his voice hushed but not quite a whisper.

"You saw the bike." Jason said.

Jason had enjoyed the night with this crazy old couple, he had been tempted by their offer. Now he knew any such notion was folly, he had to move on.

"No, horses, can you ride horses?" Tom asked again.

"I've ridden a few times, but that was years ago," Jason answered, his own voice barely audible.

"I'll saddle Bess," Tom said.

"Oh Tom, you foaled Bess." Margaret's frown spoke volumes of sadness, "Are you sure you can part with the old girl?"

"She's got the best temper; can you imagine an inexperienced rider taking Charger? I'll saddle Bess," Tom repeated, looking down at the terracotta tiles that covered the kitchen floor. "Besides, you're only borrowing her lad," he added looking to Jason.

"I can take the bike," Jason said, not wanting to put the old couple in any inconvenience.

"Some thing's not right lad, they've not left yet, I haven't heard the fuel cells power up on the main road." Tom said as he walked down the short corridor to the back door.

"Now young man, we'd love you to stay, but you can't," Margaret had sobered up considerably.

"Yes I know, and thanks again for not giving me away," Jason knelt down to lace his boots up.

"Nonsense young man, you're practically family. Now, my

son owns a farm about twenty miles north, big old place, lots of outhouses. High Peaks Farm it's called, it's the one with that ancient site, Aamor," Margaret fidgeted with the seam of her thick winter shirt.

"Yes I know the place, I used to go there years ago before I got married, never paid the toll though," Jason smiled at the memory. "It's a beautiful place that."

"Ride there, you can leave the horse with them. We'll fetch her back and don't worry, they won't betray you." Margaret turned to a hat stand, and took down a shabby leather hat and a riding crop and offered them to Jason.

"Why help me so much?" Jason asked taking the hat and riding crop.

"Why not?" The old lady asked, defiant.

"It's the honour of the thing lad, and besides, like most people around these parts we've had enough. If the government carry on with their do good laws, nothing will be sacred", Tom was proud as he made his statement. "Life never dulls unless you let it."

Jason was left wondering about Tom's last statement as they made their way outside to the rear of the farm. Tied to a gate post outside the back door was a large horse, its black coat shone with a green tint under Serene's eerie glow. Cold air enveloped them, and their breath billowed white as they exhaled.

Margaret turned to him smiling in the green tinted darkness. "You remember now, High Peaks Farm at Aamor, we'll let them know you're on your way." The old wrinkled woman stepped back, giving Jason room to mount.

"I'll remember," he said, talking quietly as he continued to sober up in the cold night air.

"What will you do then?" Tom asked.

"I have no idea," Jason answered, shrugging his shoulders and making ready to mount the horse. "I'll just keep moving I guess."

disappear. When the whining of the fuel cells faded from his earshot, Jason coaxed Bess on once more. They walked a further fifty yards in the shadows of the trees and high hedgerows before they came to a gap in the hedge. It was large enough to get the horse through.

Jason dismounted, and led Bess on foot as the first signs of daylight pushed back the night. Jason walked Bess across the field to give the old nag a rest from his weight. Light began to show on the horizon and he stumbled upon an old horse trail.

Jason stopped and patting Bess's nose, "Just a while longer before we look for some shelter." He spoke as much to reassure himself as he did the horse, then as calmly as he could, he remounted. Jason's legs and groin ached from the miles he'd already ridden, but he couldn't hide in the open daylight.

Another mile passed as they plodded on. Off to his right in the middle of a field, he saw an old oak shepherd's hut. One wall was missing and most of the roof had fallen in, but it was far enough away from the roads to be sufficient for Jason's needs.

"It will have to do," Jason said to himself as he felt weariness deep in his bones and muscles from the hours he had spent without rest.

On dismounting Jason realised how sore his arse and legs had become, it had been years since he'd been in the saddle and he had forgotten how painful it could be.

Gripping the reins tight, Jason steadied himself against the horse's neck and shoulder as his tired legs threatened to give way. Frost covered grass had made the going slippery. Jason fought against his fatigue, but eventually he pulled his mount into the small ruined shack.

He struggled as he unsaddled the horse, his tired legs almost buckling beneath him. Margaret and Tom had loaded up saddle bags and up until now, Jason hadn't opened them. Carefully he placed them on the ground and let the saddle slide off the left flank. Undoing the bridle annoyed Jason, as the horse kept nodding its head. He spent five minutes messing about with the horse's bridle and reins, but eventually he re-fastened the bridle around the horse's neck and secured her reins so that she could graze but not wander off. The last thing Jason wanted to find when he woke up was that his mount had gone back home as he slept. Then he was finally ready to settle down.

Jason sat down, letting Bess wander out onto the grass; he opened the saddle bags. Inside the saddle bags he found a packed lunch and a can of ale, placing that aside he pulled out a sleeping bag and a small torch.

"How will I ever repay those two?" he muttered to himself.

Jason ate the small lunch, putting the alcohol to one side, not daring to drink it after the night before. Feeling the last vestige of his energy leaving him, Jason quickly got into the sleeping bag and settled down to sleep.

Jason's eyes opened and he could feel winter's elements frosting his eyelashes. The sun rode high in the sky and by its position Jason assumed it to be early afternoon. Jason shivered as he sat up, holding the sleeping bag tight around his neck. Looking outside he saw Bess eating grass, he was relieved to see the horse had not broken free of her makeshift tether.

Jason braved the cold and removed himself from the sleeping bag. He picked up the saddle and walked over to Bess, speaking encouragements as he approached her "Good lass," he said as he threw the saddle across her back. He fitted the bridle back into place in a short time which surprised him, as he'd never done it before.

Before long he'd packed up his meagre belongings and gotten under way but in only a short time, he was wincing, the soreness from the day before still with him.

For about a mile they steadily meandered along the horse trail, Jason allowed the horse to pick its own way. Then up ahead, a farm appeared, close between two hills. Smoke plumes spiralled upwards from the short chimney stack into a windless sky.

Pulling his hat over his face he carried on at the same pace. His fear was that a change of pace might look suspicious. Then as he closed in on the farm yard, two eager dogs began barking. The barn doors shuddered as they were slammed open. A middle aged man came out of the barn kicking at the dogs to make them stop their noise.

"Good morning lad," the farmer said as he looked at Jason's horse.

"Good morning Sir." Jason replied, not too sure on what to say.

"Don't get many on horseback in these parts, least not in winter." The farmer said, drawing close.

"What's this place called? Where am I?" Jason asked.

"This is Orchard Farm lad, you got Cooper's Town 'bout ten miles behind ye and up ahead you got nothing but farming country, with Hurtsford off over there and Bankley Fells over there." the farmer pointed in all directions as he explained the lay of the land.

Jason knew the lay of the land but he tried not to arouse suspicion and hoped he had managed that as he feigned interest in what the farmer was saying.

"Thank you, I'll be on my way then." Jason turned the horse, desperate to get away.

"Close all me gates for me will ye?" the farmer said to Jason's already retreating back.

"Of course," Jason called over his shoulder as he rode away from the farm.

"Bess likes carrots Mr de Silva!" The farmer reached his porch and, producing a clay pipe, he sat in an ancient rocking chair.

Jason pulled the horse up and looked back; the farmer looked down into a leather pouch, fumbling pipe tobacco into his clay pipe.

"'Bout a mile north, there's a road block. Them constables got the roads hereabouts as tight as a virgin," the farmer began to rock in his chair, no emotion showing on his face. He lit his pipe with a match as the dogs curled at his feet.

Jason turned away from the farmer and his dogs, *'At least everyone is trying to help me,'* he thought.

"It would appear everybody hates Skavs," Jason patted Bess as he spoke, stroking her neck. Nodding her agreement the old mare took a pace or two sideways as Jason shifted his weight in the saddle.

Bankley Fells was a large town four miles west of Jason's current position; Jacky sat looking out of her mother's window, as traffic and the day buzzed by in tranquil serenity. Two constables sat in their vehicle, watching the house for any signs of her husband. They had arrived some hours before and Jacky's mother, Sheryl Cope, a short fat lady with facial hair, had taken them more than one cup of tea.

"You bastards," Jacky whispered under her breath, as yet another tear rolled down her cheek.

"It'll be all right love." Sheryl said, bringing her a cup of tea.

"How can you say that? It'll never be all right." Jacky said, not bothering to hide her tears. "Where is he mum? He could be dead! Why hasn't he called," Jacky asked not managing to hide the worry in her voice from her mother.

Both ladies sat on the sofa, looking out of the window. The only sounds were those of the boys playing upstairs. Mother and daughter shared an uncomfortable silence and Jacky shed yet another scatter of tears.

"Hector, bless him he hasn't got a clue what's going on, but Louis on the other hand," Sheryl stopped herself, Jacky was upset enough.

Jacky sat there looking out into the cold as the day wore on.

Sheryl made another round of tea, filling a tea pot for the

constables, "I'm just nipping those nice coppers a cup of tea dear," Sheryl tried to sound cheery.

"Let the bastards die of thirst." Jacky called after her mother as the door closed.

Back on the street where a few days earlier, life had been so peaceful, Old Ma Smith thrashed her way through her house, wailing and weeping, "My boys, my boys!" she shrieked, rivers of tears made streaks through the dirt on her face. "That fucking bastard should feel how I feel! I want revenge!" The last of the tirade trailed away as she slumped into her chair, her audience was nothing short of grim and deadly as they shared Old Ma's pain.

Sitting anywhere they could, straight faced Skavs looked at Old Ma Smith, as she ranted and raved in her living room. They wore dirty tracksuits, caps and hooded tops. None smiled as they thought of Reggie lying on his hospital bed, wires attached to his body and pipes in his nose and throat. Reggie slept the deep sleep of the comatose, although the doctors were confident he would pull through, they had no time frame.

Old Ma Smith was distraught, beside herself with worry but at the same time she was furious and aggrieved, she sought satisfaction.

Estendale, the small town not far south of Cooper's Town from which they all hailed, secretly laughed behind their closed doors. Reginald Smith had got a taste of his own medicine, and his situation was the popular gossip. Reggie was the muscle of the family, and because Jason de Silva had so easily embarrassed Reggie and his gang, they had lost their edge and for now at least, had become a laughing stock.

"Bastards, they're all laughing at ya, can't you do anything right?" Old Ma Smith scowled at the amassed Skavs, directing her anger and frustration at them instead of the absent Jason de Silva.

Jason rode west for a few miles, avoiding the road block the farmer at Orchard farm had warned him about. He considered his options as he rode, he felt obligated to Tom and Margaret and felt that he should return Bess to High Peaks Farm at Aamor.

On the other hand Jacky's mother Sheryl lived at Bankley Fells not too far from where he was at that moment. In the end he couldn't resist the need to see his family, Bankley Fells lay a few miles west, over the next set of hills.

"Just a small detour," he told himself.

Jason dismounted and walked for most of the day, giving the horse a well earned rest. He stopped often to rest because Jason wanted the darkness of night time to overtake the day before he made a move, it made sense to approach under cover of darkness. He hoped for a cloudy sky, but no matter how hard he thought, he couldn't remember if Albion's third moon was above him or below. If Serene was still in the night sky, he hoped the slow orbit of Albion's second moon would pass in front, to block out all moonlight for a time.

Finally just as night began to close in and the clouds began to gather, Jason topped the small hills. Looking over the rooftops Jason thought he could see the red tiles of his mother in laws house. Riding on slowly as to let the darkness hide his approach, Jason moved down a series of foot paths and alleys. Staying away from the roads should reduce his chances of capture.

Though an approach on horseback was not the most stealthy that Jason had ever made, he seemed to attract no attention and at length came to the end of the alley that faced Sheryl's front door.

He tied Bess to a post and then he stuck his head out, to see if the coast was clear.

'*Shit*,' Jason thought, as he withdrew back into the shadows. He saw the constables, one sat in their unmarked vehicle, the other standing at the side of the road smoking a cigar. He prayed neither had seen him, and he ducked down in the dark shadows, almost daring not to breathe.

Jason heard the rustle of feet approaching his hiding place.

"I'm telling you I saw something." One constable, the one in the vehicle, said to his colleague as he pulled rank and sent him to look.

"It's in your mind mate. Wait a minute, that's a horse's head." The second constable blurted out, amazement evident in his voice.

No sooner had he spoken than two vehicles came hurtling around the corner and down the street. At the controls of the lead vehicle was Tommy Smith, who had taken temporary control of the Smith gang and now led them on a revenge attack.

Distracted by the Skavs, the constable turned from the horses head and from Jason who, still unnoticed crouched a few feet away. Jason and the constables watched, transfixed as the two vehicles skidded to a halt in front of Sheryl's house.

Jumping out of the vehicles, the Skavs wasted no time in brandishing weapons. Tommy Smith held a short sword, his eyes wide with adrenalin fuelled anger, his laugh was loud and his cackling resembled that of his mother.

"It's the Smith gang, call for back-up!" the first constable yelled.

"Constable Reece, Bankley stakeout, we're under attack, need assistance." the second constable shouted down his radio, as the two police officers ran towards the Smith gang.

Jason had mounted Bess before he realised what he was doing and he spurred the horse forward as a claw hammer smashed Sheryl's large front window.

"Gonna end ya, me'n me homies!" Tommy Smith shouted, holding the hammer up as he yelled at the top of his lungs.

Sheryl appeared at the window wearing her nightgown, "Please stop!" Sheryl flung her arms out, palms outwards in a sign of surrender.

Tommy Smith, grabbed the window pane, leaned forward

where the glass had been and thrust forward with his sword arm. Tommy put everything he had into that thrust and his short sword pierced Sheryl clean through the heart.

Shocked by what they had just witnessed, and surprised at the same time by Jason thundering past on Bess, the two constables slowed almost to a stop.

Jason charged Bess straight into the gang of thugs as Tommy pulled his sword from Sheryl's chest. Sheryl looked blank, as life fled her dying body; she lived long enough to feel the sensation of falling as her body gave up.

Skavs dived out of the way as Bess thundered into them; she hit two unlucky lads and sent them flying. One Skav landed on the grass of the front lawn but the second wasn't so lucky. He was thrown up into the broken window, shards of glass quivered above him. One shard cracked loose and fell into his eye socket and through to pierce the thug's brain. Soundlessly the Skav gagged and gulped in air, air that would be his last breath as he too died instantly.

Turning towards the unexpected noise, members of the Smith gang faced the last thing they expected to see, Jason de Silva on horseback bearing down on them like a mounted avenger. There were six of the Smith gang still standing, and they were still up for the fight, confident they would overcome their foe.

Pulling Bess to turn her back around, Jason headed back to the group of angry youths; he dived from Bess's back onto one of the Estendale Skavs allowing Bess to go past.

One of the Skavs that bore down on Jason suddenly fell away, shaking he was being electrocuted by a police probe. Smiling and grimacing at the same time, the constable looked like he was enjoying his job.

Keeping the head of the Skav that he'd jumped onto in a head lock, Jason looked at the surviving members of the gang as they began to overwhelm him. His arm burned hot like fire drawing across it, as a blade sliced through his coat and shirt and into the flesh. His face became devoid of emotion as his arm tensed, forcing the Skav in his arms to go limp as his brain was starved of oxygen and he lost consciousness. Jason heard two snaps simultaneously, one sound entirely inside his own head and the other as the Skav's neck broke. The first was something inside of Jason's self. A mental barrier was gone, snapped with more difficulty than the Skav's neck had been but it was something that Jason had not been aware of before, a blood lust not seen for centuries on Albion, entered Jason's consciousness.

"New breed", he heard one Skav say as he thrust his machete towards Jason. Jason easily side-stepped the thrust, and grabbed the Skav's wrist as it passed. Using brute strength Jason twisted the youth around, and grabbed the hand holding the weapon and forced it up into the lads own back. The Skav fell to the ground and bled to death where he fell.

Another Skav had been floored by the shock tactics of the constables but Tommy Smith evaded them and swung his short sword at Jason's head. Jason caught Tommy's sword arm, and almost picked the young Skav up off the ground. Jason smiled at Tommy and Tommy didn't like what he saw in Jason's eyes.

Tommy had time to look around and he saw the remains of his Skav gang attacking the constables. One of the officers had been stabbed in the stomach and was staggering away from the fight. Jason disarmed his captive and drew the blade across Tommy's body.

Tommy's arrogant yelling of before was replaced by the squealing of a young child as the contents of his abdomen emptied out in a steaming tangle of guts and spattered onto the glass-strewn footpath.

The uninjured constable dragged his partner away from the battlefield and he administered first aid by trying to apply pressure to the open wound in his stomach. It was no use, blood seeped through his fingers and the stabbed constable coughed up blood and his body went into violent convulsions and he died on the ground in front of the Police Vehicle.

Jason and the one remaining Skav squared off, they circled briefly and then, with grim smiles on their faces, both raised their short swords and battle commenced. As gladiatorial combat goes, it didn't last long. As they passed each other, Jason parried the Skav's inexpert slash and then swiped the Skavs weapon away, allowing the Skav to pass him completely. He was off-balance and half-falling forward and Jason took the opportunity to slice into the back of the lad's neck as he encouraged him forward. Jason was still wearing his smile as the Skav's head rolled and bounced away from the body. Jason felt sick and excited at the same time when he felt blood spurt onto his hands and face as blade cut through the Skav's spine.

There were three Skavites still alive; one was out cold, knocked unconscious by Jason's initial charge. Two others had been tasered by the police probes, one had managed to stagger to his feet and the other was trying to crawl away.

Jason walked up to the one standing Skav as he was still trying to regain his senses. The Skav's mouth was trying to form words but his body was in shock, so his lips were moving but there was no sound. Without giving any quarter, Jason raised his short sword and stabbed the Skav through his open mouth.

"Sorry, what was that?" Jason mocked the lad as he gurgled, blood spilling out of the ragged mess that was left of his face.

Jason removed the blade and raised one foot to kick the Skav away from him.

"Stop de Silva, haven't you done enough already?" Constable Reece yelled, still cradling his deceased comrade.

"Nope, not nearly." Jason walked over to the Skav that was frantically trying to crawl away; his limbs were not working as they should. Jason pulled the thug's head back and ran the sharpened blade across his throat, with slow and vicious precision. That was the last of the gang, all but one lay dead outside the family home they had intended to ruin.

Sirens sounded from all directions suddenly, or maybe it was that Jason had just noticed them? Now that he had calmed from his temporary madness, he knew that he would feel no regret for the killings; he just felt the need to have the nightmare finished. The blaring sirens would force him to move on, before he had chance to hold his family again.

Jason ran to Bess and mounted her quickly as the sirens came closer. He turned in the saddle to look at Sheryl's house. His wife stood there, her hair was a mess, her clothes were covered in blood and Jason felt a deep longing to hold her and never let her go. Jacky held Louis; and she pressed his face to her shoulder to prevent him from seeing the carnage. She had stood in the doorway of the house, watching Jason as he despatched the helpless youth.

"Love you daddy," Louis shouted, his was voice muffled because his mother refused to let his head up, she refused to let him see the carnage.

"Love ya mate", Jason shouted back as the police vehicles screamed around the corner at the top of the road. Jason dug his heels into Bess's flanks, not caring for the mare's age and Bess responded like she didn't care about her age either, she sprang away and they galloped back down the alley as flashing lights and sirens filled the road.

Adrenalin coursed, pulsing through his veins eliminating the tiredness and pain. Jason no longer had need of stealth and he threw caution to the wind. He galloped head long down the alleys and was whipped and thrashed by low hanging branches. He steered Bess wildly first left then right, all the time low walls threatened to dismount him.

Rounding the corner, Constable West steered the vehicle at full throttle. Inspector Kingsley leaned into the corner, holding on to the hand rails above his head, for fear of falling into Constable West.

Constable West straightened up the vehicle, just in time to see a flash of the horse's flank disappear down a narrow alley.

"What the fuck, I'm sure that was de Silva?" Inspector Kingsley's incredulity was obvious as he gawked at the fleeing horseman.

Coming to a stop, the two policemen jumped out of the vehicle, what they saw was a scene of utter carnage.

"What the fuck!" Inspector Kingsley looked from Jacky de Silva, then at the corpses lay about, then at the constables, then back to Jacky de Silva. The Inspector was dumbstruck.

"They killed my mum," Jacky yelled at the Inspector.

More vehicles arrived, two medical vehicles and another police vehicle. Inspector Kingsley walked over to Constable Reece, who still held his partner, the lifeless body was slowly cooling.

"What the hell happened here? Who was the horseman?" Inspector Kingsley asked the constable as calmly as he could, his voice shaky.

Through eyes full of tears, the constable managed to look at his superior, "de Silva's what's happened, Sir," the constable answered, looking down he closed the staring eyes of his partner. "He came from nowhere," he added without looking up.

"I fucking knew it," the Inspector quickly lifted the radio to his mouth, having already wasted enough time.

"All units, this is an all units bulletin. Jason de Silva is in the Bankley area, riding a horse." Inspector Kingsley turned back to look at the bodies strewn before him. Taking his hand away from the radio, he looked at Jacky de Silva. She cradled her eldest son; whose eyes were wide and shedding silent tears as he stared off into the night.

"They killed my mum, would have killed us all if it wasn't for my Jason!" Jacky said, grinning manically at the Inspector.

Jason by this time had reached the edge of Bankley Fells. Sensing his mood, Bess refused to slow down, she galloped into the night along the main road that led north into the countryside. Leaning forward into the horse's neck, he pulled tight on the reins and managed to pull the horse to a stop a mile away from Bankley. He guided the horse off the road and through an open gateway. Spurring Bess on again, the lights of Bankley Fells began to dwindle. On and on into the night he rode, trying to put as much distance between himself and the murder he'd just committed.

Eventually he slowed, daring to let up his flight. Bess was near to breaking, her neck and flanks were lathered with sweat. Jason looked up at the night sky, the clouds had all but dissipated and he could better gauge his position by Albion's moons. To his left, the giant Dunstan sat behind Serene, her constant shine was comforting. To his right and level with the others, Cerise's dark red surface ominously loomed.

Jason sighed; he was relieved that he was still for the most part, headed due north. Jason didn't recognise the area at all, but he knew if he headed north for another day or so, he would be near Aamor. All he'd have to do was climb to high ground and find a vantage point from which, the stones of Aamor should be clearly visible.

Dismounting, Jason led Bess for a while to cool her down. Some miles behind him, he could hear the loud hover jets over Bankley Fells, flying in ever increasing circles as they searched for him. As he walked north Jason passed the occasional farm, and he gave them a wide berth. He headed into the high hills of Cooper's town district because he thought it best to drop out of sight if he could; especially now he knew his family was safe.

Running the events of the evening before, over and over in his mind, Jason realised how lucky he had been. Not only in saving his family, but also in his escape. Fate or the influence of some outside force, he thanked the gods for their support. As he allowed his thoughts to run, he came to the conclusion, that yet again he had had no choice. He had to defend his family or they would have died. His decisions dictated to him because of the thuggish behaviour of the gang mentality of the Skavs.

Jason stopped walking and mounted Bess as the first glimpse of the new day began to appear on the horizon. "Sorry Bess, my need is greater than yours," he said as he stroked the mare's neck.

The sights and sounds of civilisation were far behind him as he crested a rise approximately two miles east of Mount Aamor. The peak rose proudly out of the landscape. The rocks and boulders that were scattered at the foot of the mountain looked tiny at this distance and beyond them and out of sight was the other farm owned by the Robinson Clan.

Jason pulled his coat tight against early morning chill and let Bess graze for a moment. He watched as the first rays of the sun's majestic beams broke behind Aamor. For a moment the outline of Aamor split the light, and the sun bathed the valley with powerful contrasts of brightness and shadow.

Jason spent a little time marvelling over the beauty of nature but as the sun broke the skyline proper and ruined the effect, he wondered if he would see a sight so beautiful again and as the ancient stones sat at the front of the long and stark shadows cast by the sun's light, Jason moved onwards.

With just a few miles to go, Jason trotted Bess and covered the distance in half an hour. Their progress was only slowed by the opening and closing of gates. Eventually he reached the foot of Mount Aamor. Jason decided on a whim that he needed a closer look at the stones and so he began to climb. The horse was not the most sure-footed beast and Jason took great care as he guided the horse slowly up the side of the steep hill.

Cresting the rise at the top of the hill, Jason looked at the huge stones in front of him. In any light they looked eerie and powerful; in this light the smooth stones gleamed and could be seen for miles around.

Jason dismounted and led the horse to the nearest stone;

there he ran his right hand across its surface. It felt warm to the touch. The stone seemed to resonate, and react to his skin. Jason wondered as to the purpose of the stones, they lay in a perfect circle, just as if they had been placed there yesterday, not all those lost millennia ago.

Crossing the stone circle, Jason looked down the hill. High Peaks Farm lay below him, the fields steaming as the morning frost was evaporated by the sun's heat.

Wandering about in the mist was the farmer going about his business. Looking up, the man was silhouetted by the winter sun, he stood stock-still, and looked up directly at Jason. Then he began to wave, beckoning Jason down off the hill. Bess took one look at the farmer and High Peaks Farm; she acted on her own from that point and made her own way forward down the hill.

Jason let the reins fall from his hand and then followed Bess as she descended. It didn't take long to get from their high vantage point, even though the footing was still a little icy.

Standing at the edge of the field with his hands on his hips, Tom and Margaret's son waited to greet him.

"Jason de Silva, I take it," the man took hold of Bess's reins. He was huge, about the same size as Sergeant Bernard Willis. He had a thick shock of grey hair, cut in a straight line about his head and covering half his ears. His face was lined with years of hard work and toiling on a remote farm. But the man's most impressive feature was his nose; it was so large it cast a shadow in the morning sun.

"In the flesh," Jason replied, "brought you ya dads horse," he added.

"Go inside, the door's open. I'll see to Bess," Mr Robinson said.

Jason patted Bess on the side of the neck, and she nodded in response. Jason crossed the farm's cobbled courtyard and went towards the door and it opened with just a push.

"Morning," Jason spoke loudly as he entered, warning anyone inside of his entry.

"Morning young man, you must be Jason. Our mum warned us you were on your way," pulling the door wide, a middle aged woman stood in the kitchen, she wore a long farmer's apron. She looked older than the age that Jason estimated she should be because of the years of hard farm labour, and like her husband, she carried a little too much weight around her midriff. Her long brown hair had a sprinkling of grey and her face told a story, a story of a lady that in her youth possessed great beauty.

"I'm Heather Robinson," the lady stepped aside, showing Jason a view of her kitchen, "and these are my boys," Heather added, smiling.

Four young men sat around the kitchen table, they all smiled and nodded at Jason in greeting.

"Hello lads," Jason waved, stepping in out of the cold. It was a welcome relief after spending so much time outdoors in winter.

"Hello," they said together, all of them staring at him like they expected him to breathe fire and shoot lightning from his finger tips.

"Seen you on the television," one of the brothers said, he had side burns barely visible below his long dark hair. His face was slim, which matched his small frame but it was a frame that was heavily muscled below his tight t-shirt. He pointed to his own chest and said: "Phil."

"Phil for short, his birth name's Philip, although you wouldn't know it," Heather complained.

"Is it true, did you kill all those Skavs?" Another of the Robinson boys asked. He was the tallest of the boys by a good foot. His hair was a shade lighter than the rest and he resembled his father more than any of the others. Like his father, he didn't smile.

"Randell, don't be so rude," Heather Robinson scowled.

The other two boys looked at each other and then back to Jason. They were in their early twenties and obviously twins and they smiled as they said in unison: "Well did ya?"

Jason was taken aback by the candid nature of this family but at the same time he appreciated their honesty.

Being as tall as Philip and as broad as Randell the twins seemed friendly enough. They were well muscled and strikingly handsome, one carried slightly more weight than the other and he had a double chin but they were identical for all that.

"Trevor, Dominic, please leave Mr de Silva alone." Heather commanded obedience from her boys without raising her voice, "And don't stare like that, you're not at the zoo."

"I'm sorry Mr de Silva, we're an inquisitive lot. We don't get too many people out this way," Heather turned to Jason and she surprised him because she smiled nervously at him.

"It's ok; I think I'd want to know too, if the boot was on the other foot." Jason tried his best to return the smile, and wondered if he should talk about it or not.

"Anyway, you must be tired. I've made you a bed up in the guest room. Its small but you'll be cosy and warm,." Heather rescued him from a conversation he wasn't ready to have. "Follow me please, I'll show you your room." she said as she walked out of the kitchen.

Jason nodded to the Robinson boys as he left. He was led away through a sitting room that Jason assumed to be the living room, and into another that was small and warm, just as Heather had promised. The fold-down bed looked welcoming with its home-made quilted blanket on top.

"Sweet dreams." Heather said as she backed out of the room and closed the door behind her.

"Thank you," Jason said even as she had closed the door. He needed no prompting as tired as he was and he lay down on the bed. Fully clothed, he closed his eyes and pulled the blanket up around his chin. He drifted off into a deep but troubled sleep.

Jason woke with a start; the carnage of his dreams was as violent and nightmarish as his life of the past few days.

Jason lay on the bed for a while, collecting his thoughts. He could hear sounds of animals in the farmyard outside his window. Early evening light filtered in through the curtains and Jason made a move to get out of bed, there was an unusual weight on his legs and as he moved, a ginger cat reluctantly stood up and stretched. It curled up, back on the spot it had been in as Jason swung his legs from beneath the quilt.

Jason walked into the living room where Mr and Mrs Robinson sat watching the television.

"Hello Mr de Silva," Mr Robinson looked up at Jason, he looked relaxed in his arm chair.

"Hello dear, come sit down," Heather said cheerily, "you're on the television."

Jason sat down on the sofa and his attention was immediately absorbed by the voices of the news presenters.

"The incredible events of last night can only be described as ultra violent. All over the nation, the police and armed forces battled with Skavite gangs. Arrests were made but as yet no charges have been brought against the rioters." The images of rioting Skavs and police enforcers stopped and the television cameras returned to the studio where the usual presenter shuffled papers.

"In other news, the sleepy town of Bankley Fells is still in chaos from Jason de Silva's attack last night. Nine died as de Silva went berserk. The deaths include a police constable, who bravely sacrificed his own life in the line of duty. Jason de Silva was seen riding from the scene on horseback. Police are calling the incident a gangland slaughter, leaving local residents scared to leave their homes."

A picture inset of Jason appeared in the top left hand corner of the television and the presenter continued. "This is the latest picture of Jason de Silva. Police warn that if any members of

"Thank you for your hospitality, and I won't stay any longer than I have to." Jason said, looking at the couple. Secretly wanting to stay, but fearful of the risks the Robinson's were putting themselves in.

"Nonsense dear," Heather turned and smiled. "You can stay for as long as you like."

"Besides lad, you won't be putting on us. There's plenty needs doin out there, frost's almost gone, there's always loads to do on a farm in spring." Mr Robinson put his pipe to his mouth and lit it.

"You be leaving him alone, I ain't given you all those sons so they can layabout." Heather didn't turn from what she was doing; she was concentrating on chopping the vegetables.

The outside door opened and Randell and Phil walked into the kitchen from the farmyard. They wiped their boots on the doormat as they entered.

"That's the cows done." Randell said.

"Don't get cow shit on me clean floor." Heather said and this time, she shook her ladle in their direction.

"Sorry ma." Philip said and backed outside, taking his boots off on the cold stones.

"What about me wall?" Mr Robinson asked, as his sons left their boots outside.

"It's still there father," Randell answered, smiling at his own cheek.

"It's just on the ground." Philip added, smiling as he joined in with the jest.

Both Robinson boys grinned as they sat down at the table.

"Well tomorrow, someone's building the bloody thing." Mr Robinson's voice became gruffer and his two sons stopped smiling.

"We'll build it," his sons said together.

"I'll help." Jason said to the two young men. Glad of the opportunity to repay the Robinson's in part for all they had given.

Even before the rest of her boys turned up for supper, Heather was busy delivering the meal to the table; she placed large plates filled with salad in front of them. They waited for Heather to sit before they began to eat and then they ate in silence for a short time; Jason especially liked the red tubers and cold meats.

Philip looked up from his food, his fork filled with green vegetables. "Tell me Jason, what's it like to kill someone?" he asked.

"Don't ask such questions." Heather didn't look up as she spoke.

"It's all right, I don't mind answering." Jason stared at his food. "It'll be good to get it off my chest.

They all looked at Jason, fascinated, even Heather who was trying not to be curious.

Jason stared at the table, not wanting to make eye contact lest it put him off his answers. "I'm not quite sure to be honest, at first I was upset, but now I'm cold to the fact. I've come to the conclusion that I was doing what was necessary." He looked up; they were all staring at him, hanging on his every word.

"Tis same as killing your favourite calf," Mr Robinson was the first to speak.

"What about when you're actually there?" Philip asked.

"I'll be honest, I suppose I enjoyed the violence, it's the adrenalin you see." Jason said.

There was a blast of cold air, as Trevor and Dominic came in from the outside. They quickly shut the cold behind them.

Jason was pleased with the distraction, as Heather busied herself with the twins' dinner, the conversation turned to more mundane and farm-related events of the day.

Chapter 4

"Over here Sir, in the barn," the constable shouted.

Inspector Kingsley held the search warrant in front of him; Tom and Margaret were both reading it, trying to make sense of the document. Inspector Kingsley wouldn't let the old couple hold the document, but for legal reasons he had no choice but to let them examine it.

"Well they must have found some evidence. I told you we wouldn't be long." Kingsley said with a nasty smile.

Kingsley's arrogance was too much for Tom; he crossed his arms and he levelled as evil a stare as he could manage. Inspector Kingsley pursed his lips; he was neither frightened nor impressed by the silent threat. Margaret threaded her arm through Tom's as the Inspector turned to walk in the direction of the barn.

On entering the barn, the Inspector saw two constables examining an energybike. A tarpaulin lay at the side of it; its identity code matched that of the bike Jason de Silva had stolen on the morning of his escape. The Inspector crouched down at the side of the energybike; he picked the keys up with the end of his pen.

'We're getting closer, de Silva, I'll have you soon.' He thought.

Then he noticed the hay loft ladder. He put the keys in an evidence bag and sealed the top. Handing a constable the bag he climbed the ladder to the loft. It didn't take a great detective to find were Jason de Silva spent his first night on the run.

He looked around him, at the disturbed hay and frowned.

"That's enough for me, take them in, let's see what they have to say for themselves." Inspector Kingsley walked back out into the winter sun, followed closely by his two constables.

"I'll get forensics on it Sir," one constable suggested.

"Arrest those two for aiding and abetting an escaped villain." Inspector Kingsley's order upset Tom, who struggled in vain, the strength of his youth long in his past.

Margaret put up no resistance, but her tongue was much worse, nagging her annoyance at the arresting constables. "There'll be the devil to pay, mark my words there will!" She promised.

Inspector Kingsley watched as Tom and Margaret were driven away, then he turned and walked into the farm house.

"Get me a cup of tea first constable, then we'll search this shack" He said to the first of a line of constables entering the house.

Jason was with the four brothers in one of the out buildings at the back of the farm. Night crept in, the last glimmer of the day almost gone below the horizon.

Jason sat in a dirty old armchair, mindful of the cold. He wore some of Randell's clothes as Heather had ordered Jason to hand his over and they were now in the wash. He watched as the four Robinson brothers worked on an old fuel-celled vehicle. It looked like an old rust bucket but its power source whined and sounded as beautiful as it had the day it came off the production line.

"That sounds good, doesn't it Jay?" Trevor asked, excitement gleaming in his eyes.

"It does sound amazing for its age." Jason nodded.

"It'll look good soon, too." Randell held a grinder against the bumpy surface of a rough weld and sparks flew. Philip and Dominic were having a heated conversation and it wasn't long before they started pushing each other. The pushing soon turned into a full blown punch up.

Moments later, Heather came bursting into the building, out of breath. Her usual cheer had gone. "Lads, lads come quick." She was flustered but as soon as she had their attention, she rushed back out.

They all felt their mother's panic and turned to face the cold rush of air. All stopped what they were doing and raced out into the night to follow her.

Jason ran to the vehicle, pressing the off button he turned to see the Robinsons had already disappeared into the dark.

Jason followed as quickly as he dared on the cobbled yard. By the time he reached the kitchen, the Robinson boys had already taken off their boots. They had gone to the living room, to the television. The news was on and they all stared at the images on the screen.

"Thomas and Margaret Robinson are helping the police with their enquiries into this matter. If the shocking developments of yesterday are anything to go by, then this unbelievable story could yet again take an unexpected twist." The news reporter's expression was grave as she recited the message. Then as she moved on to another subject, the Robinsons all turned to look at Jason de Silva standing in the living room doorway.

"We gotta break 'em free." Jason said, grim faced.

"And how do you intend to do that?" Mr Robinson asked.

"Oh dear, oh dear." Heather wiped her hands on her apron as she walked past Jason, in a fluster as she made for the kitchen.

"I don't know, but their arrest is because of me, I feel responsible." Jason didn't move from the doorway, he could feel the tension inside the room.

"Don't be hard on yourself; it was their choice to help ya." Mr Robinson said. He was thoughtful and stared off into the darkness beyond the window as he thought of what they could do.

"What to do, that's the thing." Jason carried on, not hearing Mr Robinson. "And what if my trail leads the coppers to here? I've got to leave as soon as possible."

"Well lad you're welcome to stay, and it's our choice to help ya." Mr Robinson didn't turn from his view of the night, but he did shut it out as he drew the curtains.

"Father, I'm gonna break Gramps free." Randell said. His voice was determined but he waited for an argument from his father.

The other Robinson boys gathered around Randell. They were obviously worried that they were in defiance of their father's wishes, but were determined to stand by their brother.

A crooked smile slowly creased Mr Robinson's face.

"Damned right you are! The family's honour is at stake." Mr Robinson stepped forward to embrace his sons.

"I'll help." Jason's words were almost lost as the Robinsons held each other. Jason felt strange looking at the people who were risking everything to help someone they didn't know, people who he may or may not be related to.

'I suppose they didn't know it was going to get this serious', he thought.

The brothers took their turn to slap Jason on the shoulder and shake his hand.

"Do you have any weapons?" Jason asked.

"Do we have any weapons?" Mr Robinson repeated Jason's question and his boys laughed. "Show him the gun cupboard."

They filed out into the kitchen, Heather Robinson stood with a shotgun in her hands, an open door behind her, the small room housed a wall of rifles, blunderbuss's and other types of gun and the other wall had all manner of hand held weapons, boxes of ammunition were piled in one corner.

"If they're gonna take ma 'n' pa, they're gonna answer to me." she said, cocking the weapon she held, putting a live round into the weapon.

“What’s the plan then?” Mr Robinson asked.

“Well whatever we do, we’ll need a diversion.” Jason sat at the kitchen table, deep in thought.

Chapter 5

Randell and Philip looked at each other, they sat in complete silence, their faces glowed green, lit by Serene's luminescence. The previous night they had heard of their grandparents incarceration and they had quickly formulated a plan, which they were about to put to the test.

Lying on the back seat of the vehicle were a rifle and a blunderbuss, the two young men hoped they wouldn't need them, they were purely precautionary.

Sat between Philip's legs was a glass bottle, the strip of cloth protruding from its metal cap and the smell of oil meant only one thing - home made explosives.

Philip played with the lighter, rolling the flint back and forth across the dash board, causing sparks.

"Will you stop doing that; do you want to blow us the fuck up?" Randell asked.

"Yeah, sorry," Philip put the lighter in his pocket, "I'm nervous, I've never thrown a bomb before."

"Just remember why we're doing this, that's all you need to do, and to throw the bottle straight of course!" Randell said.

"Right, it's time." Randell pulled down his woollen mask, his eyes the only part of his face visible.

Philip pulled down his own mask as Randell engaged the vehicle's power, the fuel cells whined as the vehicle's drive blossomed bright. They began to move up the street at a crawl till they pulled up outside Old Ma Smith's house in Estendale.

They exited the vehicle without saying a word and Philip lit the rag that stuck out of the bottle. Randell pulled the blunderbuss from the back seat of the vehicle. They looked at each other for a couple of seconds, and then turned away as Philip lit the rag and Randell blasted the blunderbuss skyward. The kick of the powerful weapon nearly staggered Randell, but he managed to hold it only by sheer strength. Philip counted to three before he took aim and launched the bottle at the house wall.

The front door was yanked open and banged against its frame. Old Ma Smith had woken up in the night; she had got up to get a drink and saw the movement at the front of the house. She got to the front door just as Randell discharged his weapon.

Old Ma Smith stood exposed in the doorway at the same time as the bomb was flying through the air. Philip's aim couldn't have been worse; the bottle hit the frame above Old Ma Smith's head. Flames sprayed the air around the fat woman's head as the oil ignited around her. Old Ma Smith screamed and fell back into the house and slammed the door shut. She beat at the flames that melted her eyes as her greasy hair burst into flames.

Randell and Philip jumped back into their vehicle, house lights all along the streets switched on. Both Robinson boys looked at the Smith residence. Old Ma Smith was running around her living room, ablaze from head to toe. Julian Smith chased his mother around uselessly, his jaw wired from the fight outside Jason's home.

"Fuck me; look at that fat slag burn." Philip held back his tears and his voice cracked. Murder was not what he intended.

"Fuck me, you murdered the bitch." Randell screamed as he engaged the vehicle.

"I killed her." Philip held his hands in front of his face, his eyes rolled as what he had done began to sink in, "I killed her." he repeated, tears rolled down his cheeks.

They turned the corner at the end of the road and Randell raced away from Estendale, the brothers sped into the night.

A constable sat reading his paper and sipping at his coffee as the phone rang. He picked up the phone, "Hello."

He felt his face drain of colour as he listened to the report coming in, then to make his evening even better, Sergeant Bernard Willis entered the room, his moustaches twitching as if he were talking to himself.

"Sarge, it's the Smith residence, it's been attacked and is burning down." the constable carried on listening, "Reports of gunfire." He placed the phone down without thanking the caller.

"Right, get armed response on the blower, and call Inspector Kingsley. Get to it constable," Sergeant Willis went into the room next door.

"Right you lot, follow me, at the double." he gave the order to the three officers on the night watch.

"What's up Sarge?" one officer asked.

"Gunshots in Estendale, at the Smith place." Sergeant Willis gave the curt reply even as he rushed out of the room and into the corridor.

With his constables behind him, the Sergeant threw open the outside door to the station courtyard. They didn't get far. Before they had set one foot outside the door, a blunderbuss was pushed beneath the Sergeant's nose. Three armed, masked men forced the policemen back into the station.

"Back pig!" Jason bellowed, his fingers stroking the trigger of his weapon.

Sergeant Willis and his constables stepped back, throwing their hands up in surrender.

Heather Robinson stepped forward and relieved the Sergeant of his keys. "I'll be taking those," she said with a confidence she didn't feel.

"You'll not get away with this," Sergeant Willis looked at Heather's eyes, trying to recognise her.

Turning his rifle around, Mr Robinson stepped forward and hit the Sergeant with the butt of his rifle. The Sergeant fell to the corridor floor, out cold with blood welling up in the gash in his forehead.

"Cuffs!" Heather bellowed as she levelled her rifle at the faces of the constables.

They needed no prompting. The constables quickly handcuffed each other, not wanting to suffer the same fate as Sergeant Willis. Heather hurried past them, trying all the keys for the door to the inner corridor.

Jason looked at Mr Robinson; he took his eyes off the constables for only a brief moment. The one constable still not shackled, lunged forward and caught him off guard.

"Yes Sir, that's right, Old Ma Smith's place." the constable was talking down the phone to Inspector Kingsley.

As the constable leaned over his desk, a blast that could only have come from a blunderbuss sounded from somewhere inside the station. The constable ducked involuntarily, then turned to check the security screens on the wall in front of him.

"Sir, Sir, we're under attack." the constable yelled and dived behind his desk. "I say again, we are under attack."

Inspector Kingsley jumped from his bed and reached for his clothes that were folded neatly on the dresser.

"What is it dear?" his wife asked, rubbing her eyes.

"I'm needed at the station." He tried to sound calm. He rushed out of the room, buttoning up his trousers and headed for the stairs.

Jason de Silva pushed the constable away from him as plaster rained down from the ceiling. He slammed the constable into the wall, the blunderbuss pressed against the constable's chest. He fell next to his handcuffed colleagues gasping for air. Heather pointed her rifle in his face.

Mr Robinson found the right key, unlocked it and swung the

door open. Jason followed him as they charged into the inner corridor, surprise still on their side. Seconds later an alarm began to sound, ear splitting sirens announced that the surprise they relied upon had gone.

The pair ran down the inner corridor and located the cells that held Tom and Margaret Robinson. Jason pulled back the iron bolts and they both burst into the cells.

"Come on Tom; let's get the fuck outta here!" Jason yelled at the frightened old man.

Tom stared wide-eyed at Jason; his inertia worried Jason, he knew they needed to move fast. Jason did the only thing he could; he lifted his mask showing the old man his face.

"It's me, come on." Jason said as he grabbed the old man and hauled him to his feet.

As they rushed from the cell, they nearly ran headlong into Mr Robinson, who carried his mother, wide eyed and a little shaken up by the breakout.

Without saying another word, they quickly entered the outer corridor, and passed through the security door. They passed Heather who backed away still holding her weapon levelled at the constables lying prone before her.

Running across the courtyard, they left the police compound through the footman's gate, the one that was never locked. Two vehicles waited on the street outside, the twins Trevor and Dominic waited patiently to execute their part of the planned breakout.

"Come on pa!" Heather yelled at Tom, as she opened the door to Trevor's vehicle.

Heather hurried her parents-in-law into the back seat of the vehicle and then jumped into the front seat. Trevor engaged the fuel cells, applying full power. The idling hum turned to a whirling whine, as the vehicle burned rubber, they made their escape.

Jason and Mr Robinson were already in the second vehicle,

the door was slammed as Dominic accelerated to follow his brother.

"What the hell do you think you're doing?" old Tom was flustered as his daughter-in-law removed her mask.

"We couldn't do it pa!" Heather turned and looked at her husband's parents, people she had long regarded as close to her own as possible, they looked tired and frightened.

"Couldn't do what?" Margaret snapped, unhappy at their daughter-in-law's involvement.

"Leave you in that cell." she answered.

The interior of the other vehicle couldn't have been more different. They whooped and cheered, as the vehicles sped to the edge of Coopers Town. There was no sign of pursuit as they headed out into the countryside. They passed another vehicle going in the other direction at full speed. Jason looked at Inspector Kingsley for a split second, but he looked straight ahead, concentrating on what he was doing.

Forty five minutes later, the three vehicles had arrived back at High Peaks Farm.

The wintry night drew in and it threatened snow. The nine fugitives trudged into the living room and sat down, finding space wherever they could.

"Well that was stupid of you." Tom said, he sat next to Margaret on the sofa.

"Would you have preferred prison?" Jason asked, his hands were spread apart, imploring understanding "I, we couldn't leave you in those cold cells, and I felt responsible."

"I would rather have gone to prison, than you all make criminals of yourselves. There'll be the devil to pay, mark my words," Margaret said angrily, "The very devil."

"I'll go make some tea." Heather said cheerily.

Jason stood and cleared his throat, "Well in that case, I've decided, I'm gonna hand myself in. I can make a deal, get them to leave you all alone." He looked dejected, the decades of sharing a prison with criminals stretching out in his mind.

"You'll do nothing of the sort." Tom stood and shook his fist. He pointed an angry finger at Jason's chest. "We got ourselves into this mess, and we're in it proper but we're in it together!" he shouted.

"Shhhh, shush a minute," Dominic interrupted; he had turned the television on and now waved his grandfather into silence.

They turned to the television and fell silent. The news reporter spoke on the screen; "This video clearly shows what happened that night last week, outside the de Silva residence. It shows the attack on de Silva's home that sparked the violent defence from the local man that has swiftly become a legend in his neighbourhood: Jason de Silva."

The news reporter turned to the big screen behind her. The picture switched from a still photo of Jason to footage of the night that the Smith gang attacked his home. It clearly showed them charging at Jason and of Jacky getting injured.

"So as you can see, Jason de Silva was attacked by the gang. The laws of hearth and home spring to my mind, or rather the inability of the law to come into effect. The police opting to arrest de Silva, causing him to turn rogue and to leave a trail of death and destruction in his wake have more to answer to in this debacle than does de Silva, or so it would seem to me."

"Wow." Philip said and sat back on his heels, amazed at the footage of Jason fighting a gang of thugs single-handedly.

"That's rather fortunate; the nation can now see that you acted legally." Mr Robinson cracked a smile, "This changes everything."

"I went berserk, didn't I?" Jason was amazed, he hadn't realised how aggressive he had been that night.

"That's an understatement." Tom said, "You remind me of your granddad Sydney."

"At least now everybody can see you're not at fault." Randell said.

"I got some twenty year old Mead, in the cellar; I've been waiting for an occasion to crack it open." Mr Robinson was smiling as Heather returned carrying a tray of steaming mugs, "Take 'em back, we're having that mead I've been saving."

"Right you are." Heather turned back around and her eyes were gleaming with delight.

Heather and Mr Robinson disappeared into the kitchen and returned a few minutes later. They carried three bottles and nine small glasses. The living room was silent as Jason and the Robinson clan waited to sample the strong alcohol.

Mr Robinson filled the glasses and passed round the first round of drinks.

Jason knocked back his glass, emptying it of the warm liquid and nodded as the rest did the same.

Just as Mr Robinson was about to pour another round, a vehicle turned onto the lane, its headlights shone for a moment on the curtains.

"Shit, the guns!" Randell said.

Everybody looked around in panic; the guns had been left in the vehicles. Nobody thought of them in their rush to get inside to congratulate themselves on the success of their mission.

In the minute that followed, there was a mad scramble as the lights and the television were turned off. Everybody dived for cover, holding their breath, praying they hadn't been caught unawares.

The vehicle came to a halt just beyond the stone wall that separated the farmyard from the fields. Jason dared to peep through the crack in the curtain, making sure he kept low and in shadow. His heart soared with joy, behind the wheel of the vehicle sat his wife, Jacky.

"What the fuck, how the hell?" Jason turned to the waiting Robinsons, "It's my wife."

"I stole the number from ya phone." Mr Robinson answered

Jason's unasked question. "I thought you wouldn't mind."

Jason bolted from the farmhouse, and ran into the courtyard, and vaulted the stone wall. Jason was more than ready to embrace his family. His face-splitting smile was the first thing that Jacky saw as she turned with Hector asleep in her arms.

"Jacky!" He yelled, and the tears streamed down his cheeks.

He held her and kissed her but was careful not to wake Hector. Then he went to the vehicle to scoop Louis into his arms to hold him close.

Randell appeared at the stone wall. "Mrs de Silva, can I have your keys please?" He held his large hand over the wall.

"Oh yes, here." She blushed as she fumbled her keys when she looked up at the tall stranger.

Randell got in the vehicle and drove it through the open gateway into the courtyard.

"That's Randell, he's a friend." Jason said, as they started walking towards the farm house. They held a child each; Louis yawned but tried to stay awake in Jason's arms.

They went into the kitchen and Mr Robinson and Heather stood just inside to greet the new arrivals.

"Here dear, let me put the little ones down." Heather smiled, taking Louis first. Then with her free arm, she cradled Hector as Jacky passed him over.

"What about the police that were watching you?" Jason asked, worried that she had been followed.

He pulled her close, kissed her forehead, and then released her so she could sit down at the kitchen table.

Jason sat next to his wife, whilst Mr Robinson sat across from Jacky.

"Well that's the thing about tonight; they disappeared about an hour ago." Jacky said, and then she leaned over to kiss Jason once more. "And the strangest thing is that just after they left, a man rang me up."

"Did he now?" Mr Robinson looked at Jason, they exchanged

a nod.

"He sounded just like you; he told me that they would not be watching me the entire night. So be ready to escape, to here were I'd find you," Jacky smiled as she realised it was the large farmer that had been the one on the phone.

"How did you get the constables to move?" Jacky asked.

Before he could answer, Heather returned and the Robinson boys trooped into the house, carrying the guns from the vehicles. Jacky looked at the weapons and her eyes followed the farmers as they moved through the kitchen.

"Let's just say we caused a distraction. The directions I gave you were all right then?" he asked, changing the subject.

"We've been here a few times to picnic up at the stone circle." Jacky answered.

Heather was busy rustling around the kitchen, "I'm making a snack, all of you go in there," she ordered.

Margaret came back into the kitchen and without needing to ask, she began helping her daughter-in-law with the food.

Jason and all the others went into the living room, dragging the kitchen chairs with them so they'd all have a seat.

They started chatting about the events of the past week; everyone took their turn to tell their version of events. Philip got upset when he told of the burning of Old Ma Smith. He didn't know whether she survived or not. They talked on into the night and they came to realise that the events of last night and the murders they had committed had created an unbreakable bond. They drank the Mead till it was all gone as they sat in front of the open fire, sometimes in silence. The firelight was the only thing that showed their faces, the moons were hidden by thick clouds that had gathered and blocked out even Serene's luminescence.

"Well, its sounds to me like we're at war then." Dominic spoke from the corner of the room he sat forward and rested his chin in his hands.

"Sounds like it." Jason said.

They all nodded in agreement.

"This is insane." Jacky said. "You can't beat the establishment." She sounded panicky, and she wondered if she was the only sane person in the room.

"It's an insanity of their doing." Heather said, her smile in the firelight making her even look insane.

"And if they want it they can have it." Mr Robinson continued for his wife. "They're not taking our Philip!"

Jason saw the concern on his wife's face. "Let's not get ahead of ourselves, I can say it was me that burnt Old Ma Smith and still broker a deal," he said.

"It's too late for that." Trevor spoke from the shadows.

"Trevor's right." Mr Robinson turned to Jason. "For better or worse, we're in this together."

Old Tom stood, he had been holding his tongue in the impromptu conference, but now he had something to say. "What we need is a plan; we've got to have a plan." Tom said. He paused to give everyone the chance to speak and when no one did, he continued. "If we're at war, we may as well declare war."

Silence filled the room, Tom stood grim and proud as he announced his intentions, "That's not the response I was looking for, but hey I think it's a good idea." he said.

"No good will come of that, you old fool." Margaret glared at her husband until he sat back down beside her. "What will you do, ring up the Prime Minister and say: excuse me Peter but we're at war now?" She admonished Tom, but his blushes couldn't be seen in dim light.

"The media!" Jacky said.

"An interview, I can give an interview. The country already knows I've been fitted up." Jason jumped on Jacky's suggestion, "It's the only reasonable course of action to take."

Harold de Silva stood with his fists on his hips in front of his son Jason as Jacky loaded Louis and Hector into their grandfather's vehicle, then she kissed them both goodbye.

"Good luck son." Harold offered his hand.

"Thank you father, I thought you'd be pissed with me." Jason said as he took his father's hand.

"I am, but this might be the last time I see you alive." Harold seemed cold and distant, as though he already thought his son was gone.

"We ain't dead yet." Jason looked past his father at his two sons. Louis cried, his tears rolling unabated as he sobbed.

"They'll be well looked after, they're certainly better off with us right now." Harold looked at Jacky as she comforted Louis, then he turned back to his son. "'Bye son."

Jacky came to Jason's side, her tears threatened to fall as they brimmed in her eyes as Harold got into the vehicle. She waved and tried to smile and her boys waved back as they were driven away. The vehicle turned out of sight just as a hover jet came into view. The hover's jets blasted the ground as it powered low over the farm from behind the hills.

The hover jet coasted low to the ground and finally came to rest. It skidded on the frosty grass as its turbines disengaged.

As the engines turned skywards and clicked loudly as they locked, the doors beneath the wings slid open. Three people jumped from the hover jet and made their way straight to Jason and Jacky. One of the three held a large video camera, the type used by the media. Another man carried a hard case and the third, a woman, wore a figure hugging dress and high heels. She wasn't dressed for the terrain or the harsh weather.

"Hello Mr de Silva." The woman said as she got close enough to hear over the gusting wind.

Jacky touched the scar on her forehead involuntarily as the two beautiful women exchanged glances. They would have looked very similar but for the healing wounds on Jacky's face.

"Lindsey Sumter." The woman said as she shook hands with Jason.

"Shall we go inside?" Jason said.

Jason led the way into the courtyard toward the farmhouse kitchen, the news team and Jacky followed.

Tom and his son sat in the kitchen and as the news team entered, they put down their pipes.

"Hello, it's cold isn't it?" The pretty news reporter said to the farmers.

"You should try putting some clothes on." Tom said, "It is winter."

"Yes well." Lindsey was taken aback and she blushed, everyone looked at her as though waiting for her smart retort but she had none.

"Shall we start the interview?" Jason asked.

Lindsey flashed him a smile in thanks for coming to her rescue. "Are you ready?" she asked.

"I was born ready." he replied and smiled as Jacky rolled her eyes at his clichéd response.

Inspector Kingsley paced his office. *'How can this be happening?'* he thought as he looked through the glass to the next room. Every constable he had at his disposal awaited him in that room. He steeled himself to head the meeting, and then went in to brief his small force.

He looked around the room at his troops; finally he began to speak to the silent assembly. "Never in all my years on the force, have I failed to solve a case given to me and I never will." He paused and then raised his voice "So why the hell is this one eluding me? I want answers, I want to know where Jason de Silva is, I want to know who is helping him and I want to know today!" Spittle hung from his lip and he slammed his fist onto the table.

As he finished his tirade, a constable ran into the room,

ignoring Inspector Kingsley's angry arm-waving, the constable picked up the remote and turned on the television that was suspended from the wall.

"Sorry for the interruption Sir, I thought you might want to see this." The constable said.

They all turned to look at the screen; the image had been paused from the other room. The constable pressed the remote and the programme started again. "So Mr de Silva, what's your story and why all the carnage? Surely there's a better way?" Lindsey Sumter held her microphone away from her, close to Jason de Silva's mouth.

"Well Lindsey, my house was attacked; my family were persecuted and bullied. We all saw it on your news programme. There's always some poor family being picked on by these bastards but not my family! The scum attacked my family and I invoked the laws of Hearth and Home. Yes I killed those men, the Skav trash that invaded the lives of my family and they killed my mother in law and were about to execute the rest of my family. I justify myself and my actions, in the defence of my flesh and blood." Jason paused but Lindsey gave him the tiniest of nods to encourage him and he continued.

"The question I want everyone to consider is this: why is this happening in our society today? It's happening because of the do-gooders that pressure our government and the government officials that write the legislation that tie the hands of the police. The police have become an almost useless element in our society; the law protects the criminals and damns the weak. I think perhaps that's why they go so heavy-handed when someone does fight back against the thug scum, it's because the law-abiding citizen that has hit back is easier to prosecute. But I am asking difficult questions. What about the victims? What about the raped and the murdered? What about the elderly, too frightened to go out in the daylight let alone in the moons light? What about the persecuted such as me and my family? I say no to the courts of human rights, unless they're gonna consider the victims more than the criminal Skavs. It's high time our once great planet reformed its laws to suit the decent hard working citizen. The scum that wishes to feed off everyone else should be cast down into the pit of despair!" Jason's anger had been building as he spoke and as he finished, his face was red with that anger and his fists, off-camera, were clenched tight.

Lindsey moved the microphone to speak into it as Jason paused for breath.

"They are strong words Mr de Silva, but tell me what your intentions are?"

"I intend to fight." Jason's face remained angry and defiant as he folded his arms.

"Excuse me?" Lindsey's smile slipped a little as she became nervous that this report had become more serious than she had imagined.

"I am declaring war on the government legislation of the Kingdom of the Five Moons and the Land of Albion. Let all those who support the laws beware. I also declare war on the criminal Skavs that plague the decent peoples of Albion." Jason pointed at the camera. "The devil awaits you in the pit of despair." He looked grim as the camera panned away from him to face Lindsey Sumter.

"This is Lindsey Sumter, reporting from somewhere in Albion." Lindsey looked uncomfortable as the screen returned to the news room.

You could hear the constable's finger as it pressed the remote to turn the television off; the room was so silent you could have heard a pin dropping onto cotton.

"Well I think that's kinda final then." Mr Robinson turned away from the television.

"It is for me, but you all could still pull out." Jason sat back in his arm chair. "It's odd watching yourself on the television; I don't sound like me at all."

"That's something to do with the inner ear." Philip shouted from the kitchen.

"I'll take your word for it." Jason shouted back.

Mr Robinson picked up his pipe and began to fill it. "We appreciate your concern Jay, but we've all made our choices to help ya. Besides there ain't no way they're gonna let this drop, they'll hunt us down till we're dead or in prison. We may as well go down fighting." Mr Robinson lit a match to light the tobacco.

Trevor came in from the kitchen followed by Dominic, Randell and Philip.

"So what happens now?" Trevor asked and he sat on the floor next to the open fire.

"I guess it's their move, and as long as me and your grandparents stay hidden they shouldn't find us, at least not for a while anyway." Jason said.

"They'll be looking for me too." Jacky said and went to sit on Jason's lap to make more room for the Robinsons.

"Yes of course, we have to stay out of sight; anyhow we're well hidden up here." Jason put his arms around her as she leaned into his chest.

"What about that reporter, I don't trust that one, she's only out for herself." Randell said.

"She swore a holy oath, something about Thalia and the Sisters of the Five Moons." Jason said.

The family nodded, no one made an oath like that and broke it.

Inspector Kingsley sat at his desk as he pondered his next move. The phone rang and roused him from his thoughts.

"Hello?" he said snappishly.

"There's a caller on line two for you Sir." The constable on reception sounded nervous. The phone's tone changed as the caller was put through.

"Hello, Kingsley here." The Inspector said.

"High Peaks Farm." A quiet voice said.

"Excuse me, who is this?" Inspector Kingsley was in no mood for pranks.

"That's where Jason de Silva is hiding." The line went dead as the caller hung up.

Chapter 6

Spring had arrived; the frost had been forced upwards to the highest ground where the wild goats frolicked on the edge of the precipice. The four Robinson boys went about their chores on the farm. The other Robinson men sat around the kitchen table, oiling and honing their collection of swords. The gun racks were full again; the rifles and blunderbuss gleamed.

Jason and Jacky had walked to the top of the stone circle, wrapped up well against the cold spring afternoon.

"Do you remember, before the kids..." Jacky looked skyward as a few snowflakes floated towards the ground, defying the spring.

"Up here, on warm summer days?" Jason took her hand in his as they walked around the stones. Jason touched one of the massive stones that stood tall at the edge of the circle. He could feel it resonating beneath his touch; he was one of a few that claimed he could feel the stones vibrating warmth. Most, like Jacky, remained sceptical. She frowned at Jason as he turned, daring him to make his claim.

Jason removed his hand from the stone, he decided against starting that particular debate and instead he turned to look northward, towards the beauty of the mountains.

"Beautiful isn't it." he said; his troubles for the moment at least, pushed to the back of his mind.

"Yes." she said, following his gaze.

They surveyed the landscape together, seeing for miles from

their high vantage point. A hover jet came into view; it was flying low and following the line of the road.

"That's odd." Jacky frowned as she spoke.

Then a line of police vehicles came into view. They followed the hover jet, matching its pace. Their lights were flashing but the sirens were silent at that distance.

"Shit! Jacky run!"

They took off running down hill as fast as they could. Jason lost his balance and fell; he rolled down the slope for twenty metres before he managed to regain his footing.

"Cops, cops!" Jacky yelled as they neared the bottom of the hill. The Robinson boys looked up and their gaze followed Jacky's pointing finger.

Jason and Jacky scrambled into the cobbled courtyard as the hover jet flew overhead. It banked hard left, the faces of the policemen clearly visible as they watched them. Flashing lights crested the ridges close to the farm; they blocked any chance of escape by road as the frantic de Silvas burst into the farmhouse.

Jason and Jacky bent over and leaned on their knees as they panted for breath. The Robinsons were running to grab guns and load weapons. Heather rushed about closing blinds and drawing all the curtains.

"It's just like in the movies." Trevor's stupid grin showed his excitement as he ran upstairs, a rifle and a box of ammunition in his hands.

Dominic dived behind his father's overturned armchair beneath the living room window. Randell and Philip burst outside, running to the farmyard wall, armed to the teeth.

Jason straightened up, and old Tom threw a shot gun into his hands.

"Careful lad, its loaded." The old man grinned.

"There are no more guns." Jacky said to Tom.

"It's time for you to go," Jason took her hand in his. "The kids need their mum, and besides, you ain't done nothing wrong."

"I want to stay here with you." A tear ran down her face as she held Jason tight.

"We're all gonna die here sweety, I ain't goin to prison." Jason pulled himself away and held her at arm's length.

Mr Robinson came in from the living room; he put his gun on the table. He laid a massive arm across Jacky's shoulders; she looked like a dwarf in his embrace. "Hush there lass," he said, consoling her as she sobbed.

"You've done nothing wrong." Jason stepped back, "There's no reason for you to be here."

"I suppose." Jacky's shoulders slumped as she resigned herself to the truth of the matter, *'It's time to leave my love to his fate,'* she thought.

Mr Robinson relaxed his hold on Jacky as she pulled her coat up around her chin. She stepped close to Jason, and wrapped her arms around him. She kissed him once. "I love you," she managed between sobs.

"Love you more," he replied, he smiled at her and she tried to return the smile.

She turned and walked away from her husband, through the door leading outside into the farmyard.

Philip and Randell lay on the ground against the wall, guns in their hands, waiting for something to happen.

"They ain't taking me alive, I killed already!" Philip looked maniacal as he spoke, his eyes wide with rage.

"I'm with you bro." Randell leaned over and the brothers clasped right hands.

"Good luck boys." Jacky saw them through blurry eyes and she nervously approached the gate leading out onto the lane. The police were everywhere; she lifted her hands above her head, to show them she had no weapons.

Inspector Kingsley smiled, *'case closed,'* he thought.

His men lined the wall that ran along the lane a hundred feet away from the farm house. All wore police issue assault armour and all looked menacing in their hard, black, storm troopers uniform. Every constable sported a short sword, hilted at his hip in a black scabbard. Forty carried army standard, semi automatic assault rifles.

"I want the perimeter closed down!" Inspector Kingsley yelled his orders. "Sergeant Willis, get some men around the back, cut off any retreat."

"Yes Sir." The Sergeant that had been injured in Jason's attack on the station saluted as he turned, "You three come with me," he barked the order as he set off he was careful as he placed his helmet over his bandages as he ran.

Then Jacky de Silva appeared, walking slowly away from the farm house. She raised her arms with her fingers splayed wide to show that she was hiding nothing then stepped out onto the lane in clear sight. The jet hovered high above the farm, out of range of the guns.

"She's unarmed!" The observer's voice came over the radio.

"Hold your fire men." Kingsley ordered, pressing the button on the radio that was incorporated into his body armour.

'I'll get a promotion for cracking this one.' Inspector Kingsley thought, as the constable next to him sneezed.

The constable was resting on the wall, his rifle pointing at the farm. As he sneezed his body tensed and caused his fingers to clench – including his trigger finger. The crack of rifle fire echoed around the valley as the bullet shot from its chamber. Birds broke cover and the wildlife seemed to duck from the sound.

The single shot hit Jacky de Silva, her hands still in the air; she had reached the half way point. Jacky spun around, her body thrown off balance and she hit the ground and lay still.

Jason looked on, peeking through the curtains, as his wife was gunned down. "No! NO!" Jason burst from the safety of the farm house into the cold air. He reached the wall and levelled his shotgun at the police.

A second hover jet flew over head and almost skimmed the roof of the farmhouse. Jason swivelled around and raised his weapon. He let off a round which hit the hover jet with a spray of pellets. There was a camera protruding from its open door and the media jet banked sharply and made haste out of range. Then Jason brought his weapon back around to face the police and as he bore down the gentle slope he fired again. Splinters of stone flew in all directions as pellets peppered the wall.

Then all hell broke loose, as shots burst forth in a crescendo of chaos. Glass shattered and wood splintered as bullets ricocheted off hard cover. The air filled with carbine smoke from the heat of barrels and blasts of the blunderbuss.

Philip and Randell dragged Jason down behind the farmyard wall; lead was flying through the air just above their heads.

"Let me go!" Jason yelled as he reloaded the pump action shot gun

"You'll get yourself killed," Randell shouted over the cacophony.

Philip leaned around the wall to poke his gun through a gap between the wall and the gate. He fired a shot and bullets peppered the wall as Philip ducked back behind cover.

"Into the house!" Philip yelled.

Randell and Philip took hold of Jason's arms, it was an effort to drag him back, protesting and trying to get to his wife. With a huge effort they managed to get into the farmhouse and Phillip slammed the kitchen door shut with his foot as the bullets sprayed.

"A proper storm we've brewed up here lad." Tom looked up briefly from reloading a rifle.

"Jacky!" Jason screamed as he ran to the window, the glass already gone.

"She's only winded." Margaret said as she touched Jason's arm.

There was a lull in the firing and from both inside and outside of the farmhouse, the sounds of weapons being reloaded was silent to them as the shooting still rang in their ears.

"Stop firing. Stop firing!" Inspector Kingsley walked the line of his men, he slapped at those that didn't hear his yells. As the last few shots rang out, the Inspector walked up to the constable that had sneezed.

"What the fuck was that, you fucking moron?" he screeched as he hauled the constable to his feet.

Jacky half crawled, half slithered down the gentle slope toward the police lines.

"Will somebody help her?" A man's voice shouted from inside the farm house.

"Twat!" the Inspector pushed the constable back onto the wall. He climbed over the wall and ran unarmed to Jacky.

Curtains twitched in windows on both floors of the two storey building as he reached the injured woman. "Hold your fire," he yelled, waving at the farm.

"That wasn't meant to happen." Inspector Kingsley said, cradling her head.

"None of this was meant to happen." Jacky winced as the Inspector applied pressure to the open wound in Jacky's shoulder.

"Is she all right?" Jason asked, yelling from inside the house.

"I think so; she's not losing too much blood." Inspector Kingsley shouted back, he smiled and tried to keep Jacky at ease.

Two medics ran through the police line carrying a stretcher to take Jacky to the waiting medical vehicle. It had been brought forward as soon as the firing had ceased.

"De Silva," Inspector Kingsley shouted as the medics took over Jacky's treatment.

"What?" Jason de Silva shouted.

"That was an accident." Kingsley said.

The medics picked Jacky up and took her away. They jogged down the lane seeming to spare no thought for Jacky's comfort.

Jason stood in the large open window to the living room. "Is she ok?" The concern for his wife got the better of his anger.

"She's going to be fine, now why don't you all lay your guns down and come out? We can sort this out, we know you didn't start this mess, but you can't go around like vigilantes." Kingsley stepped forward, his hands out to his sides, he was close enough to see de Silva's face clearly. "There are laws!"

"If it's all right with you I'll fight my cause." de Silva looked almost Skavish, as he rolled his muscled shoulders. "And besides, I'm an enemy of the state now. I ain't spending the rest of my life in prison, with those I've declared war on. I'm better off dead."

"But," Inspector Kingsley started.

"You've got thirty seconds to get back behind that wall." de Silva said. Kingsley took the hint.

Ducking back down behind cover, Jason looked at Tom and Margaret. "Sorry you got drawn into all of this mess."

"Don't be silly dear; we wouldn't have missed it for the world." Margaret said with a glint in her eye.

"We're always spoiling for a fight, us farming folk." Tom reached over and patted Jason on the shoulder.

They ducked as the police started firing into the house.

Mr Robinson crawled into the living room. "Come on, we're making a break for it!" He yelled and he ducked instinctively as his grandfather clock took a direct hit. He looked up and shook his head and he started to turn. They made their way into the kitchen, slow and low. Jason was the last one as the Robinsons gathered at the back door. He shut the connecting door behind him and it took hits that splintered the wood.

"We can't stay here, we'll die for sure!" Heather yelled. She sported a rifle that was nearly as long as she was tall.

"We can still surrender." Jason said.

They looked at him with blank expressions on their faces.

"On three." Dominic shouted and took hold of the door

handle.

"One, two, three!" The four brothers counted down together.

The police shooting at the farm couldn't see them because the road was a few feet below the courtyard. They burst out of the kitchen, running away from the farm, heading for the out houses. The hover jet turned and circled above them. The police inside it pointed at them as the spotlight hit the same ground as their feet did. The four brothers covered their retreat, the sound of the gun fire from the road lessening. Margaret led the way next, she ran around the corner where their vehicles were in full view. From behind the first vehicle, a constable wearing a full assault kit appeared.

The constable raised his gun and he prepared to fire at close range. Old Tom beat him to it, his gun already raised as he walked around the corner. Tom fired his shotgun over his wife's shoulder. Tom hit the constable from just feet away and the constable's body armour was no match for the shotgun at point blank range. He flew backwards in the air; dead with his lungs and neck peppered with shot.

Then a second constable, with his own weapon raised, appeared from behind the second vehicle. He yelled a battle cry, his high powered semi automatic blazing away. Tom and Margaret danced wildly as their bodies were riddled with bullets and their blood sprayed the air.

Heather was next around the corner, screaming like a banshee at the sight of her in-law's deaths. The constable had emptied the magazine into Tom and Margaret and he threw his weapon to the floor and drew his sword.

"Bastard!" Heather screamed, and she pulled the trigger, her rifle fired a single shot. The constable's forward motion was halted as the bullet hit his body armour. Cocking her rifle she fired a second shot before the man could recover. The bullet hit the man in the groin just below his armour. He fell, holding his leg and blood spurted through his hands from the severed artery.

Mr Robinson pulled his wife away as the rest of the Robinsons rounded the corner with Jason. Mr Robinson slipped on the liquid that was the blood of his parents; Mr Robinson dragged Heather to the first vehicle. Two more policemen rounded the corner at the far end of the line of outhouses. One carried a semi automatic but the Robinson brothers were ready, their weapons were already trained in his direction. The second policeman ducked back behind the outhouses as the brothers let off a volley. The constable's weapon fired at the ground as he fell backwards as he was hit by the shots from blunderbuss, a shotgun and two rifles.

Jason got into the passenger seat of the first vehicle; Randell jumped in beside him and engaged the fuel cells. With a helpful push from his dad, Philip dived across his mother and Mr Robinson slammed the rear door behind them. He turned to get to the second vehicle, Trevor and Dominic had jumped into the front seats. Dominic was at the controls and they too began to move. Mr Robinson was just getting into the back seat when the policeman reappeared from behind the end of the line of buildings. He drew his sword and removed his full faced helmet.

"Bernard." Mr Robinson paused with one foot in the vehicle.

Bernard Willis swung his broad sword. He had a vicious smile as he offered Mr Robinson single combat.

"Come on dad!" Trevor yelled.

"Bastard!" Mr Robinson yelled, as he dived into the vehicle's back seat.

Randell smashed through the gate at the rear of the farmyard, obliterating it. Two hover jets followed them overhead and as the two vehicles burst out into the field that the farms cattle grazed. They skidded forward, fighting the slippery surface as the ground gave way to their frantic driving.

As they rounded Aamor, they heard gun shots behind them. Sergeant Willis was shooting at them with a rifle he'd retrieved from a dead colleague. Then they were out of sight and headed for freedom.

"What the fuck, is going on?" Inspector Kingsley fumed and ducked down behind the stone wall.

It looked like the De Silva gang hadn't returned fire for a few minutes.

He tried again and pressed the button on his radio. "Sergeant Willis, are you receiving?"

All around him, thirty three armed response officers fired their weapons, relentlessly firing bullet after bullet at the old stone building. Then the hover jets started to move toward the rear of the building, their roaring engines inaudible because the sounds of gunshots drowned out everything.

"They are on the move, this is 'Eye in the sky' and I repeat they are on the move." One of the hover jet personnel spoke over the radio. All down the police line, the constables stopped firing within a few seconds of the message. They looked to the Inspector and awaited orders.

"Man down, man down!" The voice from the hover jet broke over the radio again but this time he sounded distressed.

Inspector Kingsley jumped to his feet. "Charge!" he bellowed as he ran around the end of the wall.

'I've always wanted to do that,' he thought as he ran and a smile creased his face. His men followed him.

The two vehicles, adapted for life on the farm, were suited for off road all terrain activity, but the wet conditions made it difficult as they struggled on the slippery grass.

"Slow down, by Dark Ceinlys, you'll get us all killed." Jason cursed as the vehicle listed badly, turning toward the wall at the bottom of Aamor hill.

"I'm losing control!" Randell yelled, sounding panicked, and he lost control of the four wheeled drive vehicle. Fish-tailing wildly, the vehicle slammed into the low stone wall that separated Aamor from the fields at its base. Luckily the vehicle didn't stall as they smashed through the wall and Randell engaged full power. They shot forward and the vehicle headed for the stones at the top of the hill.

Following behind, the second vehicle nudged the first's rear end to help it along. It took only half a minute at full power to get to the top of Aamor and they crested the ridge at the top. They took off and the passengers yelled in fear as they were thrown from their seats. They flew past the outer ring of huge upright stones and missed the top ones by only inches. Both vehicles landed and skidded along the grass. The first Vehicle came to rest as it slammed into one of the smaller inner stones.

Randell, Philip and Jason were thrown forward with the impact then seconds later; they were thrown about again as the second vehicle crashed into them.

The fuel cells gave way and the lights dimmed fast and went out. For a time Jason's sight blurred, his head throbbed and his back ached from the crash. He watched in stunned silence as the police hover jet came close. Hanging out of the side was a constable, trying to aim a pistol but the hover jet was buffeted by a strong gust of wind.

Jason's hearing was impaired but he only noticed as first Randell and then Dominic opened fire from their seats inside the vehicles. The sound was muted and muffled. Then all his senses came rushing back as Randell screamed a battle cry and fired round after round at the hover jet. Then the hover jet pulled away and banked off down the hillside in a desperate attempt to avoid the gunshots.

Jason opened the rear door of the vehicle and half climbed, half fell out onto the ground. He stumbled as he walked over to the edge of the top of the small plateau. He was unsteady on his feet as he looked out over the landscape below, watching the hover jet's running lights sweeping the ground as it flew low over the farmland. He watched as an ambulance disappeared, driving out of view toward the lowlands.

"Jacky." He whispered her name as a tear rolled down his cheek; he assumed correctly that she was in the medical vehicle.

Mr Robinson appeared at his side, and he turned his attention to the farm below. Constables swarmed over the farm, kicking in doors and pointing guns into every room and outhouse they entered.

Jason walked to the nearest stone and rested his back against it and as he slid down he watched as the Robinsons ran around the stone circle, hiding behind the stones. Mr Robinson walked unsteadily over to Heather, who wailed continuously, sobbing for the deceased parents-in-law. He hugged his wife and rocked her in his arms as a parent consoling a young child would.

Trevor's face was bleeding but he knelt down at Jason's side. "They're surrounding us Jay." His face was blank, whether from shock or resignation, Jason couldn't tell.

"So much for the revolution!" Jason smiled in spite of his injuries.

Trevor slumped beside him and laughed at Jason's unintended joke.

Jason laughed too.

"I guess this is it then?" Trevor said.

"Well they ain't taking me alive." Jason stopped laughing.

"Me nether." Trevor felt at his forehead, and his fingers came away bloody from a shallow cut.

"Did you get all of that?" Lindsey Sumter asked the cameraman, as the hover jet they had chartered circled high above Aamor.

"Yeah, I got it," he replied, staring out at the history they were witnessing.

'*What have I done*?' she thought, and she was surprised to feel a pang of guilt. Lindsey thought of the phone call she had made, all in the interest of freedom of speech and enhancing her own career.

"We'll be up for awards after this," she said, hiding her shame behind her practiced smile.

"That's for sure," her cameraman agreed.

"Well, keep filming, I've got a feeling this story has just begun." Lindsey looked in every direction as the hover jet continued its lazy circles. "There must be hundreds of coppers down there."

"And the rest, they'll want to set an example with this lot." The pilot looked over his shoulder to add his opinion.

Lindsey sat and looked at the pilot and he smiled back at her. She was deep in thought, with an idea forming. "How close do you think you can get us?" she asked.

"Well they ain't shooting any more, I guess we could get pretty close," the pilot replied, he wanted to please this famous news reporter who fluttered her pretty eyes at him. "Why?" he asked as an afterthought.

"I've had an idea." She winked.

"Inspector, Sir." The constable saluted and came to attention in front of Inspector Kingsley.

"Yes?" Kingsley decided to ignore the constable's salute.

"We've got the hill surrounded, Sir."

"Good, good. Don't let the men get too close; charging up that hill would be suicide." The Inspector looked the constable in the face, "I don't need any more casualties."

"Er, Sir." The constable's attention was diverted and he pointed towards the top of Aamor.

Kingsley turned to look up and he saw the hover jet just a few feet above the top of the hill, its jets barely audible in the distance.

"What the hell are they doing?" He asked no one, and as he looked on in shock and horror. Lindsey Sumter and her cameraman threw equipment out of the hover jet and then both jumped from the craft. "What the fuck is that silly bitch doing?"

The cameraman pointed his camera at the two men pointing their guns at his face as soon as he'd landed. He jumped out onto the hill top, careful not to tread on the bags he'd just thrown out of the hover jet. He put the camera over his shoulder and turned to film Lindsey as she lowered herself onto the grassy hill top.

"Lindsey Sumter." Jason said as he stepped forward. He offered her his hand and smiled like they'd just met under more normal circumstances.

"Mr de Silva." Lindsey said as she straightened her clothing.

Trevor and Dominic lowered their guns and ran back to the edge of Aamor to keep watch over the lands below them.

"What are you doing here?" Jason asked.

"I could ask you the same thing," she bent down to take her shoes off as the hover jet left them and flew south.

"Ain't you cold?" Jason asked.

"I'm always cold around you." Lindsey answered tartly, and instantly regretted her tone.

"Thank you very much." Jason tried to sound sarcastic but he was too weary. He looked at her and almost laughed at what she was wearing, her clothes were totally unsuitable but she took his smile for admiration.

"If you must know, I've come to document your fight," Lindsey looked at the cameraman and nodded. "I had to come to you, the hover jets fuel wouldn't have lasted." She spoke to Jason without looking at him.

The cameraman put his heavy camera on the floor and turned it off with a flick of a switch. He took a small transmitter from a small case and wired it into the camera. Next he changed the battery, before turning it back on.

Mr Robinson wandered over, interested in the only activity on the plateau.

"How's Heather?" Jason asked and turned to him as he approached.

"She's sat in the vehicle keeping warm." Mr Robinson's face was full of hurt; he was worried for his wife and broken at the barbarism dealt to his parents at the hands of the authorities.

"Talking of warmth, how are you all going to keep warm tonight?" Lindsey interrupted, tact not one of her many talents.

"We have food for a few days, tents and blankets and a lot of weapons." Mr Robinson answered her and then turned back to Jason. "The lads loaded them up, just in case."

"Here," Philip appeared and handed Lindsey a thick coat.

"Thank you." Lindsey smiled as she struggled with the weight of the huge coat.

The rest of the Robinson brothers jogged up, weapons still in hands.

"They're not moving at us," Dominic said to Jason.

"But they have got us surrounded," Trevor continued for his twin.

The Robinson clan looked at Jason and waited for him to speak. Jason frowned, as he thought.

"They ain't gonna rush us, especially now we have hostages. We can make demands." Jason smiled at the reporter and the cameraman, who suddenly looked worried.

Chapter 7

Inspector Kingsley sat at Heather's kitchen table, he had taken occupancy of High Peaks Farm, using it as a makeshift head quarters and he thought it only appropriate to use their stored goods. After all, the Robinsons wouldn't need the stores, not where they were going.

'Well, I'd best go talk to them,' he thought. The only reason he adhered to protocol was to make any action legal.

He left the farm house and walked out into the farmyard. He had asked for a volunteer to go unarmed, up to the heights of Aamor but understandably, none had come forward.

Forensic police milled about collecting evidence, their activity centred on the area at the back of a line of outhouses, where the killings had occurred.

'Not much point to that cos there ain't gonna be a trial,' he thought, in his opinion, those that he faced now had resigned themselves to an early death.

"Sir," Constable West stamped to attention in front of him.

"What is it West?"

"Your megaphone Sir, and I prepared some food bundles in case they ask." West stood and awaited further orders.

"Thank you and good work West." Inspector Kingsley took the megaphone of the constable, and walked toward Aamor, West followed on his heels.

"Jason, there's a man carrying a white flag, he's climbing the hill from the farm side." Dominic ran to Jason, excited at the new developments.

Jason followed Dominic to the edge of the stone circle; and everyone came to see what was happening.

"It's that Inspector," Jason said. "I bet he's coming to talk us down."

They waited as Inspector Kingsley climbed slowly; he leaned into the slope as he came. He stopped a third of the way up the hill, to catch his breath before raising the megaphone to his mouth.

"De Silva!" Kingsley's voice boomed, enhanced by the megaphone.

Jason stepped to the edge, in plain view of the land below. He felt rather than saw the red dots of the police rifles on his chest. "What do you want Kingsley?" he raised both hands to his mouth to help project his voice.

"What do *you* want?" Kingsley answered Jason's question with his own.

"Some food, and a stove, tents and camping stuff."

"What about the hostages?" Kingsley shouted, his voice sounded louder, carried on a gust of wind.

Jason turned, confused for a moment.

Philip went to Lindsey and pulled the coat off her back. She started to complain, but then the cold steel of Philip's short sword pressed into her chest. He spun her around, and his left arm curled around her neck, choking off the air supply. Her face was suddenly white with terror as she was forced to the edge to stand beside Jason.

"Easy." Jason said to Philip as he noticed the tip of the short sword had nicked the skin at Lindsey's cleavage.

"It's got to look real," Philip smiled, and pressed himself close to Lindsey as she went limp.

"I'll see what I can do!" Kingsley's voice sounded once more, and then he lowered the megaphone and walked back down the hill.

Philip dragged Lindsey back from the edge and released her when he was out of sight from the world below.

The red lights from the laser sights on the police rifles winked out and Jason turned from the edge.

Lindsey checked herself for injuries and she turned and slapped Philip across the face. "Bastard!" she yelled.

The Robinson clan laughed, Jason laughed too, although he was a little concerned with the violence shown to the reporter.

Lindsey's camera man jogged up to the group. "I'm ready," he said, then was shocked at the dot of blood on Lindsey's white shirt.

"Give me a minute." Lindsey snapped, and put the coat back on.

The cameraman had set up a tripod with the camera pointing at the centre of the stone circle. Half an hour later, Jason stood with Lindsey in front of the camera. "What do I say?" he asked, his eyes were wide and hands clammy.

"Be as normal as you can, and say what you feel," Lindsey advised him.

"Do I look all right?" he turned to Heather, she had come to watch, and she nodded, but didn't show too much interest.

"We go live in five, four, three," the cameraman finished the countdown silently, motioning with his fingers.

The camera's signal light turned from red to green.

"Good evening, this is Lindsey Sumter, coming to you live from a little known and picturesque corner of Albion called Aamor and it's where the now infamous Jason de Silva and is gang are holed up. They are surrounded by an army of determined policemen and women, intent on the capture of this modern day outlaw." She moved slowly to Jason's side as she spoke to the camera. The inner circle of stones shone under the bright camera light and glinted off their flanks. "Mr de Silva, what do you hope to prove? I mean you must realise that your position here is untenable?" Lindsey finished, and held the microphone to Jason's face.

It was getting late in the evening, many people in the nation by habit, were in front of their television, many more than usual were watching with rapt attention because they had been forewarned of the impending interview. They sat glued to their screens watching history as it unfolded before their eyes.

Jason stood straight and tall, defiant and proud, "Everyone in the nation has by now heard of my plight. My five minutes of fame, turned into five minutes of pain. In the face of adversity and against all the odds I've made it this far, I couldn't have done it without the help of my friends the Robinsons, some of whom have died this day," he paused to get the next line right in his mind. "Today I will fall, but I won't have failed, for my wife and children are no longer tormented by the possibility of their murders. I only ask this, that when I fall dead, fighting for what I have come to believe in, that my body be cremated and that my ashes be scattered here at Aamor. To be thrown into the breeze so that my children can hear my voice on the wind."

There was a collective pause, as those present marvelled at Jason's short speech. The cameraman turned off his camera, Lindsey for once, was lost for words.

It was getting late when the hover jet hung low over Aamor. Jason and Randell pointed their guns at the police vehicle; the doors swung open to reveal two unarmed constables wearing short sleeved shirts and no armour. They started throwing bags of supplies onto Aamor. The craft moved slightly, as the pilot fought to keep his craft steady in the wind. They made short work of the bags and the last one was the biggest, sent by the television company.

Swinging away from Aamor the hover jet lifted high. Randell never took either his eyes or the muzzle of his rifle off it.

Jason dragged the big media bag over to Lindsey. "Here, this must be for you," he said, as he bent to open it. He had a quick look inside before he returned to the air drop.

Lindsey was quick; she dragged a winter survival suit out of the bag, instantly feeling happier as she slipped into it. She walked over to the ridge feeling much better, her pampered skin already beginning to warm. Lindsey looked beyond the farm as the moons began to rise behind them. The headlamps of a thousand cars lined the road of this usually quiet part of Albion's countryside.

"Look at all that traffic!" She said in excitement.

"They're just spectators." The cameraman walked up behind her, pulling on a winter coat. "We did do a live feed to the nation."

"Yes, but I've never seen anything like this before, Tim." She was breathless as she realised that her career was on the brink of greatness.

"Have you ever done an interview like that before? He touched a string in my heart," Timothy whispered, looking over his shoulder, feeling embarrassed at his own emotions.

"Didn't it just, even so, why would they come up here? Just to watch this man die?" Lindsey whispered too, not wanting Jason to know they were talking about him.

"Maybe they believe in his cause," Timothy shrugged.

"Do you?" she asked, turning to face him.

"Yes, don't you?" he smiled at her then, he couldn't remember having such a deep conversation with his boss.

Lindsey paused and looked over to where the Robinsons and Jason where erecting a camp. It looked as though the group of wanted criminals were having a meeting.

"Is the camera still running?" she asked quietly.

"Nope but it can be," he said and drifted off towards the camera which was still pointing at the group.

They stopped talking at Lindsey's approach, and only Jason smiled.

"Lindsey," Jason said.

"Mr de Silva, Jason," she tried to distract him, looking past at the camp fire that was partially built.

"Are we live again?" he nodded past her, toward her cameraman who was trying to activate the camera.

"Not right now," Lindsey blushed and gave her lie away.

"I guess you want to know what I think of all the people that have come to watch my death." Jason de Silva had changed; the events of the last week had altered him forever. He seemed to have resigned himself to the fact that he was going to die. At the same time, he displayed an air of invulnerability and a die-hard attitude, devoid of smugness.

'Like the hero from a tale,' she thought, and she lowered her eyes because she didn't want to betray her thoughts.

"Why not have some witnesses? The more the merrier, I say." Mr Robinson looked out, his land illuminated by Serene, Albion's third moon as it started its march across the night sky.

Inspector Kingsley stood at the foot of the lane, thinking. With the arrival of reinforcements and the departure of a full shift of his constables, he had the logistical nightmare of supervising his new officers into their positions.

The crowds had begun to arrive an hour ago, which he had expected as soon as the media had got involved. This time though, there was something different with the people that came to watch the show. He'd had no choice but to ask his superiors for reinforcements. The crowds of spectators did as they were asked and kept a respectful distance from the police lines. That at least helped matters if only because Inspector Kingsley had one less thing to worry about.

The Inspector looked on as the few men he had ordered to keep control, laughed and joked with the crowd. There was an almost festive atmosphere, which seemed surreal and in stark contrast to what was actually taking place.

"Inspector, look over there," one of his constables stepped up behind him, and pointed off to his right.

Kingsley looked and saw that a burger van had pulled up and

had begun opening for business.

"This is turning into a circus, I don't like it," Inspector Kingsley was thin-lipped as he spoke. "I don't like it one bit," Inspector Kingsley repeated himself, thinking he hadn't been heard.

"It's warm food for the lads Sir," the constable said.

Kingsley looked at his man, then back to the van; he pursed his lips in disapproval but said: "Very well, go and inform the burger vendor to set up a running tab and bring me back a burger."

When the constable returned, he was looking up at Aamor. The gloom hid the shapes of de Silva's people, but the Inspector couldn't shake the feeling that someone up there was watching him.

"Sir, he's refusing the tab, wants cash only." The constable was worried about the Inspectors reaction.

Inspector Kingsley rounded on the constable, his nostrils flaring, "The cheeky bastard," he fumed, then turned away headed for the burger van.

The crowd's mood changed as the evening wore on; Jason looked out as elements of the gathering had become more hostile. Although they hadn't become violent, some people openly jeered the police while they worked.

The police had surrounded them with floodlights and secured a perimeter around the bottom of the hill. Obviously this was to prevent a night time escape, albeit Serene lit the landscape green, there was never any guarantee it wasn't going to be cloudy and therefore a dark night.

Fires sprung up, most of them small ones. There was even a metal bin that was an improvised brazier, stuffed with kindling and fire wood, a constable fed the flames with sticks. Pockets of spectators drifted around the hill, some congregated opposite the farm, chatting and sharing the occasional pipe. The police indulged this, they weren't doing any harm. To those atop

Aamor, they could have been the army, hidden by the shining of the floodlights.

"Phil," Jason hissed.

"What?" Philip replied talking to the monolith that Jason stood behind.

"Do you see them?" Jason strained to see against the glare of the light.

"I got em," Philip answered.

"Don't shoot anyone, will ya?" Jason beseeched.

"Of course I won't, well not until they charge," Philip had crawled to the edge; he lay down and pointed his rifle at the gathered mob.

'I might get the lads over here,' he thought, and then the crowd surged forward, pressing the police lines. The police rallied, trying to contain the mob and fighting broke out.

Shouts and jeers broke the peace, the noise barely reaching the silence at the top of Aamor. Batons were raised and brought down onto the unruly mob. A few broke through the police ranks, and they danced and cavorted like daft animals, jumping and whooping in the floodlit no man's land.

Police were sent to repel the mob and reinforce that particular weak point. This sent the men into a panic, and the crowd, in support of those that were 'just having a bit of a laugh' overwhelmed the police. Vicious fighting broke out, floodlights were thrown down and the men poured onto the hillside.

Then the police reinforcements arrived and closed ranks, they threw back the unruly citizens with unnecessary force and violence, hitting them with batons and gun butts. Some police approached the men on the hillside and they turned and fled up the hill and the police gave chase.

"What the fuck?" Philip said as his brothers joined him, they were curious and had come to see where the noises of battle were coming from.

Jason looked over his shoulder, the camera's light shining

past him, Lindsey gave her narrative as she documented events.

Jason looked over the edge. "Lads, lads!" he yelled, urging them forward.

The mob neared the halfway point, their number lessening as they were picked off, grabbed from behind by the police. Jason lifted his shotgun pointing it skywards, he fired three rounds into the air. Everyone on the hillside ducked, and looked like the ebb of a wave. Then the men got up like a trained unit and came on as one, as the police fell back, dragging a few of the mob back down the hill.

The Robinson men stood at the edge of the small plateau and trained their weapons on the advancing mob. Lindsey and Timothy stepped back away from the edge as the group crested the ridge, gaining the heights of Aamor.

"Trevor," Jason didn't take his eyes off the men that had come to join them. "Go check the perimeter will you?"

"On my way." Trevor jogged off, looking down to the farmland.

"You lot," Mr Robinson shook the blunderbuss menacingly at the faces of the newcomers and it became clear that they had no weapons to speak of.

"Please, please," a man stepped forward. "We want to join you." he tried his best to smile in the face of the blunderbuss.

"Join us, are you mad? We're all going to die here," Jason lowered his gun, more because his arms ached than out of trust.

"Wait a minute; you're the butcher from Hurtsford. I've sold you cattle before now," Mr Robinson relaxed his stance, also lowered his gun.

"We're all from Hurtsford, I run the pub there," another man stepped forward, nodding his head at Jason. "Business not good right now though."

Another man stepped forward, offering Jason his hand. "All the able bodied men in the town had a meeting. We decided to come join you, those that ain't cowards anyhow." The man smiled, his long moustaches twitching as he did.

"And you, what did you do, before you decided to commit suicide?" Jason smiled, shaking the man's hand.

"I was the village constable," he said, his smile vanishing. Jason jumped away from him, as the Robinsons lifted their guns once more.

Nervously, the middle aged man stood in front of Jason. He bowed and lowered his eyes to the ground, and then back to Jason's, imploring Jason to listen. "I used to be a policeman, and a good one at that. But for too long, my actions as a constable have been pointless, my hands tied by government legislation. Like so many others, police or otherwise I have become disillusioned with how the nation is being run. This is why I have thrown my lot in with you. I'm your man now."

"Stand up straight man, you don't have to bow to me," Jason blushed.

"Our whole town has thrown their lot in with you, we voted unanimously," the constable turned outlaw stood up again and then smiled. "You're a hero to us!"

They moved to the centre of the stone circle, Jason counted heads as they went. Fifty one men, new arrivals had come to join Jason at Aamor. Jason watched the light of Serene dance across their awestruck faces, some with drying blood from where the constables had hit them with their batons.

He looked at Heather as she dished out food from the air drop. He then looked to Lindsey, who frantically talked to the camera, her words lost to him. He couldn't help feeling he was part of something that was growing but that for the moment resembled a group of trapped outlaws.

'What do I do?' he thought, *'I can't turn them all away now.'* Jason felt responsible for them all, guilty with the thoughts of so many deaths he would cause.

One of the Hurtsford men limped past him, the look of awe and admiration in his eyes was obvious.

"What the fuck is happening?" Inspector Kingsley paced up and down the farmyard.

The Inspector watched as a constable approached and almost fell over as he stopped a yard away from him.

"Sir, a large group of men from Hurtsford just broke through our lines," the constable stepped back, fearing the Inspectors wrath.

"How many?" Kingsley asked, his voice was calm but his eyes were wide and furious.

"Not sure Sir, I couldn't tell with the fighting going on around me." The constable seemed about to say more but he clammed up and took another step back.

Inspector Kingsley turned, following the constables stare and he saw his commanding officer, Superintendent Victor Rogers. Kingsley had always resented Rogers; he believed that Rogers had taken his job. Rogers was a product of the private education system and two years younger than Kingsley, he had joined the force much later in life, but his progression through the ranks was rapid.

He came from a rich background and his early life was pampered and privileged, though the years spent on the force had hardened him to the realities of life, Kingsley still thought of the Superintendent as a spoiled rich-kid. He had broadened across the shoulders as he aged and his short cropped hair was greying a little more with each passing year.

Flanked on either side by two smartly dressed constables, Victor Rogers was striding up the lane between the country road and the farm. He swung his elaborately carved cane, used purely as a fashion accessory and he smiled in Inspector Kingsley's direction.

"Kingsley, old chap!" He yelled, his posh voice one of the few things he'd never lost. "Damn cold up here, hey?" And he reached the gate to the farmyard.

A line of civilians were escorted into the farmyard, they

were marched through the rear gate with a line of constables on either side. Sergeant Bernard Willis marched at the head of the line. There were more than a hundred of them, most in handcuffs and nearly all of them sporting injuries with blood mingling with the mud that stained their clothes.

A few injured constables followed up behind, one half sat, half lay in a wheel barrow as he was pushed by another uninjured constable. He moaned and it was clear that he was drifting in and out of consciousness.

"It won't do Kingsley, simply won't do old chap!" Rogers sighed heavily as he walked past Kingsley.

Without being told, the Inspector knew that he had been relieved of his command.

"Well come on Kingsley!" Rogers ordered without turning around.

Inspector Kingsley followed his superior officer, he felt angry as he followed him into the kitchen and geared himself up for an argument. They sat down facing each other at the kitchen table.

The Superintendent slipped off his gloves and smiled, the gap between his two front teeth always attracted Inspector Kingsley's attention and that's where his focus stayed as the superior officer spoke. "Well Kingsley, what to do?" he said and relaxed back into a chair that creaked as the leverage threatened to lift up its front legs.

"I don't know Sir, there are more of them now," Inspector Kingsley was snide, and tried to goad his superior officer.

"Well they have the high ground, hey! We could always starve 'em out," Rogers gave his upper crust laugh and with it, he refused the argument that Kingsley wanted.

"Sir," Kingsley was surprised; he didn't think Rogers was so naïve.

"No, no, no, simply won't do! This media farce works against a man, hey?" Rogers looked to one of the constables in attendance and gave an order that sounded like a request: "Cup of tea, hey?"

"There's irony in that," Kingsley smiled. "With a nation of do-gooders looking on through the eyes of the media, how can we act violently against a few dissidents that oppose them?"

Rogers cocked an eyebrow. "Yes, damned if we do, damned if we don't, hey?" he chortled again.

Rogers stood and went over to the window. "The brass has been at me Mr Kingsley, it's becoming a circus. I didn't want to come here; they gave me no choice, hey?" The superintendant pulled back the curtains, and looked up at the heights of Aamor; Serene was bright in the night sky behind the mount.

"You think it's a circus now Sir? There's going to be thousands of 'em here by morning," Kingsley crossed his arms, he was at a loss.

"Well, this situation needs to be resolved soonest! Those damn royals seem to be interested in this one." Rogers said and became deadly serious. "We have no choice but to end it quickly."

"Why, have you heard something?" Inspector Kingsley looked up from following the grain in the table top.

The constable placed a pot of tea on the table, then turned to fetch the cups and milk as the Superintendent sat back down.

"Ah tea, marvellous," Rogers said. "They want full control, that king of theirs wants an army on every corner."

It was late in the night, the cold air made his breath billow white as he locked his vehicle doors. He walked away from the black sporty number, its opaque blacked out tinted windows showing his reflection in which he made sure of his appearance.

He turned towards the massive country house, his feet crunching the stone chippings under foot. The middle-aged man adjusted his suit as he reached the door. He wasn't used to wearing such clothing and he fiddled constantly with his shirt cuffs.

As he reached the door, he paused, collected himself and took a deep breath, then knocked three times on the wood. He waited and looked at his watch, more for something to do than to check the time. Then he heard the sound of oiled metal being slid open and a pair of eyes stared out through the peep hole.

"Mr A," a voice rasped from behind the door.

"Yo blad," the suited Skav said in reply.

The door opened, to reveal a plush interior with elegant furnishing. The door was held open by a monster of a man, his beady eyes and high voice didn't fit with the physique. Mr A felt intimidated by the giant and for all his muscular attributes and fighting skills, Mr A felt like this fat giant could tear him apart if he wished.

"New breed," Mr A said, hiding his thoughts, he smiled and sucked through his teeth, then he gave the giant his best intimidating look and asked: "Where's the meet?"

The over sized, shaven-headed goliath nodded towards a door. "Down there through that door."

"Safe!" Mr A said and smiled at the high-pitched sound of the giant's voice, then he limped past the giant bodyguard.

Mr A stepped up to the door and opened it, beyond was a short corridor with wood panelled walls. He heard voices and decided not to wait for an invite; he swaggered for a few steps then resumed his limp, the well practised limp of the Skav.

He entered the room and he paused in the doorway to watch. He wore a tight lipped grin as everyone in the room turned to look at him.

"Mr A, you're late," Gavin Jones lounged in his chair; he pointed to the only empty chair in the room.

Gavin Jones looked like an ordinary man, smartly dressed with a medium build. His black hair was shot through with grey. He was in his mid fifties and he could walk down any high street and pass himself off as a bank manager, accountant or lawyer.

In reality he was a ruthless business man, capable of any act to gain his own ends and a criminal crime boss. He demanded respect and revelled in the act of setting examples.

The others in the room looked more like well dressed thugs; they were all Gavin Jones's Captains that ran areas of his criminal network. They would all love the top job, but that could only be granted from the top man in capital city.

"Yo, yo," Mr A nodded as he swaggered over to his chair. "How's it hanging boss man?" he pointed at Mr Jones, then sat and smiled to show off his gold teeth.

"Now that we're all here," Mr Jones looked over at Mr A, and his brow furrowed. "We can get started."

Everyone in the room looked mean; all of them were intimidating men and not one of them fools. They hung on everything Mr Jones said, they wanted to know why the meeting had been called. Goliath appeared in the doorway to stand guard over the proceedings and the atmosphere changed dramatically.

"Have any of you been watching the news recently? If you haven't, maybe you've heard of the Smith family and their recent troubles?" Mr Jones started the meeting and hoped that he wouldn't have to go through the whole saga.

Mr A jumped to his feet. "They my soldiers, my soldiers." he said as he posed like the gangster he was.

"Sit down Mr A," Mr Jones ordered.

Mr A sat down but glanced over his shoulder to give Goliath a warning look.

"Foot soldiers gentlemen, foot soldiers. They're the scum of the earth, but they're *our* scum and without them we have no income," Mr Jones leaned back in his chair, and gave time for the information to sink in. He watched the grim faces of his men as they thought about what he had said. When he had given sufficient time for the message to have registered, he continued: "Without them we're fucked and our business will fail. I've had orders, from Farrell himself, we're to go to Aamor tomorrow and we are to crush everyone there. At this moment, we are putting together the biggest crew that's ever been seen and tomorrow, De Silva dies!"

"Mans is barre buzzing like, ya get me," a young Skav spoke, his ill fitting suit jacket bulged as his muscles flexed.

"For the first time in history," Mr Jones continued, without looking at the speaker. "The gangs of Albion are united and at peace. All the top people answer to one man. That man, Douglass Farrell has given me a task. It's rather simple, to go to Aamor and kill Jason de Silva."

"What's so special about dat punk?" the young Skav asked.

"What's so special about that punk?" Mr Jones repeated the young man's question. "It's probably something to do with his ideals; this one man's thoughts threaten our very existence, so sit the fuck down!" Mr Jones spoke louder than necessary and he spat out the last phrase, he rounded on the young muscled Skav and made him look and feel stupid.

"Let's cut to the chase lads," Mr Jones regained his usual calm. "You're all to get your best one hundred lads, because you're to go to Aamor and kill Jason de Silva, and anyone that tries to stop you. You are to protect our way of life."

"Datz sic man, propa sic blud!" Mr A forgot himself and talked over his boss.

"You Mr A, you're going to lead them, after all it's your district," Mr Jones smiled. "Right then lads, get your boys tooled up and hooded up, we're going to war."

Chapter 8

A thin thread of light appeared on the horizon, Serene had long deserted the night sky and left darkness that most could not abide.

Jason had woken from his sleep cold and dampened by the thin veil of mist that hung in the air. He'd got up to check on the perimeter and as he reached the first huge outer monolith, he paused and silently observed two of the men from Hurtsford. They sat at the edge, looking out into the darkness below. They had their sleeping blankets wrapped tightly around them. Both men were a little overweight but they carried their pot bellies well due to their large frames. The blonde haired fellow had long flowing hair, whilst the other had dark short cropped hair and a few days worth of beard on his face.

Jason listened to their conversation.

"Yes mate, I agree but it's not necessarily the only outcome. I mean we all believe in Mr de Silva and his cause," Dave Hibert, the dark haired one said as he rubbed his stubble.

"Our cause, it's *our* cause," Ethan Clifford said.

"Yes of course, sorry. Anyway we might actually change things for the better; we might actually change a few laws." Dave said.

"You think we could win?" Ethan asked in a dubious tone.

"Well, why not?" Dave said.

"I admit, nothing's beyond the realms of possibility, but in this, I've resigned myself to dying on this hill," the blond haired man smiled; in his mind he had won the argument.

At that, Jason stepped out of the shadows of the stone. “Morning gents, how’s the watch been?”

“Morning Sir.” Both men spoke at the same time, and they allowed their blankets to fall as they stood.

“You don’t have to call me Sir, my mother gave me a name, I would prefer you to use it.” Jason crouched down, careful not to wet the seat of his trousers on the dew moist grass.

Jason looked down to the land below, seeing the barest of movements, as patrols moved behind the line of spotlights.

“You know there’s no food left,” Jason said.

“They’ll send some more, they can’t starve us.” Ethan said, as both he and his comrade retrieved their blankets, and crouched beside Jason.

“Another air drop, like yesterday, I hope that will be the case.”

“They have to be seen to be politically correct.” Ethan said, as he tied his hair back.

“Political correctness be damned,” Jason said. “We need laws that are just, laws that serve the people’s rights.”

“That’s why Hurtsford joined you, for our children and our children’s children,” Dave scratched at his chin again.

“Will you stop that?” Ethan said to his friend even as he scratched at his arm.

“You don’t have to stay here; nobody else has to die, not for me anyway.” Jason looked at them, still plagued with the thought of blood on his hands.

“Jason Sir, we told you. We’re here for our children and the state of the nation.” Ethan said.

“We ain’t going any place, if truth be told, I think the whole nation would love to be here right now,” Dave stopped scratching, and looked out at the world beneath them. “See, you’ve got an audience already.”

They looked out into the coming dawn and fell silent; deep in their own thoughts as they watched the crowds from the night before that had already begun to increase. Jason knew the crowds would only increase from the day before. The few tents that had sprung up like a little town were mainly the media. There were quite a few people walking about, going to the burger bar, to bang on its shuttered door. A fresh troop had just arrived and the night shift were getting ready to depart.

"There must be seven hundred of them," Ethan pointed at the ranks of the police.

"Easily, and see there are no guns, the armed response must have pulled out!" Even as Dave said that, the spotlights blinked out.

"They're still down there," Jason scanned the area in front of him. "I bet they're inside the farm house, they couldn't have left, not with all the weapons we've got up here."

"I guess they're holding out for a peaceful resolution," Ethan wondered.

"I'd have to agree, but we've already decided me and the Robinsons, we're gonna fight to the death if need be." Jason looked out as he spoke; he watched a line of personnel carriers.

Eleven of the large vehicles pulled over, a mile from the farmhouse.

"Look there, that's strange," Jason pointed.

"Isn't it?" Mr Robinson said. He had walked up behind them as they talked.

Then the doors of the personnel carriers began to open, lowering slowly to crush the hedges at the side of the road. Men poured out onto the field of a farm that neighboured High Peaks. Scattering wildly, the cattle that grazed on the field raised the alarm. Even so, the people in the valley seemed oblivious to the hundreds of men disembarking from their vehicles less than a mile away.

"That's a lot of men, are they police?" Ethan asked.

"Well if they are, they're not in uniform." Dave said.

"You've got better eyesight than me if you can tell that they don't have uniforms on, they're too far away at the moment, but if they aren't police, who are they?" Ethan asked.

"I'm not sure, but I've got a bad feeling about this." Jason said.

"Those reporters down there, they can't see that field. It's hidden by those hills," Mr Robinson looked out as more of the large vehicles arrived.

"They're certainly wrapped up against the cold." Mr Robinson said, commenting on their masked faces.

"Or hiding from the cameras," Jason said.

Within minutes all those on Aamor had come for a look, the arrival of the unusually large force created a lot of excitement.

Mr A looked up at Aamor, all around him Skavites gathered in the field as clouds began to gather in the sky.

'Fuck me it's cold', Mr A thought, as he waited for his cocktail of narcotics to kick in.

The Skavs shivered too, whether through the cold or because stimuli were making their muscles dance, he didn't know and didn't really care as long as they did as he ordered. He couldn't help but think his men resembled insects, the hoods on their Black Jackets covered their faces and even their eye sockets were covered by dark tinted circles to hide them completely.

He looked around as more of the heavy vehicles arrived, then he looked down at the white armband on his jacket, it was the only thing telling him apart from the others. The sides of the personnel carriers lowered onto the field and more of the Skavites jumped clear into the fresh morning.

They waited for Mr A, milling about laughing and joking. Fighting broke out between two sworn enemies, two small gangs pushing and shoving, squaring up to settle an old argument, they were soon parted. "Remember why we're here!" a voice yelled as they squared up to start again.

"Alright, pussy gonna get fucked!" Mr A lifted his right arm so everyone could see who he was. "New breed!" he yelled, as he turned to walk in the direction of Aamor, his shout was emulated and swelled to a roar by the throng about him.

The largest criminal gathering ever to take place outside of a prison was happening in the countryside in the district of Cooper's Town. Over two thousand Skavite foot soldiers gathered behind him, all ready to march across the field with a sole intent to kill one man.

What a sight they made; the ranks of the damned swaggering to do battle, an army of chaos come to sweep all before them.

"What the hell is that?" Inspector Kingsley asked but no one was close enough to hear him. He had heard a muted shout minutes before but he'd ignored it as he ran around doing Victor Rogers's bidding as they prepared to start negotiations.

He looked up as the first Skavs crested the hill, their shouts muffled by the masks they wore.

'By the five moons!' he thought, caught off guard as more Skavs followed.

Inspector Kingsley lifted his radio to his mouth: "I want every constable at the farm in full riot gear," he spoke calmly and clearly so every policeman would understand. The camp in front of the farm began to empty as the Skavs approached it. People were leaving their belongings and fleeing from the threat that had appeared. Most of the media that had camped out did their duty, cameras flashed, film rolled and reporters talked into microphones.

Constables ran to gather at the farm, pulling on equipment and fastening belt buckles as they ran. Victor Rogers ran from the farmhouse, he still carried his cane in his right hand. No longer tired, the night shift of police constables had got a good shot of adrenalin.

"New breed! New breed!" The Skavites were still chanting as they reached the edge of the camp. Most of the civilians were running from the menace. One unfortunate photographer snapped a picture right in front of Mr A, who ran forward to 'clothes line' the man. He fell to the floor holding his throat and the next Skav to reach him stamped on his face. Blood gushed from his broken mouth as his jaw was smashed to hang uselessly. He was screaming as another thug swung in from the side with an iron bar, caving in his skull, brains squirted out like a popped boil and the screaming stopped.

At the death of the photographer, those that had not run turned to flee. A terrified mass of men and women milled around behind the gathering police lines in an overcrowded farmyard. A pretty reporter stood in the path of the Skavs, rooted in fear. She turned as if to speak to her camera but her cameraman had fled. She turned back as a Skav ran at her and then she tried to flee at the last minute. She was far too late and he tripped her with an outstretched foot and she crawled desperately to try to hide in a nearby tent but it was soon overrun by the Skavites. Some Skavs spent a little time to drag her from her tent; her clothes were ripped open to expose her breasts. She was punched in the mouth and as she disappeared under the tide of Skavs, her screams could be heard from somewhere within the melee.

High above the farmlands, with a vantage point second to none, Ethan shook his head in disbelief. "What the fuck is going on?" He was unable to take his eyes off the scene below. Nobody blocked off their escape now that all the police had regrouped to the farm and many of the spectators ran to join Jason at the top of the hill. Many more ran off into the countryside, heading south and away from danger. The huge swell of black-clad thugs squared off against the police who were outnumbered four to one.

"Jason!" Mr Robinson yelled, thinking of freedom.

"I ain't going nowhere!" Jason yelled back, knowing what the old man was going to say, and although tempted, he knew these Skavs were here for him.

"Fair enough, but I have a bad feeling."

A large man with huge shoulders pushed in beside Jason, he

had a claw hammer in one hand and a short sword in the other, the smile he wore looked strange on his square face. "Jason de Silva?" he asked his eyes were wide and menacing.

"In the flesh," Jason answered, looking at the massively muscled man. "And you are?"

"I'm Ilan, Ilan Ferris," the man said proudly. "And this, this is my sister Shereze." Ilan motioned behind him.

She was not quite as tall as Ilan and she was near as opposite to him as possible. Lithe and beautiful, her tear drop face was framed by long flowing black hair. She carried a pistol in her hand, its long barrel easily a foot long.

"How da do," she nodded a greeting to Jason and he was surprised at her accent. It did not match her beauty at all and she sounded as common as a street urchin.

"Glad to make your acquaintance," Jason offered Ilan his hand, still taken aback by how broad Ilan was.

Jason turned back to the scene at the farm, thinking better of shaking Shereze's hand which involuntarily stroked the hilt of the short sword at her side.

Thousands of Skavites had trampled the media camp and were amassing at the bottom of the lane in front of the farm. They jeered at the police lines that had formed up in neat lines four men deep. Even from that distance, the sound of the batons striking the shields irritated the ear drums, like a freight train travelling at high speed over fire crackers. The police tactics were being put to the test, as they tried to intimidate their enemy, whose crazed, drug-fuelled chanting could be heard over the shield bashing from the police. The crescendo took on a rhythm, and there were no non-combatants to witness the spectacle because they had fled the farm for the fields beyond.

Suddenly everyone twitched involuntarily as a gun was fired into the air.

"This is fucking serious." Randell said.

"It's been serious for a week now; this has just got to

ludicrous." Jason said.

Inspector Kingsley stood in front of his men and looked on at the Skavs as they jeered and mocked the law, mocked the honour of the force, mocked him.

'Insolent bastards, how dare they?' he thought and as though on cue, a brick sailed through the air to bounce harmlessly off a riot shield to his right.

He gritted his teeth and studied the brick's trajectory, grimacing and wanting the scum army to attack. It was then an arm was raised, a pistol in the hands of one of the Skavs. Everything seemed to slow down as the hand recoiled, the bullet shot skywards and his ears seemed to split with the sound.

Everyone flinched at the gunshot as the involuntary motion of shock took over. Even the highly trained constables beating their shields momentarily lost their rhythm. Then everything seemed to speed up again as Victor Rogers marched past him.

Victor Rogers held the police megaphone that Kingsley had used the previous day.

Inspector Kingsley watched as his superior officer raised the megaphone to his mouth, although he could hear the words, the meaning was lost on him, as the Inspectors attention was seized by the shooter of the pistol, then others in the Skavite mob as more guns were brandished above their heads.

Then Kingsley heard the words come from his own mouth even without realising, in the face of the Skavs brandishing weapons, he gave the order to fall back: "All officers pull back. I repeat. All officers pull back into the farmyard behind the walls."

Inspector Kingsley looked at the back of the Super's head and half expected him to turn around and countermand his orders. To his surprise he didn't, he stood defiant, cane in one hand, megaphone in the other. The Superintendent even took a couple of steps forward as he faced down the Skavite horde that continuously chanted as the police retreated behind the stone wall.

The retreat of the police into the farmyard seemed to fuel the bravery of the Skavs and they surged towards the super. His stalwart presence steadied their advance as the front of the press seemed to hold back just feet away from his cane as he swept it defiantly at the mob.

"Armed Response, ready your weapons!" Kingsley spoke into his radio as he shut the gate and ducked down, with the last of his officers clambering over the wall behind cover.

"Affirmative." The response came as another shot rang out.

Inspector Kingsley watched with his face pressed up to the gate to look through a knothole in the wood. His eyes were wide as Superintendent Victor Rogers fell back slowly, stiff and straight, as though he lay on a falling plank. Both arms were limp, his cane and the megaphone flew out of his hands. He landed on the uneven surface of the lane, and his head lolled back in the dirt, exposing the bullet hole in the dead centre of his forehead.

Inspector Kingsley held his radio to his mouth. "Fire." he said softly, admiration soaring for a man he had long disliked.

The armed response team was positioned inside the farmhouse and had remained hidden. At the order from Inspector Kingsley to make ready, they had lifted their rifles to the windows. At the order to 'Fire', they needed no further prompting and their bullets ripped into the Skavite mob. The Skavs returned fire; hundreds of them produced guns, and those that were not already taken out in the first wave fired at the farm wall and the farmhouse. Chaos reigned.

"All personnel retreat, everyone back, use the covering fire!" The Inspector ordered, keeping low as he moved towards the rear of the farm.

The Skavs overturned vehicles as they tried to find cover; many ran to the side of the farm. Those at the back retreated from the gun fight, running back towards the hills. Hundreds of Skavs were shot by the expert marksmen, who were handed the gift of so many targets. As tightly packed as they were, the rapid fire of the police exacted huge casualties in a short period of time.

Bullets pinged off walls and ricocheted off stone cobbles as the Inspector crouched and urged his constables to get to safety. He pulled on an officers arm, who then fell down dead, the back of his skull gone, his spongy brain tissue destroyed by a large calibre round.

Within minutes the farmyard retreat caused a bottleneck as Inspector Kingsley and his men escaped from the line of fire. Nearly seven hundred police pushed and squeezed through a narrow gap, only just wide enough for a vehicle to fit through and police poured onto the field beyond to take what little cover there could be found behind the out-buildings.

It took a few minutes for the farmyard to clear, Inspector Kingsley being the last man. He looked behind him, counting the twenty dead officers that lay on dirty cobbled stones. He turned and gained the relative safety of the field behind the farm. The police lines had already begun to form up, their training taking over, but in the chaos they had formed up dangerously close to the outhouses of High Peaks Farm.

"Get back," Kingsley yelled, as the gunfire threatened to drown out his voice.

With hand motions he managed to get his men moving, stepping backwards the lines wavered and then straightened as they neared the opposite side of the field.

'That only leaves the snipers,' Kingsley thought, looking back at the farm.

"I'm out, I'm out," a voice screamed over the radio.

"I'm hit," another voice screamed, and the radio became silent.

Through the gap in the outhouses, Inspector Kingsley could see the part of the farmyard; the armed response team appeared, falling out of the kitchen door. An almighty shout went up from beyond the farm, as the Skavite horde charged. The Skavs ran across the cobbled stones and ten constables attempted to flee, they were nearly at the gap and into the field when the Skavites reached the wall, firing at the backs of the fleeing police. Only two made it into the field, one of those falling into the dirt, a bullet had splintered his knee joint, his knee cap ripped through his trousers, flying in three different directions.

Inspector Kingsley couldn't believe what was happening to them, none of them could.

'Law and order must be upheld,' he thought, as he ran forward to drag the screaming man away. Bullets fizzed about his head as Kingsley tried to lift the constable. He pressed something into Kingsley's hand as two bullets silenced his pain.

Kingsley backed away looking at the hand gun that sat in the palm of his hand.

Skavs burst into the farmyard, hundreds of them. Others flanked the buildings of High Peaks Farm as the drug-crazed, blood-hungry mob waged into the fight.

Kingsley took a look up to the plateau at the top of Aamor in the hope of seeing de Silva but the horde was growing and if he was there, Kingsley could not pick him out of the crowd.

The numbers atop the heights of Aamor had grown massively, swelled by the retreating masses from the farm. Others, mainly men from Hurtsford, had lay hidden out of sight from the police cordon. They brought their weapons with them and were eager to help swell the ranks of Jason's small force. Some that had been in the media camp had had no intention of joining Jason, but now felt compelled to do so and to put down their cameras and notebooks to take up whatever weapons they could find. It hadn't taken long for the festive attitude in the camp to change, horror and fear replacing it. The mad rush up the hill had, at one point, become contagious, people fled, following others that didn't know where they were going. Many more fled around Aamor, passing those that wished to fight at Jason's side.

As it cruised into view, the police hover had its jets locked at full speed and at the sight and sound of it, the police lines cheered loudly and raised their shields to re-start the baton bashing again, given fresh hope by the arrival of their air support.

Then from behind the farm, back in the direction of the main road, a rocket propelled grenade shot skywards, its white smoke trailing behind. As the hover jet passed over the farm the missile hit, exploding at the rear of the air vehicle, blowing a gaping hole in its tail section.

Rudderless, the hover jet veered wildly over the farm house, to slam into the field to the right of Aamor. Some civilians were caught in the crash, they were cut down by shrapnel, their shredded bodies flung aside like rag dolls.

Jason turned from the crash, back to the scene between Aamor and the farm, Inspector Kingsley turned for a second time, waving up at them. He knew the policeman was signalling him, caught between the hammer and the anvil as he was. Then the Inspector noticed Jason, locking his eyes on his, as the Skavs began to enter the field, he raised his hand at Jason in what appeared to be a salute.

Jason took a step forward, looking down he raised his own hand, copying the Inspectors salute. "Come on then!" he shouted as loud as he could.

As one, the hundreds of people that had crowded the stone circle, urged the police to join them at the top of the hill. The Inspector lowered his arm to his radio, barking an order as he turned to face the Skavite horde. As one the police force turned, retreating in an orderly fashion over the low stone wall. The flood lights were knocked over as they began the ascent, at their head marched the impressive bulk that was Sergeant Bernard Willis.

As Jason watched, the Skavites began to charge, the Inspector raised his hand, and he fired his pistol. Hundreds of Skavites bore down upon him, all wanting his blood. A little way from the farm's outhouses was a large chemical tanker, a flammable insignia, almost hidden by dried mud was imprinted on its end. The sword wielding charge of the Skavs stopped dead in its tracks as the tanker that the Inspector shot at exploded.

Everyone ducked down away from the flare, even on Aamor the blast could be felt, as the cold morning was turned into a warm spring day. The shock wave from the explosion spread outwards, as the small mushroom cloud reached forty metres into the air.

Nobody dared take their eyes off the field below, as Skavs were thrown spiralling into the air, everything from limbless, lifeless bodies to body parts bounced across the hard ground. Others, incinerated by the flames, died instantly, their charred flesh becoming ashes in the wind. As he was thrown backwards, the Inspector didn't escape the blast, he flew head over heels ten feet into the air coming back to rest, unmoving, thirty feet from where he had been standing.

After the initial blast had settled and the mushroom cloud evaporated into the sky, Jason looked down at what could only be described as horrific chaos. The outhouses had disappeared; the farm house was burning, all the windows blown out by the blast. Around one hundred of the Skavites no longer existed, over two hundred more lay dead, small fires still burning on some corpses as the chemicals stuck to the lifeless flesh. Many more screamed as they wiped at their bodies or rolled around on the ground, unable to put out the fires or get rid of the acid-like chemicals as the flesh was seared to the bone.

Sergeant Bernard Willis reached the top of the hill and stood before Jason, his men massed around him at the top of Aamor.

"Mr de Silva," his moustaches twitched as he spoke. He looked Jason square in the eyes and with an expression of frustration and annoyance, he said: "When this is over, I'm having you in cuffs!"

Jason said nothing, the uneasy truce was all they had and he couldn't allow it to falter, not with the Skavite horde regrouping below. Jason watched, the constables that hadn't already turned, did then and together they witnessed a large muscular Skav marshalling the others. The Skav wore the same clothes as the rest but he had one distinguishing feature, a white armband.

'*That's their leader*,' Jason thought as the Skavs avoided the flames and skirted around the farm to approach the hill from both sides. They seemed unperturbed by what had just happened.

'*Not really drug fuelled then*!' Jason thought sarcastically as he walked a little distance down the hill.

He walked past everyone, turned, raised both hands and motioned for silence. "Everyone, listen to me!"

Behind him, the Skavs started to move up the hill, hundreds of them had died but they still easily outnumbered the people on Aamor two to one. Their frenzied howls unnerved those that watched their steady advance, Jason saw the fear in their eyes.

Jason smiled as he calmly addressed his audience. "Those of you that fear this fight, this tide of death that approaches, you may leave. I will fight these Skavites by myself if necessary. I am the one they want."

Nobody moved. They hung on to every word Jason had to say, his smiling face and calmness in the face of death gave them courage. Jason carried on: "This is what our nation has become. Do our children follow in their footsteps and become lawless scum? Stand with me against the coming tide of chaos, fight for justice and the freedom to live decently and without fear. Fight for your children's right to not have to join with that Skavite hoard."

Their faces changed as Jason addressed them, their fears replaced by true grit and a will to fight. Jason looked over his shoulder for a moment, to look at the Skavites that had reached a full quarter way up the slope. Then Jason turned back to his followers, he was forced to shout out of necessity, to compete with the Skavite battle cries: "Who will fight with me? Who will die with me?"

They all yelled together, most raised their hands in defiant salute and even Bernard Willis showed a little emotion, excitement almost showing on his face.

"Fight with me, for our children, our honour and the blood of our ancestors!" Jason had worked himself into a frenzy and he screamed the last words of his pep talk.

Jason turned and broke into a run, to charge at the Skavites that still numbered more than he could guess at. They had reached half way up the hill, and they picked up speed as Jason headed towards them. Jason dared not turn around; he feared that he was charging alone.

Mr A charged uphill, screaming his battle cry which was drowned by a thousand other battle cries all merging into one cacophony, the sound of death to come. He looked uphill at the heights of Aamor and became confused as to why those he charged at and sought to do battle with were not fleeing for their lives. Then he saw Jason de Silva turn with fist raised and start to run towards him. Mr A was unperturbed, he ran on up the hill with colleagues and fellow criminals around him.

The voice of reason began to pound on the locked door of his mind, but the cocktail of drugs had long since taken over, to dominate his thought process. He was a god, a lord amongst men, and all he wanted to do was kill his enemies, or make them kneel before him as a sign of fealty. But as those he wished to maim charged down the hill, coming closer with every heart beat, he saw something in them he had never witnessed before; a grim determination on the faces of those before him when he was used to seeing fear.

'Why do they not fear me?' he thought, and the first seeds of doubt were sown in his tempestuous mind.

Jason de Silva charged head long down the hill; he carried his shotgun and a broad sword. He dared not look to either side for fear of losing his footing to fall at the feet of someone that would kill him without hesitation.

'This is all fucked up,' he thought as he picked out his first target. The opposing sides were within seconds of violent and brutal hand to hand combat.

Two more hover jets appeared and they turned higher in the sky than the hover jet before had done. They saw the wreck that burned in the fields at the side of Aamor and learned from that pilot's error.

As the two forces came together in battle, shots rang out from both sides. Men fell dead before they hit the ground; faces were torn from near point blank shots. A Skav in front of Jason had his shoulder removed by one of the Hurtsford men blasting him with a shotgun. The yells and battle cries drowned out any screams of pain. The battle roar was deafening, a symphony of death that made no sense. The hooded man that Jason was aiming towards fell back, the black glass of one of the eye sockets in his hood shattered as a bullet smashed through it. The impact of the bullet snapped back the Skav's head as it disintegrated his brain.

Jason had no time to think, he changed his target at the last second. He raised his shot gun and pulled the trigger. The two armies met, colliding with a ferocity that only history books remembered, recounting the conflicts of ancient past. The three Skavs in front of Jason were tightly packed and took the shotgun blast in their chests. They would have fallen backwards because of their injuries but were unable to with so many of their allies charging up behind them, they were compelled to fall forwards. Jason gripped the used weapon tightly in his hand and lifted the broad sword; he hefted it and swung it above his head. Moving his arm full circle, he brought the broad sword around, to bring it down on the head of another of the masked Skavites. The skull parted effortlessly and Jason felt rather than heard the bone splintering beneath the weight of his blade as the Skav's brainbox was cleaved in two.

Jason didn't hear himself screaming battle cries and curses, as fighting ensued all around and the opposing forces merged. The yellow jackets of the police flashed in Jason's line of sight and they were joined by the good people of Albion and they all came together to mix it up with the Skavs, the police and ordinary people fighting for their lives.

'How the fuck did it come to this?' Jason thought as he punched a Skav in his face, the tinted glass that was built into the hood broke on impact, a shard of glass piercing the Skavs eyeball. As he fell to the cold ground, the hooded face seemed to fix on Jason's. Jason lifted his heavy boot and brought it down onto the Skavite's face and with a sickening crunch; he knew the lad's neck was broken.

Jason had no immediate threat after that kill and took a few seconds to survey the battle field. He saw a chaotic maelstrom that hadn't been seen in Albion since the invention of gunpowder was being played out. Death filled the air, the smell of blood in his nostrils almost made him gag and everywhere around him; the bodies were beginning to pile up.

A policeman looked Jason right in the eye as he spun around with his throat slit. He clutched his fingers to the wound in his neck, and Jason saw the life as it left his eyes before Jason could take his gaze away from the man. Jason turned away to see Ilan Ferris hacking at four Skavs whilst his sister Shereze, stood close behind him, making her targets with her two long barrelled pistols. Ilan's smile sickened Jason, the thought that anyone could enjoy this slaughter irked his sensibilities. Yet at the same time he gained hope from their savagery; the sick determination on their faces frightened the Skavs that faced them as they tried to avoid his ferocious attack. Jason looked about him at the swinging arms of death as they scythed a deadly melody, the chaos continued and Jason began to rage, adrenalin tasting finer than any drug ever concocted.

Two Skavs rounded on him and charged; their blood stained

blades raised for the kill, their crazy eyes covered by hoods. The hard ground of the hill had turned to mush, heated by the spilled blood of the fallen and trodden into a bloody quagmire by the thousands of stamping feet. Jason tried to turn to face his assailants but he slipped in the mud as he did so, then Jason panicked, his feet flailed upwards and a moment later, his back hit the slope. Mud was flung into the air from the bottom of his boots to hit the hooded masks and cover the tinted glass of the Skavs who bore down upon him. The two Skavs stopped, blinded by Jason's blind luck. He managed to stand, slipping slightly, as one Skav tried to wipe the mud away while the other pulled his hood back, to reveal twisted, manic features. Jason wasted no time; he head butted the unmasked Skav and sent him reeling backwards. The other Skav swung his sword around crazily as he anticipated Jason's attack, but Jason leaned backwards and turned his head to try to avoid the blind swing. The blade cut his cheek and the wound burned with an intensity that only fuelled his rage. His anger and rage exploded, his sanity turned on its head, and as the blade arced away from him, he stepped backwards to draw his arm back; then he thrust his sword arm forward, and struck the Skav's sternum square with the point of his blade. The Skav convulsed and collapsed under the weight of his own death as his ribcage was shattered, his heart bursting under the pressure. Jason threw back his head, his chest out and arms back, and he roared like an angry beast, the Skavs around him falling away from him, their morale finally broken.

"Ya wanna piece of me, motherfucker?" Mr A yelled. He stepped over the constable who lay bleeding at his feet as Mr Robinson approached him holding his shot gun like a club, the ammunition used up. The old farmer and the young Skavite commander faced off against one another as the battle spread out down and around Aamor hill. The old man had been busy, he was covered in blood, none of it his own. Mr A was also covered in the warm sticky liquid that he had drained from so many of his victims.

After circling for a few seconds, Mr Robinson lunged forward to swipe at his opponent with his improvised weapon. Mr A was taken aback by the speed of the fat old farmer, but his startled expression was hidden behind his mask. Mr Robinson knew he had surprised him and he seized the advantage, he followed up his attack, and again swung at the Skav leader with the butt of his shot gun. Mr A dived, and rolled away from the attack, tucking his sword into his body, trying not to stab himself.

'*Fuck this*,' he thought as he came to his feet and he knew he had only just managed to roll out of the way. He drew the pistol he'd been saving from inside his coat, and levelled it at Mr Robinson's chest.

"New breed, motherfucker!" Mr A shouted, smiling beneath his hood.

Mr Robinson smiled, knowing his time had come to leave this world; his eyes went blank as he raised the gun above his head. He stepped forward as the pistol rang out, expelling its deadly bullet that hit him in the chest. The giant farmer that was Mr Robinson fell, dead the instant the bullet pierced his heart, and he hit the side of the hill, to roll to a stop. His eyes were wide as they saw nothing but the afterlife.

Mr A turned just in time, to see an elderly woman charging him. She was howling like a banshee, not caring for her own safety. He raised the hand gun but he had to fire three times before he could stop her. The last bullet killed her and like her husband, Heather Robinson was dead before she hit the ground.

Mr A watched as the old woman rolled down the hill and came to rest at the side of her husband that he had just killed. He smiled, amused at all the death around him, as on both sides the casualties were building up. Then, with his shield raised and his baton held above his head, a constable charged. His pristine yellow jacket was spattered by a thousand flecks of blood.

"You want it bitch?" Mr A yelled as he shot the policeman in the face. "Motherfucker!" he spat on the constable's upturned ruined face as he walked past the fresh corpse.

Still the fighting raged about him, but was more spread out, breaking into one-on-one combats. Something caught his eye up the hill and he saw Jason de Silva twenty metres away from him. He was shouting something unintelligible and the Skavs about him retreated down the hill, running in fear from him, their drugs turned against them. de Silva looked fearless, brave and psychotic.

'Ain't havin you upstage me!' Mr A thought, he was more concerned for his own image of superiority than the fact his men were beginning to rout. He lifted his hand to his head and quickly undid the zip, pulling his hood off his face revealing to the world exactly who he was.

A media hover jet, with cameras rolling, hovered close above filming his every move.

Mr A raised his sword, the tip pointed at the camera that was pointed at him. "Watch this motherfucker!" he yelled, his face contorted in his rage. He chewed on the inside of his cheeks as he walked uphill towards the yelling Jason de Silva. His own men ran past him, running from the wild man, *'Motherfucker's gotta die, gotta die, gotta die!'* Mr A's mind whispered.

Jason de Silva turned to look at him, his roar coming to an abrupt end as his lungs emptied; the big man that opposed Skavite-kind looked majestic as he smiled at his sworn foe.

Mr A stopped short of Jason, knowing what he needed to do. "It's a new breed, innit!" Mr A smiled, lifted his hand gun and pulled the trigger. Click, click, the gun was empty, its bullets all used up on other victims.

'Never mind' he thought and raised his sword, he threw down his useless hand gun. Then there was shock and pain as a sword erupted from his chest before his eyes. His ribs broke outward and his blood sprayed forward, bits of his flesh sticking to the heavy blade and gore dripping from it. He tried to turn and he

took hold of the blade that had killed him, unconsciously he seemed to realise that it was only that that was keeping him on his feet.

"Innit," Randell mocked the killer of his parents and pulled his sword free. He made certain that the dead Skav lay face down as he told the back of the late Mr A's head: "Say hello to the underworld, motherfucker!" his voice never wavered but tears poured down his cheeks. Then he ripped the armband from the corpse and stuffed it in his pocket. Mr A would remain anonymous if it had anything to do with Randell Robinson.

Jason and Randell looked at each other briefly and shared a moment of mutual and unspoken respect, before Randell turned to run off to kill someone else.

Jason looked all around him, the fighting had started to move downhill, a few even fought in the field between the base of Aamor and High Peaks Farm. The outhouses were all but gone, the cattle were charred lumps of steak, and the farmhouse wouldn't be long before it too was destroyed, the flames were rising above the highest point of its roof, which threatened collapse and the dead and injured lay all about him like a writhing carpet as men lay waiting for help to arrive or for death.

Another Skav charged him, he stumbled on one of the bodies and Jason took advantage and in one smooth motion leaned to one side bringing his arm around and up from behind him. He timed his sword stroke to perfection, the blade's edge, honed as it was, sliced through flesh and bone, smashing through the Skavs spine and completely severing the man's head. It spun into the air, spiralling in perfect circles, until it landed, coming to rest hood-less, the eyes expressionless and staring and the mouth slack.

Hundreds of people had gathered opposite the farm, ordinary people from all parts of the land, they were surprised at what they saw and in awe of the people that were doing what they only dreamed of doing, killing Skavs.

Then the Skavites started to pull away from the fighting, the first few gathered in the heat of the farmhouse, milling about in the field. Then the rest routed, beaten by the determination of the ordinary people of Albion. The effect of their drugs started to wane and as the effects lessened, so did their courage, the Skavite force grouped together in the field leaderless and uncertain of what to do.

"Let 'em be." Jason ordered, he bellowed out above the sounds of shouts and moans of the dying. Jason handled his broad sword like a throwing dagger, point first and threw it at the ground. It stuck through the abdomen of a dying Skav, finishing him off. Jason stretched his weary muscles as he watched the Skavite force gather in one spot, he estimated their number at over a thousand, still.

He could see his own force was still clearly out numbered. There were very few constables left, perhaps less than two hundred he guessed. What was left of their force gathered around Sergeant Willis, Jason saw that he held two police batons, one in each hand, held loosely at his side.

The Skavs gained courage, when they realised they outnumbered their enemy, they started jeering and shouting, and the chant of "New breed!" was beginning again, it was obvious that the mindless thugs did not know how else to behave.

Jason could see out across the valley, at the roads that were choked with vehicles, many abandoned on grass verges or driven off the road and left in fields. Sirens and flashing lights tried to navigate down the blocked highway, their progress impossible even as fresh police tried to reach the battle zone.

'It's too bloody late for reinforcements now!' Jason thought.

The hundreds of citizens that had gathered beyond the farm suddenly charged without warning. They spilled into the field at either side of the burning farm. Jason saw but couldn't understand why they now acted as a collective rather than as individuals. Their hatred for the Skavites must have untied them he thought.

Looking around him, Jason could see his comrades were battle-weary, hurt and exhausted. He pulled his broad sword free of the corpse, and began to walk downhill, even now; he did not want those charging onto the field to face the Skavs alone, the adrenalin started pumping through his veins once more.

"Let's have it then, one more dance!" Jason yelled as he picked up speed, running at a fast jog, raising his broad sword above his head.

His exhausted army followed him; they yelled and screamed at the top of their voices as they too charged downhill at what remained of the Skavites. Jason chanced a look behind him and he realised that the rag-tag band of shopkeepers and family men had become an army – his army - and his heart swelled with pride. It was all too much for most of the Skavites, they flung their weapons down and they turned to flee, their morale was finally shattered and the rout was complete. They ran in all directions trying to escape certain death at the hands of the vengeful mob. Most ran to either side, where the new arrivals met them, they were grabbed and beaten with improvised weapons and chased into the neighbouring fields. Some had their heads held in ditches filled with water; some were desperate enough to run the gauntlet of flame, and they ran into the inferno that was High Peaks Farm, where the buildings still burned with fierce intensity.

One hundred stood their ground, but in the end the result was the same, the Skavs were grabbed by groups of crazed people who wanted justice at last to be served. All around the surrounding countryside Skavs were chased and hunted down. They were cornered and killed like diseased and mangy dogs, and they were stamped on and beaten until their heads burst open and their limbs snapped.

Jason walked this way and that, stabbing at injured Skavs as they tried to crawl away. One Skav had been wrestled to the ground by a group of justice-seeking citizens. Jason walked over to the struggling group, picked up a small wooden bat and without a word he started to hit the Skav. Jason heard himself as he laughed wildly as he struck the Skavite, but he was buried under the horror and violence of the previous few hours and the decent part of Jason would not emerge for a few hours yet. He beat the Skav to a bloody morass of bone and blood, all the while being encouraged by his audience. Jason pounded on the Skav long after he had died, sending warm blood droplets into the air about him. Then his rage began to ebb, fading back into his subconscious, to wait and fester till it once again was released.

Then Jason was startled and caught momentarily off guard as a burning Skav ran back into the field.

"Let him burn!" A man yelled, he held back his friend who had moved to put the Skav out of his agony.

Gathering around the fallen and screaming Skav, a small group looked on as the fabric covering the Skav's face melted and the eyeballs stuck to the tinted visor. The smell of melting flesh filled the air as the young man screamed for his mother. He desperately rolled around on the ground and the Skav at last extinguished his own fire but his ordeal was far from over. The crowd were in no hurry to end his agonies and he continued screaming as they looked on in grotesque curiosity. Jason thought then that there would be many people thoroughly ashamed of their actions from this day, he hoped that he would not be one of them.

Jason took another look around the field and made certain that there were no more Skavs close enough to be a threat to him, he saw some in their death throes with people hacking and bashing at them with anything they had to hand and he contemplated how easily civilisation fell to violence.

While he was scanning the field, he saw what remained of the police force gathering around the spot were Inspector

Kingsley had fallen. Jason took his time and turned away from the slaughter to pick his way through the corpse-littered field over to the group. As he walked, people began to follow and then to surround him, and as the crowd swelled, the chant began. They cheered his name and the People's Army celebrated their hard won victory.

"Let him through," Inspector Kingsley croaked, Jason barely heard the order over the noise and was surprised that Kingsley had managed to survive. *'He's one tough bastard, that one.'* he thought.

Only Sergeant Bernard Willis dared look into Jason's eyes, the constables all lowered their eyes and they parted as ordered, then the people surrounding Jason stopped chanting.

"I thought you were dead," Jason looked Kingsley in the eyes; the respect he felt for the police commander was extreme at that moment.

"Mr de Silva, you're mad you know." Kingsley wheezed the statement and held his chest at the effort. He smiled and tried in vain to ignore his pain. "Here, the cuffs on my belt, take em, put 'em on, you're under arrest."

Jason smiled and saw the humour. "I would but I got some issues that need attending to."

"Like what, haven't you done enough?" A blood stained constable dared to ask.

Jason searched in the crowd of constables for the one who had spoken, when he couldn't, he addressed them all; "I'm guessing all these Skav bastards have committed crimes before today. I've just made your life so much easier; you should give me a fucking medal." When he saw that none of the officers were openly opposed him, he continued. "And besides, I've got an army now and a war to fight."

"Don't do it, de Silva, we can help you, it's not too late." Inspector Kingsley implored.

"It is too late, it's way too late. And help? You already did, at the cost of the lives of so many of your friends and colleagues, for that I thank you." Jason saluted in the police fashion.

"I can't move de Silva, I'm in too much pain, but if I could I would arrest you." Inspector Kingsley winced as he smiled and his voice was growing weak. "Today was a matter of survival; that scum was out for blood, that's for sure, de Silva, but there are laws that have to be upheld."

"Join us," Jason surprised himself with his statement as he pleaded to the Inspector.

The crowd around him was silenced; they waited for an answer with baited breath.

"I appreciate the sentiment," Inspector Kingsley said and he did seem to think for a moment as he looked past de Silva. Then he turned his gaze back to his enemy; "The answer's no, it's still my intention to arrest you."

"Just not today," Jason turned and walked away, disappointed.

"The next time we meet, it will end with you in custody de Silva," Kingsley yelled after him, instantly regretting making the effort to shout as pain coursed through his chest and back.

Jason stopped, waited for a moment and then turned around. "Without you, this fight wouldn't have happened; it's as much your war as it is mine. When you're ready, come and join us." Jason waited, giving the Inspector the chance to change his mind.

He was helped up by two constables and eventually Inspector Kingsley managed to sit up. "Whatever it is that you're trying to achieve, its madness, you talk of war and treason; there must be law and order!"

"I agree, but the laws that govern us must be just, must be fair and with proper retribution for crimes committed. The laws that govern us now ain't worth having." Jason walked away.

The throng resumed their cheering and the chanting of his name, their yelling became louder and louder and the police retreated from the field.

Chapter 9

The live feed came through on the television. The suited gentlemen around the table were silent and sullen as the battle scene played out. In disbelief they sat open mouthed, unable to take their eyes from the visions of chaos and slaughter.

The large man at the head of the table turned from the television. He leaned back in his chair; it creaked like an old door under his weight. "What the fuck are we supposed to do about that?" he asked in a stunned and quiet voice.

The ministers remained silent as they looked at each other nervously.

Then Peter Dickenson, their fat Prime Minister struggled to his feet, and then began to pace laboriously up and down the Cabinet room. He had to stop before he spoke because he was out of breath from the unusual exercise. "Right then," he said, trying not to wheeze. "Gag the press. I want a gagging order on the press." Then he resumed his pacing.

The Cabinet remained silent, a little in shock at the events of the morning at Aamor. They waited for the rest of the Prime Minister's orders and sure enough, he barked again: "And I want every available officer in Albion bringing here!" he stopped pacing and turned to look at his most trusted advisors.

"The whole force?" one man asked the question, though the entire Cabinet were wondering the same thing. He voiced the concern of all present but the rest were wise enough to keep quiet.

"This is going to blow up in our faces! This is the excuse the Royals need to take over the government of Albion," Dickenson returned to his chair and lowered himself into it. "I want every copper in Capital City, I want them armed to the teeth and I want them here yesterday!"

"You're talking about war Sir?" Gerald Fontaine, the Minister for War asked.

They sat motionless, frightened for their careers because of what was happening during their time in office.

"Right, you lot get your heads together, accommodation and sustenance, ammunition and weaponry," the Prime Minister pointed a finger at them. "Go! Now!" He yelled and glared at his Cabinet of trusted men through weary eyes.

Five Cabinet ministers jumped up, and rushed headlong from the room to do the Prime Ministers bidding. Only the Minister for War stayed behind.

"Gerald," the Prime Minister said.

"Yes Prime Minister." the Minister of War looked at his boss.

"Do we have any troops near this little rebellion?" he stood again and began the laboured pacing of before.

"I have no idea Sir." Gerald was smug and spoke calmly, 'You're mine now you fat twat, it's getting close to the time when I can call for a vote of no confidence,' he thought.

Sensing Gerald's mood the Prime Minister leaned forward and placed the palms of his hands on the table; "Well go find out, get your people on the phone and find out!" he yelled, leaning further forward, right into his right-hand-man's face.

"Mr Prime Minister," Gerald Fontaine stood, his face a perfect mask of composure; "Right away Sir." then he turned away.

"Gerald," the Prime Minister called after him, having calmed his voice; "Don't be so smug."

Picking up his phone, the Prime Minister didn't watch his main rival shut the door behind him as he left the room.

"Get me the king!" he yelled at the aide that was unfortunate enough to answer the call.

Lindsey and Timothy were still filming; they edged their way down the hill just out of arms reach of any combat. Luckily for them, everyone had treated them as non combatants, too busy with their task at hand to bother the media and they fared better than some of the other reporters had at the hands of the Skav hoard. They reached the bottom of the hill with Lindsey giving a running commentary like she was reporting at a sports event. Her excitement was obvious, and at times the violence seemed to appeal to her.

"Jason de Silva is now talking to the police and those that have survived seem almost reluctant to make a move against him." Lindsey stumbled and almost lost her footing as she neared the masses of Jason de Silva's supporters chanting his name.

Jason turned away from the police, straight towards her.

Lindsey stepped up to the smiling warrior. "Jason de Silva." She said as though expecting an exclusive.

"Lindsey," Jason said and waited for her to start the questions.

"How do you feel to have survived such a horrific morning?" she held the microphone to his face.

He leaned forward slightly, making sure everything he said was captured. "I feel alive," he replied, and the crowd around him cheered and shouted their agreement with his statement.

He turned, holding his hands up for silence, when he'd quieted the throng he turned back to the mud covered reporter; he was smiling and obviously happy.

"Let the world be aware, no longer are the good people of Albion going to stand idly by. No longer will the rule of government and their shitty do-gooder legislation hold down the masses. Beware the criminal and those who believe they're beyond the law, no longer are we going to take their shit!" he bellowed every word, his eyes wild and his followers cheered and shouted and whistled as they pulsed forward to press around their hero.

"There you have it!" Lindsey's eyes were pricked with tears at the emotion of it all. "On this cold winter's morning, you saw him here first, with me, Lindsey Sumter, at the battle of Mount Aamor."

'What now though?' Jason thought. He stood in the middle of a chaotic dance as his followers and supporters thronged him. 'We'll need to organize some food and shelter, I could do with a dinner and a warm bed, and to get out of these wet clothes would be good.' he smiled at his new family, in spite of his worries. "Folks, quiet please," he raised his arms, his words going unheard, it took a while but eventually he managed to quieten the crowd.

"Today we have won a great victory over the scum of Albion!" he had to wait for the cheer to die down before he continued and his arms would ache by the time he had finished if he could not lower them because of the crowd's noise. "Hear me now!" he yelled over their ruckus, and then the crowd quieted so that not even a whisper was heard and Jason became more serious. "Ahead of me lies a road of death and carnage, where at any time my life could be forfeit."

Jason had to lower his arms and stop speaking because a police hover jet was coming in to land near Inspector Kingsley and the engines were too much for him to compete with. Within minutes the Inspector had been stretchered aboard, and the hover jet took off again.

Jason took advantage of the crowd's quietened mood and continued his speech. "As long as is necessary, I promise to dedicate my life to the eradication of the organised criminal element and the laws that protect them. I say down with the Skavite threat and death to the scum that intimidate our sons and daughters!" The crowd were wild in their agreement of

Jason's words and showed it in an ear-splitting round of cheers.

Jason's legend had grown internationally and everyone seemed to know his name. To most he had become a hero and after the battle of Mount Aamor an aura of invincibility would follow him for the rest of his days.

Even in the surrounding fields, the cheering could be heard clearly and Jason let them cheer and he waited, wanting the people to fully comprehend what his message was.

"We need to organize ourselves," Jason said, after they had grown quiet again. "We need shelter and food."

Jimmy Fowler, the landlord of the Ox and Cart ale house at Hurtsford stepped forward. "Hurtsford, there's food and warmth for you there." The man was loud and jolly, his overbearing confidence and charisma not damaged by his large belly and slicked black hair.

"We'll go to Hurtsford then, for food and warmth by the landlord's hearth." Randell yelled.

The masses cheered, which soon turned into a chant as they headed for the vehicles that lined and blocked the road.

Jason turned to the Robinsons, a look of pity in his eyes. "I saw them fall," he said, and his eyes welled and a tear for his fallen friends rolled down his cheek.

"So did I, I was too far away to help them." Dominic held his face in his hands and sobbed.

"In war there are always casualties." Philip looked up to the heavens and his face was patterned by tear-streaked grime.

"Our father wanted this war; he's talked about it for long enough." Randell spoke to his brothers, looking at each one in turn. "We can't shed any more tears; you know how father hated them." Randell had taken over his father's role as head of the family; he wouldn't let them fall apart.

"Come on, let's go and give them a decent burial." Trevor walked past Jason, and Jason saw the toll his parents' deaths were taking on him and knew the other brothers would be suffering the same way but they held their heads high as their father had taught them and Jason knew they would battle on to the end. Jason watched the four young men file past him, making their way up the hill to where their parents lay. Medical vehicles appeared to tend the injured and priests appeared as if on cue walking from one corpse to the next, giving whatever blessings were suitable under the extraordinary circumstances.

An injured man tried to stand some metres away from Jason, Jason turned to look the Skav in the eyes as he drew back his hood. The young man's tattooed face was the very image of agony as he twisted and fell back down. Jason walked over to the man, not sure whether to laugh at the youth or pity him.

Breathing through clenched teeth, the Skav looked up at Jason, his muscled chest heaving as he spoke; "Mercy, mercy." was all the Skav could say, as he coughed up blood.

Jason levelled his sword point with the thug's throat. "No, no mercy. You would not have shown us any if the positions were reversed." Jason spoke calmly as he looked the Skav in the eye. With a single movement it was over, Jason pushed his broad sword through the gurgling throat of the Skav and into the ground underneath. There was a brief look of shock on the man's face, and then nothing as the light of life left the Skav's eyes.

Jason looked up to see the camera filming his actions, Lindsey Sumter again slack mouthed and lost for words.

"All Skavs must die." Jason walked past them, his face grim, as he looked directly into the camera. "I declared war on the Skavs and I meant all of them."

Douglass Farrell, the crime boss of Albion, sat behind his desk; his massive fingers drummed the surface and his jewelled rings clinked together. He waited for news, watching the various channels and listening to the main radio station. Up until now nothing worth listening to had been broadcast, the only thing coming through was that an incident had occurred, in the Midlands near Cooper's Town.

Then the phone rang, making him jump.

"Yes?" he said, anxious for news, then his face became slack as he listened to a voice shouting at him.

"Fuck you, you pompous fuck! You fucking know what I'm capable of, you cunt!" Farrell's reaction was swift and straight to the point; nobody spoke to him like that and lived.

There was a prolonged silence as both men waited weighing up their options.

"Right then, that's better." Farrell calmed himself and took a deep breath. "You will respect me, you pompous bastard."

Farrell's face turned from crimson to white as the other man spoke.

"What do you mean, all dead, wiped out?" Farrell slammed the phone down, and splinters of plastic flew from the handset. Everything about Farrell was loud and large, he was used to being obeyed and his orders carried out exactly as he gave them. He was not used to receiving bad news like that and he was stumped for a way to move forward from that disaster but he would recover, he always did.

He paced his office, and paused only to open his cigar case.

Then the television caught his attention, as the reporter on the screen appeared out of programme, with a special news bulletin, Farrell listened.

"In an unprecedented chain of events, the Royals have left Capital City. King Edmund and his family are said to be headed for the Isle of Cadida, to spend some time in their royal residence on the island."

Farrell sat back in his reinforced armchair. He lit his cigar as he payed rapt attention to the news now that it was getting interesting.

"Also, unusually high numbers of armed troops have been sighted headed north on all main highways, causing traffic problems due to the long convoys of troop vehicles used to move men and supplies. It has been confirmed that earlier today a violent and bloody battle has taken place on the mainland of Albion, the first since the civil wars four hundred years ago. Although at this time we can not show any footage due to the horrific nature of the conflict, I can say that an army made up of followers of Jason de Silva and the police force defeated an army made up of unknown mercenaries, believed to be Skavs. This is an historic moment in these times of political unrest. The exact number of deaths and casualties can not be confirmed at this time, we will keep you informed as the story unfolds."

"So, Mr Jones, it would seem that I must have your head now," Farrell spoke out loud, as he leaned forward to turn off the television.

He picked up his custom-made phone; the one he had had made for his huge hands and he dialled. "Brendan, get me the Heads of State, tell 'em to get here with as many of their lads as they can." Farrell's deep booming voice paused while the other man spoke.

"Yes I mean everyone. Yes I've seen it, and yes I mean Capital City." Farrell paused again as the other man tried to interrupt.

"Brendan, Brendan," Farrell stopped him. "Listen to me, the army's moving north, I want all our boys here. All those that have said that they'd follow me, let them know, cus I'm taking over."

He placed back the phone gently and picked up a piece of plastic that had been shattered the last time he hung up, then Farrell took a long draw on his cigar and blew out the smoke as he murmured to himself: "It's time for the strong to rule." He smiled at the swirls of smoke in the air above him and leaned back in the chair that creaked under his massive weight.

Jason drove the commandeered vehicle in thoughtful silence. He had watched the Robinson brothers bury their parents and grandparents in the lea by the front of the burnt out shell that was High Peaks Farm. By the time they had finished, most of the people that had planned to travel to Hurtsford had left and now they sat at the edge of the little town, trying to get into it. The traffic was queued bumper to bumper as the gates to the fields at the edge of town were opened to allow vehicles to pour onto them.

Jason drove his vehicle onto one of the fields, and then walked the rest of the way; they got to the centre of Hurtsford in a matter of minutes. Tents were being erected on every available piece of grass, lawns and fields covered in white canvas, which gave Hurtsford the look of a refugee camp.

Everyone that saw Jason walking with the four brothers stopped to stare. Jason didn't know how to react as some people even pointed as they passed.

A marquee was being erected on the village green, it was conveniently placed outside the local ale house and the smell of cooking meats wafted on the air. A group of women stood around a number of cauldrons, stirring the contents with long metal ladles and Jason's stomach growled.

"Look over there." Philip pointed.

"It's that inn keeper and the ex-copper." Randell said and started to walk over the road, between the grid locked vehicles. "Are you coming then or what?" he asked as he looked back to where Jason was still standing and looking.

Jason looked at the others and then strode over the traffic-filled carriageway.

"Landlord, what are you doing and where did all these tents come from?" Jason asked.

"We've got a store of tents in Hurtsford, for the holiday season, we rent 'em out to the tourists. We get lots up here you see. Oh, I'm Jimmy Fowler, the pub landlord. I didn't introduce myself the last time we met." He held out his hand to Jason and Jason didn't hesitate to shake it. Then Jimmy looked at two men carrying a large wooden table. "Put it down over there will you lads?"

Jimmy was in his mid forties and obese to the point of bursting but seemed to manage his bulk for the time-being. Jason wondered how he'd survived the battle, let alone the day, with so much weight to carry.

Jimmy looked at Jason and he sighed. "I'm organising Sir, it's what I do best, organise. It's the key to any large operation Mr de Silva Sir!" the landlord nervously wrung the towel he used to keep his hands dry and free of sweat.

"Logistics then," Jason said and he smiled, "That'll save me a job, you're my head of logistics and organising stuff." Jason was more than happy to give Mr Fowler the job and until now hadn't given the subject any consideration.

"It would be an honour to serve, Sir." Jimmy bobbed his head a few times, and then with his head held high, he told Jason that it was too late in the day for breakfast and so brunch would be served as soon as possible.

Jason then turned to Teddy Williams, the small town's constable-turned-revolutionary, he had been silent during the exchange with the pub landlord, listening to what Jason and Jimmy had to say.

"We need a security strategy for this lot, will you help me?" Jason asked.

Teddy Williams wasn't much older than Jason, he'd kept fit all his life and he was a capable man who always thought his skills were wasted stuck in Hurstford.

"Of course Mr de Silva, it would be an honour." Teddy looked over his shoulder toward the idyllic town's inn. "We've got two local louts in custody; they've been causing trouble in this town for years. We've got them tied up in the Ox and Cart."

"What are they like?" Jason asked, impressed that Teddy had already took on his old role.

"They would steal the fillings from a corpse if they weren't too lazy to dig the hole." Teddy said. "They stole a small bag of coppers from their grandmother and their mother's last silver piece just to buy drugs. They've bullied everyone and terrorised the town since they were young boys."

"Let's go see them shall we?" Jason said and nodded for Teddy to lead the way.

They filed into the old pub where a group of people teased two tall and heavily built Skavs. Although the young men were in their twenties, they resembled adolescents; their dirty tracksuits looked worn and scruffy. They kicked out and spat at anyone that got too close.

Silence fell as the crowd noticed the change in mood of the captured Skavs and they turned to see the reason for it, first a few and then everyone. The fear on the faces of the Skavs was obvious to Jason when they recognised him.

"Hello lads," Jason said, as he worked his way through the crowded bar. "I hear you two are the lawless scum of this town!"

"Get fucked de Silva." one of the Skavs spat on the floor. He was used to getting his own way without suffering any consequences.

"Let my boys go, they'll be good from now on." a voice croaked from a table at the window at the far end of the pub.

Everyone inside the Ox and Cart laughed. "They don't know how to behave, cus you never taught 'em!" one man shouted and the crowd parted so that Jason could see who had spoken up for the captured Skavs.

The parents of the Skavites were the picture of hopelessness; they were dirty and middle aged versions of their sons, the law protected what it called the disillusioned and unfortunate.

"Hang 'em." Jason ordered and began to turn away to leave the room.

"That's illegal!" the Skav's father said, jumping to his feet. The mother remained seated but wailed her objections.

"By whose law?" Jason asked as he spun around to answer

the father's question and the room became deathly silent. Jason had to calm himself before he continued. "Tell me, what you do, for a job?" Jason spoke softly, yet his words still seemed to echo around the room.

The little skinny man with home-made tattoos covering his dirty arms sat back down on the bench next to his wife, he stared down at his feet as he mumbled his reply. "Nothing."

"So the good people of Albion pay your way. If you had been grateful and raised your offspring properly, none of this would be happening now. They are scum and are following in the footsteps of their parents. I wouldn't be surprised if you two aren't siblings." Jason paused, waiting for the sudden burst of laughter to die down, "Hang 'em."

Bursting into sudden fits of sobbing, the two tearaway Skavs struggled against their bonds and captors. Their parents tried to reach them and they even made an attempt to rushed the mob, then the whole bar area erupted as Jason's followers beat them back, and pinned them to the cold, stone floor.

"Hang 'em all, the parents as well." Jason stepped back and his followers became enthused, chanting the word 'death' over and over as they dragged the family outside. Jason followed them out and the Robinsons went with him. The odd procession walked around the pub into the back yard where an old oak had stood for hundreds of years.

'I bet this old tree has been used for this before,' Jason thought and he saw that the tree's thick limbs reached out at a perfect distance from the ground. The four Skavs were dragged to the base of the tree and bound, the mother proving the most difficult; she was sickly and fat and had numerous health problems in her near future by the look of her waxy, yellowed skin. Her massive arms wouldn't come together behind her and her captors had to use more rope on her than on any of the rest of the dysfunctional family.

"Jason?" Lindsey Sumter gave Jason's arm the softest of

touches. "What are you doing?" she was clearly concerned with what she witnessed.

"Were going to watch them hang, because if the whole family dies, they can't breed any more wasters." Jason's face was crazed and manic.

The father of the family was suddenly hoisted from the ground by his neck. The rope yanked tight and after a few seconds, urine stained the front of his trousers and his body jerked and shuddered.

"Don't you think you're going too far?" Lindsey asked, her voice was strained and panic was close to the surface of her usually controlled self, her hand went to his arm, as she pleaded for their lives. "What about the law, don't you think they have right to a fair trial?"

Jason rounded on her. "Look Lindsey, what is this all about? What about this morning? Have you understood nothing of what's happening here?" he was angry and aggressive in his stance and she backed off a step in the face of it.

Cheers and laughter erupted behind him, and they looked. The Robinson brothers were smiling and enjoying the show. The second of the screaming Skavs was silenced by the tightening of the noose and Lindsey crossed her arms and felt responsible for the murder that was being committed and used as entertainment and she felt guilty at being the one that had made the call to Inspector Kingsley, telling him the whereabouts of Jason de Silva at High Peaks Farm and starting the battle.

'*There was going to be war anyway*,' she thought, justifying her actions if only to herself.

"This has turned into open warfare and you know what they say, it's all fair in love and war, well they started on my loved ones and now, they've got a war." Jason motioned towards the old oak. "This is what it's all about, the prey becoming predator, the victims have had enough." He read her silence as a protest.

"But..." she started to tell Jason the truth of how she helped start the fight at Aamor.

"No buts Lindsey, we're taking the country back for the good of the people." Jason interrupted.

"I'll see you in the pit of despair, de Silva you..." her words were cut short as the elder brother was jerked skywards; he danced on the end of his rope, in much the same way as his family had before him and he looked into his mothers dead face before the world turned dark for him.

Jason turned back to face Lindsey. "If you don't like it, maybe you're with the wrong people; maybe you should go report on the Skavite cause."

Lindsey turned her back on Jason and the scene of vigilantism and walked back in the direction of the village green. Jason turned back to look at the faces of the four Skavs swinging from the tree's thick branch. Their faces were as red as beetroot's as they swung, some of their limbs still moving with the tiniest of twitches. Jason turned around to look at the growing crowd who had come to see the village problem being eradicated as old nuisances paid for their crimes.

Jason woke from his nap, the sunlight barely peeped over the horizon as it hung low in the late afternoon. He swung his legs from the sofa in the back room of the inn, and then he stood and allowed the cold air to hug his naked upper body. He dressed, donning the clean shirt that Jimmy's wife Lizzy had left out for him, (she said Jimmy wouldn't mind donating it from his own wardrobe), and then he left the room. Jason walked through to the bar where a large crowd had packed out the pub's spacious room. The crowd had started to become rowdy as the ale flowed freely in celebration at the victory of the battle of Mount Aamor.

"Mr de Silva!" Jimmy shouted and then frowned as he recognised the shirt that Jason was wearing.

Jason turned to look at the landlord and he smiled when he

saw that he was holding out a pewter tankard brimming with ale for him.

"What's in that?" Jason asked and had to raise his voice to be heard above the ruckus.

"It's home made mead!" the landlord yelled back, as singing began around them. "It's strong stuff!"

"Thanks!" Jason shouted and took the proffered drink.

'*Strong? It's bloody lethal*.' Jason thought after sipping from the tankard. He left the landlord busy rushing around, serving drinks and taking money and he made his way across the room. He headed for the far wall where he saw the Robinson brothers sat around a table, it took quite a while to reach them as everyone in between Jason and the Robinsons wanted to shake his hand.

Jason had almost made it to their table when Randell stood up. He looked at the large television screen which hung on the opposite wall and with only a glance to acknowledge Jason, he made off towards it. Randell was trying to get Jimmy's attention as he made his way over to the television and once there, he climbed up onto the table beneath it to point at the screen. "The television!" Randell yelled, still trying to catch Jimmy's attention.

Jimmy stood behind the bar with the remote in his hand; he pressed the Pause button and halted the live feed and waited for the last murmurs to fall silent before he pressed Play.

"Although it can not be confirmed at this time, reports that King Edmund of Albion has refused to talk to our Prime Minister are coming through. Peter Dickinson is said to be livid with the Royals and the whole affair has sparked serious political debate in Government House. I ask you this, who leads us on this day of chaos and crisis? The government has declared a state of emergency and are urging people to stay calm and go about their daily business. And here we have the first pictures of the Battle at Mount Aamor." The reporter continued as the camera panned over the corpse-littered battle field. "As you can see, the farm has been completely destroyed; the livestock are dead inside the walled compound. The body count is unknown at this time, but it is thought to be in the thousands and one can only imagine the horror that the people involved must have witnessed as the opposing factions collided on that hillside below the ancient stone circle." The scene behind the reporter switched to the hundreds of black body bags that were being placed in long lines. "And here we see the dead being taken away from what must have been hell, may the light steer them from the pit of despair."

Then the scene switched again, back to the studio where two elderly and smartly dressed women sat across from the reporter.

"Joining me today is political analyst Sarah Thatcher and renowned Royalist, Claire Wortle." The news reporter smiled, he looked forward to the forthcoming argument that he knew would soon be taking place. The women were already blatantly hostile toward one another if their body language was anything to go by.

"Miss Thatcher, can you give us your thoughts as to why this is happening and how it can be stopped?" the reporter asked.

"It's as simple as this, anarchy ruled at Aamor and if you allow something like this to happen and continue to happen, there will be a complete breakdown in society. Albion's streets will run red with blood." The prim and proper socialite sat with her back straight and her knees together, she expected to continue her speech but she was wrong if she thought that she'd have her say without interruption.

"Good." Claire Wortle said.

"Good? What do you mean by that?" Sarah Thatcher asked.

"The laws in this country, our Albion, are pathetic! It is common knowledge that the real criminals get away with their crimes and that crime is on the increase because the penalties no longer fit the crime." Claire Wortle said, showing complete disdain for her counterpart.

"Albion's laws are civilized, for a civilized future." Miss

Thatcher said in a pompous tone as she looked down her nose at the other woman.

"It's only civilized if you have the money to live in a nice area." Mrs Wortle said, talking over Miss Thatcher.

"The laws are put in place to support those communities and provide civil rights for the needy." Miss Thatcher argued.

Mrs Wortle remained calm. "Those laws didn't help my fifteen year old boy, he was stabbed to death with no provocation, he was walking on the streets of Capital City."

Miss Thatcher held her tongue for a moment whilst she collected her thoughts. "I'm sorry for your loss," she said. "But I feel we need to be careful, we can't criminalize an entire generation of young people."

"I agree, we can't but the criminal element has to be stopped, I say let's all fall in with Jason de Silva and kill all of the criminals. That won't affect the vast majority of our tracksuit wearing youth, who at heart are nice kids, it's the minority that are at fault and if we eradicate the problem, the solution will be so much easier to come to." Claire Wortle was satisfied that she had managed to get her point across.

"But," Sarah Thatcher began.

"No, you won't drown out my opinions with political agendas. I say kill all the criminals and let's have an end to organised crime." Mrs Wortle interrupted.

"So you would like to see the return of the death penalty?" Miss Thatcher mocked.

"Yes I would, for those who deserve it, and I'll tell you something else. If there was a general election today, then Jason de Silva would win a landslide victory, whether he was standing or not!" Claire Wortle openly laughed at the slack-jawed reaction of her opponent.

Jason looked around him, as the sound from the television was drowned out by the cheers of the crowd who then started to chant his name. He raised his arms and motioned for silence, it seemed that was all he was doing of late, raising his arms, asking for silence, giving speeches, but it was some minutes later that he was able to be heard, this time even his own people refused to quieten.

He opened his mouth to speak, but he didn't get a chance. The doors to the pub slammed open and a clean cut man wearing camouflage trousers and a black coat burst into the room.

"Army supply vehicles, three of 'em, wearing the King's five moon emblem," he said. He didn't wait for a reply of any sort and he turned on his heels and left the pub.

The bar emptied in minutes, the revellers surging outside. Jason was swept through the bottleneck of the doorway, into the cold and dark of late evening. He forced his way through the crowd, making his way to the village green. He saw six men lying face down in the grass, they were soldiers of the Kings own guard, their three trucks stood motionless, their fuel cells powered down.

Jason ran across to the soldiers who were surrounded by a mob of Hurtsford men. "Move out of the way," he said, pushing his way through as his men fell back.

"We got em, Mr de Silva Sir," Teddy Williams said, pleased with the efforts of his troops, he prodded one of the soldiers with the barrel of his shotgun.

"Enough of that, these lads aren't the enemy." Jason said to Teddy. "Get up off the grass." he said, offering the closest of the King's guard his hand.

The gathered crowd moved back to give the young soldiers some room, and he wasted no time in standing up.

The soldiers stood in front of Jason, they looked splendid in pristine uniforms. Jason estimated the man he had helped up to be in his mid thirties. The man stepped forward offering Jason some papers. Jason took them and started to read the top sheet, his eyes widening as he did so.

"Mr de Silva," a voice called from the rear of the first army truck. "You gotta see this, Mr de Silva!"

Jason looked up to see Lizzy standing close by and he gave her instructions. "Take these lads inside get 'em a beer and a meal. Do you fancy a beer, lads?" he turned to the soldiers who all nodded.

Without hesitation, the six soldiers followed the ageing landlady into the Ox and Cart inn. Jason watched them go, and then looked at the document again.

The paper was headed, 'A little something for a revolutionary' , the letter was written by one of the King's aides, it outlined the cargo sent by King Edmund to help Jason de Silva in his quest for glory and then wished him the greatest of luck.

Jason folded the papers up and slid them into his pocket; he then forced his way through the crowd to the rear of the first truck.

"Well then," Philip looked down at Jason from the tailgate of the truck; he held a brand new assault rifle in his hands. "I guess we're an army now!"

Philip prised open the crates and passed the contents to the crowd and together they began removing the weapons, holding them above their heads chanting fake battle cries. Then Jimmy jumped onto the tailgate of the truck and fended off any further removal of the weapons.

"Give 'em all back." Jimmy said in a voice more like a schoolteacher than a commanding officer. He smiled as he gave the order and everyone that held a gun became sheepish and good-naturedly handed them back.

Philip jumped down from the truck, a huge smile on his sallow cheeks.

"Here, read this." Jason handed Philip the letter.

The crowd hushed, waiting to hear the reading.

"To the People's Army of Albion, we place in your care one truck load of assault rifles and two truck loads of ammunition. Good luck in your endeavours to bring a crime free peace to our once great nation." Philip read the letter's opening statement, the crowd cheered happily. The Royalists appeared to have shown where their allegiance lay.

Jason quickly opened the second letter; he read it quickly, and then put it in his pocket. It was not something he wished to share.

Chapter 10

Inspector Kingsley sat in the police vehicle. He travelled south down the main highway that bridged the gap between north and south. He had been ordered to Police Headquarters in capital city, just north of the Tallulah, Albion's main water way. He suspected it was to answer for his failures at Aamor and to answer for the police losses.

"Look, more army personnel carriers." Inspector Kingsley moved uncomfortably, fidgeting with the neck brace.

"Sir, most of the army are moving northwards, to side with the Royalists." Constable West said, glancing at the Inspector but concentrating on his driving.

"Not all of 'em lad." Bernard Willis leaned forward from the back seat. "It's about fifty-fifty."

Inspector Kingsley tried to turn around, with little success as the pain in his neck made him wince.

"Most of the southern based regiments have stayed behind, to protect their home towns," the Sergeant said "Whether they are friendly or not I couldn't tell ya." His deep voice rumbled as he had to sit back, because he was too tall for the height of the vehicle.

"It would be nice if they were allies, but you know what these army types are like, they are 'King and country boys', through and through." Inspector Kingsley mocked the soldier mentality, rubbing at his temples.

"There's an awful lot of traffic heading north." Constable

West rubber necked often, looking at the masses of vehicles queuing on the opposite carriageway.

"They're getting out of the Capital City." Inspector Kingsley looked across the driver to see clearer just as a modified speeder full of Skavs drove past them, its fuel cells burning energy at an alarming rate. The Skavs wore caps with their hoods pulled up over them. One of the passengers of the high performance vehicle stuck his middle finger up, gesturing at the police vehicle as they raced past.

"Oh no you didn't, Skavite scum!" Sergeant Willis frowned, wondering how he could get hold of the youth.

"The cheeky bastard," the Inspector said and watched as they sped past. Then another speeder raced past and then another. All of a sudden the three lanes were lit up in front of them, as the fuel cells blazed at the rear of a hundred speeders. The Skavs obviously had no regard for the law, breaking as many of them as they could, including the speed limits on the highways.

"Well this lot's not fleeing from Capital City," Constable West said. "I bet they're up to no good, Sir."

"Like rats in the sewer, hey? And stop calling me Sir, I've been suspended remember." The Inspector sighed, watching as the speeders disappeared into the distance, '*Like rats in the sewer*,' he thought.

The rest of the journey passed without incident, and the three police officers eventually reached Police Headquarters in Capital City.

As their vehicle pulled up in front of the headquarters of Albion's police force, a convoy of vehicles turned around the corner at the top of the street. At their head were four police energy bikes, their sirens sounding as the riders, members of the elite light riders, guided the convoy to a stop in front of the Headquarters. Inspector Kingsley refused help from the police usher who opened his vehicle's door and instead, opted to struggle as he hauled himself out. He stood watching as the convoy came to a stop in front of their vehicle. Constables and high ranking officers rushed to the vehicles, their highly polished brass glinting. The first vehicle's door opened kerb side. The officer in attendance nearly scraped the tarmac as he grovelled at the feet of the vehicle's occupant. The Inspector looked to the roof tops, and saw the police snipers and Peter Dickinson climbed out of the lead vehicle.

'*What a time to arrive*,' Inspector Kingsley thought, as Albion's senior policeman, Sir Edward Parker, walked from the building, flanked on either side by a ceremonial guard of honour.

Sir Parker shook hands with the Prime Minister. Then the Chancellor stepped from the vehicle and finally, the Cabinet emptied out onto the footpath from the other vehicles. The Ministers, led by the Prime Minister, were ushered inside flanked by the honour guard, the two most powerful men in the land looked like best friends as they walked and chatted.

Inspector Kingsley looked at Willis and West. "I think some thing's happening and before you ask, I haven't got a clue, so shall we go and see?" he said leading the way.

West and Willis stepped in behind him, and followed the Inspector towards the impressive glass fronted building.

Albion's hard man and crime boss, Douglass 'I'll have ya fingers' Farrell, 'Fingers' for short, stood against the railing at the top of the block of high rise flats. He was surrounded mostly by smartly dressed men, with just a few younger ones dressed in tracksuits and hoodies.

"All that answer to my call are to be put in the flats, here!" Douglass Farrell said. His smile told that he was pleased with the progression of the aggressive take over.

People hurried from the flats, their bags and belongings in their hands. Thugs and hoodlums pushed them along and they saw their possessions and clothes being thrown from the balconies to the ground below. Screams and yells of protest could be heard echoing across from another tower block. Those standing with the crime boss of Albion laughed as a naked girl ran screaming from a doorway with a gang of Skavs chasing after her. From this distance they looked like tiny figurines, the screams and shouts indistinct as they chased the young woman into another door.

"I'm not leaving, I've lived here all my life, you've got no right!" a little old man said as he was pushed out of his flat behind Douglass Farrell and his gang. The old man was clean shaven and unsteady on his feet, he clasped a dog ornament close to his chest; it was of no monetary value.

"Just get ya shit and get going, man!" A young Skavite shouted as he pushed the old man onto the rail.

Douglass Farrell walked over to the odd looking pair, who struggled against the iron barrier.

"What's up old man?" Farrell asked, putting his massive hand across the man's back.

"Mr Farrell Sir." The old man stuttered. "I ain't got no one, or nowhere to go Sir!" He pleaded his case, hoping for mercy.

"Well, you ain't got anyone hey?" Farrell guided the man away from his door to look out at the city. "So no one will miss ya then." He pushed the old man over the rail. He screamed for a moment as he fell from the balcony and the scream silenced as he hit the concrete.

The Skavites laughed again as Farrell rounded on the young Skav.

"Ruthless, ya hear? Ya gotta be ruthless!" He yelled as he slapped the young Skav open handed across the jaw. The youth dropped like an iron ball.

"Next time I'll throw you off, you hear me boy?" Douglass Farrell's booming voice echoed across the space between the high rises as he headed for the stairway. "Come on lads, I'm hungry."

Farrell and his men left the flats and walked out onto the

road, they heard the sirens before the police vehicle rounded the corner. The police were responding to an emergency call made by one of the residents of the high rise complex. The police were not prepared for what they saw.

As one, Farrell and his men drew their handguns, the approaching vehicle never slowed, it's occupants knowing their time had come. The gang peppered the vehicle with hundreds of bullets and the two constables thrashed as they took multiple hits in a matter of seconds. The dead driver slumped forward and fell across the controls. The vehicle sped up, careering down the road past Farrell and his henchmen on its way into the wall of the high rise; it exploded in a shower of deadly flame.

"I guess the revolution has begun." Farrell said, as a hover jet appeared above the flats, its cameras filmed the vehicle as it exploded.

Police Headquarters were buzzing with activity as the Inspector entered the building; the Cabinet were nowhere to be seen as the Inspector walked to the reception desk.

"Excuse me," he said, getting the attention of the skinny blonde receptionist busy typing at her station.

"Inspector, you're to go straight up, fifth floor room five." The receptionist wore a well practised smile; she did not look up from her work. Inspector Kingsley and his escort went to the lift and as the doors closed, the Inspector turned around to look through the gap in the doors as a group of policemen carrying assault rifles ran past the lift.

"What the fuck is going on?" The Inspector asked his Sergeant.

"I'd say war is close to breaking out, if it hasn't already." Sergeant Willis said and exchanged a glance with Constable West.

"That's not funny, not after what happened on Aamor." The Inspector looked at his two friends and colleagues. "We survived a terrible day; let's hope the nation learns by our experience."

The lift stopped at the fifth floor and the three men stepped into a corridor which stretched out to either side. Although the fifth floor was calmer than the foyer, people were still moving with a certain amount of urgency.

"You two can wait here," the Inspector said.

"Sir." They said simultaneously.

Inspector Kingsley knew where to go; he had been in the building on many occasions. He walked a little way down the corridor. He came to a stop in front of the conference room and he raised his hand to knock on the door. The door was opened by a female constable to reveal the room inside before he had time to knock.

"Inspector Kingsley, please, please come in my fine friend." Sir Edward Parker said as he took to his feet behind a long meeting table. Inspector Kingsley was caught completely off guard, he'd never met the highest ranking policeman in all of Albion and the last thing he expected was for the man to address him in such a familiar manner.

The woman who had opened the door moved aside and left the room and as the Inspector entered the room, she shut the door behind her.

"Sir," Inspector Kingsley walked forward to face the man who held his future in his hands.

"I saw you on the television, Inspector," Sir Parker said. "Please sit." He motioned to a chair opposite him.

"What's happening Sir?" The Inspector asked, confused as to why he was being treated so well.

"You're getting an award Kingsley, a commendation," Sir Parker sat back down, the smile never left his face.

"Excuse me Sir, but I thought I was going to get a dressing down," Inspector Kingsley dropped into the chair, forgetting his injuries and suffering pain for his forgetfulness.

"We're doing it on the television, Kingsley; you're going to receive it from the boss. That's right Kingsley, you should feel honoured." Sir Parker nodded enthusiastically as he ignored what the Inspector was saying.

"If you don't mind my asking Sir, why is everyone running around like headless chickens?" The Inspector said. He removed his neck brace then, its irritating itch had become too much.

"Is that such a good idea Kingsley, what about your injuries?" Sir Parker asked, his face showing what seemed to be genuine concern for the Inspector's well-being.

"It's just a precaution Sir, nothings broken but I am sore as hell, not to mention battered and bruised," Inspector Kingsley rubbed his sore neck, his movement was slow and deliberate as he tried not to aggravate his injuries.

"Very good, Kingsley we need to be off for the interview now," Sir Parker said.

"Sir, about the… what about Aamor?" Inspector Kingsley asked.

"We're at war Kingsley, that's right, war!" Sir Parker stood, and walked around the end of the table. He helped the Inspector to his feet. "We've lost control of a large portion of Capital City, gangland Albion rose up this morning, hundreds have died, mainly the citizenry. You're our first war hero; you single-handedly defeated the Skavite horde at Aamor and eliminated the criminal element there."

"But what about Jason de Silva?" The Inspector protested, thinking of how the man took control and led the charge, '*How can I take all the credit for that?*' he wondered as he got to his feet.

"Yes, yes, we'll have him Kingsley, don't you worry about that." Sir Parker said knowingly, he did not want Kingsley to admit his thoughts; he needed him to take all the credit.

"But..." Inspector Kingsley argued, but was interrupted.

"One war at a time, Kingsley," Sir Parker said, emphasising the Inspectors name.

The Inspector knew that the conversation was over and

that he was being ordered to keep his mouth shut. Although the Inspector thought himself a hero from that day, he didn't feel completely happy taking all of the credit. Then the doors leading to an adjacent room were opened, and he saw a camera crew had turned the room into a studio as riggers laid cables this way and that, getting the makeshift studio operational.

Chapter 11

Jason de Silva sat with the Robinson brothers and the pub landlord drinking a pint and having a bite to eat; it was noon three days after the battle of Mount Aamor.

"How long is the food going to last?" Jason asked, looking at the pub landlord whilst chewing on a cut of beef.

"We've got enough food to last for months for thousands and everything you could wish for." Jimmy said with his mouth full.

"How big did you say that warehouse was?" Jason asked, still surprised at the answer, having already asked the same question not half an hour earlier.

"It's a distribution centre for the supermarkets," Jimmy said, wondering how he could make Jason believe him.

"I've seen it!" Trevor said, coming to Jimmy's aid but not looking up from his food. "It's massive."

"Well, in weeks, how long do we have?" Jason asked, pushing for an answer.

"Honestly Mr de Silva, I couldn't tell ya. I mean we got new arrivals coming in all the time." Jimmy remembered to cover his mouth as he answered.

"The People's Army does seem rather fashionable, doesn't it?" Philip said between bites.

Dominic put his fork on his plate, and leaned back. "I'm sorry for changing the subject, but there's something I find really weird. For the most part, Albion continues, going about its business peacefully as if nothing has happened, yet there are small portions of the country that's in absolute chaos."

Jason opened his mouth to speak, when Lizzy turned the sound up on the television and drowned out the murmuring chit chat that drifted around the room. Everyone in the room turned to look at the television, to watch Peter Dickinson. He stood with his hands crossed in front of him, holding a small flat box which looked as if it rested on his massive gut.

"Good people of Albion," he began. "I stand here before you as your leader and Prime Minister. I have grave news, which will resonate down through the ages and into the history books of Albion."

Peter Dickinson paused, changing his posture slightly. Not a single sound could be heard as everyone in the Ox and Cart Inn waited.

"As most of you have probably heard, King Edmund and his court have removed themselves to the island fortress of Cadida, opting to flee mainland Albion. I can tell you now that King Edmund and the aristocracy have abdicated the throne of Albion, leaving me and my Cabinet to fill the power vacuum they have left behind. With the help of the armed forces that have stayed loyal to Albion, I intend to bring all the rebellious factions of Albion to heel and if necessary wipe them out. I will use extreme prejudice and they will be brought back within the confines of the law. I only ask for calm and peace, from all of you, as I deal with these criminal gangs and to commiserate with all of the families that have lost loved ones in these troubled times." The Prime Minister paused again and looked to his left and then back to the camera. "Three days ago a battle was fought near the picturesque site at Aamor. A small force of well trained policemen won against all the odds, against an army of well organised Skavites four times their number. I give you the police commander and my good friend, Inspector Kingsley."

Peter Dickinson walked tall and proud as he left the podium

and the camera panned to follow his departure. Sir Edward Parker and Inspector Kingsley had been standing to the left of the camera shot, now all three men stood in the camera's range, with the Inspector in the middle.

The Prime Minster smiled, opened the small box he'd held through his speech and took a medal from it, then he pinned it to the front of Inspector Kingsley's uniform.

"Ladies and gentlemen, I give you the hero of the battle of Mount Aamor." Peter Dickinson said as both he and Sir Edward Parker stepped away, applauding the newly decorated police officer.

The customers in the Ox and Cart erupted and insults were hurled at the television. Everyone, including Jason, were on the feet shouting for the head of the Prime Minister who was stealing their glory before the eyes of the world.

The sound of a television smashing on the pavement outside and across the road silenced the yells inside the pub it would seem that everyone in the village felt the insult like a blow to the head.

The screen changed and the picture returned to the news room.

"We have an emergency announcement." The reporter looked serious as everyone looked back to the television. "We have confirmed reports that two constables have been shot in Capital City, they were attacked by criminal gangs that have taken over parts of the capital south of the Tallulah River. The gang is said to number into the high hundreds, but as yet we have no confirmation as to their identity and sources from the military say they have not been asked to intervene."

Inside the Ox and Cart, the people fell silent and you could have heard a pin drop. Jason stood and spoke. "Are you ready for a war?" There was a broad grin on his face.

Roaring their approval, the crowd spilled outside, as Jason walked toward the doors. "War! War! War!" the crowd chanted and soon they were joined enthusiastically by the rest of the town.

"We'll give 'em hell, and send them reeling into the pit of despair!" Jason shouted above the noise, sending the gathering crowd into a frenzy.

Jason walked across the green with his people around him. "People's Army!" They chanted over and over. Long into the night they celebrated, there were a little over five thousand people dancing under Serene's glow as she made her way across the sky. Eventually though, the mead and ale stopped flowing and everyone went to their beds. Serene was eclipsed by the dark Ceinlys, and there was no one to see the spectacle of Ceinlys with a perfect halo glittering around its edges as it passed in front of Serene. No one except Jason de Silva who was unable to sleep; he saw the eclipse as he wandered around the village, breathing in the spring air as he wondered and worried about his family. He was glad when someone distracted him.

A man stepped from the shadows. "Evening Mr de Silva," a middle aged man stepped forward and snapped to attention, he was short, skinny and pale skinned.

"Stand easy friend," Jason said.

"Sir," the man relaxed and waited for Jason to speak.

"Why are you about tonight?" Jason asked.

"Guard duty Sir," the man replied.

"And you are?" Jason asked, not wanting the little man to feel intimidated.

"Jonathan Spalding," he looked both ways up and down the street.

"Who put you on guard duty, I thought everyone was partying?" Jason asked and he yawned, thinking about sleep.

"Captain Eric put me out here. I don't mind, I stopped drinking years ago."

"Captain Eric hey?" Jason didn't know who Captain Eric or the man in front of him was and suddenly he felt a pang of guilt for dragging this and other strangers into a war.

"Yes Sir, Captain Eric." Jonathan looked nervous, his hands clenched together to prevent him from fidgeting.

"Tell me Jonathan, what did you do before you came here?" Jason smiled trying to look friendly to calm the man's nerves.

"I was an accountant." Jonathan said, and was apparently proud of the achievement. "My wife is too." he said, unable to resist the boast.

Jason whistled through his teeth, counting precious metals was a sought after trade, and one of the best jobs a man could have. "Where's the Mrs now?"

"She's at home with the kids." Jonathan said, thinking of them as he looked skywards, his eyes rested on Albion's first moon, Cerise, its red shine dominated the sky, Serene still sat behind Ceinlys.

"I've got kids, I think of them every day," Jason looked up, also captivated by the dark red sky. "They've seen too much already."

"Yes, it was all over the news, you're very famous Mr de Silva." Jonathan looked at his feet and kicked at a stone.

"And what does Mrs Spalding think of your adventuring?" Jason turned his gaze from the red moon, back to the man that he had taken a liking to.

"She wanted to come, but somebody had to stay at home and run the business." Jonathan said. "You see we're rich, I'm a millionaire on the silver scale, but I had to come. I'm the same as everyone here in this camp following you Mr de Silva. We've all had enough, Albion society has hit rock bottom, and something needs to be done for our future generations. The laws that protect this 'new breed', as they call themselves, are destroying the very fabric of our culture. Mankind just isn't ready for the government's softly softly approach, I wish it was but it isn't. And I, like so many others, think you're our best hope outside of the royalist camp of course, and I think like everyone here, that this cause is worth dying for." Jonathan blushed when he realised how much he'd said and that maybe he'd said too much.

"Next time I need a speech writing, I'm coming to you," Jason was moved by Jonathan Spalding's honesty. "Tell me Jonathan, were you at Mount Aamor?"

"No Sir, if only I was. I just arrived two days ago," Mr Spalding turned away. "If you'll excuse me Sir, I've got some more patrolling to do."

"Yes of course, thank you for the chat," Jason was pleased he had spoken to the accountant, he watched as this seemingly unimpressive man walked into the night. Jason returned to the Inn and to his bed, he lay down and thought of his family and especially of his wife, his last thought was a memory of Jacky smiling as they snuggled up in bed.

Jacky lay awake looking out of the window, she saw clouds beginning to gather, blocking out the view of Cerise, the grey clouds took on a red tinge because of Cerise's glow. She lay in a hospital bed, in The City of Kalverstone's Royal Hospital and she worried about Jason as she recovered from her injuries. The bullet had been removed, fortunately it hadn't hit any major organs and she hoped to be released soon. Although she did wonder about the armed guards posted at her door, were they there to protect her or to hold her captive? Only time would tell.

The door to her private room opened, the guard looked inside and smiled. "You all right Mrs de Silva?" he asked.

"Struggling for sleep, worrying about my husband, besides that I'm fine," Jacky said.

"If I can get you anything, just give me a shout," his moustaches twitched as he spoke, but the smile faded from his face as he closed the door.

Jacky turned back to the red night, and waited for Serene to reappear. She thought of her family and the news that had filtered in about the battle at Aamor.

Jason woke late; he had struggled with his sleep all night. He could hear noise outside his window and he dressed quickly. He ran down the stairs and wasted no time going around to the back, he used the front door of the Inn. The noise increased as he walked out of the front door onto the street, Hurtsford was alive with activity.

All around him thousands of people ate breakfast or worked. Some loaded vehicles with all manner of equipment and many stood around debating their next destination.

A little distance from the village green, down the road outside the post office, a small troop of horsemen and women steadied their mounts.

'*Where did they come from?*' Jason wondered as he stared at the rifles strapped to their backs. He shaded his eyes to look across the green at the group.

Next to the army trucks was a small circle of men, the Robinson brothers, Teddy Williams, Jimmy fowler and others he recognised but wasn't sure of their names, some of them he knew from Aamor.

"Are you off now then?" Lindsey appeared behind him from inside the inn.

"Lindsey, I thought you'd left," he said, surprised that the reporter had stayed on.

"No, still here, it's one hell of a story." she said, she smiled, having apparently forgiven him for his barbarous acts. "Winter's done at last, no more frost." She looked past him to the snow covered mountains, some miles to the north.

"Where's your cameraman? What's his name, Timothy?" Jason asked, wondering if he was going to show up too.

"He's off trying to find some parts for the camera. I haven't seen him since yesterday, it's all right though, I've done with reporting." she looked into his eyes, to gauge his reaction to her news.

"Seen too much death? I know I have," he said in a matter

of fact tone.

"Not at all, well yes actually I have. But that's not what I meant. I want to write the story and this will make one hell of a book. By the five moons I'll be famous." Her lips thinned as she pressed them tight, she was worried he'd have an objection.

"Warts and all?" he asked, thinking of all the gory details.

"I'm going to tell the truth, if you..." Lindsey started.

"Of course I don't mind." Jason said. "Write it as it is, I'm not here to win a popularity contest."

"Thank you." Lindsey put a hand on Jason's arm, she lowered her eyes, and she turned and walked back into the Inn.

Jason watched her go until she entered the back room. He remembered her reaction to the hangings three days previously. '*Ah well, should be a good read*,' he thought, and turned his attention back to the small group of men standing next to the trucks.

Jason made his way through the crowds that rushed about getting prepared to move out. As he approached the gathering, they looked up.

"Morning Jason," Randell spoke first.

"Morning gentlemen, what's the debate?" Jason asked, he raised an eyebrow at the map of the Midlands that lay atop a crate.

"This is Ethan," Philip introduced a man standing next to him.

"Yes, I remember you from Aamor; we chatted as the Skavites arrived." Jason smiled politely, but wondered why they were having a council without his presence.

Randell sensed his mood. "Nobody wanted to wake you, we were waiting for you to arrive, discussing our next move and Ethan here is a tactician," he said by way of explaining their actions.

"That's fortunate, because I haven't got a fucking clue, seriously." Jason said and he smiled as they laughed at his jest.

"What do you suggest?" Jason asked Ethan, satisfied with

Randell's explanation.

Ethan bent over the map of the Midlands and pointed at a spot. "I suggest we go here," he said.

"Ramby? Why do you want to go to Ramby?" Jason asked, not sure of Ethans reasoning, "That's the Midlands second city, how do you expect to take Ramby?" He scratched his head, his expression was blank.

"You wanted a war, you've got little resources and fewer men," Ethan explained.

"So why such a large target?" Jason asked, he realised that he sounded as though he was interrogating the Hurtsford genius but he needed to know the reasons behind the advice.

"It's the last place they'll expect you to attack; you can't afford to fight in little towns such as this one." Ethan answered Jason and a bead of sweat rolled down his temple.

"Please explain." Jason quizzed the man, he was hungry for answers.

"Because your fight will falter, but if you go for the large gain, and stab the Hydra in the heart then the heads will fail. Mr de Silva, let them know you mean business." Ethan finished with a flourish, and then waited for a reply.

Jason looked at everyone in turn as he thought, and then a smile creased his face. "I like it, Ethan your counsel in military tactics will be sought after from now on, if you don't mind?"

"Of course Mr de Silva Sir, it would be my honour to serve you." Ethan said, happy with his sudden elevation and overjoyed that Jason de Silva would hold him in such high regard.

"So how do you suggest we do this thing?" Jason asked Ethan, looking at the map.

"You have too many vehicles for one column, especially when there are other options open to us. We can approach from three different directions, synchronising our time of arrival so we meet here." Ethan pointed at the map.

"That's Ramby park and nature reserve," Jason's brow

furrowed, he was thinking about what was being suggested. "So you want to come from here, here and here." Jason ran his finger down the jagged lines on the map.

"Yes," Ethan said, brushing strands of blonde hair off his face.

"Well then, it looks like we need to divide our forces, we need to have people to command each column and agree a time of arrival." Jason looked at the assembled group of men, waiting for suggestions.

"We've already done that." Randell said, he instantly hoped Jason wouldn't be too upset about their preliminary planning.

"We've already sorted out a command structure as well." Philip said.

Jason looked bemused, and was a little put out by all the decisions made in his absence. He'd started the damn movement, why were they keeping things from him?

"We've got ranking officers and Sergeants leading squads," Dominic said. "We didn't want to bore you with the details."

"You can't do it all by yourself, Mr de Silva," Jimmy fowler said. "If you don't mind my saying so."

"Yes, yes, of course you're right, you're all right but it would be nice to be informed of what's happening," Jason said, trying not to lose his temper. "Well, when you're ready." he calmed himself down, he realised that there was no point getting angry.

"We're ready when you are," a man Jason didn't know spoke from the back.

"Which column am I leading?" Jason asked, ignoring the man.

"This one here, down this highway," Ethan pointed at the map again; he smiled nervously at Jason's anger, but was happy that his plan was being put into action.

Chapter 12

Inspector Kingsley looked up into the sky, and watched the hover jet fly overhead, at the same time he listened to the radio chatter. The movements of the criminals were relayed to the police forces. The Inspector had been given a commission; he had been put in charge of a large task force and ordered to move against a neighbourhood that lay north of the river.

"What's it look like?" the Inspector spoke into his radio; he looked at the hover jet as though that would speed up the response. The hover jet circled high above the ground, well out of range of any bullets that might be shot at it.

"They're on the roof tops, and positioned in every window," there was a short pause; the speaker's radio was still engaged. "And there's something else Sir, they've erected barricades from overturned vehicles and tied women and children to them.

"Return to base," he ordered the hover jet pilot. *'The crafty bastards, human shields'*, he thought.

"Right lads, pull back. Pass the word, pull back, and do not engage!" The Inspector looked at the tall buildings that lined the streets, and then turned to his bag man who stood behind him. "Get me PHQ!"

"Sir," the constable said, raising his phone to his ear whilst pressing the key pad in front of him.

'This is going to be messy, too much chance of collateral damage,' the Inspector thought, not wanting to go forward and put innocent lives on the line.

"Yes, this is Kingsley unit one, requesting audio conference with PHQ1," the bag man fell silent, waiting.

After a short pause, the constable offered him the radio. "Sir."

Inspector Kingsley took the offered phone. "Sir we can not go forward, they have hostages tied to barricades."

Inspector Kingsley couldn't believe his ears, as his commanding officer ordered him forward.

"Yes Sir I'm well aware we're at war. Yes Sir, save what we can," the Inspector handed the phone back to his bag man. "I'll give the bastard collateral damage." he said to no one in particular.

His bag man was stunned, the shocked expression made his emotions apparent. "Sir, there are innocents down there." The Inspector clearly heard the pleading in his voice.

"It would appear collateral damage is to be the theme of the day. We have our orders constable, and to be fair to our illustrious leader, we can't let the criminal bastards take over." Inspector Kingsley showed no emotion as he turned and walked a short distance up the road. He lifted his radio to his mouth and spoke the orders with a certain amount of regret for the loss of life to come and the real casualties of war, the innocents and the non combatants.

"Forward! All squads forward, take no prisoners; kill 'em all!" Inspector Kingsley ordered as he peered around the corner at the barricades and the people that at this distance screamed silently, their naked and bleeding bodies thrashing in complaint to their situation.

A battalion of battle ready constables marched past him into the open space and formed into four lines. They held their full length bullet proof shields before them and began to stamp forward with heavy and short steps, each step taken was accompanied by the batons bashing onto shields. The shield bashing and stamping feet made a hell of a noise, it filled the senses of the hundreds of police moving forward. Bullets began to hit the bullet proof screens as the riot police moved forward and a thousand sword wielding constables followed to form up in ranks behind them.

An officer that ran past the Inspector fell clutching his abdomen, shot by a Skavite sniper from a third-floor window, the flash of his gun gave away his position some hundreds of feet away.

Moments later, a rocket propelled grenade slammed through the opening into the Skavite shooter's position. The blast that followed shook the building, blowing bricks and dust outwards. There was no scream from the Skav, he died instantly but the body parts flew with the debris that showered the street below.

Edging forward, the police hit their batons on their shields and they sounded like a locomotive of old. The Inspector left the relative safety of his cover, to walk into the street, with his bag man and a core of selected constables surrounding him.

"Sir," one man shouted, concerned for Inspector Kingsley's move.

"Don't worry, I'm still too sore to fight," he shouted back. "I just want a closer look."

Past the ranks of policemen, he could just make out a Skavite horde, forming up ranks in front of the riot police. They fell back slowly, one small step at a time, towards their own defences as the police advanced.

The barrage of enemy fire intensified as they edged closer and closer to the Skavite positions. For the most part they bounced harmlessly away, but some inevitably found their mark. The Skavite snipers in turn, took fire from the police snipers. Many lost their lives to the highly trained constables. Another rocket propelled grenade was launched and it slammed into the masses of Skavs and the air was awash with a shower of blood and gore, as the blast caused carnage in the ranks of the damned.

From a side street, Skavs backed away from another

formation of riot police to join with the ones retreating down the main street, swelling the numbers of the opposing Skavs.

'*This time a fortnight ago, I was sat at home drinking tea,*' the Inspector thought, but yelled: "This is madness, there are thousands of them!"

The Skavs began climbing their own barricades as they were pushed back. Desperate Skavites pushed at the police shields and the police pushed into the Skavs. There were thousands of them, just as Inspector had estimated, trapped by their own defences. The police continued their relentless short stepped march, playing the tune of 'Bash Bash Bash' on their shields.

Glass bottles filled with flammable liquids arced into the sky, to come down into the ranks of the police. Many of the constables ignited, their clothes bursting into flames.

Intentional gaps were opened in the shield wall and Skavs were pulled through, a few at a time. They were passed back through the lines of riot police, to waiting groups of constables who beat the hapless youths to death, hitting and stabbing them until they stopped moving.

One Skav managed to evade the police and fled for his life. He ran straight at the Inspector and his guard of a hundred men. He slowed to a stop and threw his hands up in a desperate attempt at surrender even as the Inspectors men levelled their guns at him.

The Skav opened his mouth to speak, but didn't get a word out, a constable giving chase barrelled into the youth and knocked him to the ground. The constable kicked the Skav in the face, causing the Skavite to flip onto his back, his head rested on the kerb like it was a pillow. The constable raised his heavy boot and stamped on the Skavs head repeatedly until he was certain that the Skav was dead.

"This is proper policing," the constable said, Kingsley noticed the madness behind the smile as the constable enjoyed his work.

'*It would appear we are winning,*' Inspector Kingsley thought, as a grenade was thrown over the barricades, to land in the middle of the assembled police. The blast ripped up the road and shattered the police ranks. Constables were thrown into the air, many of them dead before they hit the ground. A legless constable crawled across the road, his limbs taken by the explosion. He screamed for his mother, the intensity of his shock and agony written on his face, the man breathed his last as he uttered something guttural and died.

They were at the barricades now, stabbing at the last of the Skavites with their short swords.

"Forward men, over 'n at em! No mercy, kill 'em all!" The Inspector screamed his orders into his radio, lusting for blood as his adrenalin took over.

Constables began to climb onto the barricades; Inspector Kingsley rejected his own impulse to move forward, despite his instinctive desperation to engage the unseen enemy. One constable reached the top of the barricade and turned back toward his colleagues, he was holding his groin and he managed to pull the knife from his private parts as he fell from the wall. Another gained the top, firing his hand gun into the Skavs, his head snapped back and Kingsley saw that his face was shot away. The wound spewed forth a spray of blood and gore as he fell back into his fellows.

Then the barricade was breached, the strength of the police ranks eventually forced it apart. Pushing the vehicles aside they revealed a path that the riot police could take advantage of and the gap widened as the shield wall rammed forward. The shield carrying constables thronged around the breach.

'*This is chaos*,' the Inspector thought, as his men pushed against the wall of Skavs who were trying to hold the police back.

Shots still rang out and men on both sides fell dead and the casualties continued to rise. The police pushed forward through the breach and began to make ground against the criminal enemy.

Another grenade exploded in the breach, the police packed in there were blown to pieces as the shrapnel tore through their flesh. As this happened, the doors to a large department store behind the police lines slammed open, and, not waiting to be challenged, Skavs poured out onto the city street; they attacked the nearest constables and took them completely by surprise. Hundreds of the hooded thugs charged out of the shop doorway, not giving the police chance to respond, they fell upon the rear of the police formations, stabbing and slashing men. Many fell in those first dreadful moments, and then the police marksmen opened fire on the new threat, as the rear of the police turned to face and fight on two fronts.

"Forward, now," the Inspector yelled his face screwed up into a mask of pure fury.

The Inspector started to move forward, his guard moving forward with him. They carried police issue hand guns and opened fire indiscriminately. They killed the thugs and perhaps a few of their own. The surprise attack failed right there as the poorly armed thugs were cut to pieces by the quick thinking actions of the police.

Then it was over. Their morale broken, the Skavites behind the barricade resigned themselves to defeat and in seconds they turned, the battle lost. Some fell over their comrades in their desperate attempt to escape the long and deadly arm of the law.

Inspector Kingsley walked forward and had to step over corpses with every foot he placed down, thousands lay dead at his feet.

"That's enough, do not give chase," he ordered, speaking into his radio.

Moaning, a Skav moved slightly, trying to get away from the Inspector but not actually going anywhere. Lifting his boot, the Inspector stamped repeatedly on the Skavs face until the Skav stopped moving, the face near gone, battered into an unrecognisable and bloodied mess.

"See to the wounded, kill all surviving Skavs," Inspector Kingsley ordered. His face was deliberately neutral; he refused to show any remorse for the murder he had committed.

A good many of his men had watched him despatch the Skav, who was little more than a child. Kingsley walked over to the barricade and he looked at the thousands of dead constables. His face was still devoid of emotion. '*How many have to die before this is over? Was de Silva right?*' he thought, questioning his own ideals for the first time.

Then he looked at the bodies strapped to the barricade, most were dead and those that did survive had terrible injuries, whether sustained before or after the battle he didn't know. '*Albion bleeds,*' he thought, as the hostages were rescued and blankets wrapped around their naked bodies.

Chapter 13

Camouflage hid the man from plain sight as he lay motionless in the long grass at the edge of the small wood. He watched the road as the people walked along it. They carried everything they could, their lives in a suitcase, children dragged behind crying for their home comforts. The roads leaving Capital City were thick with its residents, as they headed away from Albion's capital, fearful of the troubles that had flared up.

Traffic stood idle for the most part, the vehicles inching forward at a snail's pace. Not much travelled in the other direction to enter the city. The traffic sped along in that direction but they were mainly Skavs and their families answering the call of their master. Eventually the soldier had seen enough and he crawled back into the wood, to blend into the shadows and disappear.

The spring sun had finally defeated the last of the frost and it had failed to show for the last week or more. The sun's rays were split by the trees and its rays hinted at a glimpse of heaven as the beams finally reached down over the cliffs that sat above the woodland. The natural chasm had been carved for millions of years and only recently had man put a road through it. The People's Army travelled down the road in a column of vehicles, trucks and personnel carriers on their way to Ramby.

"It's beautiful, it takes your breath away. Look how the beams of light play through the trees," Jason said to those travelling with him. He was travelling in the lead vehicle, sitting next to a man in his fifties who hadn't spoken a word since they had left Hurtsford. The man's name was Horace Brown, he was a short skinny little fellow with a hook nose, and he had shoulder length, black, greasy hair and no smile. He hadn't fought a single fight in his life, not even a fist fight, but like so many others, he had volunteered to join the People's Army and for that Jason held the man in high regard.

"Sir, what's this stretch of road called? It's been winding down through these hills for miles now," Horace finally got over his nerves for his proximity to Jason de Silva.

"Its name is the 'Heulwen Pass', more commonly called the chasm of the hundred bridges, see how the river switches under the road," Philip said, leaning forward from the back seat.

"Has it got a hundred bridges though?" Jason asked.

"I don't know," Philip said. Then they saw that buildings had begun to appear on either side of them and the cliffs dropped away dramatically. The river ended in a small lake surrounded by a low stone wall and they passed through a small village. There were people going about their daily business and they stopped to look at the convoy as it passed.

"What is this place?" Horace asked.

"Winford," Jason said.

"Peaceful place, picturesque," Philip said, he always found the picture postcard views enjoyable.

"Let's hope it stays this way." Jason said as they were leaving the tiny little hamlet.

"How long till we get to Ramby?" Philip asked.

"About an hour from here, not long," Jason said. "The road gets better from here, but there are a few towns to pass through, one of them is quite big."

They drove on at a steady pace, following the line of the river Eirwen which meandered down the centre of the valley. After a few miles, the convoy crossed the river via a switchback bridge and they took the opportunity to watch the line of the convoy that stretched out behind them. To the men that were inexperienced in army manoeuvres, it was an awesome sight. Then, just five more minutes of driving and they entered a town that covered the slope of the hill to their left.

A crowd began to gather as Jason ordered Horace to slow down and then to stop. Jason wound his window down and leaned out of his window. "Hello," he said, in his best, friendliest manner.

"It's de Silva!" one man yelled.

"It's the People's Army!" another shouted.

Then the cheering began as the people on the heights above them stood up from their hiding places. Doors began to open, people rushed out onto the street, yelling his name.

One long haired young man carried a green flag with the picture of a red winged beast upon it.

"What's that flag?" Jason asked the man nearest to him.

"It's something the young men in the town made up, they couldn't decide who to support," the man said, he came closer so that Jason could hear him over the din.

"But what does it mean?" Jason asked again and it seemed that the whole town surrounded his vehicle.

"They say the green is for King Edmund and the red dragon is for you!" the man laughed, unable to contain his happiness.

"So you support us and the Royals then?" Jason looked puzzled. "But we ain't at war with the King!"

"Perfect," the man said, he took Jason's hand in his, and gave it a good shake.

"We're at war with the Skavite bastards and the stupid laws that protect them," Jason's words were lost, as the man was swept away by the cheering crowd.

After a few minutes, order began to return to the main road and the town on the hill. Jason opened his door and got out of the vehicle and was instantly surrounded by members of the People's Army, acting in a purely precautionary role as guards for their leader. Jason climbed onto the top of the vehicle's roof.

'*Another speech*,' he thought as he steadied himself. Then he raised his hands to quiet the crowd, '*I'm beginning to feel like a bureaucrat*.' The crowd became silent and they looked at Jason as if he were a demigod, sent from the heavens to give them a message.

"People of the Eirwen valley," Jason began. "I thank you for your obvious support and for the flag that depicts me as a beast." He smiled as the crowd laughed.

"I hope that you can carry on as normal in these troubled times and I hope this conflict will end soon, with the government changing its legislation regarding crime and criminals." He was forced to pause as the crowd cheered. "I hope to put an end to the criminal culture that holds Albion in its clutches but for now, we march on Ramby. Hold this town in the name of King Edmund, and if you catch any Skavite bastards, hang 'em high and hang 'em quick!" with that said the crowd erupted once more, they went berserk as their chanting and dancing resumed.

Jason climbed down from the roof of his vehicle and was surrounded by some of Teddy Williams' men, Jason recognised them by their long black leather Jackets. The people stopped dancing around Jason as the crowd parted and they were pushed aside by a grizzly looking bunch of townsfolk. An old man with long greying dreadlocks stepped forward. He was a large man with a round face, his nose squashed flat to it. He walked with a thick staff, and he planted it firmly in front of Jason, his legs in a wide and strong stance which defied his ancient appearance.

"Mr de Silva," the man said. "Welcome to the town of Hillsgate, we hold fast for the People's Army and for King Edmund. We stand against the government that we feel has for too long let us down and we shall hold fast, to the death if need be. It's the principle of the thing Sir." the man finished and bowed low.

"Thank you Sir and you are?" Jason asked.

"My name is Denzil, Denzil Humphries. I'm the elected mayor of Hillsgate and I should warn you, up ahead is our parent town, the town of Leakfield. The Skavites and criminals from here about have taken up residence there." The old mayor spat on the ground.

"How many of them are there?" Jason asked, a troubled look crossing his face even as Philip spoke to one of his men, to send him down the line of the convoy to spread the word.

"We're not sure, but most of the townsfolk got out before they took complete control, some are with us now. If I had to guess I'd say close to a thousand, some came through here yesterday. They didn't stay long, not with all the bullets that we fired at em!" Denzil Humphries smiled as his people laughed at the memory of the fleeing Skavs.

"Well then Mr Humphries, I will bid you farewell and we'll rid Leakfield of its Skavite infestation on our way through." Jason's face was set as stone as he spat the last words out.

"Some of our lads are gearing up Sir; they are getting ready to join the back of your convoy as I speak. They have a young leader, Jacob, he's the one with that flag, he's a good lad, albeit a little arrogant, and he's good in a scrap," Denzil stepped back, giving Jason room to open the vehicle's door.

"Right, no problem," Jason said. "Do you think you can move your people back? I've got some Skavite scum to clean up." Jason was keen to push on, all thoughts of synchronised columns were suddenly pushed to the back of his mind.

"Of course Sir," the old Mayor bowed again and his dreadlocks fell forward over his shoulder.

Jason watched as the mayor of Hillsgate, helped by his lackeys, pushed the crowd back away from the road.

"Let's roll," Jason said, and sat back in his seat and closed his door.

They set out once more at a quickened pace and the fuel cells blazed a little brighter. They soon passed a line of modified vehicles filled with the young men of Hillsgate who wished to join the fight. A large youth with shoulder length hair stood against the lead vehicle, he held the red and green flag. '*That'll be Jacob then,*' Jason thought as he exchanged a brief glance with the youngster as they passed.

They soon left Hillsgate behind on their route to Ramby, down the Eirwen valley to follow the course of the river. Another few minutes' driving saw the roof tops of Leakfield coming into view above the tree tops. The town of Leakfield was divided by the river, which at that point, slowed and widened as it approached the town's dam, which provided the town with electricity. Across the top of the dam ran the town's main road, which Jason and his men could see through the trees. Jason pulled the convoy to a halt before they turned around the last corner, keeping the People's Army out of sight; he hoped to keep the element of surprise.

Jason got out and walked a short distance with Philip. Randell soon joined them, jogging up from a vehicle further down the line. They rounded the last corner, keeping to the tree-lined side of the road. They looked down the hill and they could see straight into the town. They saw smoke rising above the smouldering ruins of some burnt out houses that once belonged to residents of the tranquil town.

"Would you look at that," Randell said as he kept close to the hedge, to stay hidden.

On either end of the dam was a barricade of overturned vehicles and all manner of objects that had been utilised by the defenders of each side of the town. On the other side of the river the barricade was manned by a few hundred men and women, some of whom carried guns. On Jason's side of the river the barricade was manned by a host of Skavs who seemed to have no guns at all. On the road between the two barriers were the corpses of near on a hundred Skavs that seemed to have been shot.

"It seems that the good people of Leakfield held out against the scum," Philip said.

"Those that didn't run," Jason said, formulating a plan to free the town of its Skavite infestation.

As they watched from their hide in the hedge bottom, a man was dragged to the edge of the barricade, by a group of Skavs. The man tried to escape but the Skavs had too good a grip.

A large and muscular Skav climbed on top of his barricade, his shouts echoed across the small lake and up the valley to where the People's Army waited.

"Are you fuckers goin ta surrender? This is my fuckin town ya fat fucks. I'll do it, I swear I will!" The Skavite leader yelled and even at that distance, his voice seemed too high-pitched for his size.

"Don't listen to him," the captive man yelled as he struggled, until he was silenced by another Skav who punched the defenceless man in the face using knuckle duster. The man spat blood and teeth and fell silent.

"We're not surrendering to you!" came the reply from the other side of the dam.

With that, the lead Skav jumped off the top of his barricade, he walked over to the man bleeding from his mouth and punched him five times in quick succession. He then ripped open the man's shirt, drew a large dagger and ran it down the man's chest and belly to open him up. The man's eyes widened and he let out an agonised scream. The knife reached the man's groin and cut straight through and as the victim looked down at his own mutilated flesh, his guts spilled out onto the road. The Skavs laughed as the man was released. He dropped to his knees and tried desperately to put himself back together.

Jason, Randell and Philip looked on, horrified by the needless torture; they looked on as the man finally fell forward and died in the puddle of his own guts. They stood and returned to the convoy without a word. They rounded the corner to find two hundred of their men already formed up in the tight space that was the main road.

"With me then," Jason said, grimacing at the memory of the man's death. He turned to march back down the road. "Let's have it, give no mercy." He drew the short sword he'd liberated from Mr A's corpse after the battle of Mount Aamor and advanced, his men fell in behind him, they carried the rifles that had been gifted to him from the King and they marched around the corner, liberators and executioners both.

As they came into view from the town half a mile down the hill, Jason looked over his shoulder, '*Just like a proper army*,' he thought as his men formed up in neat lines, they showed discipline as they came on behind him. Falling in behind them were yet more of the People's Army wanting to get into the action. All needed satisfaction, blood and revenge for some past indiscretions. It was impossible for them to stay hidden any longer as the thousand or so soldiers stamped down the hill and the Skavites finally saw them.

The Skavs formed up in equal numbers to Jason's men and they threatened to halt the march of liberty. Jason quickened his pace and then he was jogging, his men matched his gait and his mood, and death was the only thought on their minds.

Fifty metres away from the Skavite line which stood at the edge of this once idyllic town, Jason raised his sword. He lowered it point forward, but did not try to shout over the tumult of yelling battle cries, he simply charged. The image of the tortured man was still fresh on his mind. Yells and the battle cries split the air which stirred with the expectation of the coming slaughter. They charged headlong into the Skavs and Jason stabbed a youth in front of him in the throat and fired his hand gun in the face of the man next to him. He couldn't miss at that range and neither could his men; they opened fire at near to point blank range. The dead were five deep in front of Jason, riddled with bullets.

Jason didn't break stride and he withdrew his sword from his victim as he ran on. Then he swung it behind him in a wide arc and brought his sword down onto the next Skav, a middle aged man wearing a dirty tracksuit. The sword hit the man in the top of his skull and stuck there. It shuddered in Jason's hand as the ageing Skav quivered. He looked at Jason and his upper lip moved, trying to form words as both his arms grabbed Jason's sword arm.

Then the two opposing factions mingled, fighting with the determination only known to those that experience hand to hand combat. Jason spun around, jerking his blade from the old Skavs head and he fell dead at his feet. Then Jason saw him, the Skavite leader, he was busy smashing in the skull of one of the People's Army with a blunt object that looked like a crowbar. Jason started to head toward him when two Skavs jumped at him.

"Mother fucker," one screamed, as he thrust a dagger at Jason's face.

Jason dodged the blade but was caught by the other, his shoulder burned with pain as the blade ran across his shirt, cutting through it and into his shoulder, drawing a ragged line of blood in his flesh. Jason let his sword trail as he swung around and pulled away from the blades. He spun around using his own momentum and at head height, Jason's blade hit the first Skav with all the power and strength he could put behind it and it completely severed the man's head.

The second Skav ducked beneath the blow and in one movement he drew back his own dagger, Jason had left himself completely exposed and facing certain death. '*This is my time then*,' he thought as the Skav was blown sideways, leaving just a spray of blood in the air. The people of Leakfield had charged and taken the barricade, a tall man stood looking down at Jason from the top of the barricade and he smiled as he reloaded the shot gun he held.

"Watch ya mate," the balding man said, and then he laughed as he jumped from the barricade, firing at the next Skav that ran at him.

Jason stood and held his shoulder, trying to staunch the blood that flowed over his fingers. He looked wildly around him, searching for the brute that commanded the rabble of Skavite scum. He desperately longed for single combat with the man who tortured the innocent; it was in direct opposition of all the ideals Jason held dear. He also hoped the Skavs would give up the fight when their leader was dead.

The number of guns soon began to make a difference as the Skavites were overwhelmed by the superior fire power of the People's Army and were cut down easily, massacred and butchered by an eager foe.

Then Jason saw him again, the Skavite leader, he was trying to marshal his men as they tried to flee a fight that was obviously lost. The muscular Skav backed off and pushed at his own fleeing men, trying to turn them around to face their enemy. Jason started towards the man and he grimaced as the two of them locked eyes.

Then it was all over, the people of Leakfield swamped the well muscled Skav and clubbed their tormentor as his men fled the battle field. The Skavite commander tried to fend off the blows with his raised arms, but it was no use with so many striking him at the same time. Before too long he was on the ground, no longer fending off any blows as he slipped into an unconscious stupor. He would never again see the light of day, his body soon gave way to death as the mob, like a flock of avenging angels, tore his body apart.

Jason had to sit down as his blood loss made him feel faint.

"He deserved that," the balding man said as he knelt down beside Jason, ripping at his shirt to give proper attention to the wound.

Jason opened his mouth to speak, but the man that attended him continued.

"It's ok, I'm a doctor!" the man said, pushing his spectacles back to the bridge of his nose. The man was easily six foot two inches, with a little pot belly, his blood-soaked sweater wasn't the sort of garment you'd expect a warrior to wear. He looked quite average except for the twinkle in the man's eye.

"Aren't doctors meant to preserve life?" Jason asked, wincing at the pain.

"And by killing these parasites, am I not preserving life?" the doctor answered with a question and then said to a man behind him: "Go fetch my bag."

Jason smiled as he saw the man's point of view.

The tall balding man turned back to Jason, pressing on the open wound with his hands, "it's not caused any serious damage, but it does need stitches."

"Get on with it," Jason looked up at the sky, trying to relax and to think of anything but the fire in his shoulder.

"Thank you for coming to help us," the doctor said after a few minutes.

"You're lucky," Jason looked at the doctor. "You're on our route to Ramby."

"Luck and twice luck then," the doctor looked behind him, as the man returned with the doctor's bag.

"Here, get this padded and take over compressing the wound while I stitch it," the doctor told his assistant.

Moving aside, the doctor made room for the young dark haired lad who quickly knelt down as he obeyed his mentor. It wasn't long before the doctor was stitching the wound carefully as a crowd began to gather to watch the open air surgery and their ranks were swelled by the People's Army who were also curious.

Philip appeared at Jason's side. "That's a tidy cut," he said smiling, but Jason saw the concern behind the humour and allowed the jest at his expense.

"It was only a matter of time before I got one," Jason said.

It took twelve stitches to close the wound and end the

bleeding, Jason watched the people around him as they began removing the dead, clearing the battle field. Non combatants came to help with the tidy up, having left their hiding places from the other side of the river Eirwen.

"We lost one hundred and twenty one men." Randell sat beside Jason as the doctor finished with his bandages.

"There, all done," the doctor stood and wiped his hands.

"Thanks," Jason said and nodded to the man who'd just sewn him up. He stood using the hand that Randell offered to him to help him up. Some of the towns folk doused a pile of corpses with flammable oils, "Do they have to do that?" Jason asked the doctor. "Do they have to burn the corpses I mean?"

"Yes they do, because I told them to," the doctor replied. "They're dead, what use are their bodies now? They aren't in there anymore, and anyway, long before we can bury them all, infection will lead to disease. Having piles of rotting corpses around is not my idea of healthy living, we have to cleanse the foulness." The doctor packed his equipment into his bag then turned away to walk over to the next person who lay waiting for treatment.

"How many dead Skavs?" Jason asked Randell

"He's got a bit of an attitude, hasn't he?" Randell spoke to the man's back, not caring if the doctor heard him, then answered Jason's question. "I'm not sure, close on a thousand."

"That's a result then, what do you think of burning the dead?" Jason asked Philip, who had remained silent throughout the conversation.

"We always burn dead cattle to prevent disease, it's the same principle," Philip answered, as Randell tied Jason's sling behind his neck for him.

Jason nursed his injured shoulder and tried to keep his arm still as the convoy pulled into town. The People's Army recovered what equipment they could from their dead and started climbing back into their vehicles. The doctor reappeared without his bag, his sleeves rolled up and arms covered in blood. Jason was just about to climb back into the convoys lead vehicle.

"You off then?" the doctor asked.

"We're behind schedule now; we have to get to Ramby and possibly a much bigger fight." Jason offered the doctor his hand.

The doctor held his arms up in front of him, "I've got blood on my hands you know."

Jason smiled back at him, "Yes, and I've got blood on mine."

"Well, thanks for saving my town." The doctor said, wiping his hands on his apron.

"It's my pleasure; just support our cause will you?" Jason asked, climbing into the passenger seat, careful not to catch his arm.

"How would you have me do that?" the doctor answered with a question again, he didn't seem to care if his words were taken as rude.

"Fly our flag, red dragon on a green background," Jason closed his door and wound the window down.

"Of course I will. Good luck Jason de Silva." The doctor removed his spectacles and stood back from the road.

"See you doctor, and good luck to you," Jason said.

Horace engaged the vehicle's power cell and they moved off down Leakfield's high street. It wasn't long before they were driving through beautiful countryside once more, a stark contrast to the ravaged town they had just left behind.

Chapter 14

Jason's column was behind schedule by a good two hours when it finally reached the outskirts of the city of Ramby.

Philip's phone rang and he answered with: "About ten minutes!" and hung up.

"Trevor?" Jason asked, looking over his uninjured shoulder.

"Nope, Dominic," Philip replied.

People turned out to line the streets; it was the same reception as everywhere else, smiles and cheers greeted the convoy, the residents were always happy to see the arrival of Jason and his followers. The convoy met no resistance of any kind, either political or military and Jason slowed the convoy down to allow his people to soak in the good atmosphere.

They soon left the residential area, and increased their speed for a short distance to reach the sprawling National Park of Ramby. The other two convoys had reached the city without incident; they sat about in the spring sun, chilling out with the locals. All manner of food stuffs were being prepared, by residents and businesses. Children played happily, their parents glad to let them play, their safety assured.

The convoy pulled into the park and was directed to a parking area by some of Teddy Williams' Black Jackets, who took their work seriously. Jason's men disembarked, their mood soon brightening as they sauntered around the park, taking in the festive atmosphere. Jason and Philip joined Randell at the side of their vehicle, they stood looking at the hordes of people enjoying the warm spring morning. Trevor, Dominic and Ethan walked toward them, followed by a mass of people, some of whom Jason didn't recognise.

"What's happening then?" Jason asked, as the throng of people stopped before him.

"We've taken Ramby for you," Ethan said proudly.

"And without a shot being fired," Dominic added.

"Well that's excellent news, but may I remind you it's for Albion and everyone, not just for me." Though Jason was delighted at the news, he wore his business face; he felt he had to remind them what he was doing was for the good of all, not just for his own sake.

Nobody said a word; they looked at him and his injured arm, wondering as to the cause of his mood.

"Ah well, don't worry about it," Jason added. "I can be over sensitive."

Jason felt a little embarrassed at the silence, "Ok then," he said, trying to end the melancholy mood of the crowd he felt he had caused. "Tell me, how did we take the city?"

"They've joined our cause," Trevor said. "The whole city."

A small man stepped forward, his scrawny features suited his tiny frame, at five feet tall he was short for a man of Albion. He was well dressed in the finest suit money could buy; he smiled nervously as he looked up into Jason's eyes. "Jason de Silva, on behalf of the fair city of Ramby, I pledge allegiance to your cause and the People's Army," he said, choosing his words carefully.

The assembled crowd started to clap, appraising the spokesman's words.

"And you are?" Jason asked, offering the man his hand.

"I am Alfred Carnell, the elected mayor of Ramby," the man took Jason's hand, shaking it vigorously.

"Well Alfred Carnell, as the leader of the People's Army of Albion I accept," Jason didn't know if what he had said was correct, or even if there was a protocol for this situation, but it sounded good to him and the applause verified that he was right.

Then the crowd began to disperse and fragment into smaller groups, chatting amongst themselves. The Robinson brothers and Ethan gathered around Jason as they discussed the battle at Leakfield. Jason's attention was taken by a group of men standing ten yards away; they stared at Jason with blank expressions.

Jason chose to ignore them and turned back to Alfred, with a question. "Mr mayor, where's your police force?" Jason interrupted the conversation Alfred was having with the Robinson brothers. "I haven't seen any security force since we arrived, I'm wondering how you keep order over the tens of thousands of people that live within the city."

"They left, right after what remained of the Skavites fled," the Mayor said and smiled.

"They just left?" Jason asked, he was confused as to why they would leave.

"Most of them," Alfred answered. "Those that stayed behind pulled back into their head quarters, when they heard you were coming they fled."

Jason fell silent; he rubbed his chin deep in thought.

Alfred Carnell took his silence as a cue to continue, "Most of our city's Skavs were at Aamor, in less than one week crime in this city has been eradicated and it's all down to your revolt, that's why we decided to throw our lot in with you."

"Well if there ain't much in the way of security, how are you keeping order?" Jason questioned further, he had a feeling that he hadn't been answered properly.

"Well now, Mr de Silva Sir," Alfred began.

"Please, call me Jason."

"Ok then, Jason. The strange thing is everybody that has remained in Ramby seems to be obeying the law, by choice and to the letter. All the bad people fled the day after Mount

Aamor," Alfred explained.

"It appears that everyone has had enough of the bastards that have ruled us unjustly for so long," Jason said, those around him nodding their agreement.

"Everyone's ready for a change," Trevor agreed.

"Makes our job easier," Jason replied. His attention drifted back to the group of strangers who stood a respectful distance away but stared rudely at him and he became distracted again.

"I'm sorry, but who are you lot?" Jason shouted, his curiosity finally got the better of him.

The group started forward, but the mayor held up his hand to order them to remain where they were. "If I may be so bold as to answer your question, those gentlemen are from the Northern Isles, they are refugees that have fled from Kalverstone city."

"Stop talking now Alfred," Jason interrupted.

Alfred stopped talking and stepped back nervously, and a giant of a man stepped forward. He was broad across the shoulder and near to seven feet tall. He offered Jason his hand and it was the size of a shovel.

Jason shook the man's hand. "Hello and you are?"

"I'm Jonas," the man's thick accent gave him away; he was definitely from those far off Northern Isles.

Jason was pleased to meet Jonas, but was a little confused as to why the mayor seemed so nervous, "So Jonas, where in the world are you from?" he asked the giant.

"I'm from Kalverstone," the northerner replied.

"No, I meant what island are you from, originally?" Jason asked again.

"Oh, I see. Me and my people, we hail from Dragandisland," the pale skinned man smiled, showing a mouth full of jagged and uneven teeth. "Tis my pleasure to be meeting with you."

"And I you," Jason smiled back, as he noticed Ilan and Shereze Ferris standing with Jonas's people. Jason waved at the pair, Shereze smiled and waved back whilst her brother nodded.

"Ah, you remember my spies then?" Jonas smiled.

"I remember them very well," Jason answered.

Alfred let out a breath he had been holding and Jason turned to him.

"Alfred, tell me, why are you so nervous?" he asked.

"Well to be honest with you , we weren't sure how you viewed the foreigners, some don't like those that migrate from the far off shores," the Mayor tried to smile, but he was so nervous it turned into a frightful scowl, which he stifled quickly lest he offend one of the giants he stood amongst.

"What?" Jason was truly surprised by the thought that somebody might consider him to be a racist.

"I'm sorry Jason, Mr de Silva Sir," the Mayor looked Jason in the eye, then quickly at his feet.

"No, it's all right, I suppose it's a reasonable question due to the chaotic times that have been thrust upon us, but no I'm no xenophobe."

Jonas and his fellow islanders stared at Jason with blank faces.

"Are you all decent people?" Jason asked them.

They nodded as one.

"So you're not criminals and you're all law abiding and honourable people. Then you're all good in my book," Jason smiled, happy that the Dragandislanders wished to befriend him.

The crowd of oversized, pale-skinned warriors cheered, attracting more attention than they usually did, and Jason heard his name called out more than once.

"For my people I thank you," Jonas lifted Jason's hand and bent his forehead to meet it in a sign of great respect, then he stepped back and gave a traditional bow, a slight nod of his head.

"You honour me too highly," Jason said, a little embarrassed but pleased.

"I wish it very much, that you let me and my Islanders fight in your army," Jonas asked, the Islander accent suited the giant, who looked like even his stare could kill. It seemed alien as the man acted subservient.

"I would be a fool to turn you and yours away, your people are legendary in the art of warfare." Jason's smile was genuine, as nothing else could please him more than two hundred fighting men from the Northern Islands.

Jonas' smile transformed his face and made him so much more human, even approachable. Jason turned around to see the Robinson boys smiling too. The Mayor had wandered off with Jimmy Fowler to talk about logistical matters, the two men had their heads together trying to organise beds for the five thousand men of the People's Army.

"I doubt that could have gone any better," Randell said, watching as their new allies departed.

"One thing though, he told me he was from Kalverstone, what's he doing here in Ramby?" Jason asked.

The mayor looked puzzled as he rejoined Jason.

"Alfred?" Jason looked at the mayor.

"Refugees from Kalverstone have been pouring into Ramby for the past few days," the Mayor swallowed hard before he continued. "There's nothing on the news, but Kalverstone has been overrun by our unsavoury enemy."

"By unsavoury, you mean Skav criminal bastards." Jason suddenly became angry. "A city, a whole fucking city."

"There'll be a gagging order I should think, because of Aamor," Lindsey appeared from behind the Robinson brothers, she had been writing notes in a little black book.

"It's not just that though," Alfred looked at Lindsey. "All the national broadcasters have gone off line."

"Off line, stopped broadcasting? They wouldn't do that!" she laughed and turned and walked off, still writing in her book.

"They have, it's just the local media that's still broadcasting," Alfred said.

"So Alfred, tell me what you know about Kalverstone?" Jason said.

"I only know what the people who escaped the city have told me, and it's not good," Alfred paused, the five men waited. "Imagine all of the very worst people in society running amok and there you have it."

"Rape, murder and pillage?" Dominic asked, disgust and dismay on his face.

"Pretty much yes, they came from all over the Midlands to attack the city, apparently there's tens of thousands of the bastards," the Mayor almost seemed pleased with himself, a little smug knowing something no one else knew.

"Why Kalverstone?" Jason thought out loud, Kalverstone was only twenty miles away.

"What is there to think about now?" Trevor asked his voice tense and becoming angry. "Now is not the time for thought, we need decisive action. We've got every Skavite bastard from the Midlands in one place."

"You're right, of course," Jason began to get excited too. "Get the message out, I want all commanding officers here, let's have a council of war. The day's not too cold lads, lets hold it there, under that tree."

Only Randell remained, the other three brothers scurried off to spread the news.

Jason watched them run off in different directions, '*They hang on my every word*,' he thought.

Henry Sumter pottered around his study, sorting through some paper work. He was a slim middle aged man; his black hair had started to turn grey above his ears. His mobile phone began to ring in his trouser pocket. He quickly removed his phone to check the screen to see who was calling him.

Pressing the conference button, he placed the phone in front off him. "It's about fucking time, where the hell have you been?" he asked, agitated.

"I'm still reporting on Jason de Silva." Lindsey's voice sounded distorted through the phone's speakers.

"Are you all right?" he asked.

"Yes I'm fine, listen Henry is it true about the blackout?" she asked.

"Yes it's true; everything's been shut down, and not just the media. Capital City is in chaos, the Royalists have fled and government are trying to fill the void," Henry sounded thoughtful, "when are you coming home?"

"I'm not sure; I've still got work to do."

"Well, where are you? I can come to you, when I fled Capital City I took the hover jet."

"We're in Ramby, but I don't know how long for. Listen darling, de Silva's got thousands of followers now. It's all gotten out of control." Her voice sounded strained.

"Stay calm, the main thing is we're safe, love you sweetie." Henry said as the door to his office opened.

"Love you too, see you soon," Lindsey said.

Henry's phone was silent as the conference call ended. He looked up as the pretty weather girl entered the room carrying a bottle of wine and two glasses. She wore one of his tee shirts which only just covered her bare behind; she closed the door behind her.

Chapter 15

All the cities in the south of Albion were under government control as the blossom broke from their buds and the flowers burst forth in a rainbow of colours. The cities and towns were protected by armed forces, whether it was army, navy, air force, or government militia. They all sang from the same song sheet, "It's for your own protection." Realistically though, the government had secretly passed a mandate to stop the support for the Royalist cause and the growing popularity for the People's Army and its ideals.

In extreme cases, where military was sparse, even the neighbourhood watch had been deputised with guns thrust into their hands. Whoever had control, the orders on the streets in the government controlled areas were the same, keep command at all cost and execute with extreme prejudice. The leading politicians of Albion had been able to keep such a strangle hold thanks only to the military officers that had refused the orders of their Field Marshal, King Edmund the first. In the first few hours of the conflict that threatened to destabilise the nation, the gangland boss of Albion, Douglass Farrell, called his followers to him to wage a war against all that opposed him. Farrell was a megalomaniac, who greatly underestimated the will of the people and the government, who up until that point had proven to be dire. But in the face of a changing political climate, with battles taking place on the streets, it proved more than up to the task, fighting Farrell's Skavite hordes with all the men it could gather.

Most of the Skavs had answered Farrell's call; they raced to Capital City without second thoughts. Those that stayed found themselves persecuted by the populace and either died or ran to one of the Skavite held towns or cities, taking their families with them.

Douglass Farrell walked through the city park, a huge retinue of followers fawning at his heels; every one of them carried guns and blades to protect their leader. The Skav leader walked to a line of trees, where a nondescript building stood, a grey brick pavilion hidden by the park's greenery. Outside the park building stood a line of black vehicles and body guards surrounded them. They were pristine in their black suits and shiny black shoes. They gave nothing away, their body language perfected by years of training. As the gangland procession approached the pavilion, some of the body guards pulled hand guns from inside their jackets.

"Where's the Minister?" Farrell asked, unperturbed by their defensive stance.

"He's inside," one body guard answered and stepped aside.

The large group of criminals entered the small building where Gerald Fontaine, the Minister of War and the Deputy Leader of the government sat. He was flanked by ten body guards as he rested on a park bench that had been half painted. Opposite the Minister was a large chair which Farrell wasted no time in occupying. "Minister," he said, his gruff voice starting the conversation.

"How are you?" Gerald Fontaine asked, he crossed his legs and relaxed with a smile as his arms rested across the back of the bench.

Farrell leaned forward to put one huge forearm across his knees. "Let's get straight to the point."

"Yes let's get straight to the point," the Minister mirrored Farrell's forcefulness. "Can you tell me what the fuck do you think you are doing?"

Farrell bristled with anger at the Minister's words. "What I'm doing?" he yelled. "You said the armies of Albion were retreating north of the border, you fucking loon."

"And they have," the Minister remained calm as he lied through his ever present and carefully practiced smile.

Farrell sat up and tried to remain calm, he clicked his fingers and one of his men dragged a girl by a choke chain to stand at Farrell's side. The gangland boss reached up to take hold of her long dark hair, and then he pulled her down so she sat on his knees. He unbuttoned the girl's coat and revealed her naked flesh. Fontaine could only guess but she didn't seem to be too far into her teens. Farrell sighed as he began to stroke her breasts with two fat fingers. Farrell looked relieved and much calmer as the girls eyes darted, searching for an escape route.

"Then why are my people beaten everywhere except for Capital City and Kalverstone?" Farrell's eyes stared straight into the Minister's, but if the Minister was intimidated he didn't show it.

Ignoring the fact that the gangland boss had a naked young girl sat in his lap, the Minister continued. "All your people want to do is rob, rape and pillage. There are millions of law abiding citizens that are bound to oppose you, did you really think the people would stand idly by and watch as the daughters of Albion were raped by your hand?" the Minister didn't move, but the smile had left his face. "Why the fuck did you rise up anyway?" Fontaine asked.

"Every man with a gun appeared to be leaving the country, why shouldn't I take control?" Farrell smiled, his hand moved down the girl's body to rest on her thigh.

"Because you people don't know how to rule." The Minister smiled again, as he answered before Farrell finished.

"Are you calling me inadequate and simple?" Douglass Farrell's volume increased at the insult.

"Not at all Douglass, you're a very clever man. But in this case I think you certainly read the situation wrong, you allowed your mind to go overboard with delusions of grandeur and thoughts of conquest. The people of Albion won't let you rule, we've seen the evidence of that fact." The Minister was smug.

"The Kings of old took power at the tip of a blade and only kept it by showing strength," the gangland boss squeezed the girl in his lap; she did not dare to squeal for fear of punishment.

"You great oaf," the Minister lost all composure; he raised his voice, uncrossed his legs and leaned forward as a bead of sweat ran down his face from his temple.

The sight of the young girl had sickened the guards that up until now had managed to keep their feelings under control. One guard struggled with his neutrality. He was a father to three daughters and his mind twitched to think of his own girls living under Skavite rule. It all became too much for him, the sight of the girl on Farrell's knee, too scared to cry or struggle as the pain passed across her ashen features.

He drew his pistol and fired, too quickly for any reaction in the room other than that of Douglass Farrell who already gripped his improvised shield in his hands. All hell broke loose in the dusty store room as the perfectly aimed bullet tore into the chest of the young girl. She died in an instant, her heart exploded as the bullet tore through it. Men on both sides wasted no time, guns were drawn and fired, and men began to fall dead. The Minister sat rooted to his park bench as his guards died around him. The crime boss stared as a bullet hit Gerald Fontaine in the throat severing an artery. As the Minister raised his hand to the wound he was hit again, this time in his belly, dark blood running from the man's liver.

Then the bullets stopped flying. The only sounds of gunshots came from outside until a vehicle sped away, then only silence. Farrell looked down to see the girl was dead and riddled with bullets; he was hit three times in one arm but for the moment, chose to ignore the injuries. He let the girl's corpse fall to the floor. Then he walked over to the Minister and felt for a cigar in his jacket pocket. He sat next to the Minister of War and lit the cigar with a match. The smell of sulphur and warm blood mingled for a few seconds. The Minister strained as he turned to face Farrell, his breath came in short and pained gasps as he held his neck, unable to hold back the flow of his lifeblood.

"This is my land now, I will rule. We are going to overthrow your police army tonight," the gangland boss stood up and left the room with what was left of his guard, four men, all injured.

The Minister for war fumbled with his phone in his free hand, as he watched them leave. He dropped the phone on the floor and it came apart and the battery slid across the room to stop in a pool of blood.

Gerald Fontaine, one of the most powerful men living in Albion, closed his eyes to die alone. A single bead of blood dripped onto the back of his hand, his arms flopped to his side and the darkness claimed him.

The afternoon sun shone down upon the land of Albion, and at the same time as the war Minister was dying, one of his commanding officers, Colonel John Blithe Dempsey left the large green canvas tent that was serving as his field head quarters. He strode to the edge of the road and looked out past the fields towards Capital City. He could see the edge of the distant suburbs and plumes of smoke rose from the horizon. He was trailed by some of his subordinates, mainly Captains and lieutenants with two Majors; and they all waited for orders or for something to happen.

Colonel Dempsey looked away from distant evidence of warfare; he turned towards the makeshift holding camp that had been set up for the Skavs they had captured. "My god, there must be hundreds of the blighters," he said.

A Captain marched forward and stamped his feet in the dirt as he stood to attention. "Two thousand one hundred and eleven, Sir," the soldier said, saluted and then marched back into line.

"How many men do we have?" the Colonel wondered out loud as he looked at his men. The Colonel was an impressive man when he wore his uniform; he still looked fit and healthy. He was in his early fifties and he had the posture and pep of a man in his twenties. His greying side burns were the only thing that gave away a hint of his age, that and the crow's feet that lined his face below the eyes.

The Captain stamped out of line again, his rigid hand forming a salute as his boots came together. "Five and a half thousand, posted on all the major routes in and out of Capital City. Five hundred are here at HQ Sir."

"It won't hold Sir," a lieutenant said, standing at ease, and then quickly to attention, saluting as the Colonel frowned at him. "The overseas troops are arriving back on Albion soil all the time Sir, most joining us, but some heading north to join up with the King's lot."

"My god what a mess," the Colonel said to his officers. He looked towards the camp, trying to collect his thoughts. "And with that idiot Minister of war ordering the troops everywhere but where the enemy is…" he stopped talking and looked down the hill at the mass of Skavs that had been detained trying to enter Capital City.

'What would history say of me?' Colonel Dempsey thought with accusations of war crimes on his mind.

Another young Captain displayed the pomp that Colonel Dempsey required as he stood to attention beside his commander. The Captain saluted. "If I may be so bold Sir," he waited while the Colonel looked him over.

"Yes, go on," the Colonel said.

"These scum we've captured, they're threatening the entire operation, and it's obvious that they've become part of the problem. Well Sir, the mission comes first." The Captain stood tall and straight, confident that he was correct in his assumptions; but he would not make eye contact with his commanding officer.

"What would you have me do?" the Colonel asked. He lifted his cane to trap it in his armpit as he deliberated his choices. He glanced over to the captured foe, a fleeting glimpse and he made his decision. "Kill them."

"Yes Sir." The Captain didn't dare move; he waited for the Colonel's response.

"My god man, stand easy," the Colonel sighed, deflated. "Stand at ease, all of you."

'*I guess we had the same thoughts, but there was just one man that dared to say it out loud*,' the Colonel thought as he considered his options and thought of the possible future charges against him.

"Give the order," Colonel Dempsey said, he read the Captains name on the front of his jacket, "Captain Dawkins."

"Sir." Dawkins stood to attention and saluted.

"When you've executed the orders come back and see me, I've a different uniform for you to wear, Major Dawkins." The Colonel knew he should be happy, a promotion was always a joyous occasion, but the mass murder he had just ordered worried him greatly.

"Sir." Major Dawkins turned on his heels, also unable to smile. He was nothing special to look at, an ordinary man in a soldier's uniform, but he was ruthless to all that opposed him.

Colonel Dempsey and the rest of the officers watched as soldiers ran to carry out their orders. Squads of soldiers surrounded the prisoner's enclosure and the prisoners became restless, moving into the centre of the field and away from the guns that were trained on them.

"Should be quite a spectacle from here," Colonel Dempsey managed a wry smile, his humour gone.

"Fire!" The newly-promoted Major Dawkins sounded muted at the distance.

Machine gun fire rattled and the Skavs were cut down where

they stood and although the murder was dark in essence, it didn't dampen the spring sun which shone on regardless.

"My god, they got what they deserve hey!" Colonel Dempsey thrust his cane out in front of him, trying to make sense of the situation, if only in his own mind.

Then the guns fell silent. The soldiers entered the enclosure with the new Major at the fore and they shot any Skav that still breathed.

"It should make a marvellous fire," one of the officers dared to comment.

Chapter 16

Inspector Kingsley opened the door; he was in awe as he walked into the room. He was daunted by the people who sat around the table; they were the most powerful people in the country. They talked to one another and discussed the orders that they were about to hand to officers who stood waiting for their names to be called out. The Inspector waited his turn at the back as one by one the names of the officers were called out and they stepped forward to receive their orders.

Eventually, Kingsley was the only one left. He stood patiently as the panel of people in front of him discussed his future.

"Come forward Inspector," Sir Edward Parker smiled; he looked up as the Cabinet sat easy, their discussion over.

"Yes Sir." Kingsley walked forward; he came to a stop in front of the long table.

"Please take a seat Kingsley," Sir Parker motioned to a chair.

"Thank you Sir," as Kingsley sat in the chair he noticed he was being scrutinised by the Prime Minister, his hands resting on his giant gut.

"I've left you till last because your mission is the most important and the most secretive." Sir Parker leaned forward, resting his hands on the table.

The Cabinet all looked at the Inspector and their conversation ceased whilst the Inspector was being dealt with.

Sir Parker continued. "As you must be aware, we are running out of ammunition, but so are the enemy, we think, but as to the state of their supply we haven't got a clue. In the light of the obvious dangers, you're to help evacuate and escort the Cabinet and government north where you will join up with a military outpost and report to Colonel John Blithe Dempsey. When you get to him, give him this letter." Sir Parker was solemn as he handed the Inspector a sealed envelope. "You are taking a thousand men, handpicked for your mission. That will be all Inspector, you're to be at the front of Head Quarters in two hours."

Sir Parker turned to talk with the Prime Minister and Kingsley knew he had been dismissed, but he had a nagging question that couldn't wait.

"Begging your pardon Sir," Kingsley said and all heads turned to him once more. He felt a bead of sweat forming on his brow. "Why so many men? After all, we have the Skavites contained south of the Tallulah River and we hold all the bridges."

"That'll be all Inspector. All will become clear when you reach your destination." Sir Parker raised his voice only slightly but it was stern enough to let the Inspector know he'd been dismissed, again.

As he left the room, the Inspector closed the door behind him and tucked the letter into his pocket. He walked down the corridor towards the elevator and Sergeant Bernard Willis and the newly promoted Sergeant Stephen West fell in behind him.

"What are our orders Sir?" West asked.

"You'll find out soon enough, but I can tell you we're leaving Capital City." The Inspector smiled as he relished the thought of a respite from fighting.

"Thank god for that," Sergeant West said, the Inspector was not the only one that was more than happy to leave the chaos behind.

Afternoon spring rays broke through the rain clouds that scudded overhead. Jason de Silva sat with his back to a tree trunk. Alone at last, he had time to think and contemplate his next move; all around him the park was abuzz with the People's Army and their allies, the citizens of their adopted city of Ramby. Jason had thought of food, but opted instead for the relative peace of the tree.

Jason watched as a stage was erected, the huge scaffold structure was covered with large square boards that were fixed with heavy duty bolts. Electric cables were being fed into all sorts of gadgetry that were positioned on and off the stage, large spot lights were hoisted onto a frame that overlooked the stage.

'*By the five moons, anyone would think we were having a music festival*,' he thought as a group of children darted past him, one of them tripped over his outstretched legs.

"Sorry Sir," the young lad jumped to his feet and bowed, he was red-faced with blushes.

"It's all right lad," Jason put on his friendliest smile as he remembered his own boys.

The young lad beamed as he ran off. "Did you hear Mr de Silva speak to me?" the young lad shouted to his friends.

Jason got to his feet, 'I guess that's what we're fighting for,' he thought. 'The next generation'

A large crowd began to gather around the stage as the afternoon wore on. Jason felt a little useless, standing around, not knowing what to do. People passed him and he noticed that more than a few of them bowed in his direction and many a 'my lord' was spoken, and he felt like a spare peg on a clothesline and uncomfortable at the reverence shown to him.

In the end, Jason became so bored with the waiting that he picked up a hooded top that lay across the back of a chair. He put the top on and as his head appeared through the neck, he looked around and saw a young man staring at him, worried.

"Begging your pardon my lord," the ashen faced youth stuttered.

"Is this your top?" Jason asked, pushing his arms through the sleeves. "Can I borrow it?"

"Of course my lord," the young man dipped his head in a sign of fealty and respect.

"How do I look?" Jason asked. His face was partially hidden by the hood.

"You look all good Mr de Silva Sir," the youth stuttered again.

Jason stepped close and spoke quietly. "Call me Jay will you? I want a burger without all the bowing and scraping and 'my lords'. I'm starving and fed up with the people all ducking their heads at me." He stepped back from the lad. "Well come on, let's go get some food."

"Sir…" the young man's incredulous look and inability to call him 'Jay' threatened to give him away.

"Come on, that's an order," Jason turned away and the young man fell in at his side.

"I've got work to do," the youth said, matching Jason's stride.

"You have haven't you and you're doing it. I'm ordering you to help me have half an hour without people treating me like King Edmund, all I want is a burger." Jason stepped out from behind the stage, the noise was that of tens of thousands of people chatting and mingling as they waited, the crowd was huge and growing.

Walking into the massed crowd was easy enough; there was no press of bodies because the crowd spread across the vast expanse of the parkland.

"What's your name lad?" Jason asked, and he pulled his hood lower over his face.

"Jacob, Jacob Adams, Sir," he whispered and he tried to be covert, to obey his lord's command.

Jacob Adams was a big lad, almost as big as Jason, but where Jason trained for his physique, Jacob's was natural.

"No need to whisper, just get me the burger, lots of onions and sauce." Jason looked around him as the throng buzzed with excitement, '*Just like a festival*' he thought.

They threaded their way through the crowd in silence for a few minutes; then they came to an area that was set out like a market town, with row upon row of food vendors selling all manner of food stuffs.

Jacob looked at Jason as he stepped in front of a burger bar. "Can I have two burgers please with lots of onions and ketchup?" Jacob spoke to the vendor but gave Jason a backward glance. Jason looked at the floor and he smiled, happy with the ruse and the chance to mingle without being swamped. He also smiled because he liked the way that Jacob was a polite young man, his upbringing had been based on manners, just like his own. Minutes passed while the vendor prepared their food.

"That'll be six coppers mate," the vendor said, handing Jacob the food.

"Thank you." Jacob handed the copper pieces over then he turned back to Jason and handed him his share of the meal. Then they walked between the lines of stalls and Jason had time to take in the atmosphere and he relished the happiness of the crowds.

"What now?" Jacob asked, wondering what his duties should be.

"We eat," Jason said as he took a bite out of the burger, he walked a few feet as he chewed, then heard a familiar voice.

"Do you think Jason is happy with everything?" Alfred Carnell spoke to a man who walked slowly with him. They were also grabbing a bite to eat and held their food carefully as they avoided people walking towards the food wagons.

"Well if he isn't, he hasn't said a word to me and believe me he would have." Jimmy spat food everywhere, failing to close his mouth as he bragged.

Jason turned away he did not want to hear any more. "Don't you just hate that?" he asked, directing his question to Jacob.

"What? The eating and talking, yeah man gross. I don't wanna see what he's chewing." Jacob smiled, he was truly jubilant as he walked with his hero, he felt as though the gods themselves had blessed his soul.

They walked back in the direction of the stage and the safety of Teddy Williams' black jacketed troops; Jason finished his snack and licked his fingers. "Marvellous, if we do change Albion's way of thinking, this is one thing that's staying the same."

Once they had finished their meal, they picked up their pace and headed back to the rear of the stage. On his return, Jason was swamped by his followers; at their head was a worried Randell.

"Where the hell have you been? We've been worried to death." Randell remained calm as he berated his leader, then instantly felt daft, he sounded like the older man's keeper.

"I needed a bit of 'me' time, Randell," Jason said, shaking his head at all the fuss. "It was just a burger for fuck's sake."

Jason handed the borrowed top back to Jacob and with a wink and a nod he dismissed the youth.

"You're due on stage in half an hour," Trevor said, his arms folded in front of him.

"Look, don't worry, I just wanted a burger without the fussing," Jason raised his hand to quieten them. "Enough, I'm fine. Besides, I can look after myself ya know."

Jason's command was final; he turned away from the whining and the fretting.

The old man sat in his vehicle and waited. He looked in the back at his two grandsons as they slept. Louis and Hector de Silva hadn't seen their father for some weeks and the thing that Louis remembered of him most was a chaotic scene of death and destruction in which his father had gone crazy. In the fight his grandmother had been killed, stabbed by one of the Smith boys. The whole affair had started with him being bullied by one of the Smiths and Louis blamed himself. Needless to say, the six year old boy spent a lot of time crying lately. He suffered from lack of sleep and when he finally did drift off from exhaustion, he had nightmares that made him waken to the sound of his own screams.

Fred de Silva stepped from his vehicle and stretched and rubbed at his aching back. He opened the vehicle's rear door to wake Louis and then he lifted Hector from his safety chair even as the littlest one still slept.

Louis stood and rubbed at his eyes as they adjusted to the light, his saw his brother cling to his grandfather and close his eyes to fall back to sleep. Louis wanted to be picked up and held tight too.

"I'm sorry Louis, I can't carry you both, it's my back," the old man said, understanding his grandson's tiredness.

"Grandad?" Louis looked at his grandfather, unsure as to what the old man meant.

"It don't matter Louis. Here watch your brother a mo will you?" the old man put the baby wrapped in the blanket on the grass while Louis sat next to him stroking his hair. Fred then opened the rear storage compartment and removed the toddler's stroller; he set it up next to the two children. Hector still refused to wake even up as his grandfather lifted him off the ground and strapped him into his seat.

"Come on then, let's go find your father." The old man said and he took hold of the stroller's handles. Louis also took hold of the stroller as he had been instructed by his father and they moved forward. They were surrounded by lines of vehicles of varying designs and ages, but it didn't take long to navigate through the gaps. Before too long they walked through a line of large oak trees and into a vast field filled with tens of thousands of people.

"Don't let go Louis, I don't want to lose you." The old man said, leaning over to make sure the lad was listening.

"I won't let go, Grandad." Louis promised, his eyes were wide and he was daunted by the crowds.

They made their way into the park and no one gave them a second glance, unaware that the little group were the father and the seed of the man they were all there to see. They walked on for a quarter of an hour through ever more dense crowds and eventually they saw a stage.

"I bet that's where your father is," Fred looked at Louis and ruffled his hair and the boy smiled at him.

Leading them forward, Fred tried to skirt around the thickest parts of the crowds, worried that the children might be trodden on. It took a while but eventually they came to an area level with the rear of the stage, off to the right, near a big old tree. The area behind the stage was fenced off by poles and some flimsy tape, men in long black leather jackets stood around or walked its length, they were obviously the guards, they looked serious and even dangerous to Fred.

One of the guards stepped forward as Fred approached with the children and halted Fred's progress.

"Sorry mate, no one's to go any further." The man looked solemn; he looked like he took his job seriously. Fred was not to know that a short time before his arrival, the guard was subjected to a severe dressing down from Teddy Williams over the incident involving their leader's disappearance.

"But I'm…" Fred started.

"No buts old man." The guard interrupted Fred and though he didn't need to, he smiled menacingly.

"Does this mean I can't see my daddy?" Louis looked from the guard to his grandfather.

"And who might that be?" The guard's smile softened as he looked down at Louis.

"Daddy." Louis said, smiling back.

"And what's your name?" The guard asked Louis, mocking the old man with a wink and a smile.

"I'm Louis de Silva." Louis looked up at his grandfather. "Can I see my daddy now?"

The guard's smile froze as the colour drained from his face. He stammered "de Silva…" and then redness flooded to his cheeks in his embarrassment.

The black jacket didn't turn his head; he just stepped aside and seemed to look past Fred and the children. "Would you like to go through, I'm sorry for any inconvenience." The man's eyes were steady but concerned; it wasn't a good day for him.

Louis broke free and ran past the guard.

"Thank you," Fred said, as he hurried after Louis.

At the rear of the stage, Fred caught sight of Louis as he ran into his father's arms. Both Jason and Louis began to cry, their arms wrapped around the other in a seemingly unbreakable embrace. The baby remained sound asleep despite the noise of so many people and Fred pushed Hector to his son's side.

Jason looked at Hector then to his father. "Thank you," he managed as he lifted Louis into his arms as he stood upright.

Someone began speaking on the stage but the words were ignored by the small group, then a man with a clip board came rushing over. The man didn't want to disturb such a beautiful moment and he opened his mouth to speak then closed it again. Then the crowds beyond the stage began to cheer and his hand was forced.

"Mr de Silva Sir, you're needed on stage." He sounded apologetic and held his paper work close to his chest.

It was clear to Jason that the reuniting of him and his children had to come second under the circumstances. "Yes of course." Jason said. "I'm on my way."

Jason put Louis back on the ground and held the lad's hand. He walked towards the steps leading up to the stage and he could hear the crowd chanting his name over and over. The noise became deafening as Dominic Robinson finished his introduction and climbed down the steps.

"There, I've introduced you," Dominic smiled. "That's one hell of a welcome you're going up to."

Jason lifted Louis again, he held the boy in one arm as he climbed to the stage above, holding tightly onto the rail.

The noise that was already deafening increased in volume. It seemed to Jason as though the population of Ramby had all turned out to greet the people's hero in this modern day revolution. The huge expanse of parkland stretched as far as the eye could see and was covered with waving, screaming and chanting people. Jason looked at the camera pointing at his face and he turned to look behind him at the massive screen, only to see the back of his own head. Jason then looked back at the throng, the massed multitude of supporters singing and dancing. He stood for a moment and allowed his own name to wash over him as Louis tried to bury his face in Jason's chest.

When the chanting finally began to ebb towards silence, Jason lifted his free hand.

At length the massive mob quietened enough for Jason to make himself heard and he stepped forward to the microphone clearing his throat. "Hello," he said.

The crowd cheered for a half minute.

"People of Ramby, be quiet please, I have a few things I wish to share with you." Jason made his voice as soft as he could and the tens of thousands of people fell silent at his gentle command. "This boy I'm holding, this beautiful little lad, is my son. They tried to bully and intimidate him and when I found out, I said 'no'." Jason paused and looked out at what seemed to be a million statues, all motionless and hanging on his every word. "So then they came at me and they tried to bully and intimidate me, and again I said 'no'. They attacked my family and my home, and I said 'no'. Then the police came for me, and I said 'NO!'" Jason was about to continue but the crowd had caught his message and as he said the last word, they yelled "NO!" with him in a wave of noise. He stepped back for a moment and grinned down at his son's head, and then he stepped up to the microphone again and finished his speech.

"I will have justice, for me and for all of you!" His voice gradually became louder, and he took a deep breath to shout. "Because I am still saying 'NO!'" He emphasized every word in this last sentence as he bellowed and the crowd exploded. They had a new chant now, he could hear them, it was 'Jason says NO! Jason says NO!'

Shouting over the microphone in order to be heard, he continued. "This is what it's all about, our children and our children's children. No longer will we or our future generations allow ourselves to be victims of the criminal evil that is protected by government legislation." Sweat dampened his shirt and he paused again. Then he leaned forward to shout over the multitudes of cheering supporters. "No longer will I feel the shame of inactivity and think myself a coward. I have fought my demons, I have taken on the devil and I have beaten him!" Jason put Louis down and then he thrust both his clenched fists into the air.

The crowd's joy could not be contained any longer; the noise rocked the air to make the stage quiver with its power. It was some minutes before he could speak again, the noise was almost unbearable as his supporters chanted and sang. He took the time to send Louis back to his grandfather who was waiting in the wings and reflected on the support he had from the people.

He held his hands up for silence and got it. "Good people of Albion," he was calm again, the anger he had displayed a few minutes before, gone. "Good people of Albion who have followed me into the jaws of death, I can not thank you enough, for I know you are with me till the end of your days as I am with you. Together we will rid our nation, this beautiful isle, of those who would take away our liberty, our happiness, our hopes and our dreams." Jason paused for effect and felt surreal as if he were reciting a poem.

"Well my friends, because you are, every one of you, my friends and countrymen, who amongst you has the courage to follow me to the gates of hell?" This last question was asked almost in a whisper, but it carried over the silence.

Like a tidal wave of sound, the roaring approval hit him and he was lifted by its power. Again he raised his hands for silence and it came instantly as the crowd seemed to obey his very thoughts. He spoke in a calm voice. "Not too far away from here, in the city of Kalverstone, chaos and evil reign and people are suffering." His voice began to shake as he raised his voice once more. "If the Skavite hordes have taken Kalverstone, then that's where I'm going. Who is with me?"

Again the crowd cheered their affirmation and he yelled to compete with them. "I will bash down those black gates to the Pit of Despair and I will fight the hordes of hell. I will take the devil by the horns and rip them from his skull. Who is with me?" If Jason had any more to say, it would have been wasted because the crowd, finally, would not be silenced. They were at the point of no return as they went berserk and it seemed that every single one in the crowd yelled his name back at him.

"Who's with me?" he asked again, but he couldn't hear his own words because they were lost to the tumultuous chanting.

Jason left the stage exhausted and emotionally drained. He felt like he'd already fought the battle. Alfred Carnell climbed the steps and Jason waited at the top to descend. Alfred hurried over to the microphone as Jason disappeared out of view. The mayor of Ramby took the microphone and said: "Our hero Jason de Silva!" his strong public speaking voice was barely heard over the sound system, it was still drowned by the celebrations and he had to wait a few minutes for the noise to abate so that he could continue. "If you want to fight at Jason de Silva's side and join the People's Army, it's really simple. Get tooled up and be here at sun up." The little old man was in his element, the crowd went berserk again in approval of his every word. "But tonight I urge you to party; we have some local musicians here to entertain you, so enjoy the celebration." The crowd of thousands began to chant 'de Silva' over and over as the little old mayor climbed back down the steps and the first of the bands took to the stage.

Jason was there to meet Alfred at the bottom of the steps.

"Sun rise is at seven, I was thinking more like eleven," Jason mock-complained to the Mayor.

"With all due respect my lord, you should have said," the little old man grinned at his leader, he was still buzzing with adrenalin. "And besides my lord, it will take hours to prepare for the march according to Ethan."

"I suppose you're right," Jason looked down at the floor then back at the mayor. "Alfred, can you sort out some accommodation for my father and my sons?"

"I've been meaning to ask you my lord, but it would be my honour if you were to stay with me, at the manor house at the edge of the parkland." Alfred suggested. He was still smiling after his performance on stage, he could see himself never out of office, winning every election hence and perhaps becoming almost like a lord perhaps.

"That would be great, thank you." Jason said as the music started on the stage.

Jason left Alfred and went to seek out his family. He didn't have far to go, his father was waiting for him with the children and Louis was smiling whilst Hector cried, he had woken prematurely, nothing could sleep with so much noise.

"Father, we're staying at the parkland manor house as guests of the mayor." Jason said and Fred could see that he was ecstatic to be reunited with his children; he picked Hector up who hugged him.

"That's nice of him." Fred looked to the floor, an anguished look on his face.

"What's wrong father?" Jason asked.

"It's Jacky." Fred said.

"What, is she all right?" Jason asked, desperately needing a straight answer from his father.

"She was admitted to Kalverstone Royal Hospital, after she was shot at Aamor, she's still there as far as I know." Fred de Silva forgot himself, the children were next to him and he spoke without thinking.

The smile dropped from his face and Jason looked out towards Kalverstone to where his wife was.

Chapter 17

What Fred could not have known as he told Jason about her, was that Jacky de Silva had been moved by her guards when the Skavites attacked the hospital. They moved her to a public ward, so they could better guard all patients but they were slaughtered later, whilst trying to prevent the rape of two pretty nurses. Their deaths were in vain, the nurses were raped anyway.

Jacky tried to look inconspicuous as the hospital staff were pushed around and beaten by groups of rampaging Skavs. All around her, the patients lay in fear as the oppressed hospital staff tried to care for them. The smell of rotting flesh and soiled sheets was almost unbearable. A nurse limped onto the ward holding her tunic together, her nose bleeding heavily, her tear filled eyes told volumes.

Jacky was not in too much pain but was still sore where the bullet had entered her body. She considered her options, '*Do I stay or do I try to leave? It's insanity to stay*' she thought, she knew that a few of the less dedicated staff and the more mobile patients had made it across the road to safety.

Across the front of the hospital ran a dual carriageway and on the other side of the main road was the University of Kalverstone where government forces had occupied. The forces were unable to move any closer to the city as their numbers were too small but the soldiers and the Skavs occasionally exchanged fire but neither side dared to try a full on assault.

Jacky came to her decision late in the afternoon, she resolved to escape and she waited, listening until she was certain that the coast was clear. The nurse that had been violated was asleep in the chair and Jacky tried to be as quiet as possible. She edged her way off her bed, dropping her feet to the cold floor.

In her bedside cabinet she found some clothes which she decided to take. She dressed quickly into the jeans and shirt, which were for a taller and bigger woman and didn't fit properly. The shirt sleeves covered her hands and the jeans would have to be rolled up. She also found a pair of shoes that fit perfectly, but decided to go bare foot for the sake of silence.

"What are you doing?" the nurse asked. "You're not well enough to move yet. Maybe in a couple of days Mrs de Silva."

"I've got to go, I can't bear it any longer," Jacky struggled with the top buttons on her shirt, her arm was still not working properly. "You couldn't button me up could you?"

"Yes of course," the nurse got to her feet and buttoned up Jacky's borrowed blouse.

"Thank you," Jacky spoke softly; as much in sympathy for the other woman as to not be heard, "Did they..." she stopped herself from stating the obvious.

The nurse looked down nodding, fresh tears streaming down her face.

"Why don't you come with me?" Jacky pleaded.

"The patients, I have to care for them, too many have gone already. Besides it's too late for me now, at least ten of them have been inside me." She turned away from Jacky. The pretty blonde nurse wiped her eyes and wandered off in a stupor, she stopped at the next bed. "Are you ok dear? Can I get you anything?" she asked an elderly lady that had been dead for at least a day.

Jacky gave up at that point and left the ward. In the corridor, the screams of the victimized were numerous but fortunately, that part of the hospital appeared clear. She followed the overhead signs and headed for the stairway and as she rounded a corner of the ward the stairs were in full view. There were still no Skavs as she passed the lifts; she feared the use of them in case she got stuck or worse, that the lift doors would open up onto a group of the foul criminal scum that roamed the hospital.

Jacky crept to the top of the stairs and paused to look down them. She stood silently and could only hear the sounds of distant torment and shrill screams somewhere down a far-off corridor.

Jacky tentatively crept down the stairs as quietly as she could, listening for the slightest of noises. She made it to the ground floor without hearing so much as a pin drop, then she heard heavy footsteps heading her way fast.

"Get the fucker, bastard doctor!" A rough voice yelled.

"Yeah man, gimme ya drugs," another Skav said.

Jacky fled down the stairs to the basement level and out of sight, she heard the doors that she had been standing next to burst open.

"No please, you've had all the drugs, there's nothing left," crying, the doctor pleaded.

"Fuck you, where's the drugs?" the first Skav insisted.

"It's all in the pharmacy, please I've got kids," the doctor begged for mercy, he would have tried anything to ensure his survival, even lying about the children he did not yet have.

"Pharmacies bled dry, fuck you," the Skav shouted, nose to nose with the cowering doctor.

Then Jacky heard a gunshot and she almost jumped out of her skin, then the thud of the body as it hit the hard floor and the doctor would never see those imaginary kids of his. A short burst of laughter came next and the doors closed behind the Skavs as they left the staircase.

Jacky waited a few minutes, not daring to move. When she had courage enough, she left the relative safety from beneath the stairs almost at a crawl. She gained the ground floor level once more and she forced herself to ignore the dead body, stepping over the doctor's corpse. She looked through the rectangular strip of glass in the door to the corridor to make sure that the Skavs had gone.

Jacky pushed the door open and stepped through but it slipped from her sweat-slick fingers and the door banged shut. Jacky froze and didn't dare to breathe, fearful that the noise she had just made would bring Skavs running but there was not a sound.

Jacky began to hope for her freedom, she could see the fire escape twenty metres away and she trotted down the corridor towards it, looking out through the glass to the sun soaked grass beyond. She burst out of the confines of the hospital of nightmares into the open air and the afternoon coolness, into a blessing of normality almost.

She gave a little laugh and almost began to skip. She could ignore the nagging pain from her wound as she rounded the corner of the hospital and there it was the university and safety. As she came around the corner, she ran head long into twenty Skavs, who grabbed her arms and stopped her from falling onto the ground.

"Well fuck me, it's Jacky de Silva." Reginald Smith stepped forward, there was a mixture of shock and surprise on his face and that turned into a nasty leer. He couldn't believe his luck.

"Oh my god, no, I thought you were all dead!" Jacky was shocked to her core, the futility of her efforts was now apparent and she tried to escape, knowing she couldn't be in worse company.

"It's time for a bit of revenge, slag," Reginald stepped forward, and punched her square on the jaw. Jacky fell to the floor dazed and as she passed into unconsciousness, the last thing she remembered was the hands ripping at her clothes.

Inspector Kingsley looked up and down the lines of men and women, as if at a parade, inspecting them for their worthiness. The lines of constables stood to attention; they resembled a military unit on the parade ground.

"The government is leaving." The Inspector paced the line and spoke in a clear voice. "We have been assigned to protect them on their journey. We are to give them safe passage to their destination. That will be all, mount up."

Sergeant Bernard Willis stepped from the end of the line. "Sergeants get your squads together." He gave the order in his usual roar.

They broke up their lines and grouped together into their squads. They lifted their kit bags onto their shoulders and marched towards the waiting vehicles. Three quarters of the vehicles they boarded were police vehicle personnel carriers the remainder were commandeered trucks; the drivers had volunteered to help, they were more than happy to do their bit in the war against crime.

Inspector Kingsley and his two Sergeants watched as the squads of newly deployed men, one thousand of the best constables in the country, lined up to board their vehicles.

"I feel like an army officer in a war," the Inspector frowned as he looked at his trusted companions. "I suppose I am, given the present circumstances."

"It'll be over soon enough Sir." The newly promoted Sergeant West assured him.

"I don't know about that, I feel the winds of change and although I know I'm righteous in the side we fight for, I'm not sure we're on the winning side." The Inspector looked to the sky; night was creeping in, Cerise's red glow becoming brighter in the dimming light.

'Can anything stop the darkness coming?' he thought.

"Can I drive?" Sergeant West said, breaking the Inspectors contemplation as he voiced his admiration for the powerful off road police vehicle. "I'm dying to drive one of those."

"Certainly not," Inspector Kingsley turned towards the powerful vehicle to hide his smile from his colleagues, '*I am too*,' he thought.

The three of them walked to the vehicle and climbed into it. They had to wait a few minutes before all the men had taken their seats in their vehicles. Inspector Kingsley took the controls and engaged the fuel cells. The powerful engine whined into life.

"All loaded Sir!" a voice said over the vehicle's intercom.

"Let's get this show on the road," the Inspector said and released the vehicle's brakes. As he moved off in the direction of police headquarters he was almost tempted to give a battle cry.

"It's been confirmed Sir," the aide fidgeted with the bottom button of his suit jacket.

"So his body guard has been found dead and there is no sign of the Minister, well he's missing and I can only assume he's met his end. We can't wait for him to reappear; we have to make other arrangements then." Peter Dickinson said as he looked out of the window, into the gathering gloom.

"If I may be so bold," Sarah Johnson, Minister for education joined him at the window.

"Go on," the Prime Minster turned his head to look at her.

"Maybe it would be prudent to wait here for Gerald, after all he's a friend as well as a colleague," Sarah suggested to her leader.

"No, we have to assume he's dead. Why else would his guard be found riddled with bullet holes," the Prime Minister made his decision as he turned back to the gathering night outside. "Besides, the convoy will be here soon, shall we go downstairs and wait in reception?"

No sooner had the Prime Minister finished talking than the lead vehicles appeared and turned the corner at the bottom of the road.

"They're arriving Sir," the young aide pointed out at the approaching convoy.

"Speak of the devil," the Prime Minister looked up the road, then back at Sarah Johnson and smiled. "That settles it then."

The group of fifty people picked up their bags and suitcases and started to file out of the room, heading for the lifts. Some minutes later they stood in the foyer of the headquarters where Sir Edward Parker was waiting to escort them to the convoy.

"Peter, are you ready? The convoy's waiting." Sir Parker said, approaching his long time friend.

"Yes, thank you Edward," the Prime Minister offered his Chief of Police his hand and as the two hands clasped, he said. "Good luck old friend."

"Good luck, we'll be back at government house before you know it!" Edward Parker said, stepping back from the Prime Minister.

"Let's hope so hey, I'm missing my tuck shop," the Prime Minister joked.

Sir Parker escorted the Prime Minister outside into the red tinged night. In the middle of the convoy was an empty personnel vehicle which had been assigned to the Cabinet, the two most senior men in Capital City didn't speak again as the Prime Minister boarded the vehicle the two friends shared a brief smile. The Prime Minister looked out of the window at the front of the vehicle and the hero of mount Aamor, or so it was spun, stood at the side of the lead vehicle. Sir Parker had walked to the Inspector and they stood talking as the vehicle's door closed. Inspector Kingsley climbed back into his vehicle after he had shared a short conversation with his superior.

The Prime Minister jumped up from his seat. For someone so fat he showed amazing agility by jumping from the personnel carrier and running along the line of the convoy.

"Hold up," he shouted, as he reached the side of Inspector Kingsley's vehicle.

"Mr Prime Minister Sir?" Sir Parker ran to his side.

The Prime Minister looked around, as Inspector Kingsley

disengaged the power cells and brought his vehicle to a halt. Everyone was staring at the prime Minister.

"I've never liked those large vehicles, they give me travel sickness," he yelled over the sound of so many fuel cells whining. "And besides, on a vehicle with all those politicians, it'd bore me to death."

The joke wasn't lost on his old friend, Sir Parker and he barked out a quick laugh as he patted the Prime Minister on the back. The Prime Minister got a little excited as he jumped into the back seat of Inspector Kingsley's off road vehicle. "I've always wanted to drive one of these," he said.

"Mr Prime Minister Sir, begging your pardon, but I'm next," Sergeant West blushed, his smile leaving his face as soon as he'd finished talking.

"Oh no you didn't Sergeant West," Sergeant Bernard Willis said, his deep voice sounding almost surprised as the convoy moved on. Inspector Kingsley smiled at his Sergeant's gaffe.

Chapter 18

Lindsey frantically jotted down notes in short hand, as she listened to the conversations in the privileged area she had managed to con her way into. Black jackets, the People's Army enforcers, had cordoned off the area at the back of the stage and she was on the inside. A band rocked on the stage, making it difficult for her to concentrate and she looked up to watch Jason playing with his kids, they all looked so happy after being reunited. It must have seemed like a lifetime to Jason.

Lindsey looked past Jason de Silva, her attention caught by a man she knew standing beyond the line of Black Jackets, her husband waved at her and smiled to show off his perfect teeth.

She was overwhelmed and dropped her notepad to the grass at her feet. She ran over to him, skipping through the crowds of the privileged and the leaders of the People's Army. Some heads turned to watch her progress because she cared nothing for the people she bumped into.

"Lindsey," he yelled over the din, and his smile widened.

"Henry," she squealed, forgetting herself as she became almost girl like.

The guards came between them and raised their arms to prevent the hug.

"He's my husband," she shouted at them, slapping at their arms.

"Sorry Miss Sumter, I can't let him through, not without the proper authority." It was the same guard that had stopped the de

Silva family and he was determined to stop someone, perhaps he thought it would prove him worthy of the jacket he wore.

"It's ok, let him through," Teddy Williams had appeared at the guard's side.

He blushed and stepped to one side to let the couple come together.

Lindsey pulled away from him and she kissed her husband. Their lips came together and she took his hands in hers and realized the guards were looking at them, but for once she didn't care, she was happy to be safe in Henry's embrace.

She looked at Teddy. "Thank you," she said, as she led her husband into the enclosure.

"Lindsey, sweetheart," Henry started.

Lindsey quickly interrupted. "How, by the five moons are you here?" she asked.

"The roads are still there you know, I couldn't bear it any longer, I had to be with you," he kissed her again.

Lindsey nestled into his chest. "I've missed you too you're the love of my life."

"Lindsey," Henry held her away from him.

"Yes?" she looked lovingly into his eyes.

"We started up again," his smile was gone and he looked at her with an expression more businesslike.

"What do you mean, 'started up again'?"

"Capital City has collapsed under the weight of the troubles, the criminal gangs are on the verge of taking over and the people need to know," he said, holding his wife by her shoulders.

"Yes I know all that, it's a common thought that the People's Army is going to have to stop the evil." Her smile was gone too; she was disappointed that her husband had brought business into their conversation so soon.

"Most of the people that can have left the city, the financial district has collapsed and the media have stopped functioning. Everything's a complete fuck up!" Henry said.

"So what? Are you saying you've started up a news channel?" She laughed at the very idea.

"That's exactly what I'm saying. Me and some of the other heads of the media have banded together to form a new firm, Celtica Global News," he smiled, confident that she would be impressed.

"And you thought you'd come here to use my influence to get close to Jason?" Lindsey crossed her arms and screwed up her face. Her romantic reunion was turning out to be nothing like she'd imagined.

"No, that's not it my love," Henry hastily answered, looking contrite; he couldn't afford Lindsey to be angry with him. "The new firm is based in Ramby."

"Who's this then Lindsey?" Jason had walked up beside the loving couple and caught them by surprise.

Startled, Lindsey pushed her husband away from her as if caught in a clandestine tryst but she quickly regained her composure and introduced the men. "Jason de Silva, this is Henry, my husband," she smiled and swept her long black hair over her shoulders.

Henry, in comparison to Jason was half the size but prettier, with his handsome and boyish good looks, fashionable style and dashing charm.

"No introductions necessary, everyone knows the face of Jason de Silva, hero and leader of the People's Army." Henry offered Jason his hand. "I'm pleased to meet you."

"The pleasure's all mine," Jason took Henry's hand. "I couldn't help overhearing your conversation, about the news station in Ramby," Jason quizzed the pair, interested in any way that he could speak to the nation uncensored.

"Yes, that's right; we're going to tell it as it is!" Henry began with enthusiasm.

"Warts and all?" Jason interrupted, raising an eyebrow to look at Lindsey. "Where have I heard that before?"

"What's that?" Henry asked, smiling uncomfortably at the joke between his wife and another man.

"I'm writing a book on the troubles of Albion, telling it as it is," Lindsey said.

"Warts and all," Henry finished for her.

"Yes, makes me out to be a war criminal, it's going to damn me I'm afraid," Jason looked at Henry, trying to gauge the newsman's thoughts.

"Oh," was all Henry could manage, amazed that the leader of the People's Army would allow such a publication. Like others that had met him, Henry was taken aback at how normal Jason de Silva seemed, on the inside he was apparently no different to any other man.

"Mr de Silva, how would you like an interview to be aired to the nation?" Henry asked, nothing could start Celtica Global News off better than an interview with the people's hero. Not in their wildest dreams could they expect to better that.

"I'm sure Jason has better things to do," Lindsey pointed out, feeling a little offended and insulted by her husband's move, after all, Jason de Silva was her story.

"On one condition," Jason became serious, business like.

"Name it, anything, if I can do it I will," Henry couldn't believe his luck, and he nervously ran his hand through his greying hair.

"Lindsey does the interview," Jason named his terms and allowed himself to be a little smug at the shocked expression on Henry's face.

Lindsey's heart missed a beat and the smile returned to her face, as she waited for her husband's answer.

'*Don't you dare refuse*,' Lindsey's thoughts must have shown on her face because Henry cast his eyes downwards briefly as he looked at her.

"Of course, I wouldn't have it any other way." Henry smiled at his wife's response, her face lighting up with a beaming smile.

"After all, she knows your story better than anyone else."

Jason nodded his approval but his attention was partially diverted as his father approached. "I'm putting the kids to bed, Alfred has kindly offered to show me the way to the manor house." Fred de Silva put a hand on his son's back. "Good night son."

"Goodnight father, thanks again for bringing the kids to me," Jason looked at the older version of himself, both nodding to each other.

Jason watched the old man leave with the tired children. "Well I can only thank the gods for the old man's dedication, he truly loves the little beggars," he spoke to no one in particular, but his words weren't lost with Henry and Lindsey Sumter hanging on his every word.

"I can't do the interview tonight and tomorrow we're moving on Kalverstone, to remove the criminal evil that infests it," Jason said, getting back to the matter at hand.

"Well, to be honest, it's going to be a few days till we're set up anyway. We're taking over an old studio next to the university, it's got a large mast capable of broadcasting and that'll marry up to the network, it has everything we need really," Henry paused, thinking. "So if you give us a few days, we should be all ready for you."

"Why don't you come along with some cameras and document the whole affair?" Jason said.

"I'm sorry Mr de Silva, but I have far too much to do," he replied.

Henry's answer surprised Jason; he looked at Henry, his eyes wider.

"I've got all the gear though, fancy taking a camera crew with you Lindsey?" Henry asked his wife.

"Yes I will, of course I will," Lindsey was absolutely delighted, within the last ten minutes she had been reunited with her husband, had been given the slot for the first exclusive interview with Jason de Silva and provided with all the equipment to do in-depth coverage of the next confrontation of the People's Army, "Happy days," she thought out loud and both men smiled at her response.

Chapter 19

Police snipers lay positioned on rooftops all along the Tallulah River. There were close to two hundred of them, armed with the latest available equipment. They overlooked the bridges that spanned the city's main waterway, protecting against the criminal Skavites that held sway in the southern districts of Capital City.

Lines of constables wearing bullet proof and stab proof armour stood behind blockades, they had expected attacks that up until now had not arrived. The Skavs seemed to be hiding and planning.

There was an ease that only soldiers waiting for combat can know, they sat around waiting, their weapons never far from their side. Occasionally one of the enemy dared show themselves, exposing their bodies to the sights of the snipers; they were taken out quickly, it was one less criminal Skav to deal with. The night was drawing in and spotlights were turned on to illuminate the Tallulah River and the bridges. Civilian militia formed up, their police commanders led them on patrols and all was still as it had been the night before and the night before that.

Then came a shot.

"Movement, we've got movement!" a voice yelled over the radio waves, alerting the police. Then another gunshot and another as police snipers all over the city began to discharge their rifles at the advancing lines of charging Skavs.

The police forces were almost taken by surprise and reinforcements were hastily deployed to man the barricades.

The fore-sight of the government forces meant that they had barracked their men in the buildings closest to the bridges and the necessary reinforcements rushed from those buildings as the Skavite horde charged onto the bridges along the river. Wielding all manner of weaponry, tens of thousands of the Skavs swept over the bridges to engage the police in vicious hand to hand combat.

Douglass 'I'll have ya fingers' Farrell, followed his Skavite horde, he had surrounded himself with the largest and most capable warriors, and they were well muscled and well armed. He had dressed them in the finest attire, suits and shoes of the highest quality that he could loot from the capital's stores.

"Forward, ya fuckers, have at em! Kill 'em all, the pig bastards!" Farrell yelled, and pushed forward with his massive bulk.

All around him his men and boys were falling dead, killed by the police snipers, their rifles were inflicting a heavy toll. They charged on and made it to the head of the bridges and then out over their spans. The Skavs were dying in vast amounts but making good progress, such were their number. Then they were at the barricades, trying to climb up and jump over. At first they were dragged over to be killed or they fell back dead onto their comrades, but eventually the Skavite horde's superior forces began to tell, and they climbed up and over the corpses of their fallen comrades which were piled high against the protective walls. The police were overwhelmed and had no choice but to give ground.

"That's it lads, slaughter the bastards!" Farrell yelled, his eyes had taken on a wild and insane look.

Pushing forward into the mob, Farrell reached the first barricade; his Skavs fought a ferocious hand to hand battle beyond. One of his guards mounted the concrete barricade and he fell back with a bullet hole in the middle of his forehead.

Farrell grimaced and bellowed: "Who wants to live forever?"

And he climbed the barrier to gain the other side, behind more than a thousand that were already there, fighting and dying.

An injured constable lay at Farrell's feet, curled up in a ball. Farrell took a hand gun from inside his coat and he knelt beside the injured man, then he put his pistol to the coppers forehead.

"Hold out your fucking hand!" Farrell yelled the man into consciousness.

The copper cried out in agony and he saw the barrel of the gun, then his eyes went wide when he looked at the man holding the gun. The constable shook his head, as much in fear as in answer, and he clenched his fists, trying to hide his digits.

Farrell smiled and he stood, his men poured over the bridge to either side of him. He looked the constable in the eyes, no quarter given and none asked and as he pulled the trigger to shoot the constable through the eye and blow the back of the man's head off, he laughed.

The police had backed off to the first line of buildings in order to secure their flanks with brick walls. They banged their shields, playing their rhythmic game of intimidation. Thousands of Skavs had crested the concrete barriers and gathered around their leader chanting. "Die pigs, die pigs!" They didn't seem to care that hundreds of their number were being picked off every minute whilst they sang; they played the police at their own game.

Surrounded by his guards, Farrell forced his way through his troops to the front of his army. He stood chanting with his men to allow the police to see him standing with them. Then he raised the hand that held his gun and he grinned manically, battle fever had taken full control of his senses and as the chaos that was his mind roared insanely, he charged, letting out a battle cry that matched the roar inside his head, and his Skavite horde followed.

The display was all too much for the police, they were outnumbered five to one and they knew it. They turned and ran, dropping their shields and fleeing in the face of the overwhelming odds stacked against them. Farrell stopped running, in the split second thereafter one of his guards ran between him and the sniper's bullet that had his name on it. The guard died instantly as the bullet hit his skull to penetrate his brain, turning it to mush.

"Get the fucking snipers!" Farrell yelled out his order, as another bullet buzzed past him to ricochet off the tarmac behind him. He danced to a nearby wall, pressing himself behind it, as his men entered the surrounding buildings to carry out his orders.

Farrell edged himself around the wall till he rounded a corner and faced the river. Feeling that he was out of the sniper's line of sight, he stepped away from the wall and he started walking down the road toward the next bridge. The bridge was ablaze and it lit up the darkness with its red glow. The police around the bridge had inflicted heavy casualties on the Skavites before turning them back. The Skavs destroyed the bridge in the process of their retreat and the constables had then turned away from the battle, withdrawing in an orderly fashion.

Farrell watched and knew that he had captured Capital City; the government position was untenable now he had crossed over to the north of the Tallulah. As the last of the police withdrew, a sniper's bullet hit the ground at his side but the marksman was dead before the ground broke his fall, a knife protruded from his back. The Skavs had broken through the last barricades and were making short work of the snipers.

All around him, Skavs looted the bodies of their own fallen comrades and those constables that had died, taking anything of any worth and Farrell didn't care. They deserved it, they had broken the police lines easily and the city would be his by morning.

"Capital City will be ours by daybreak!," His deep voice boomed, and he threw his head back to give forth a rumbling laughter from deep within his twisted soul.

His guards laughed with him and he bent down to pick up a police radio that had been dropped. "Pull back, pull back take up your secondary positions!" The voice on the radio said, repeating the message several times before going silent. Farrell thrust the radio into the hands of one of his guards.

"Here monitor this," he said. "Right lads, north then, let's see what the pig bastards are up to there."

They walked north along the city streets for two miles and encountered no opposition. The Skavite horde chanted "Death to the pigs!" in their monotonous collective voice.

Capital City was criss crossed by a number of wide canals and the fleeing police force and citizens had set up their second line of defence on one of these, manning further concrete barricades for Farrell's Skavite horde to try to breach. Tens of thousands of Skavites reached the canal at about the same time and issued forth from the roads along its length. Thousands of police and fleeing citizens had made it north across the river ahead of them and again, the Skavs began to drop as the police and militia opened fire, hundreds died in the first few moments, cut to pieces by the relentless fire.

"This is it then lads let's have 'em! Charge!" Farrell's shout was unmistakable and the Skavs within earshot responded, they charged past the would-be king and headed for the bridges and the north side of the canal. The canal bridges weren't as long as the bridges that spanned the Tallulah, but they were heavily defended because the militia had more time to prepare. The Skavites no longer had the element of surprise.

Douglass Farrell watched as his massive takeover bid charged the bridges, the scene of death that unfolded disturbed even his cold heart as volley after volley of bullets from behind the barricades ripped continuously into the mass of his Skavite horde. Thousands fell because the bullets just couldn't miss the biomass of human flesh pressed together. Mortar shells whistled in, aimed directly at the bridges, trying to take them out. The explosive power was not enough to succeed in destroying the bridges, but it was enough to cut swathes through the Skavs. Three times the Skavites withdrew and charged again when the gun fire halted, their drug-fuelled charges becoming slower as the bodies underfoot made their footing more treacherous each time.

The charge of the Skavs was destined to fail against the well organised defence contrived by strategic analysts. Perhaps an hour and thousands of dead Skavs later, the gunfire stopped. The Skavites rallied for a fourth charge because Douglass Farrell refused to give up the fight. The silence of the guns was the sweetest sound Farrell had heard for a long time and he looked at the defence as his men began their assault. There was no gun fire and no sound of small artillery shells trying to take out the bridges. The Skavs approached the bridge at a walk, holding back against their drug fuelled psychosis. They listened as the gun fire at a bridge further down the waterway petered out into silence too. Farrell smiled and edged forward himself, daring the charge. "They've got no fucking ammo lads! Right you bastards let's show 'em what we're really capable of!" He yelled and his face was contorted by drug induced fury.

The thousands of Skavs up and down the canal cheered as they charged against the barricades, they climbed up with their weapons drawn and they stabbed down as they dived into the police ranks with little or no self regard. To the men waiting for the assault, they sounded like baying animals, their chant lost in the howls and screams. The police shield wall was forced back slowly but surely. Farrell reached the bridge, slowed by the crush of his own men desperate to bloody their blades. Farrell was surrounded by his body guards, his best warriors. Then he passed under the bridge support on the south side of the river with his men pressed around him.

Hiding above them no one had noticed the police sniper, the

one constable who had been given the task of killing Douglass Farrell when he walked onto the bridge.

'No more fingers for you Farrell,' the sniper thought as he lined up his target in his sights. Smiling, the constable squeezed the trigger, applying pressure as he counted down, knowing this would probably be the last thing he ever did.

He had waited too long. His thoughts and mental countdown ended abruptly as his head was yanked back and his whole body jerked and his trigger finger with it. The rifle's aim put off by the surprise and he killed the guard that stood to Farrell's left. Farrell turned and looked up as he was pushed toward the relative safety on the north side of the canal. A young muscled Skav stood behind the constable; he had climbed the bridge support to get out of the crush of his own people. He had come across the sniper accidentally and had sprung into action when he saw that the man he considered to be a god was about to be shot.

Farrell watched as the two men struggled above him, he knew if his Skav lost the fight he would have nowhere to run or hide.

The constable's face went purple, he gripped the young man's arm but no matter how hard he pulled he couldn't break from the impressively well executed head lock. The constable managed to stand by pushing backwards then he head butted backwards to strike the young Skav across the bridge of the nose. The Skav staggered and let go and the constable turned on his attacker. Nothing was going to stop the drug demented Skav in his moment of glory; he stepped forward to punch the sniper in the chin. The constable's screams were lost amid the sounds of combat as he fell twenty feet onto the unfriendly crowd below.

"That piece of shit just saved my life," Farrell yelled at his guards, and he raised his hand in salute at the young man looking down at him.

"I recognise dat bruva," the guard behind Farrell said.

"You stay at the foot of the bridge and bring him to me."

Farrell ordered his guard as they exited the bottle neck to spill out onto the north shore as the barrier in front of them fell over.

Although the battle that raged was sickening to the eye and the bile rose up in most men's throats till their palate was dirtied, something inside them, some ancient feeling that society had tried so hard to quell, rose to the forefront of their mind. Tens of thousands of men, young and old, joined and locked together in a deadly dance. Douglass Farrell seemed to rise up, to grow in stature as the berserker rage took hold of the giant man. The crime lord was out of control and added credence to his hard man image. He carved a path through the crowd, constable and criminal fell to his sharp edged axe, such was his march that the crowd opened for him, trying to evade the crazed giant.

Saliva filled his mouth and spittle flew as he bellowed and shouted unintelligible battle cries. Those before him were crushed because his vision was a haze and even his own guard had backed away from the sweep of his axe. He swept left and right killing all within his axe's circumference, until his arms were caught by his own men who hauled him to the ground.

"My lord, please stop," one of his guards yelled at him.

Then another slapped him across the face, trying to bring his master out of his frenzy. This at last brought him part way out of his madness and he began to gain control of his senses once more. He relaxed, and then the ten strong Skavs that held him relaxed too.

"I liked that, I liked that a lot." he said to his guards as they released him.

He stood slowly, allowing his men to help him up and he turned, lifted the axe and swung it in one motion to bury it in the skull of the guard who had slapped him.

"What happened?" Farrell asked, still looking a little wild around the eyes.

"Ya lost it," one of his guards answered, looking nervously

at the ground.

"Ya lost it my lord." Farrell corrected the man, growling through gritted teeth.

"Of course, sorry my lord."

"My lord, we beat em!" Another Skav said, stepping forward. "The pigs have fled the battle field."

Douglass Farrell looked at himself, wiping uselessly at the blood that soaked his clothes and then he looked around at the thousands that lay dead.

"We lost a lot of our people tonight, how many did I kill?" he asked, and his guards looked anywhere but into his eyes.

"At least fifty," one voice dared to comment.

"Ah well, we've plenty for the job at hand." Farrell said.

All around him the scum of Albion were running amok, tens of thousands of them, looting shops and burning buildings. A little way up the canal, Farrell could just see the flames above Parliament House around which the battle still raged, the last few brave constables making their stand. Closer to him a few constables huddled together, disarmed and made prisoner, surrounded by a chanting mob.

"My lord, the prisoners would make useful hostages." one of Farrell's men suggested but he didn't really care what fate the constables met.

"Fuck that let the lads have their fun," the crime lord laughed.

No sooner had Farrell finished his sentence then the angry mob pulled a constable from the group, then another and another until they were all separated from one another. Farrell laughed as one constable was stripped naked and nailed to a door; he screamed as the iron was driven into his hands and feet, then finally he fainted as an iron spike was driven into his penis. Others were hacked into pieces, the Skavs taking care to keep their captives alive as long as possible.

Two female constables weren't so lucky; they were stripped and held aloft, like the trophies of some sick sport. They were carried away to be treated worse than any whore, used over and over long into the night till they wished they were dead.

"Right then lads," Farrell said, already bored of the entertainment. He looked at his guards and followers. "Let's make it official, let's go and take Police Headquarters."

He walked over to a vehicle that somehow hadn't been torched and he climbed up on top. The roof gave way a little beneath his weight.

"Right then lads, let's go give it to the pig bastards one more time!" he bellowed his order and did not much care how many men followed him, knowing it was a mere formality.

"What the fuck is going on?" Sir Parker shouted at the officers who stood around him, as dumbfounded as he was.

The doors to his office had been pinned back and left open for the comings and goings of his men. One of those men, a Sergeant in his police force came rushing in.

"Sir, Sir," the Sergeant blurted, out of breath with blood staining his face and uniform and everyone turned to look as the man stopped running.

"The bridges have been overrun, the Skavs are north of the canal defences!" the blood stained policeman fell to his knees and his hand left a blood print on the pristine carpet as his legs gave way.

No one spoke for a half minute, the realization that the battle for Capital City had been lost weighed heavily, Sir Parker turned away from the injured man and looked out of the window. He saw crowds of citizens fleeing north with nothing but the clothes on their backs. Buildings burned unchecked, no fire fighters left to put out the flames, amongst them, Government House making the finest blaze of all.

"News spreads like the wild fires, doesn't it?" Sir Parker remarked as he looked out at his own personal hell.

"Sir," Jack Finch, Parker's second in command joined him

at the window and spoke softly into the ear of his friend and colleague. "Your orders Sir?"

"Orders, yes of course, I suppose we best sort this mess out," Sir Parker looked around, away from the lit streets and into the silent faces looking at him. "How much ammunition do we have?"

They looked at each other, then one man stepped forward, standing to attention the man saluted. "Sir, only what each man carries, all the ammo went to the front lines," he stepped back and stood at ease.

"Right," Sir Parker put his hands together behind his back, to avoid fidgeting nervously then he looked out of the window again and watched as masses of fleeing citizens and constables raced up the road, bloodied and exhausted. "It would appear we have lost Capital City."

"We must evacuate the city," Jack Finch said, he put his hand on Sir Parker's shoulder to console him.

"Yes I know," Sir Parker replied quietly.

Without turning from the window, Sir Parker steeled himself, ready to give out his orders from his office at Police Headquarters one last time. "Get the word out, tell your men to evacuate the city," he said sternly.

"Where to Sir?" one of his officers asked.

Jack Finch turned from his friend. "Go north to Eldersfield, you'll meet up with the Prime Minister and Colonel John Blithe Dempsey," the order was firm and commanding and everyone responded. The officers walked from the room in an orderly fashion as quickly as they could.

The phone on Sir Parker's desk began to ring and Sir Parker turned from the window and stumbled to his seat, he sat heavily behind his desk and stared at the phone as it rang. He was defeated. Jack Finch picked the phone up to answer the call. "I'm sorry, but Sir Parker is unable to take your call at the moment," he said, not giving the caller a chance to speak then he hung up.

"Come on Sir, let's get out of here while we can," Jack Finch pleaded.

"To lose the capital to a band of pirates, rapists and murderers?" Sir Edward Parker leaned forward resting his elbows on his desk, with his face in his hands, "This is my castle, I will burn with it."

"As you wish, Sir," Jack Finch turned from the room, knowing there wasn't much time for arguing, he hoped his friend would follow on his own.

Sir Parker stood when Jack had left the room and he circled the room, looking at all its finery. At length he returned to the window, once again looking down the main highway that headed south into the darkness that hid his approaching nightmare. People still fled north along the road, carrying nothing as they hastened along.

'*Like the tide rolling high*,' he thought as he watched them running, "and the storm that follows," he said out loud.

The lift doors opened into the foyer, Jack Finch stepped out to survey the chaos. People rushed about yelling and shouting orders, the front doors swung outwards, as the civilian staff and what was left of the police force evacuated Police Headquarters to mingle with the crowds and head north. Finch looked at the receptionist who was answering the phone, he walked over to her and he took the phone from her and placed it down, she stared at him and was annoyed at being cut off in mid sentence.

"Excuse me Sir," the pretty young receptionist said, she was angry at the man who'd interfered with her work.

"Get out!" he yelled. "All of you clear the building!" Jack Finch climbed onto the receptionist's desk and every face turned up to him. "Clear the building, the enemy is upon us. This is the worst place to be in Capital City right about now! Flee, flee for your lives!" he shouted like a madman, not as a senior officer and the staff looked at him for a moment longer before his message became clear and they fled.

Jack jumped from the desk to the receptionist's side and without looking at her, he smashed the glass panel at the corner of her desk, the fire alarm began to ring throughout the building. He bent close to the pretty young lady that had displayed so much anger towards him. "What do you think will happen to a pretty thing like you, when this building is overrun by the enemy?" Jack didn't wait to see if the girl was following his meaning, he left the building in favour of his waiting vehicle outside.

The activity in the street defied the lateness of the hour and the road was full of all manner of vehicles heading out of the city. Injured constables lay atop of them with no one to hold them down as their improvised ambulances sped off. Lines of constables appeared at the bottom of the road, and then the Sergeants and Captains led an organised withdrawal.

"Sir Parker, where's Sir Parker?" the driver asked, as Jack, followed by the young receptionist, approached his vehicle.

"He's coming in the next vehicle," he answered. '*I hope*,' he thought to himself as the driver opened the door.

Inspector Kingsley waited outside the large khaki tent, he'd been kept waiting for at least an hour. The Prime Minister and Colonel Dempsey and others had entered the tent for an impromptu meeting and it was expected that they would have finished by now but as far as their agenda went, he could only guess. The Inspector paced back and forth impatiently, holding the letter he'd been given by Sir Edward Parker, while his men sat around resting or talking and keeping warm near their fires.

Major Dawkins opened the tent flaps and approached the Inspector. "Mr Kingsley, follow me please," he ordered rather than requested and he turned around without waiting to see if the Inspector did as he said.

Kingsley did follow, although he was annoyed at the order from someone that held no authority over him, he didn't want to be kept waiting any longer outside in the cool spring night. He entered the tent and he saw the Prime Minister and the Colonel bent over a table poring over maps. Ignoring protocol and the basic rules of etiquette, the Inspector did not wait to be asked, he walked over to them.

"Begging your pardon Sir, but I really must protest," Inspector Kingsley looked at the two men who stopped what they were doing to look up at him. "I've been kept waiting far too long, I need to get back into Capital City, there is work to be done there." he said, then his expression turned neutral when he remembered the letter in his hand, and he held it out to the Colonel. "Oh this is for you!"

Colonel Dempsey took the letter and opened it immediately. He turned away from the table to pace the length of the tent and then he threw the letter into the iron brazier that helped to heat the tent.

Peter Dickinson turned back to the table to look at the maps. "May I remind you of the company that you keep at this time?" the Prime Minister addressed the Inspector without looking up; he sounded just a little annoyed.

"I'm sorry, I truly am but I've been kept waiting all this time, me and my men are needed in the city," the Inspector defended his actions.

"You are not going to the city," the Prime Minister said. "You are staying here to protect your country's leader. I'm the capital of Albion."

"The cheeky bastard wants all my men and ammunition and all the armoured vehicles too. You can't take those vehicles into city streets, they'll be vulnerable," the Colonel stopped pacing and returned to the table. "He might be a good copper, but he has no idea how to fight a war."

"They have no bullets and are outnumbered," the Inspector

felt his hackles rise and he spoke louder than he meant to.

"That'll be all Inspector," the Prime Minister ordered sternly.

"But," Kingsley began.

"That will be all!" the Prime Minister spat the command as he rounded on the decorated policeman. "Go and get some rest with your men and await further orders."

There was no use in arguing and the Inspector knew it, he turned away from the two men and walked out of the tent, his head held high with the knowledge that he'd done all he could to get his point across.

Major Dawkins met him outside the tent.

"Fucking megalomaniacs," the Inspector said under his breath as he passed the officer, spitting in the tents entranceway to show his dissent.

"You need to show the proper respect to your leaders," the Major seemed to get taller as he defended his commanding officer and he barked at the Inspector like he was talking to a man under his command.

The Inspector rounded on the Major and he raised a hand to point a finger at the Major's chest. "You can fuck off!" he said and even though he was angry, his voice was calm and quiet, adding menace to the words. The Major was left open mouthed; he hadn't expected any such reaction.

'*That's one battle won*,' Inspector Kingsley thought smugly as he turned away from the Major. Kingsley rejoined his men at the brow of the hill and he looked down into the valley below at the thousands of tents. A huge refugee camp had sprung up there when the troubles in the capital began, now that previously rural part of Albion more resembled a slum, filled with those from Capital City that had nowhere else to go. Whole families were crammed into a single small tent, but anything was better than being out in the cold night.

"At least the winter has left us," Sergeant West appeared at his side to look down into the camp with him. "Any luck Sir?"

he asked.

"No luck at all, part of me wishes we had thrown our lot in with de Silva," Inspector Kingsley whispered he did not want his treasonous remarks to be heard by anyone else.

"Sir," the Sergeant looked shocked.

"Yes I know, he's a criminal and must be brought to justice," the Inspector's shoulders lifted and dropped as he sighed. "Cup of tea?" he asked.

"Of course Sir," West took the question for an order and was about to rush off when a commotion within their camp startled him. Some of the constables around one of the camp fires were causing a disturbance, something had panicked them.

"The bridges have fallen," one constable yelled.

"The city is lost," another said, almost wailing.

The Prime Minister and the Colonel appeared at the tent entrance and looked at the constables, wondering what the shouting was about. Around the camps the news was spreading, both soldiers and police felt the distress of the fall of Capital City.

"It's fallen, you arrogant bastards," the Inspector said quietly fearing that if he was heard, he would be put under arrest.

The two senior officials turned back to the relative warmth of the head quarters, they seemed unsurprised by the night's developments. Then the constables were brought to order. Sergeant Bernard Willis brought them to heel as he roamed about the camp fires. "Get some rest, that's an order," his familiar deep voice barked.

Jacky de Silva woke from a nightmare, she was tired and sore and she was not fully awake as the door opened. "Jason, is that you?" she said. She tried to sit up, but the binding that had numbed her hands made her wince as fresh blood welled up where they had cut into her skin.

"No," the softly spoken but panicked word broke free from

her lips and she realised that the nightmare was real after all.

She looked down the bed, past her naked body and saw a man standing in the doorway, it was Reginald Smith. Her legs were open and wet, there was no feeling in them, but she managed to close and cross them, as the Smith boy reached the side of the bed.

"Don't worry bout dat," he said, "I ain't gonna fuck you!" he stroked the side of her face. "We done dat already."

Jacky turned her face to the wall as fresh tears ran down her cheek. More men came into the room, Jacky tried to turn her body in a futile attempt to hide herself from the smiling onlookers. Then her hands were freed, her bonds cut. The group of Skavites lifted her battered body from the bed and she felt fists punching her and hands slapping her. She couldn't have cried out even if she hadn't willed herself not to, the first few blows had knocked the breath from her fragile and punished body.

"That's enough," Reginald shouted.

Jacky was relieved that her bonds were cut, her body had been defeated and broken in the marathon ordeal and she so desperately wanted it to be at an end. She thought of the leering faces and of her dignity lost and the pain of her memories hurt more than the blows she had just received.

They took her from the room, carrying her for several minutes down corridors and through rooms filled with smiling Skavite faces, some of which she remembered from the night before. At length, she was presented to a large and muscular man with fat fingers. He was middle aged, had no hair and a long pointed nose. He cast a long shadow as he stood, the light from the spotlights streamed in from the open space behind him at his back, he smiled as he walked over to them.

"Mrs de Silva, how pleased I am that you could join us," he raised his hand and slapped her across the face; he rolled his huge muscled shoulders as Jacky recoiled from the blow.

"My name's Sharpy, you can call me Mr Sharp," he said. "Do you remember me from last night? I see you don't, ah well shame that," he laughed and punched her hard, breaking her nose and snapping her head back as her face seemed to explode with blood.

She swooned, as dazed as if she was drunk and she felt like she was floating as she was carried from the room. She tried to hold onto her consciousness, feeling that if she didn't, she may never wake up again. She felt herself lifted up higher and her head lolled backwards as something was placed over her head. The laughter was ever present as she was hoisted up and thrown, then she was falling and it felt as if she was falling for a very long time. Thoughts of her childhood spun through her mind, flashing images of her parents playing with her on the local park. Then she seemed to bounce on the air beneath her feet, her flesh defying gravity as she sprung upwards. The pain in her neck was only there for the briefest of moments before the blackness took her.

She may have had time to think '*Thank Thalia that's over with*,' before there was nothing, but perhaps not.

The sun began to illuminate Capital City as Sir Edward Parker walked down the stairs and into the reception of the Police Headquarters. The foyer was a mess, paper and bits of kit were strewn all over the floor. He sighed, he had seen the signs of defeat before, and knew his time was close at hand.

"Courage now," he said to himself, as dawn broke and he walked from the building onto the steps. He looked around at the building that had been the focal point of his life. The streets were free of people; an urban fox was the only living creature he saw, it ran across the road and stopped in the middle and turned to look at him and then it was gone, to resume its foraging journey.

Sir Parker didn't have long to wait. A procession of men and boys rounded the corner at the bottom of the road, they were armed with all manner of weapons, both purpose made and improvised. At the head of the unruly mob was a giant of a man, his height and stature made him stand out in the crowd of criminals and they came on at a walking pace, their battle already won. The large man at the head of the army of thugs stopped short of Sir Parker, he smiled nastily as the police commissioner straightened himself.

"Sir Parker, I thought pigs flew from a sinking ship," there was a ripple of laughter at Farrell's joke.

"Mr Farrell, you know my name?" Sir Parker asked. He stood defiant and he ignored the laughter.

"I've seen you on the television," Douglass Farrell said. "And you know me."

"Wanted posters," Sir Parker said and the crowd laughed as he joked too. "Well let's get it over with." He lifted his hand and slid his pistol free behind his back.

Although Sir Parker feared death, he refused to be daunted by the evil he confronted. He lifted his hand gun and fired as Farrell's men charged forward. Farrell saw the threat and pulled a young Skav in front of himself, using him as a shield. Then it was all over as two burly men wrestled the Police Chief to the ground, his attempt to finally assassinate Douglass Farrell had failed.

Farrell knelt down beside the head of Albion's Police Force, removed his cigar cutter from his Jacket pocket. One of Farrell's trusted guards forced open Sir Parker's hand with ease and Farrell slipped the thumb of the hand into his cutter.

"I'll have your fingers now," Farrell was grim and serious as he closed the cutter with a quick snap the thumb fell free. Sir Parker screamed as Farrell took the fingers of his right hand one by one. He'd heard the stories and never doubted them, but to be party to the act was a state of realism he cared nought for. Then the pain began all over again, as his left hand suffered the same terrible fate.

His captors then let him go, the pain was immense as he was lifted from the ground, and they placed him on his knees in front of the man giant who now owned his fingers. Sir Parker's blood was all over Farrell, and he nearly fainted as he looked at his ruined hands.

"Burn it, burn this fake fortress, this eyesore in front of me," Farrell said, as he put a digit in his mouth.

Farrell looked at Sir Parker and smiled to see that tears were running down the old man's face whilst he watched him as he crunched through the finger's bone. "Normally, I'd let you suffer and live a fingerless life, but not today you crazy old bastard," he lifted Sir Parker's gun off the concrete. He had gained a certain respcct for the old man who hadn't run from his fate. Sir Parker looked to the rising sun; Farrell lifted his pistol to his forehead and in front of the cheering mob pulled the trigger.

Chapter 20

Jason de Silva awoke in his bed with his children at his side and he slipped from beneath the covers, careful not to wake the sleeping youngsters. The spring morning sun warmed him as it filtered through the window. Jason dressed quietly, the peace of the day not lost on him as he left the room quietly.

Jason quickly descended the stairs to the ground floor hallway and walked to the kitchen of the parkland manor house. There he was greeted by the sight of his father chatting with Alfred over a cup of tea. The two old men sat at the kitchen table and talked to one another as if they'd known each other for years. Alfred's daughter Rebecca busied herself in the kitchen making breakfast. Rebecca wore a short woollen dress patterned like an old ladies carpet, all dark reds and blues. She was in her early twenties and had long flowing brown hair and was beautiful to behold. Jason had been introduced to her the night before and instantly liked the well mannered young lady.

"Good morning." Jason said as he sat down in the chair opposite his father.

"Morning," they all said at the same time.

Jason looked at the two old men, who looked anywhere but at each other, or him, and he instantly knew they had been talking about something they didn't want to share. "Have you been talking about me?" he asked the two old men.

They looked at each other then back to Jason; his father had a look of despair on his face.

"Son, I'm worried about you that's all," he began, then paused while he collected his thoughts. "Why can't you leave the fighting to the armed forces and the police?"

"And where are they father?" Jason answered with a question; his stance was firm but without venom.

"We have had some military come to join us," Alfred looked from Jason to Fred and back again, unsure whether to join in this conversation.

"Yes, those that are stuck here, or come to protect their families," Jason said gently, he did not want an argument with the old man over political matters.

"Do you think that'll happen a lot? Because I think it would be really cool if it did," Rebecca asked, placing two breakfasts on the table, one each in front of the old men.

"What do you mean, really cool?" Alfred asked.

Rebecca placed another hot breakfast in front of Jason and one on the table for herself and she sat down. "Well I think it would be nice if all the soldiers went home to protect their families," she answered.

"This is delicious, thank you," Fred said as he tucked into the food.

"Yes, thank you," Jason said. He did not know what to say to her statement, so he picked up his cutlery.

Rebecca ignored them, she had succeeded in diverting the men away from confrontation and she picked up the remote for the television and started flicking through the channels. "There's never a lot on at this time of day, there are still no nationals either, we've only got the district station," Rebecca said, placing the remote on the table.

The three men turned to the television as Rebecca turned the sound up. "…but is it too little, too late? The stock market prior to the freeze had already all but crashed," the news readers, a man and a woman fell silent as they put a finger to their ear pieces. After a moment of silence the screen cut to commercials.

"I wonder what's going on now for them to freeze like that?" Fred sat back in his chair, chewing thoughtfully on a piece of bacon.

"It's never good news nowadays is it?" Alfred said as the news came back on, cutting an advert in half. They fell silent to listen once again, and Hector started to cry upstairs.

"I'll fetch him," Rebecca said and stood up to skip quickly towards the crying child.

The news reporters came back on, their smiles replaced by solemn faces that were etched with dread. "We have some breaking news coming in from Capital City," the woman said.

"Capital City has fallen, it was overrun last night by what has become known as the Skavite Horde of the Criminal Underworld," the man said his piece then looked at the woman.

"The last place to fall was Police Headquarters, with the Police Commissioner, Sir Edward Parker killed. Although the details are a little sketchy at the moment, it is believed that the Skav leader, Douglass Farrell, killed Sir Edward Parker in single combat after Sir Parker called him out," a tear rolled down her face as the reality of what she was reporting hit home.

The man cleared his throat as he took over. "Government House burns and it is rumoured that the government have fled the city to go north to the city of Eldersfield. To anyone still trapped within Capital City, our hearts go out to you. With the government in retreat and the armed forces spread thinly throughout the land, we need a miracle to bring the Skavite Horde to heel. May the gods have mercy on all our souls," the news man ended, as his fellow presenter regained her composure.

The news turned to the weather, a smiling weatherman appeared but his words were ignored, as the three men turned to their unfinished breakfasts that were going cold. Rebecca stood in the doorway holding Hector in her arms, Louis stood by her side. "Is everything all right?" she asked. A look of concern was on her face as she looked at the silent men.

"Morning Louis," Jason forced a smile for his eldest son.

"Daddy," Louis laughed and ran to his father for a cuddle.

"Well look on the bright side, we don't have to fight the government if their armies are beaten!" Fred picked up his fork and stabbed another piece of bacon with it.

"We can name our own terms once we annihilate the Skavite Horde," Jason smiled at the thought, and he took Hector from Rebecca's outstretched arms and Louis climbed onto his lap.

"If they're beaten, that is." Alfred said and pushed his plate away from him, the talk of war had finally ruined his appetite.

"Alfred's right father," Jason interrupted his father as he was about to disagree with the mayor. "The government control everything south of Kalverstone, who knows what they have in reserve? And this Farrell bloke has concentrated all his efforts taking Capital City."

"But how do you know?" Fred frowned, raising his voice a little.

A loud knocking on the front door made everyone jump and took attention away from the brewing argument.

"Will you get that dear?" Alfred asked his daughter.

"Of course," Rebecca said and went to answer the front door.

"It stands to reason, I mean think about it. If the government does fail and people are left to fend for themselves, their communities ain't gonna let a few young Skavites rule them, look at the Eirwen Valley," Jason bit into a sausage, and waited for a response.

"What happened there?" Alfred asked.

"The townsfolk fought and died against the Skavs!" Ethan stood in the doorway. "I dare say it's a scenario that has repeated itself up and down the country."

Jason gave the boys to Rebecca who took them into another room.

"Have you heard the news?" Ethan asked excitedly.

"Yes, and it ain't good, so why the smiles?" Alfred asked.

"What? It's excellent news." Ethan was genuinely surprised at the old man's grumpiness. "Black coffee one sugar please." Ethan directed his request at Rebecca and wondered if there was breakfast on the menu as the pretty Mayor's daughter turned to the stove.

"How do you mean, excellent news?" Fred asked, frowning at Ethan's line of thinking.

"Two enemies going head to head, weakening each others position, we ain't strong enough to fight everybody." Ethan answered, taking the mug offered from Rebecca.

"You've got a point." Jason said and smiled at his military advisor. "We're going to Kalverstone today." But it was more of a question than a statement and he wait for Ethan to confirm the plan.

"Well, I guessed you'd want to go there, I heard about your wife." Ethan looked thoughtful as he sipped his hot brew. "The troops will be loaded and ready in two hours; we already have fifteen thousand volunteers, with new recruits signing up by the hundreds every hour."

"That's a good turn out," Fred said.

"Do you think it will be enough?" Alfred asked.

"All depends what's in Kalverstone." Ethan said.

"When we've liberated Kalverstone we march on Capital City. We can't leave any stone unturned, every Skavite bastard dies." Jason's mood changed as he thought of the Skavs spreading like a cancerous growth through the beautiful old city.

"May I advise caution, one battle at a time?" Ethan drained his mug, then he stood. "Gentlemen, I've got to get back, I promised Jimmy I wouldn't be long."

"Wait outside please Ethan, I'm coming" Jason grabbed his boots.

Rebecca, who had left the room, appeared in the doorway as Ethan left the house, she held Louis' hand.

"Are you going away again daddy?" Louis asked.

"Yes son, I'm going away, but I'll come back soon, I promise." Jason scooped Louis up, cradling the little boy and Louis clung to him.

Jason felt something at his feet and he looked down, it was Hector. He bent down and picked the toddler up with his free hand. He kissed them both gently as he went to the front door. "I'll be back in a few days, look after your grandfather for me mate?" Jason smiled lovingly at his sons and handed them to Rebecca.

"Are you going to find mummy?" Louis asked, as he took hold of Rebecca's hand.

"Don't worry about mummy, we'll find her." Jason looked down at his son's worried face and he reached down to stroke his cheek trying to soothe him.

Jason felt a pang of guilt and although he was worried about his wife, he hadn't had the time to think about Jacky too much. He also wouldn't allow himself the luxury of worrying, so as not to appear selfish. Too many had lost loved ones and still continued the fight, Jason knew that he just had to carry on in the face of adversity.

He turned once more to look at his sons; Hector and Louis gave beaming smiles as they waved at him.

Jason turned to Ethan and said; "Let's get gone then, the sooner this war's over the better."

"Goodbyes are never good are they? It's a bit of a contradiction if you ask me," Ethan said as he closed the gate behind him.

"I'm with you on that one," Jason agreed. He did not look back; he did not want to lose the mental image of his smiling sons.

"I've got no one, sometimes that's a good thing hey?" Ethan had no dependants although he was sometimes lonely, he preferred his solitary existence.

Henry and Lindsey Sumter stood at the rear of the stage watching as the cameras were loaded and the equipment was stuffed into bags. There was one vehicle for the crew of four and a slightly larger one which was rammed with the equipment for broadcasting.

"No, put that one back and get the other one," Henry shouted at the disgruntled cameraman.

"What's all this?" Jason asked as he approached Henry.

Lindsey spun around when she heard Jason's voice. "Ah Jay, can we do the interview now?"

"I said when the fight for Kalverstone is over," Jason looked at the couple and frowned.

"Please Jason, you've got plenty of time, it'll only take ten minutes," Lindsey begged, almost but not quite fawning at his feet.

"Why now though? You aren't going to be on air for a few days yet and I'd have thought you'd want me as current as possible," Jason questioned the reasoning behind what they proposed both with his words and his expression.

Henry and Lindsey turned to one another, the camera crew stopped what they were doing and they all looked at Jason.

"Well, why?" Jason asked and his voice grew more commanding.

Henry looked Jason in the eye, he straightened himself and looked sorrowful, "Because you might not make it back," he said and braced himself against Jason's wrath.

Henry was surprised because Jason's expected anger didn't materialise and instead he sighed.

"I'm well aware I'm target number one, but if I die in conflict it won't matter will it?" Jason said, knowing they were right to show caution and get their interview while they could.

"Please Jason," Lindsey took one of Jason's hands in hers as though that may sway him to reconsider.

"Actually Jason, it would matter," Ethan said, stepping

forward into the conversation.

"Explain?" Jason turned to face his advisor.

"If you die you become a martyr to the cause, your thoughts and feelings could be the driving force of your army's success or failure and by not giving the interview you risk the entire campaign." Ethan said and managed to look smug.

Jason felt trapped and he looked from one face to the next.

"Yes, of course you're right as always," he conceded with another sigh. "Let's get it done then."

"Great," Henry offered Jason his hand.

Jason shook the man's hand, although in reality he didn't really trust the man. Jason had a nagging feeling that Henry was out for Henry and nothing and no-one else. He'd met his kind before. Jason watched as the camera crew went back to work and it wasn't long before all the cables had been plugged in and the switches turned on.

"We're ready for you," Lindsey said, calling him to join her on what looked like a small film set.

Jason walked over to a chair that occupied a space in front of the camera next to Lindsey who was already seated. "I take it I sit here then?" he sat down and rubbed a hand over his stubble. '*I wish I'd shaved*,' he thought.

A man stood in front of the camera as everyone got into position and Lindsey cleared her throat.

"And in five, four, three," the man counted down from five, using his fingers as he finished silently, two, one.

Lindsey looked to the camera and smiled "Good morning, I'm Lindsey Sumter coming to you from the Ramby parkland on the morning before the battle of Kalverstone city. Here with me on this momentous day is the leader and hero of the People's Army, Jason de Silva," she turned and looked at Jason. "Good morning Jason, nice day for a war," she ended her introduction and held out the microphone for him.

Jason smiled even though he thought her statement a little

daft, he went with it. "Good morning Lindsey."

"Jason, in your own words, I think you owe the nation an explanation." Her smile had gone and Lindsey attacked Jason with verbal determination.

Jason was shocked and unprepared. He was taken aback by Lindsey's ferocity.

"You do, do you?" Jason asked, the shock was plain for everyone to see and not lost to the camera, but then Jason sighed and he recovered his composure.

"What would you like me to explain?" he asked her and mocked her with his smile. He could play the media assassin at her own game.

"For all the families of the fallen and those about to meet their death today, for the disenfranchised and displaced people on the move, whose number already runs into the hundreds of thousands? We want to know why you helped fuel the tides of conflict and fanned the flames of war?" Lindsey asked and her expression did not change.

It seemed to Jason that nobody breathed. He felt slighted by the reporter that he'd come to know, if not befriend, and he felt like standing and walking away. He visualised himself leaning across to strangle her, to cast her limp corpse to the muddy ground, and his facial expression and body language must have shown his mood in great detail.

"They are beautiful words Lindsey, very flowery," Jason soothed himself, and dismissed his unclean thoughts. "I didn't want all this trouble; I just wanted to be left alone to live in peace with my family. But *they* wouldn't leave me and mine alone. We endured a vicious assault at our family home and an even worse attack at my wife's mother's home which left my mother in law dead. So I killed them." Jason tried to look unaffected by Lindsey's line of questioning and he remained calm and business like throughout his short speech.

"So all this time you've acted in the defence of your family?"

Lindsey asked, relieved Jason had played along and not left the interview.

"After the troubles at my home and before the battle of Mount Aamor, all I wanted to do was make sure that my family was all right and then to escape the clutches of the law. It seemed as though the whole world was against me," Jason looked to the camera as he finished, his nostrils flared as he remembered the Robinsons who had sacrificed so much for their belief in him.

"That sounds a little paranoid Mr de Silva," Lindsey stated, raising an eyebrow.

"Does it? Does it really?" Jason jumped on the back of Lindsey's comment. "That's maybe how it sounds, but believe me I was running for my life."

"And when did that all change Jason? When did this adventure of yours turn from flight to fight?" Lindsey never smiled, not even a turn at the corner of her lips as she pursued Jason vehemently, seeking out answers in her verbal assault.

"At mount Aamor in the Cooper's Town District, when I realised that I had support and that entire communities were willing to throw their lot in with me. That was when the people's movement began. But I must say it was not me that started the war." Jason shifted in his chair, as he determined to answer every question quickly.

"Well, I'm sorry Jason, but I don't see any other warlords around," Lindsey mocked him as she looked around and shrugged her shoulders.

"You were there Lindsey; you saw the attack on the ranks of those men sent to arrest me. They ended up fighting on our side, against the Skavite horde. It was that event that started the war," Jason sat up and his voice rose a little as he remembered that day.

"Yes, I was there, I do remember the level of cruelty, it haunts me now and always will. That day certainly was insane," Lindsey couldn't match his stature, but she sat up in her chair to match his stance.

"Yes it was mad wasn't it? Tell me Lindsey, do you think I'm mad?" Jason relaxed and smiled as he sat back in his chair.

"I don't know, are you?" she countered his question with one of her own as the two fenced verbally.

Jason paused and became thoughtful, he collected himself again. "I guess I must be a little crazy to go through all this, if I wasn't mad at the start of this whole affair then I am now because if truth be told, I'm haunted by the faces of the men I've slain." Jason thought that was a good enough response, it showed his compassionate side.

There was a pause as their eyes locked and their battle of words had a momentary respite but Jason continued before Lindsey had a chance to ask another loaded question. "I've killed a lot of men since the troubles began and I would agree that Mount Aamor was a catalyst for everything that has gone since, but I am not to blame for all the chaos that has infected Albion." As he spoke, he softened his features and voice and he calmed his temper. "I look at it like this, all of those people whose lives I've committed to the Pit of Despair, have taken up arms against me and my family and those that have joined my crusade. If they had conformed to the ideal of decency and civility that most people feel is just, then they would still be alive today."

"Do you truly believe that?" Lindsey asked looking smug again because she had successfully guided Jason where she needed him to go.

"Yes I do, it's the only way my mind can cope with the guilt," Jason answered quietly, and he looked at the cloudless sky and then back to the camera and then finally back to Lindsey.

A large crowd had gathered around the pair, even the guards that had been posted around the perimeter had come to watch the show. People had wandered up as quietly as they could and the cameras rolled on, filming everything, capturing every breath and movement from the crowd.

"Tell me Jason, what's your stand point on religion?" Lindsey asked, changing the subject.

"I'm agnostic, I don't know what to believe in, I think there's something there and I respect all the faiths and beliefs that people hold dear." Jason answered though he was surprised by the question.

"So in Jason de Silva's world, religion wouldn't be abolished?" Lindsey continued the uncomfortable line of questioning on religion which she knew was always a controversial subject.

"Of course not, people should be free to feel and think how they want to," Jason began.

"Unless they interfere with Jason de Silva's law and not, how did you put it, conform to your ideals of decency and civility?" Lindsey interrupted rudely to finish off his sentence.

Jason felt another volley of questioning stirring in the mind of his interviewer and he considered his response carefully before he continued. "I do not care what you do, what clothes you wear, what you look like, what your beliefs or ideals are," he paused, to give Lindsey chance to pursue him further but she remained silent. "The only thing I want to change is the victims."

"Victims?" Lindsey started, trying to interrupt again, but Jason wouldn't let her, he continued talking over her.

"Yes victims. Wouldn't it be nice if nobody had to be a victim anymore?" Jason said and then fell silent, awaiting a response from Lindsey.

Lindsey was trapped; she could only go one way. "Yes," she said. '*Clever bastard*,' she thought.

Jason looked at the camera. "I don't care if you wear a tracksuit and listen to gangster music; I own a hooded sweat shirt and listen to some of the music the Skavites play at their gatherings, that doesn't make you a criminal." Jason stood then, he was fed up with the interview and Lindsey's probing assault.

The cameraman was caught off guard by the sudden movement and he wobbled slightly as he panned to follow his subject. "All I ask is that you obey the laws of common decency and let others live in peace without creating any more victims," Jason turned to the ever growing crowd around him, silent as a statue. Then he yelled. "Who's with me?"

The crowd responded to Jason's charm and they raised their weapons and their voices to the air as they yelled their approval of his words.

"If you have no honour, then maybe you deserve to die," Jason shouted at the camera as the crowd was quieting. Then Lindsey was at his side and the camera crew followed. Between them, they lifted the camera from its stand.

"What do you mean by honour?" Lindsey asked, putting her mic to Jason's mouth.

He stopped and turned towards her as the crowd chanted his name, "de Silva, de Silva."

"It's simple," he said then looked to the camera. "If you go around feeding off other's fears, intimidating people and committing crimes, then prepare to die."

"But that's how men are and always have been," Lindsey mocked him again.

"Then it's high time mankind changed, isn't it?" he countered her statement. Jason turned to leave and Lindsey grabbed his arm, he stopped himself from pulling free of her grip and turned to face her in an attempt to not look bullish.

"Yes, but look at yourself, you're a hypocrite. Now you're just as bad as they are, you want death and blood spilt all across Albion."

Jason pulled his arm free. "Sometimes radical action is required to bring about change!" he shouted out of anger as much as to make himself heard.

"How much death though Jason?" Lindsey asked trying to sound smooth and gentle as the crowd grew quiet.

"As much as it takes to change the attitudes of the criminal classes," Jason answered, he also calmed as he faced her.

"But they'll still be criminals," she said.

"They'll be dead criminals, or they will conform to the new rules our government will put into effect," Jason turned and walked away.

"So it's not your intention to replace government and rule yourself?" Lindsey asked him as she followed, the camera crew did their best to keep up and the crowd parted for the odd procession.

"It never was, I just want them to listen to reason and change their laws governing criminal behaviour," he answered as they walked.

"What now though, after all this death and civil unrest?" she asked fervently, feeling the interview was coming to its climax.

"Now they have no choice, they must give in to our demands. The winds of change have whipped up a storm, a tempest that I intend to ride until it's blown itself out," he answered as they rounded the stage that was being dismantled by workmen.

In front of them, the parkland was covered by thousands of new volunteers, being marshalled by newly appointed Captains and officers of the ever growing People's Army.

They looked at the scene in front of them, and then Jason turned as the camera panned back to him and Lindsey who gawked at the swelled ranks of the army before her.

"Lindsey, you have a nice day," Jason said, a breeze tousled his blonde hair as Ethan Clifford and Teddy Williams appeared either side of him.

"Good luck Jason, I hope you survive your war," Lindsey said then turned to the camera as she turned her microphone off.

"That was fucking superb!" the cameraman said as he lowered his equipment to the floor.

Lindsey didn't acknowledge him, but spoke to Jason who

was pointing off across the parkland. "You have cavalry," she was surprised.

Jason followed her finger. "Ah so we do," he said.

It was the same bunch of horsemen and women he'd seen at Hurtsford, but their number had swelled. There were hundreds of them, many more than the few he'd seen on the village green a few days earlier. They sat upon their mounts proudly in neat lines, all wearing clothes of varying shades of green.

"Go get everything packed and ready to move," Lindsey turned to bark orders at her crew.

"Are you coming to Kalverstone then?" Jason asked without turning from the sun drenched parkland.

Lindsey had turned and walked away. "I wouldn't miss it for all the silver in the southern isles," she yelled back at him, as the crowd flowed around them.

"Shall we?" Ethan motioned as huge vehicles waited to be loaded with their human cargo, their side ramps resting on the parkland grass.

"Yes, let's get it over with," Jason said as Horace pulled up in the new style off road power vehicle, a 'Thank You' from the city of Ramby.

Chapter 21

The lifeless corpse that was once Jacky de Silva hung by the neck and swung gently from a length of rope, her naked body was bruised from head to toe. Sharpy sat on the Mayor's chair on the balcony of City Hall his muscled figure made the chair creak as he leaned back with one foot on the low brick wall in front of him. He overlooked a city centre in chaos and ruin. The crime boss from the coastal city of Havenstock had assumed control of Kalverstone without opposition and he fiddled with his shades as he contemplated the possibility of joining up with Douglass Farrell.

Three men marched up the corridor behind him. Their boots tapped in time on the marble floor by accident rather than design. Sharpy sat up and took his shades off to look over his shoulder. Flanked by Sharpy's personal body guard, the three men marched right out onto the balcony to confront Sharpy, who looked at them down the length of his long narrow nose.

"What the fuck blud, what d'you think you're doing?" The scruffy Skav in the middle was aggressive from the start, his northern Albion accent more pronounced because of his anger as he questioned the man who assumed command.

Sharpy smiled and adjusted his position in the chair. He'd heard the rumours that there were already complaints about his actions and he was waiting for one of the groups to complain directly to him.

"What the fuck brov? Show some respect ta ya betters,"

Sharpy all but challenged the northern Skavs, he found them laughable mainly because none of them matched his strength or physique.

"Betters brov?" one skinny Skav from the Northern Reaches complained. He spat angrily in front of Sharpy.

"The de Silva lady, we could have used her," the Skav in the middle said at the same time, talking over his colleague.

"Use her, that we did brov, fucked her and hung her, we used her for entertainment brov," Sharpy laughed as did his men, remembering the fun they'd had with the de Silva woman.

"Bad mischief that brov, what with that de Silva bastard only down the road at Ramby," the northerner said.

"Listen up now brov, don't come into my yard givin me grief, show some fuckin respect," Sharpy snarled.

"You can't talk about respect," the northerner spat.

Sharpy jumped up from his throne and drew a pistol from inside his coat, in one smooth motion he raised the hand gun and shot the Northern Reaches leader straight between the eyes at point blank range.

The Skavites that revelled and raped in the city square below ducked instinctively as the sound of the shot echoed around them. Then as they looked around and upwards, they saw the Northern Reaches leader being thrown unceremoniously from City Hall's balcony. His warm corpse hit the slabs below with a sickening thud and his already mangled head burst open on contact.

The square was full of the Northern Reaches crew who had come prepared and ready for a fight, they had waited for their leader, but hadn't expected him to return to them in this fashion. Then two more shots rang out as their leader's guard met the same fate at Sharpy's hand. Naturally the Northern Reaches criminals were angered by the loss of their comrades, but their hearts were especially inflamed by the way in which their leader's corpse was treated, thrown from the balcony in such a disrespectful way. All across Kalverstone's city square, guns were drawn as men belonging to more than two factions felt the mood change.

One of Sharpy's guards leaned over the rail as he bundled another of the northerners over but he showed too much of himself. He hadn't realised that he had been targeted and he was hit by a volley of shots, one of which hit him in the eye which exploded in a fountain of blood as his head was thrown back.

All over the city square bullets began to fly. The different factions had separated quickly, taking what cover they could and soon enough, old scores were settled with the barrel of the gun and the edge of the blade. The uneasy truce of the Skavite gangs had come to an end in the city of Kalverstone. Alliances and old friendships meant nothing as the violence spread from the square into the streets beyond. The chaos spread from street to street and building to building as thousands of Skavites battled for respect.

Jason sat in the large tent that had been erected for the People's Army's headquarters whilst they waited to move. The event company gave it over willingly, along with all the furniture and Jason sat in a high backed black leather chair that rested on a dais overlooking his commanders. He truly felt important, but was determined not to let his elevated position in life go to his head.

In front of Jason, the Robinson brothers chatted and laughed with others that over the past week of the troubles had gained Jason's trust and confidence. Ethan stood laughing and talking to Jonas and the youngster's leader, Jacob, whose ranks had swelled the most with thousands of the youngsters from the city of Ramby volunteering to join the People's Army. There were many more in the tent that Jason didn't recognise, they were officers of the different divisions and corps that had been formed to cope with the ever growing numbers.

Philip broke off from those he spoke with and went to Jason's side. "Are you all right Jason? You seem quiet today."

"I'm fine mate, just wondering about Jacky," Jason looked at Philip, and was touched that his friend's face was full of sympathy.

"Have you ever ridden a horse?" Philip asked, changing the subject.

"I rode from your grandparents to your place, the horse broke into a gallop once and it scared the shit outta me."

"Well I've taken control of the cavalry," Philip hoped that Jason wouldn't disapprove.

"Yes I saw them earlier, right after that stupid interview, I can never get across what I'm trying to say," Jason said, thinking of the things he hadn't said that maybe he should have.

"From what I hear it went quite well," Philip said, then after a moment, he continued. "If you like, I'll pick one out for you, a horse that is; we have a few spare ones."

"Thanks for the offer but I'm all good, I like my comfort and besides it hurts your nuts," Jason winced at that memory.

Philip laughed and said: "I'll do it anyway, just in case." Then he looked over his shoulder and beckoned one of his men forward.

Jason recognised the man as he stepped forward; it was Dave Hilbert, Ethan's old friend that fought beside him at Mount Aamor. Jason remembered his ferocious appetite for Skavite blood.

"This is my second in command and Bannerman, Dave Hilbert," Philip said, happy to introduce his friend.

"My lord," Dave bowed a quick nod of the head. "These are our colours." he said and rolled out a small white flag with a rearing black stallion at its centre.

"Very nice," Jason was impressed. The fabric was smooth to the touch as he ran his hand across the silken material.

"Where did you get all the horses and riders from?" Jason

asked, but then they looked as the tent flap was pulled aside to show Jimmy standing in the gap, silhouetted by the sun above and behind him.

"There are thousands of horses on farms all over Albion's countryside, most of us country folk can ride, even if we don't own a horse we still learned to ride as a child," Philip said. The expression on his face showed that he was wondering how poor the city folks knowledge of country life really was.

"More horses than people hey?" Jason joked. "How many have you got signed up?"

"I'm not exactly sure, but if I had to guess I'd say more than three thousand, with more coming in all the time," Philip answered, delighted at the surprise that showed on Jason's face.

"Everybody's fed and loaded up Mr de Silva Sir," Jimmy tried not to bow, but did anyway as he approached Jason's makeshift throne.

"Three thousand?" Jason couldn't believe it, his eyes widened and a smile appeared.

"Mr de Silva Sir?" Jimmy bowed again as he waited for a response.

Jason managed to get back to the here and now. "Yes Jimmy, thank you," he said to the Hurtsford man. Jason stood and stepped from the dais, he put his arm around Philip's shoulder as they followed everyone out of the marquee. "What the fuck am I supposed to do with all those horses?" he asked Philip.

"All the great armies had cavalry," Ethan joined in the conversation as they walked.

"We're in the Digital Age, not the Stone Age, horse flesh ain't no match for bullets," Jason told the two of them and he released Philip's shoulder as they reached the tent's entrance.

"Who knows what civil war in Albion will cause when the infrastructure has collapsed along with manufacturing and energy production. I bet we run out of bullets and energy cells before we do horses." Ethan said, looking solemn.

They filed out of the large tent and walked out onto the sun bathed grass.

"I don't see three thousand horses," Jason said, shading his eyes.

"We camped at Hadden Fields last night, if you change your mind Jay, a horse will always be made available for you," Philip offered again as a man led two horses towards the group of commanders, both Philip and his Bannerman went off towards their mounts.

"Will you ride in my vehicle with me?" Jason asked Ethan as all the Robinsons went off to join their troops.

"Of course I will it would be my honour." Ethan said. Horace pulled up in Jason's posh new vehicle and they both climbed into the back of the chauffeur driven vehicle.

"I'll be very glad of the company, thank you." Jason said.

"When were cavalry last used in war?" Jason asked as Ethan settled himself beside him.

"Four centuries ago, a force from the Northern Islands attacked an Avalonian army that consisted of mechanised infantry. They were slaughtered before their charge even reached its first objective. It's well documented as being the shortest war the world has ever known," Ethan said. He loved to recite his knowledge of the history of warfare.

"I rest my case." Jason looked forward, he knew he had to indulge the people on horseback, but couldn't see where they could be used.

They moved off the grass and onto the hard tarmac and Horace accelerated as they moved off at the head of the column. They passed waiting vehicles that lined the side of the carriageway, waiting to join the end of the line. The citizens of Ramby cheered as the army passed, they celebrated Jason de Silva's presence as the long awaited morning had turned into noon. There were tens of thousands of cheering people waving their loved ones off as they went to fight a necessary war.

Jason waved back, glad of their support and friendship.

"How many men do we have in total?" Jason asked Ethan, but he was also wondering how many thousands lined their route out of the city.

"Sorry Jay?" Ethan turned from the view outside, unsure of what Jason had said.

"How many bodies do we have in our army?" Jason asked again, sighing as he repeated himself.

"Fucking shit loads. People been arriving all morning, but as to a precise number," Ethan looked thoughtful while he hazarded a guess, "I'd have to say twenty five to thirty thousand."

Jason whistled through his teeth and turned to look out of the window again. Horace drove the vehicle onto another carriageway to skirt around the city, the long line of vehicles stretched out behind them. They passed under a bridge which had a giant flag draped over the rail. The flag was the red dragon of the People's Army. The bridge was crammed with yelling and cheering people. A little way down the carriageway, they passed Philip's cavalry trotting along the hard shoulder; they passed Philip just as they passed under another bridge crammed with cheering citizens. Philip did look magnificent as he sat upon his war charger at the head of his troop, with his long green jacket spread over the horse's hindquarters behind him.

"Thank fuck for all of you," Jason thought out loud.

"Actually, the general populace was ready for a war and has been for years, war is in our nature." Ethan said without turning from his view.

"I mean thank fuck for you and Jimmy and the Robinson brothers, because without all of you, none of this would have been possible." Jason explained, he smiled as he waved at another group of onlookers. "Without you guys organising stuff, I'd still be in the Ox and Cart at Hurtsford getting pissed and contemplating my next move."

"Behind every great leader there is a chain of command,

it takes many individuals to lead a charge, no one single man in history could organise such a force," Ethan smiled, he was happy that Jason could see everyone's worth. "You're the hero that leads our charge, the Shepherd that the sheep follow."

"I was given no choice but to fight, whereas all you that follow me do so at your own free will. I ain't the hero, all of you are." Jason was pleased; he could rely on Ethan for his honesty and true point of view.

"No, they'll be the real heroes." Ethan sat up, curious to see why Horace had suddenly laughed. Jason looked too and as they slowed down for a traffic roundabout at the end of the stretch of the bypass, they saw what Horace had found so funny. They leaned forward to look out of the windscreen to see a group of young ladies wearing hot pants and tight t-shirts. They stood in a line facing their route in the middle of the roundabout. They danced under a huge banner which was tied between two poles stuck in the ground. The banner read 'WE LOVE YOU JASON' in large bold black letters.

"Bless 'em," Jason managed as he watched the large breasted young ladies jump up and down as the vehicle drove around and past them.

"Lucky bastard!" Ethan laughed.

"Yeah, lucky I love my wife and wouldn't," Jason smiled more as one of the young lasses lifted her top in the excitement.

Gavin Jones listened to the gun fire for a few minutes then he stood from his chair behind his desk and walked to the window. He didn't turn as one of his men burst into the room.

"Sir, Mr Jones, they're havin it mate!" The young skinny Skav stammered, trying to get his breath back.

"Ain't they just?" Mr Jones said, agreeing with the messenger as he looked down from his hotel window. He couldn't see the fighting, but the sounds coming from a few streets away told a story of death and carnage on an unprecedented level in the city.

Mr Jones looked over his shoulder as the door opened again. In the doorway stood his most trusted man, Henry, his body guard who watched over him faithfully.

"Henry, how many men do we have left?" he asked the giant thug.

"Two hundred or more Sir." Henry squeaked his reply, his voice had never broken.

Mr Jones looked back to the streets as off near the centre of Kalverstone, the front of a building exploded outward from a grenade blast. Then sporadic gun fire could be heard, followed by heart wrenching screams. On the streets below the hotel they had commandeered, there was no fighting taking place but Gavin Jones knew it was only a matter of time.

"I'm guessing that Sharpy started it." Mr Jones mused to himself as he looked out. He didn't turn to look at the panicked youth that had burst in. On the street he saw a young Northern Reaches Skav being dragged down by a gang of Havenstock City Skavs. The captured Skav tried to ward off the blows but eventually succumbed as his attackers beat him to death.

"Yes Mr Jones, Sharpy done dat de Silva woman, the Northern Reaches lads kicked off about it," the young Skav joined Mr Jones at the window.

"And the outcome?" Mr Jones asked.

"Sharpy shot em, dem north lads," the Skav slurred his words and he wiped his nose across his sleeve.

"Tell me why I'm not surprised," Mr Jones turned from the window. "Get the lads together and let's get the fuck out of here!"

"Where are we goin?" Henry squeaked.

"Anywhere but here, perhaps south to join up with Farrell," Mr Jones walked to his desk and took his suit jacket from the back of the chair.

The youth fled the room followed by Henry. They both shouted and kicked in doors as they went, their voices becoming fainter as they fled down the corridor.

Mr Jones walked down the corridor and Henry met him at the far end and they walked towards the stairs. Mr Jones paused at the top of the stairwell; he looked over the rail as his men made their way down to the ground floor. They both followed them down and were the last ones to reach the ground floor.

When his men had evacuated the building, Mr Jones followed Henry out into the fresh spring afternoon. "Well Henry, it's a nice day for it," Mr Jones said, pulling on a pair of thin leather gloves.

"Nice day for what Sir?" the giant squeaked, looking puzzled.

"I have no fucking idea." Mr Jones smiled in spite of himself, he longed for intellectual conversation and Henry was still trying to figure out what his boss was talking about when ten men rounded the corner, their guns drawn. Before the lax Ramby Skavs had time to react, the ten men turned to fire in the direction they had run from, gunshots and a hail of bullets was the response from an unseen group who were giving chase. Everyone dived for cover behind anything they could find and the ten fleeing men mingled with them. One of them fell dead even as he gained cover; a bullet had found his liver. The Ramby crew drew their weapons and trained them on the corner.

A group of heavily armoured Havenstock Skavs ran around the same corner and the last thing the Havenstock Skavs expected was two hundred and fifty Ramby Skavs awaiting them in ambush.

The nine fleeing Skavs fired first followed by the rest of the Ramby crew who were left with no choice but to fire in self defence. The Havenstock Skavs didn't stand a chance. They were out in the open, out gunned and outwitted. They tried in vain to lift their guns to return fire as they performed the dance of death, their bodies riddled by hundreds of bullets. Limbs fell away and bodies blew apart, they were literally shot to pieces and all were dead within a matter of seconds.

When all the guns fell silent, the Ramby Skavs and the newcomers turned their weapons on each other.

"I'm Mr Jones, you might have heard of me?" Mr Jones said with confidence, breaking the uneasy silence. "I've saved you, your lives are mine."

"I guess you me bossman then." One young Skav said, lowering his weapon, glad to serve and be alive. The rest of the guns were lowered then and the sounds of combat didn't dwindle at the cities heart, but for now didn't seem to be getting any closer.

"We're getting the fuck out of this cursed city, if you're coming, you answer to me," Mr Jones was confident in the nine men's allegiance and was determined to lay down the law.

"Boss," the first young man said and nodded his head.

They walked the short distance down the road to where they had left their vehicles; all were the latest fashionable and sporty models and all of them were stolen.

The vehicle storage depot was soon half empty as forty vehicles, their fuel cells blazing, drove out into the city away from the fighting. They raced at full power and it wasn't long before Mr Jones and his men had crossed the river Flou, Kalverstone's main waterway.

"Was this anything to do with you?" Mr Jones asked, turning in his seat, to look at the Skav that sat next to Henry.

"Nothin wrong wid fucking her," Reginald Smith said. He did not want to be accused of anything. Just a few days ago, little could he have known that his actions would have led to the chaos and so he thought it best to lie, as usual.

Chapter 22

Jason de Silva looked in the vehicle's side mirror and as far as the eye could see, the convoy stretched behind him. They had slowed and stopped at a roundabout at the outskirts of Kalverstone. A few vehicles passed in front of them at the junction. Those travellers were bemused by the convoy with the lead vehicle flying Jason's flag, a red rearing dragon on a green background.

"They don't look like Skavites and they certainly don't look suppressed," Jason leaned forward in his seat, he was confused.

Then he saw them, flashing lights approaching from the direction of the city. Jason got out of the vehicle as Horace disengaged the power cells. He was soon joined by Trevor and Dominic who were riding in the vehicle behind. Ethan also got out of the vehicle, just as Teddy Williams appeared with fifty of his Black Jackets, taking up positions around the lead vehicles, their guns pointing at the fast approaching police.

"Well this should be fun," Jason said and the Robinson boys smiled with him.

Three vehicles pulled up on the roundabout to block their progress, one military officer's vehicle and two police vehicles. Four constables jumped from their vehicles and they took cover behind them. Then four soldiers and a ranked officer carrying a cane exited the military vehicle, the four soldiers carried huge weapons with multiple barrels, the like of which Jason had never seen.

The officer stepped forward, his moustaches twitching ever so slightly as he talked, "I'm Captain Ian Flanders."

"And I'm," Jason began but was cut off by the Captain raising his hand.

"I know who you are," the Captain stepped forward and walked to within a few feet of Jason. He stood easy with his hands behind his back. "State your business," he said, showing Jason no respect.

"We're here to kill all the Skavite criminals. We've been told that you have an infestation," Jason replied, his voice was calm; his fight wasn't with these men.

The Captain had never fought in combat before Kalverstone was attacked and he was fresh from his military training. To face Jason and his People's Army was truly daunting for him. He gripped his cane in both hands, hidden behind his back as he hid his fears behind his blank expression. "Not all the city is under criminal control, obviously," Captain Flanders said authoritatively, his eyes hidden behind mirrored sun glasses.

"May we pass?" Jason asked and he smiled so as to not upset the Captain.

Flanders stared at Jason for a long minute. "I've been instructed by my superiors to arrest you on sight," Captain Flanders dared to smile, just a little twitch of his lips.

"And who do you answer to, where are your superiors?" Jason asked. "Are they here?"

"I answer to the rightful rulers of Albion," the Captain replied in a pompous tone.

"You're king Edmund's man then?" Jason asked, knowing this was not the answer to his question. "We're not your enemies," Jason continued before the Captain could answer. He took out the letter that he'd kept on his person ever since he had taken delivery of the three truck loads of weapons and ammunition. He handed the letter to the Captain, who removed the letter from its envelope and read it, scanning the contents quickly.

The Captain put the letter back into its envelope and passed it back to Jason. "You have us wrong Mr de Silva, I follow the orders of the elected government."

"Ah, so we are enemies after all if you decide to enforce farcical laws," Jason stared into the Captain's shades, looking at his own defiant face staring back at him.

Dominic stepped up, puffing his chest out threateningly. "Why the fuck are we even having this conversation?" he asked.

Captain Flanders turned his attention to Dominic, taking his sun glasses off to stare at him. "Because if you show me any signs of aggression, the military hover jets at my disposal will fly down the line of your convoy to strike it with gun and rocket fire."

"Ah, I see," Dominic sounded much calmer and his face flushed in embarrassment.

As if to enforce the Captain's words, five hover jets, bristling with weapons, flew overhead.

"They're Avalonion!" Trevor shouted over the sound of their engines as they passed close.

"Yes, they left them behind," Captain Flanders confirmed, gaining new confidence as his trump card hovered overhead.

"What do you mean left them behind?" Ethan asked from behind Jason.

"In the light of a brewing civil war, our ally has returned to Avalon, but they have left us a few gifts," Captain Flanders smiled and motioned above him with his cane.

Jason knew his troops were not geared up for this sort of confrontation, the casualties would be immense, he turned to Ethan who shook his head and mouthed the word no.

Jason looked down the long lines of vehicles; thousands of his men were taking cover at the side of the road, hundreds of guns pointing at the hovering gunships. Ethan walked past Jason and drew his attention back to the Captain.

"If I may be so bold," Ethan spoke to the Captain, bobbing

his head as he did so.

"And you are?" Captain Flanders looked Ethan up and down.

"I'm of no significance, other than I have the ear of my leader, Mr de Silva," Ethan answered, playing down his role in the People's Army.

Ethan turned to Jason. "May I have a private word with the Captain? It's to every one's benefit," he said.

Jason looked around him, the tension was palpable, you'd need a chain saw to cut the atmosphere and fingers were tight on the triggers. Both Jason and Ethan looked to the Captain who wrung the cane to near snapping point, he nodded his agreement.

"Of course," Jason said, '*Anything to resolve the situation*,' he thought as he stepped backwards leaving the two men a modicum of privacy.

Ethan and Captain Flanders turned towards each other, their heads together and away from the thousands of eyes and they talked. Their private meeting lasted only a brief time, with Ethan talking earnestly, his hands and arms waving about. The Captain held his head close and nodded. Then he said something abrupt to Ethan, stepped back and offered Ethan his hand. "Shake on it," he said.

Ethan shook the Captain's hand to seal the gentlemen's agreement. The pact was sealed, now for the trust.

Without looking at Jason or the People's Army, the Captain looked up above him and motioned to the hover jets, pointing his finger skywards and turning his arm around. By the time the Captain and his men had mounted their vehicles, the hover jets were already more than a mile distant.

Ethan smiled as he turned to Jason and the army, who had visibly relaxed.

"What by the five moons did you say to him?" Jason asked.

"I told him I knew that if he had the manpower or the resources, he would have attacked us already, and he would not have let the city fall to the Skavite horde in the first place. I also told him we would take care of his Skav infestation, which was his biggest threat. I also assured him that we would go straight into the city and out the other side and be on our way," Ethan's smile was wide and genuine; he was pleased to succeed in negotiating with the Captain.

"You just saved a lot of lives and probably the war," Jason offered Ethan his hand. "What did the Captain say?"

"The enemy of my enemy is my friend," Ethan said, still smiling.

Jason turned to the Black Jackets standing nearby. "Did you lads hear all that?" he asked.

They nodded.

"Stay here and pass the word along then, no leaving the vehicles until told to do so."

They climbed back into their vehicles, only Teddy Williams stayed behind to marshal his troops and they walked off to the nearest vehicles to spread the word.

Ethan climbed back into the vehicle beside Jason and Randell appeared, he'd come up from his corps and transferred to Jason's vehicle, he climbed into the front passenger seat.

"Are you all right Randell?" Jason leaned forward to ask.

"Yes, I just wondered what the holdup was," he smiled nervously, he wanted the waiting to end, as they all did.

Horace engaged the vehicle's fuel cells and increased its power steadily as they moved off slowly, not wanting to worry or spook anyone in the government held territory. They came to a junction, a crossroads where more police vehicles had blocked off the side roads.

"Keep going driver," Randell ordered Horace as the old man seemed to slow down, easing down on the power.

One of the military hover jets returned, thrashing the air into a frenzy twenty metres above them and kept parallel as it joined the escort, adding credence to Ethan's assurances. Then they were into the suburbs. People came out onto the streets or opened their doors to watch as they passed. Unlike Ramby, the populace of Kalverstone were quiet and although the inquisitive lined their way, there were no cheering crowds or flags flying. Fields appeared through the gaps in the houses off to the left, the grass invisible beneath the canvas of thousands of refugee homes. Thousands of people in the camp shaded their eyes against the sun, trying to see what all the fuss was about. Their hands resembled a military salute, paying respect to the People's Army as they passed.

Behind them the convoy stretched out of sight and towards the horizon.

Next was the university, the road travelled through its campus and here, the pavement was the busiest, every inch of tarmac was choked with students.

Many of the students held banners protesting at the futility of warfare, many more cheered or jeered their passing, dependent on their political inclinations.

After a few minutes, their progress slowed as they reached the end of the tree lined avenue and as the sun filtered through their untouched limbs, it seemed hard to believe that a few hundred metres in front of them, chaos reigned. Then the trees abruptly came to an end and a large concrete barricade blocked the way.

Soldiers and police were rushing about, guiding bloodied and injured civilians onto shallow sloped grass banks or back further to the shade of the trees. There were hundreds of them, dirty and tear stained faces flooded from behind the concrete barricade.

The convoy stopped and an officer approached to the side of the vehicle as Jason opened his window.

"Were going into the city," Jason said and his commanding tones were clear behind his smile.

"Yes I know, we've been informed but I must tell you Mr de Silva, there's been a lot of activity in the city today, lots of gun fire and we have retaken the hospital," the officer in command said as he motioned for the barricade to be opened.

"My wife Jacky was in the hospital, have you heard anything?" Jason asked.

"No I haven't, most of the people in the hospital made it into the camps, but I'll put the word out," the young officer said with a friendly and helpful attitude which Jason appreciated.

"Thank you," Jason replied, in a more friendly tone.

Both men looked toward the city as the barricade was moved to one side, its massive bulk shifted by industrial forklifts.

"Now then, I'd take a right just ahead, travel a mile down the dual carriageway and take the next exit," the young officer motioned ahead with his left hand pointing, he looked at the junction before them as they spoke.

"What's there?" Karl asked, leaning from his window to look at the shattered hospital building and the corpses that lay around it.

"That's the biggest precinct in Albion, it might be big enough for what you need, it's at the edge of the city across the Flou, almost strategically sound but for the highways," the officer turned without waiting for a reply, he shouted orders at his men who removed debris and started to remove the corpses on the road that were in their path.

Three unarmed squads marched past Jason's vehicle; they were rolling their sleeves up to help. Between the two groups of men, the way forward was cleared in minutes.

"Let's go Horace," Jason leaned forward to peer up the road, the peaceful surroundings denied him a look at the chaos beyond.

They drove onto the roundabout ahead of them and onto the main road that would take them to the precinct. They sped up as the city fell away beside them; everyone looked over to the city's central districts straining to see the enemy. Nothing moved and the streets were as still as death with only the smoke of a thousand fires to give any indication of the troubles within. Jason looked back in the direction they had come from, the convoy stretched as far as the eye could see, winding its path through the suburbs.

The drive down the bypass didn't take long; the next junction was only minutes from the first. They entered a huge industrial and shopping district, with giant malls providing anything a person could want. Over to his left, Jason saw a cinema and a supermarket, their shutters closed against looters.

"Look at that, at least we've got entertainment if we need it," Horace said, breaking the silence.

"Yeah, I bet that supermarkets full, it doesn't look as if anyone's been down here," Randell pointed out.

"I think I'll have a word with Jimmy," Jason said, turning to look at the vehicle that followed them, trying to spot the Hurtsford man.

"I bet he already has his crowbar ready," Randell said as he strained to see any signs of forced entry.

On either side of the bypass were huge vehicle parks surrounded by shops that sold everything from garden equipment to toys. There were easily enough parking spaces to accommodate the vehicles and the men. The convoy pulled off the main road and Horace turned to the left to drive into the middle of the nearest deserted precinct and theirs was the first vehicle to come to a full stop.

Jason looked for Jimmy's vehicle, but it had veered right to head straight for the supermarket, that meant they would eat well that evening.

As Jason's vehicle came to a stop, the personnel carriers pulled in around it, intentionally creating a shield as they powered down their fuel cells. Soldiers of the People's Army ran in all directions to secure the perimeter, even as the rest disembarked from their vehicles.

Jason stood on the tarmac and was amazed at their progress;

he wondered how long it would be before they made contact. Ethan joined him as Teddy Williams trotted up to them. The middle aged policeman from Hurtsford had changed in the last few weeks, from the quiet smiling village constable, to the calculating leader of his own troop of men, the Black Jackets. He had forgotten his old life and forged himself anew in Jason's service, he coveted his new position in life and threw himself into his work and although he hadn't become arrogant, he did have an air of superiority that most commanding officers developed.

"Jason," Teddy nodded a quick bob of his head which was not quite a bow.

"Mr Williams," Jason said. "How are your Black Jackets?"

"We're ready to serve," Teddy said and stretched to crack his back and relieve the muscle strain from sitting so long on their journey.

"Good, good, take your lads up that dual carriageway leading into the city centre," Jason ordered and pointed up the road in question.

"But don't engage the enemy," Ethan suggested as he joined in the conversation.

Teddy looked from Jason to Ethan to take stock of the man before he looked back to Jason. He didn't say a word. He'd taken Ethan's suggestion as a command and he didn't take orders from anyone else but Jason and that was plainly written on his face. Jason nodded his consent but didn't speak; he did not want to embarrass either of his friends.

"By your command," Teddy turned to jog off and bark orders at his men.

Jason looked back at Ethan who, although not angry, was red in the face.

"Why did he do that? Why did he ignore me?" Ethan asked himself through gritted teeth.

"I guess he only wants to take orders from me, don't take it personally," Jason tried to console his military strategist.

"I guess you're right, but why would he look at me like I'm nothing?" Ethan's frown smoothed a little as he agreed with Jason's explanation and he tried to put aside the perceived insult.

More vehicles arrived on the parking lot in a constant stream and the troops did not wait for orders, they disembarked and followed their Sergeants and Captains to secure the area and increase the size of the perimeter.

Jonas, flanked by two burly Northern Islanders, jogged up to Jason with a smile on his face.

"This isn't too far from my home," he said, his thick Islander accent unmistakable.

"Jonas," Jason offered his ally his hand.

"What I want to know is where the fight is? Where are the fucking cowards?" Jonas took the proffered hand and shook it with an iron grip; he looked left and right, eager for the battle to begin.

"What do you think is happening?" Jason asked, turning to Ethan who was still sulking.

"They are a group of villains thrown together by chance and their command structure would be feudal at best, if what that officer told us is true, then they're probably doing our job for us," Ethan looked skywards as he pondered on the problem of Kalverstone.

As if in answer to Ethan's statement the sound of far off fighting in the city's centre could be heard as sporadic gun fire sounded in the distance. They turned from the noise which was too far off to be of any concern. Jason turned back to address the growing number of officers in front of him, he looked up with a start, at the face of the tall broad shouldered Jacob from Eirwen valley.

"Ah, hello," Jason was startled and momentarily taken aback. "It's Jacob isn't it? I don't think we've been introduced yet, how are you?" he said and took the hand that Jacob offered.

"Ok, I guess. What do you want me and my lads to do?" the young man asked and his smile never left his face, his excitement at the coming battle was building.

Jason turned to Ethan who shrugged; he did not want to be the one to send the youngsters into combat.

"How many follow your orders?" Jason asked.

"All the young people," Jacob answered.

"What do you mean all the young people?" Ethan asked then.

"More than two thousand of your army are younger than eighteen and they follow my orders. There would have been more but I turned anyone under sixteen years away," Jacob stood proud and tall as he addressed the men that surrounded him. Although he was only eighteen, he didn't look out of place amongst the men he stood with.

"Too young to fight," Jonas said, cocking an eyebrow as he appraised Jacob.

"They're not too young to have seen their loved ones die," Jacob spat and the smile left his face. "And they're all willing to die for our cause."

"I meant no offence," Jonas countered, tempering the young man's outburst.

"Clear the buildings and if you find anything useful, commandeer it, especially anything such as food and medical supplies." Jason ordered.

"No problem," Jacob said and looked from Jason to Jonas. "No offence taken," he said to the huge Islander, he didn't want to either lose face or fight the giant that he knew he couldn't beat.

Jimmy wandered over carrying a box; he was followed by some of his men.

"Jimmy," Jason said, smiling at the commander of his logistic corps.

"Jason, my lord," he offered Jason the box.

"Wow, cream cakes!" Jason's eyes widened with delight as he

took a cake from the box, he hadn't seen a sweet treat in weeks.

Jimmy and Jonas both dipped into the box with greedy hands, Jacob licked his lips but was left wanting; the box was empty.

Jason swallowed a glob of cream he'd licked from the side of the cake. "Jimmy, you and your corps, get the buildings cleared of any enemies, increase the perimeter."

"Already on it," the ageing landlord said, licking his fingers.

"Here, take Jacob with you and put his men to good use," Jason covered his mouth as he spoke. "Make a list of anything you take and where from, they'll need reimbursing later."

"Already being done my lord," Jimmy turned to Jacob. "Come on then lad; let's see if we can find you a cake to eat."

Jimmy walked off with Jacob.

Trevor, Dominic and Randell Robinson approached next and it seemed to Jason that they were waiting their turn to come and speak with him.

"It's a good start, nobody's dead," Randell said.

The Brothers had formed their own corps during their stay in Ramby City's Parkland.

"Gentlemen, that leaves you and your corps, what do you think Ethan?" Jason asked, turning to Ethan.

"Make yourself comfortable gentlemen; I think we'd be best wait to see what Mr Williams turns up." Ethan answered with a suggestion, which was met by agreeable nods. Jason's commanding officers had come to trust Ethan's tactics, which up until now hadn't failed them.

The gang members from the Woodland Park Tenant Estate, which was a rough suburb of Kalverstone, had fought desperately to get away from the chaos. They had broken free of the main fighting and they had battled their way past the train station to leave their own city behind them.

"Fuck dis, I want my own pit!" one Skav shouted.

"The ghetto's other side of town," their leader shouted and

rested his hands on his knees as he pulled his men up for a breather.

There were less than one hundred of the Woodland Park Gang remaining, they were on the wrong side of town and they were being followed.

"They're not even from here, tis our turf!" another shouted.

"Yeah, lets av em, fucking soz hards," another said.

"I'd rather head for our yard and escape through Meddlers territory," a blonde haired youth suggested, he was visibly shaken from the day's events.

"Ain't no love lost there lads," a voice yelled from behind them, the air being sucked through his teeth was a clear sign of disrespect.

Then the pursuers rounded the corner, there were hundreds of them, jogging at a fast pace following their quarry. The pace slowed but moved with purpose and they held weapons, already red, with fierce determination. Without saying another word the Woodland Estate Skavs took off down the road, heading out of the city as fast as their legs would carry them.

The other Skavs gave chase; they outnumbered the Woodland Skavs five to one and were intent on exacting punishment upon the rival tribe, especially as the others were fewer in number and therefore, easy meat. One of the Woodland estate Skavs tripped and fell forward onto his face, none of his mates turned to help as their pursuers gained on them. As the Skav struggled to his feet, the cold and bitter touch of steel thrust through him, he looked down in disbelief at the blade that protruded from his belly, he moved to touch its tip but was too late, it was pulled back through him and he felt it as it grated on his backbone.

Then the Woodland Skavs saw a group of men coming towards them, the Skavs continued forward but the oncoming group stopped, formed up ranks across the road and blocked their path.

"We surrender!" they shouted desperately, as they neared the men dressed in black leather jackets, their lines five deep and bristling with weaponry.

Standing to the right of their front rank was an impressively large man; his face was stern as he gave the order to open fire. The Woodland Estate Skavs tried to stop running and turn aside, but the world seemed to slow for the gang as bullets ripped them apart.

The last of them ran back, pleading with their pursuers. "Mercy, mercy!" they cried but none was given as they were chopped to pieces. The last of them had his skull opened by a bull nosed hammer, wielded by their enemy's leader.

Teddy Williams moved forward, edging on his feet as his men reloaded their weapons. The front ranks stood as their leader started forward a step.

"Black Jackets, charge!" Teddy Williams shouted until his lungs needed more air.

The charging Skavs were filled with blood lust and ran over the dead and dying Woodland Skavs as the People's Army Black Jackets fired their weapons in quick bursts of fire as they ran at the aggressive Skavs. The result was devastating for the Skav force; their front ranks were shredded as the two sides collided. The Skav scum charged on, their drug induced frenzy making them impervious to fear. The Black Jackets met them with equal ferocious determination and the two sides clashed with only death in their hearts, as both sides fought to slaughter the other.

Teddy Williams led the charge, his mind flashed back to all the years of abuse dished out by criminals such as these. With hands no longer tied by the government chains of legislation, he smiled the crazed smile of the temporarily insane. He held a heavy pistol which recoiled upwards with every shot that he fired into the mass of charging Skavites and in his left hand he held a short leaf-shaped sword, his knuckles whitened by the pressure he exerted upon its hilt.

Teddy side stepped a sword thrust and in a fluid motion, he

hacked downward to cleave the attacking Skav's head almost in two. His sword stuck fast in the dead Skavs skull as the man's brain spattered over his face and upper body. He tried to yank it free and he did not see the battle raging around him or the Skav that jumped at him. Teddy Williams turned too late to move or fend off the attacker. The raised hand was already in its downward arc to bring down a huge army knife at Teddy's exposed neck.

Teddy William's life flashed before his eyes as one of his men tried to block the attack and defend him. But he missed the parry and exposed himself to the attack and he took the blow that was meant for Teddy in the chest. The black jacket didn't scream as he fell back against Teddy Williams, his face was full of shock and surprise as he gripped the hilt of the blade that had killed him.

Teddy Williams quickly lifted his pistol at the Skavs face, who was trying to retrieve his blade; he didn't hesitate in pulling the trigger to fling the Skav head over heels as he sent his would-be killer to his death. Teddy Williams yanked his sword free and the force of freeing the blade jerked his arm outward and to his right, accidentally slicing through the throat of another Skav that was trying for a kill at Teddy's expense. The Skav fell to his knees and dropped the gun that he held so as to clasp at his wound, shocked and thinking of nothing but his impending death.

Teddy Williams stepped free of the bodies that lay around his feet, he looked around him at the melee that was drawing to a close. The Peoples Army's superior fire power was beginning to tell as bullets felled the Skavites at point blank range. The People's Army had won this skirmish easily. A few Skavs managed to evade death, fleeing back in the direction they had come.

Bodies lay everywhere and the Black Jackets counted their dead. Everywhere Teddy looked he saw his men tending to their own, he couldn't have been more proud of them; they had won their first pitched battle. Teddy looked for the man that had saved his life by inadvertently giving up his own. He soon found him, still alive; his eyelids were fluttering as he clung on to his life.

Teddy rushed to the man's side and knelt down beside him. He lifted the man's head from the cold tarmac and the still warm blood that had pooled around him.

"I know you, don't I?" Teddy said, puzzled that he recognized the man from somewhere.

The man's eyes focused on Teddy, "Tim," he coughed.

"Ah yes, the cameraman," Teddy was surprised; he hadn't known the man had joined his Black Jackets. Tim's eyes glazed over and he stared past Teddy and into the blue sky above them, he coughed once, his spittle was tinged dark red and died in Teddy's arms.

"Fuck, is that all I can say to a man that just saved my life?" Teddy said to himself as he gently lowered the man's head back to the ground.

Captain Eric knelt down beside him, his skinny frame in part hidden by the leather jacket and the baggy trousers he liked to wear. The Hurtsford man was Teddy's first cousin and they were often accused of being brothers, they looked so much alike.

"Ted, I got casualty numbers," Eric said, he sounded sad that they had lost anyone at all.

"Go on," Teddy said as the two of them stood.

"Seventy five dead and wounded," he looked down at the corpse surrounded by the halo of blood.

"Get the wounded and the weapons, we'll come back to bury the dead later," Teddy ordered, his emotions were all over the place, he was happy that they had gotten a victory but distraught that they had lost so many.

"I remember enrolling this one, I didn't think he'd amount to much," Captain Eric looked down at Tim's lifeless body. "Ah well, I guess he's in a better place now."

Teddy didn't look at his cousin; he looked into those staring eyes. "Thanks, Tim" he said under his breath, and he turned to hide a solitary tear because he felt an emotion akin to love almost for the dead man that had taken his place.

Chapter 23

The gun shots and shouting could be heard less than a mile down the dual carriageway at the parking lot. "You gave him the orders!" Ethan complained, shaking his head.

"Chill out Ethan, conflict is unavoidable sometimes, you know that," Jason said tartly. As he looked about, the People's Army were forming up ranks and preparing for battle, thousands of them formed up in lines as their commanders shouted out orders.

Three of the Robinson brothers ran up to Jason.

"Do we move into the city?" Trevor asked excitedly.

"Let's wait and see what the Black Jackets have to tell us," Ethan snapped, still a little bit annoyed.

Then the sounds of combat abruptly stopped and in the silence that ensued, Jason, Ethan and the Robinson boys looked at each other and silently wondered which way the battle had gone.

"I'm not committing any more men till we know what we're facing," Jason answered Trevor's question and he looked along the road that curved behind the buildings that hid the battle from their view.

Jonas formed his troops up on the road without the need for orders. His Islanders made three lines of tall, solid and menacing warriors, the mere sight of which would be enough to strike a chill into the coldest of hearts. Jason held no authority over his foreign ally and did nothing to dissuade them. They seemed ready to take on any scum that wished to fight. They were ready to be the first to be sent into the fray if the battle that had just finished had turned out bad for the People's Army.

Then five minutes after the sounds of battle had ceased, the Black Jackets came into view, marching boldly down the centre of the road. Four abreast they stamped, their number included the walking wounded, the limping and the carried men.

The awaiting army visibly relaxed, knowing that the liberation of Kalverstone was not about to be thrust upon them without notice.

Jason watched as Teddy Williams paused to talk to Lindsey who had moved up with her camera crew to document the return of the Black Jackets. His men marched proudly past him onto the precinct, their heads held high. Lindsey's arm holding the microphone fell limp to her side as Teddy spoke; she looked to the ground nodding her head, as she wiped at the tears that ran down her face.

Jason began walking toward them and Teddy turned at the same time and waved. Jason was a little annoyed at Teddy, as he hadn't reported straight back to him. "We might get some answers today," he said sarcastically, as he turned to those he stood with. His companions smiled at the jest and Jonas ran up to join Teddy as he approached. Teddy Williams smiled as he got up to Jason. "Good news!" he shouted.

"Like what? We lost the element of surprise!" Ethan yelled and waved his arms in his anger.

Teddy stopped smiling and stepped to the front of Jason. "Who asked for your opinion?" he spat venomously towards Ethan.

"Gentlemen," Jason stepped forward, placing himself between his arguing friends.

Both men were angry and ready to come to blows.

"Shut the fuck up," Jason bellowed, instantly regretting his outburst as most people within earshot turned at his shout, both Ethan and Teddy's faces turned beetroot red with embarrassment.

Jason's face also flushed and the three of them fell silent whilst they waited for the watching crowd to resume whatever they had been doing.

"That was awkward," Jonas frowned, feeling embarrassed for the small group.

"Like your accent," Randell joked.

That broke the tension and seemed to relax everyone involved.

"Your report please," Jason turned to Teddy.

"We were scouting up the road, as you ordered," he turned unnecessarily to point to where everyone knew they'd been. "When a group of Skavs ran towards us, we formed up our ranks and opened fire as they tried to surrender,"

"Tried to surrender? So it's true about them fighting each other," Randell said.

"Well, it was then that I realised that the Skavs were two factions and not one, one group running from another, I thinks fuck it, kill 'em all," Teddy thought he had a right to be a little smug in light of the victory.

"We should strike now," Ethan jumped in.

"You were exercising caution not long ago," Jason turned to Ethan, wondering what his advisor might be thinking.

"Teddy, I'm sorry for my outburst, but tell me, did you get them all?" Ethan asked the leader of the Black Jackets, the anger having left his voice.

"Some got away," Teddy didn't look at Ethan, but he did at least answer the question.

"Some always do," Ethan said, his voice becoming frantic, "as soon as they hear we're here, they will stop their in-fighting and concentrate on us. We need to attack before that can happen," Ethan had turned as he spoke, resting his gaze on Jason, hoping he would listen. "We can take the city before the sun rises."

"Does anyone here know the road layout of the city?" Jason asked, not needing any more convincing, but managing to contain his excitement, as he bought into Ethan's enthusiasm.

No one responded to the request for intelligence until Jonas raised his hand and nodded. "I lived here for two years before the troubles began."

All eyes turned to Jonas, the irony of the situation escaped none of them. They looked at the giant Northern Islander, thousands of miles from home, informing the local men on matters of geographical importance.

"Ok," he began. "We all march up the road here," he pointed back up the road Teddy's Black Jackets had reconnoitred. "When so far up, some go left some go right some go straight on."

"What about this road?" Ethan asked, looking back down the bypass towards the hospital.

"I'm sorry Jonas, I'm getting confused," Jason rubbed his head and combed his fingers through his hair.

"Will this help?" Jimmy asked, holding up a map as he stepped from behind the Robinson brothers.

"Thank you," Ethan said, snatching the map from his friend. "Sorry Jonas, please continue," he turned back to the Islander and held up the map.

Jonas nodded and stepped back, he knew the map would help his explanation; he was well aware that people struggled to understand him. Ethan opened up the map and laid it out on the floor; they knelt down or crouched as they studied it.

Ethan rubbed his chin as he looked thoughtfully at the map for a half minute, he looked at the men in turn and then back to indicate points on the miniature bird's eye view.

"If I may be so bold?" he began before he looked up, and then paused.

"Go on," Jason said, looking at his corps commanders, trying to gauge their reaction. They seemed more than happy to listen, including Teddy Williams.

"If I was attacking this city, I would send troops up this boulevard," Ethan pointed at the map, "Dominic's corps," he said, looking up at him.

Dominic looked to Jason who nodded at him, he looked back to the map to study in more detail where he was being instructed to lead his men and then he stood and stepped back so the others would have more room.

"I would send Trevor's corps in from the east down this highway," Ethan bent his neck and cocked his head to one side, deep in thought. "Randell's corps should approach from the south west, go back down this highway and turn in when they pass the hospital. If we synchronise our attacks, we should all reach the town square at the same time," Ethan stood, he was happy with his plan.

"What about the Black Jackets?" Teddy asked.

"I'd keep your lads back in reserve," Ethan said, the smile fading fast from his face, he hadn't expected any complaints, but should have known better.

"My boys want to be in the thick of it," Teddy's stern face spoke volumes, he felt offended at the prospect of being left out of the fighting.

"No General became great by putting his best units in harm's way," Ethan was ready to defend his tactics.

The commanders, including Jason, watched the arguing pair but Jason thought it prudent to let Ethan win his own argument if he was ever going to have the respect of the men.

"What the fuck's that got to do with this?" the middle aged Teddy snapped, motioning with his arm at the waiting army, thousands of men sitting around in the warm spring sun.

"Like I was saying, you never commit your best troops, you keep them back until you find where best to use them. Mr Williams, your Black Jackets are our best troops," Ethan became calmer as he finished and this answer appeared to satisfy Teddy Williams who seemed to deflate as he conceded to Ethan's logic.

"What about this half of the city?" Randell asked, pointing at the map. "We've only covered half the city."

"We don't have the man power, and when we take the centre, the Skavs in the north of the city will flee. Cut off the monster's head, it can no longer bite you," Ethan explained.

Jason looked at everyone. "Right then that settles it, Jonas, Jimmy, Teddy and Jacob, you're with me here in reserve. I guess the Robinsons lead the charge once again," he ordered, and his men nodded as he looked at them in turn. Then they shook hands and said their goodbyes before they walked off to join their men.

North of Kalverstone Mr Jones pulled in his small force of Skavs, he slowed his vehicle to a stop and his men pulled in behind him. Then he turned off the road, crashing through an old wooden gate that had seen better days, the cattle scattering as the convoy of stolen sporty vehicles skidded on the slick ground.

Gavin Jones was at a loss at what to do, all he knew now was that he had to escape Kalverstone, but with so few men and the whole of the nation at odds with his kind, he didn't expect to last long. He climbed from his vehicle and stretched, Henry and Reginald smith joined him.

A young man approached Gavin Jones, his movements spoke of barely suppressed aggression and Gavin Jones thought that it may be directed at him. The Skav was clearly looking for an argument and he confronted his leader.

"Yo bossman, wossup?" the youth said.

"Ah, dissent among the ranks," Gavin Jones looked rather unimpressed as he walked around his vehicle. He came face to face with the youth that was challenging him and without a moment's hesitation, drew the gun from the holster strapped under his jacket and shot the Skav in the face. He didn't give the youth a chance to apologise, he wanted no apology. Although executing the lad was the last thing he wanted to do, the lad had forced his hand, Mr Jones had to retain order at all cost.

Then he waited for anyone else who found it necessary to complain, he held the gun high at the side of his face pointing skyward. He couldn't lose control now and he needed these scum as much as they needed a leader.

"There aren't enough of us here to go anywhere safely so we will wait here to see what comes out of the city before we take our chances," he said, hopeful that he wouldn't have to kill any more of his men.

"Like what boss?" one of his men asked; his loyalty evident, he did not want the same fate as the dead Skav.

"Like more men of course, so no more shooting and no killing any that I recruit, even if you've got beef with them!" Mr Jones ordered. He looked about him waiting for an argument, but his men seemed more than happy to consent to his request. "Good, I'm glad you all see my point of view. You five, there's a restaurant two miles down the road, go get us some food," Mr Jones pointed at a group of Skavs that stood around the vehicle closest to the gate. "The rest of you set up a road block; let's see if we can't increase our numbers."

They all cheered, whether at the thought of food or at his words he didn't care, as long as they did as they were told.

Jason, Ethan and Jonas stood around the little table that had been fetched from the furniture superstore in the mall. They looked over the map of Kalverstone and Ethan calculated his measurements; hoping they were all correct to scale. Jacob stood a little way from the table; his smile had gone and he sulked. Jacob wanted full combat for his youngsters The Young Guard as they had come to be known, as a mark of respect for their courage in wanting to join the war. Teddy Williams sat laughing with his men, as they lounged about waiting for further orders.

"How much longer?" Jason asked impatiently.

"Five minutes," Ethan answered looking at his pocket watch.

"HQ to corps commanders, are you in position?" Jason spoke down the hand held radio Jimmy's men had found them.

"Randells corps in position," "Dominic ready," "Not quite, give us two minutes," came the replies.

"Come on Trevor, let's not lose the daylight," Jason put the radio on the table, he was becoming anxious waiting for the fight to begin.

Two long minutes passed while they waited with silent radios.

"Trevor's corps in position," Trevor announced over the airways.

Jason wiped sweat from the palm of his hand, before picking the radio off the table.

"HQ to corps commanders, start your advance, good luck lads," he said and handed the radio to Ethan.

The affirmative responses were lost to Jason as he looked toward the skyline; the afternoon sun glinted off the tall buildings. Dunstan hung low, the world's fourth moon looked black as the daylight lost its potency.

"I think I might advance with the reserve," Jason said, watching the black moon.

"I advise caution my lord," Ethan used the title but not the name, as he urged Jason not to advance.

"I'm a man of action, not a general to be found at the rear, I need to lead from the front," Jason said.

"I'll make sure my future calculations include your wanton destruction," Ethan said automatically, for a moment forgetting who he addressed.

"How fucking dare you?" Jason snapped, fuming at his advisor.

Ethan was aghast and unsure as what to say as Jason slammed his fist into the table. An uneasy moment of silence followed, as the two men glared at each other.

"I'm sorry, it's the waiting," Jason broke the silence; he

apologised but still sounded angry.

"I'm sorry too," Ethan turned away, he looked to the sky. "In any case, the plan's already set in motion, it would be insane to deviate from what everyone else out there thinks is set in stone." he tried to make Jason see sense.

"Yes, of course," Jason conceded. "Just don't take the piss again."

"Sorry mate, I won't." Ethan said, offering Jason his hand.

Jason shook Ethan's hand and reaffirmed their friendship, but he did not look any happier.

The sun slowly dipped to touch the horizon and the light turned to the luminescence of dusk because Serene's glow announced its appearance. Trevor Robinson led his corps down the four lanes of the dual carriageway, they approached Kalverstone city centre from the east. More than four thousand men and women edged slowly down the road, their weapons drawn and expecting contact with the enemy at any moment.

For approximately ten minutes they walked before they crossed the river Floe and entered one of the city's richest suburbs. There were no people greeting their liberators, no flag waving crowds of happy citizens. Eventually they passed the train station as the tall buildings of the city's heart loomed ever closer.

No one spoke unless it was to convey essential information and then it was only a whisper, whether they kept quiet through Ethan's advice or whether through the thrill of their beating hearts, the silence added an eerie atmosphere.

Faces appeared at some of the windows from the high rises, the residents who failed to flee in time. They waved at the approaching army who flew the red dragon flag, which was the ensign of the People's Army and then disappeared back into hiding. Fortunately for the People's Army, those few residents that did appear sensed the need for quiet and stilled the celebrations of liberation.

Then they were at their first objective, the large roundabout at the city end of the eastern highway, the scene that greeted them was horrific beyond belief. The whole area was littered by countless bodies, every one of them a Skavite bastard killed by their own kind in a brutal fight for respect.

"Well if we needed proof of in-fighting amongst our enemies, this is it," Trevor said, smiling at his enemy's demise.

Then everyone ducked instinctively as gun fire shattered the calm. At Kalverstone Castle, the old stone fortress that stood at the city's highest point no more than half a mile away, a battle had begun.

'*That must be Dominic*,' Trevor thought and he pressed the button on his radio. "Trevor to HQ, I hear a gun fire, permission to march to the sound of the guns?" he let go of the radios button and waited for a reply.

The reply came instantaneously from Ethan. "Negative, stick to the plan, Jonas and his foreign corps are marching up the road to intervene as we speak," then nothing, as the radio silenced.

"Right lads up we get," Trevor ordered as he jumped to his feet, "Let's have at em!" Trevor did as he was told, like any good soldier and leader of men. He stuck to the plan and marched away from the sounds of battle, putting the life of his twin in the lap of the gods.

As they marched up the hill toward the city centre, the tower blocks loomed ever closer, black smoke rose from the blocks of flats and was accompanied by all the sounds of combat. It appeared that different groups had taken up residence in the high rises that served as fortresses. Gun and rocket fire threatened to destroy the tall residential buildings and Randell was in no hurry to stop them.

Cautiously and partially hidden by the sounds of combat, Randell edged closer to his first objective, to clear out the flats of all enemies. His corps was three thousand strong and against all odds had stayed undetected as they advanced. Randell crept to within a stone's throw of the flats, leaving most of his men a quarter mile down the road; he had taken just a handful with him.

Randell peered around the corner, at that distance he could see that the fighting wasn't contained to just a few gun shots; the ground between the flats was a scene of utter chaos. A few thousand Skavites were pitted against one another as they clashed for control of the flats and absolute madness had taken over, the fighting had developed an insanity all of its own.

"Pull back," Randell ordered and edged backwards out of sight. "Let 'em kill each other," he said as flames leapt out of the ground floor of one of the flats to engulf some of its defenders.

They remained unseen, easily avoiding detection as they made their way back to the main body of Randell's men; the Skavs were too busy killing each other to notice them.

"Randell to HQ, I'm pulling back, first objective unattainable, I repeat first objective unattainable," he sounded muffled to those around him as he needlessly covered his mouth to hide the sound from possible detection.

"Hold and await further orders," Ethan's voice replied, "Hold your ground, do not bypass the flats!"

Teddy Williams joined Ethan and Jason at the table, his men stood ready, they looked menacing in their black garb as they lined the side of the highway that led into the city's heart.

Jason started checking his weapons, preparing himself for combat as he zipped up his coat.

Ethan leaned on the table. "Jason, what are you doing?"

Jason turned aggressively, he'd heard enough. "Ethan, you don't need me to coordinate the battle plan, you move the pieces on the board, I knock them over," he was desperate to join the battle.

"I agree that I don't need you here, but the movement does,

what happens tomorrow if you die today?" Ethan asked, and they all knew he was right.

"I guess I better stay alive then!" Jason replied the anger on his face matched that in his heart.

Jacob stepped up to the table; he had come to see what was happening. "Jason," he pleaded.

"No," the reply was sharp as he snapped at and walked past the young man.

Jacob fell silent, knowing that the anger wasn't directed at him. The Black Jackets fell in with Jason as he approached them with their leader at his heels. Then they jogged up to the road in pursuit of Jonas and his Islanders. Jimmy joined Ethan and Jacob at the table, waiting by the radio for any news of the fighting within the city's centre.

"There goes our illustrious leader," Jimmy said to Ethan.

"Let's hope he doesn't go get himself shot," Ethan said more nonchalantly than he felt.

"Oh, he'll be fine," Jimmy laughed. "He's lucky, he is," and he looked away from the map towards the distant sounds of war. Ethan was silent and miserable as he looked from his map to the radio and back to the map again.

'Not such a good plan after all,' he thought.

Some managed to get away and they fled, most of those were terrified as their narcotics turned on them. They ran from the melee, fleeing from the new threat and the psychotic strangers dressed in black leathers. One of their number fell to the tarmac coughing up blood, his colleagues left him there to die.

If they gave any thought at all, they assumed correctly that the men they fought were part of the People's Army and they wasted no time as they ran back into the city's heart to inform as many of their friends that would listen. Acting together the Skavite forces managed to organise themselves into a decent defence below the heights of Kalverstone castle on the Kingsway Boulevard. They quickly blocked the road with overturned vehicles and anything else they could get their hands on. Runners were sent out into the other parts of the city in an attempt to inform the other warring groups of the massive threat poised to overrun them.

A few hundred Skavs manned the barricades, a few hundred more lay hidden playing the snipers role from across the Kingsway Canal that ran parallel to the road. They were armed with rifles, shotguns and pistols, but were low on ammunition. The bulk of their forces though, lay hidden and silent, waiting for the opportunity to ambush. Surprisingly the Skavite force managed to keep discipline and keep itself hidden.

Dominic's corps had made quick progress up the Kingsway Boulevard, believing they may have lost the element of surprise. They were proven right about that as Dominic's five thousand strong force came to a barricade that blocked their way.

Dominic heard Trevor's voice on his radio and as the airways cleared of his brother's transmission he lifted his radio to his mouth. A bullet whistled past him before he had time to speak and the man at his side dropped to the hard surface of the road. Then another bullet ricocheted off the tarmac near his feet. Before he and his men had time to think, the sounds of battle were all around him. From the side of his line and below the cliff which the castle sat upon, hundreds if not thousands of Skavs poured out from the buildings in which they had lay hidden. The ambush was complete as the snipers from across the canal opened fire, Dominic's people didn't stand a chance out in the open.

Dominic was inflamed by the death of his men and he drew his hand gun and his short sword, looking for someone to kill, it wasn't such a difficult task as Skavs were all around him and in amongst his men. One of his men fell at his feet, struggling with a Skav who held a carving knife, four arms held an opposing hand at bay as they rolled to a stop at Dominic's feet.

Dominic collected his courage and steeled his nerve and without hesitation he thrust his sword deep into the Skav's back and pulled it up into the chest cavity to make sure of the kill. Twisting around in agony the Skav let go of his knife and stared defiantly at his assassin with blood tinged spittle flying through gritted teeth as he grimaced. Dominic looked at the Skav's blue eyes staring at him as he raised his gun to the man's temple. He pulled the trigger the Skav's head whipped away from him, then back again to cover him with a shower of blood. At the same time the carving knife that his man had recovered, stuck through the Skav's abdomen.

Looking about, Dominic wasn't short of targets, although he soon realised that his corps outnumbered the men that had out foxed him. He held out his hand to help the man he'd just saved up and lifted his pistol to shoot a Skav that charged him, the Skav fell dead and dropped the hammer he held aloft.

"Thanks boss," Dominic's soldier said but as he stood, a bullet hit him in the back of the skull, the smile never left his face as he fell limp to the ground.

All around him the battle raged, he knew his corps was in trouble and would suffer greatly; he turned to look for the gunmen. Then he saw the flashes from the gun barrels, lighting from hidden positions across the canal, he realised that they had time to take their aim at his exposed flank.

'*Beautifully contrived*' Dominic thought as his larger force was pushed towards the shooters they couldn't get at. "Bastards!" he shouted as he fired three shots at the opposite bank of the man made waterway, all of them missed their intended target.

He turned; slashing at a charging Skav with his short sword and in his temper, his wild swing hit with surprising accuracy to cut the Skav at the neck and almost sever the youth's head, the blade stopped at the bone as the Skav's squeal was cut short.

Dominic, covered in other men's blood, looked like an angry demon, his emotions raged within him. He walked to the nearest melee, where four of his men were bent over a dying Skav that they were stabbing repeatedly; he didn't interfere, but moved on. One of the four men stood as he moved past, the bullet that had Dominic's name etched along its metaphorical casing hit the man, felling him, Dominic would never know the man had inadvertently saved his life and sacrificed his own.

Then two Skavs jumped at him from a small knot of fighting, Dominic only had the time to raise his hand gun, the Skavs were so close that the sound of his pistol firing was muffled by the Skav that was pressed against the barrel, he fell away clutching at his abdomen.

The second Skav was a large man in his early twenties; he was tall and fat and he caught Dominic off balance. He smashed into the corps commander and knocked him down. The Skav had Dominic at a disadvantage as he scrambled to get to his feet. He raised an aluminium bat above his head and grinned as he swung it downwards towards Dominic's head. Dominic froze and he realised that he was about to take the hit.

Fortune favoured Dominic again as the bat changed direction, the Skav had been shot by one of his own snipers and spun twisting away to fall on Dominic's side. He felt the weight of the man pressing him into the tarmac, his collar bone snapped and the sharp pain made him cry out as his free hand slapped the ground to his right.

Dominic slid from beneath his dead assailant and he tried to push the pain away as he attempted to stand. It was futile however, his shoulder crunched and ground, his collar bone a splintered mess. He struggled to keep everything in focus, but in shock and pain he fell away from his waking thoughts as he passed out, seeming to fall backwards down a black and enclosing tunnel.

It wasn't long before Jonas and his small band of foreigners, arriving at the double, reached the rear of Dominic's corps, everywhere the dead and dying lay, the injured moaned and screamed and the corps medics tended to their injuries as best they could.

The Skavs didn't have that luxury; they had been cut down and put out of their misery. The People's Army's policy of no Skav prisoners was put to good use.

Jonas and his men stormed past the lines of injured towards the sounds of fighting where, a few hundred metres ahead of them, Dominic's corps had stalled. Blood from thousands of corpses, friend and foe, stained the ground red. The battle that had been happening only minutes before made the ground slick. As they neared the front line of the battle, Jonas could see the barricade and the flashes of light from the guns that its Skav defenders held. Tracer fire left lights in his eyes from the opposite side of the canal also, one brave soldier stood at the canal's edge firing his gun at the snipers there, he was shot several times before he fell forward into the murky waters, his body lost in the half light.

Shereze Ferris, one of the Islander warrior maidens ran past the kneeling Jonas, she held her long barrelled pistol in her hand. She aimed, and took only one shot to hit the brave man's assassin, he in turn felt the bite of a bullet and fell forward slumping dead behind his grassy cover.

Four men ran passed Jonas carrying a door; Dominic Robinson lay upon the painted wood his body was still but for the heave of his chest. A bullet fizzed past him to hit one of his Islanders. He bent double and grunted with the pain. That enraged Jonas and his men and they started to unlace the double bladed war axes from their backs, they took off running toward the barricade through the ranks of the People's Army that crouched waiting for the front to press on.

Although they waved the dragon flags of the People's Army and refused to retreat, they were leaderless and made no progress. Jonas and his people reached the front line to take cover with Dominic's soldiers as the fire intensified. Two more of Jonas's men were shot dead.

For a few painful minutes, Jonas watched as the People's Army and his own soldiers struggled, trying not to get shot lying as close to the ground as possible. They were unable to press forward as the cross fire was too intense. Powering overhead they heard the unmistakable sound of the hover jets. Three flew overhead and Jonas dared to look at the barricades a few hundred feet ahead.

The hover jets flew at their optimal attack speed and took it in turns to fire volleys of air to ground anti tank rockets into the barrier with pinpoint accuracy. Parts of vehicles flew skywards and bits of flaming plastics and wood mixed with the twisting metals. The silhouetted corpses that looked as rag dolls flung about by a rabid beast were torn apart by the huge blasts that ripped into the Skavite defences.

As one, the people that had been pinned down stood and as they began to charge, some thought they were imagining Jason de Silva sprinting past them, others were lifted and elated by the sight, he already had the forward momentum and he was using it with no thought to his own safety. It gave Dominic's corps new heart and they rose up with renewed vigour to catch up to the man they had sworn to follow. Jason was pursued by Teddy Williams and his Black Jackets and they merged with the allied forces to charge the now exposed and burning Skavite defenders. Most of the Skavs that survived fled.

The cheer went up as the barricade was breached. A few injured Skavs tried to defend themselves but were quickly dispatched, run through or shot by the soldiers of the unforgiving People's Army. A small number of Skavs were brave or fool enough to make a stand but they were overwhelmed in seconds, dragged down and stabbed to death.

"Remind me to thank that Flanders fellow," Jason appeared at Jonas's side, smiling his manic grin.

"That I will my friend," Jonas answered, his words a waste of breath because Jason had already moved on to find something else to slaughter.

They heard the blasts before they saw the approaching hover jets and somewhere to the east of their position the Avalonian hover jets from the government controlled suburbs of Kalverstone had dropped their payload and blown something up. Now they headed straight for Randell and his men.

"The two faced bastards!" Randell screamed. "Take cover lads!" he yelled to his men, assuming that the government had gone back on their agreement. Then the hover jets flew over them, circling around their position. One of Randell's men, holding aloft the green red dragon flag of the People's Army, stood defiantly in the middle of the road to face the hover jets as they circled back.

They lined up above Randell's corps, which for the most part tried to hide from the impressive killing machines. Randell watched as the pilot of the first hover jet flew low and almost close enough to touch someone raising their hand, he saluted the flag bearer and Randell's man saluted back with a smile wide and jubilant.

Flying over them the hover jets headed for the tower blocks. Randell, followed by his men ran into the middle of the road for a better view. He stood next to the man who still held his flag, the proud expression still on his face, Randell thought it was the expression of a man who had proved his worth and surprised himself in doing so.

"Brave bastard ain't ya," Randell shouted at the man and grinned as his men cheered the hover jets on as they approached the Skavite killing grounds of the high raise flat complex.

The hovers let fly with their missiles and the lead hover jet hit the nearest tower block, just below half way up to blow glass and concrete into the open air as fiery destruction rained down on the embattled Skavite horde below. The hover turned away as the second one opened fire and one of its missiles hit the floor above with the other disappearing into the hole made by the first hover jet's missiles.

A split second later all the windows of the tenth floor of the tower block blew out. the building groaned as its structural integrity was weakened by the attack and the hover jets turned away from the blast as the concrete quivered, smoke and flames took hold of the super heated structure.

Randell drew the sword he carried and raised it above his head. "With me!" he yelled and he ran towards the burning buildings, his men drew their weaponry and followed suit. Without looking back Randell knew his men followed, he knew down to a man that their bravery was unquestionable. He looked up as he ran and the hover jets turned in a sharp arc to bank high above the battleground.

Before the ground at the foot of the flats came into view, the hover jets had let out another barrage of their deadly death bringers, the missiles hurtled towards the tower blocks and slammed into two more of the large buildings and they too burst into flames as the highly flammable incendiaries inflicted maximum damage.

Randell and his men charged out from the street and onto the grass in front of the flats, they slowed nearly to a halt as the first building that had taken the missile fire swayed. Three of its floors were blazing and the smoke made it difficult to see how badly damaged it was. Then its structure failed dramatically as it collapsed in on itself. Debris from the imploding masonry spread away from the ruin, reaching as far as its neighbour to blind all those that stood in the soot and dust cloud. Thousands of dead Skavs littered the ground, it was a scene of complete devastation that resembled scenes of artwork depicting the pit of despair, as the wounded still writhed and reached out with blooded hands for mercy.

The hover jets turned again, banking sharply to face the

improvised fortresses. This time, with their missiles spent, they hovered around pumping thousands of bullets at their enemy and Randell's corps watched bodies being blasted apart as the high calibre rounds strafed the ground. By that time, all the flats were ablaze, the flames burnt unchecked as they spread quickly from room to room and sparks began to fly. The hover jets continued firing, turned slowly, seemingly unaffected by the bullets fired from the Skavs that began to fire back. A lucky shot found a small gap in the side grill of one of the death dealers, the bullet ricocheted around the hover jet finding its way into the back of the pilot's skull. The hover jet banked wildly as the pilot's arm, still gripping the controls dropped to the side. It swerved slowly to the left in a wide arc, taking twenty seconds to crash against one of the flaming flats.

The two remaining hover jets veered away from the smoke engulfed scene and took off south, back towards the government controlled part of the city. No one cheered at the destruction of the hover jet, there had already been too much death brought down upon the Skavites. Those that remained turned to look at Randell and his men charging at them, they were caught completely off guard. Those Skavs that were still able bodied turned to flee from the flats they had so desperately fought over, they gave not even a second thought as their comrades screamed as they leapt to their deaths to escape the flames of the blazing infernos.

"Die Skav bastards!" Randell yelled, as he shot and stabbed a man who tried to crawl away, his tracksuit already torn and blooded.

His men needed no orders; they charged at their stunned enemies and slaughtered the injured that no longer had the power within themselves to resist as above them the tower blocks turned to raging infernos. The frenzy of death only ended when all the Skavs lay motionless. Randell led his men away from the horrific scene recklessly in pursuit of the Skavites that had shown their cowardice and ran.

Sharpy stood with his hands clasped on the concrete plinth, staring out from the balcony over the city's square. All around him his men scurried about preparing to do battle with the People's Army. Jason de Silva and his troops had announced themselves two hours previous and reports of fighting reached him from different parts of the city. The hover jets had left, but many feared their return and fled the city to head north, choosing to run before the oncoming enemy that refused to be intimidated by the city's Skavite rulers.

Day had become night as the remnants of the daylight ebbed away, replaced by the moons and their varying light displays. Tonight's being extra special, as three of the world's moons aligned. Cerise, Ceinlys and Serene eclipsed one another. Serene created an outer circle of luminescence, Ceinlys near invisible blackness sparkled in front of it whilst Cerise sat before them both to create an inner red glow. The whole effect was made even more lurid by the wisps of cloud that moved the eerie lights across the ground in varying strengths and hues.

His closest friends joined him on the city hall's balcony to watch as a few thousand of the Skavs under his control surged onto the city's old market place from the square's southern most streets. The Skavs turned as one and drew whatever weapons they had at hand. Seconds later, the People's Army, led by Jason de Silva himself, charged into the city's ancient heart with their red dragon flags flying before them.

Sharpy checked his pistol as the two sides clashed he had just three bullets left. He felt in his pockets for bullets he knew he didn't have, in the chaos he had forgotten to get some brought to him from the ammunition store he had set up.

From another direction a few hundred Skavs rushed onto the square and gave hope to the beleaguered Skavites, but the hope was short lived as the relieving force turned out to be yet another group of Skavs in full rout. The People's Army entering the battle from the west was led by a broad shouldered tall man Sharpy didn't recognise. The man wielded a heavy broad sword easily and at the distance, he resembled an ancient warrior.

Jason de Silva fought like an insane god, there was no block or parry, there didn't appear to be any style or skill to his swordplay, he was berserk and hacking away with wanton disregard for his own life. Twice as the battle unfolded before him, Sharpy saw the leader of his enemy completely exposed and both times a man wearing nothing but black threw himself into the blow. de Silva didn't seem to notice as the People's Army made steady progress and Sharpy's Skavs were cut down, one step at a time.

Gun shots and screams, metal on metal and the general din of a pitched battle filled his ears. Sharpy looked around at his loyal men standing by his side awaiting orders. He looked back to the battle that raged below and considered his own mortality. Then he looked up at the tri-eclipse and decided that it was a bad omen if ever there was one.

"Let's get the fuck outta here!" Sharpy turned and walked quickly away from the sounds of battle, his men followed and stayed close to him.

All about them, the Skavite criminals readied themselves for the last defence of their captured city, they watched as their leader hurried along with his entourage following. Seeing their leader heading out the back doors of the town hall killed their dreams of empire and the morale that was left abandoned their already damaged enthusiasm and they scattered. They fled to spill out of the doors, to run north through the streets or anywhere that the People's Army hadn't yet touched.

They took flight uphill and raced toward the old financial district of Kalverstone, away from the battle and the screams of death, they ran up the shop lined streets toward freedom. Then their advance came to an abrupt end. The fleeing Skavs halted as though they had hit a brick wall; they tried to run against the press of their allies as other factions of Skavs ran from their own fight. Four lines of soldiers from the People's Army blocked the road, and row upon row of guns were levelled at them, halting their progress.

"Fire!" a voice ordered, loud enough for the Skavs to hear, let alone the troops that the command was aimed at.

The People's Army fired at once and the guns showered the retreating Skavs with a hail of lead. Sharpy moved just in time, he dived out of the way and crashed straight through the toughened glass of a shop window. Scrambling amongst the shards of glass he managed to stand, he wasn't alone he was surrounded by fleeing Skavs. They ran through to the rear of shop, looking for another way out. He found a fire escape at the back of the shop and burst through it into a tight alleyway; he saw the street up ahead and more of his men running and began to make his way toward them. Again the order to fire came and his men fell before his eyes.

Sharpy turned around to flee back through the fire door, to see it click shut leaving him in the alley alone. "Bastards!" he yelled and felt for his gun, but it wasn't there, his holster was empty, he must have dropped it when he fell through the shop front.

He turned and realised that his lip was quivering and he felt emotions that he had thought that he'd forgotten. '*I remember this, it must be fear*,' he thought as the enemy appeared at the entrance to the alley.

Jason dodged the dagger that swung at his face, and changed the direction that his sword was travelling; he switched back the blade to slash his attacker across the chest, the Skav fell over his own feet as he tried to turn and he spun around, clutching at his chest. Jason stepped up and stabbed the Skav through the neck and blood sprayed his face to mingle with the blood of a hundred other dead Skavs.

The last line of the braver Skavs began to falter as along the line of battle the Skavs were being systematically cut to pieces. The last remaining Skavs backed away and they too turned and fled as they gave up the ghost.

The cheer went up from the People's Army and Jason de Silva looked about him and smiled at his victory. He locked eyes with Randell, the broad shouldered warrior and he saluted him, holding his broad sword above his head. Jason returned the salute holding his sword in his hand.

Then the retreat halted as the Skavs were driven back onto the square, before Trevor's corps. They were marching in an orderly fashion firing in volley fire; their progress was slow but efficient and effective. The unruly mob of Skavite criminals were not used to regimented fighting, their lives up until that point had been all about the intimidation of others, the whole incentive behind their violence was that of financial gain and false respect. The People's Army on the other hand fought for an ideal, trying to save the nation that was Albion, trying to eradicate those that would rule them by force. They fought for the future, their children and their children's children. If there had ever been a better cause, none could bring it to mind. More than two thousand Skavs were driven back into the centre of the old city of Kalverstone, the People's Army surrounded them and formed a large circle to leave a ten foot perimeter, from the air it looked like a target.

The men and women who fought in the People's Army began to chant, "Skav scum, Skav scum," over and over, stamping their feet or rattling and banging weapons. They were all there, the corps of the People's Army that had entered the city. Jonas accompanied by his foreigners and Teddy Williams with his Black Jackets. The two Robinson brothers that hadn't been injured headed their troops and the remnants of Dominic's corps. Jason watched on as the chanting continued and developed into an almost party like atmosphere as the People's Army intimidated the Skavs, playing them at their own devilish game.

Some people in their crazed state even began to dance, closing the gap between themselves and the fearful Skavs, teasing them as they laughed before returning to their own line.

Finally the festivities ended and the massively muscled Ilan of the Northern Islanders charged, his axe raised above his head and he swung it before him, cutting three Skavs in half with a single swing. Kicking another that charged him; he roared a battle cry that was engulfed by the sounds of ten thousand shouts of death as the People's Army waded into their cowering enemy.

Those that chanted smiled; their eyes were wide and manic as they revelled in the death of so many Skavs. In later years the end of this battle would be known as 'The Culling of Kalverstone' as the last of the Skavs were dragged down and beaten to death, the vengeful nature of the People's Army became almost like a sporting event. Then it was over, the last Skav alive was sliced open and his guts were sent spilling onto the old market slabs as his captors turned him to face the ground, Jason smiled as the Skav screeched as he died.

Their victory complete, the People's Army went truly wild; they danced around the square and pressed in around Jason who was lofted into the air. He was carried to the steps of the town hall to be gently set onto his feet.

Jason walked to the top of the steps and was joined by his commanding officers. They smiled and embraced and were glad to have survived where so many had fallen.

Jason hushed the masses of jubilant revellers with raised hands, it took some minutes to coerce them but eventually they fell silent. "Today, we won a great victory," he said, the crowd responded to his words. Jason waited for them smiling as they partied before him. "The forces of evil have been driven out, we have liberated this beautiful old town, let this day never be forgotten. It has been a day of death and loss in pursuit of the greater good!" Jason raised his hands in salute of those that had followed him; they cheered him like a king, a god. Jason turned as they cheered, he walked into the old town hall of Kalverstone followed by his corps commanders, and they would occupy the town hall for the remainder of their short stay.

Jason walked through the heavy wooden front doors of the liberated seat of power. At the same time ten of Trevor's men were leading a large, broad shouldered Skav down a corridor opposite him, the man was shackled and dripping with gold.

"This is their leader, a present for you," Trevor spoke from behind their captive.

"How's Dominic?" Jason asked, looking to Randell and Trevor without acknowledging the prisoner's presence.

"I haven't heard yet, but I think it's just broken bones," Randell said, if he was concerned for his brother he didn't show it.

"He'll live," Trevor added.

Jason turned to the Skavite leader and looked him up and down. He wasn't impressed by the man who stared back at him, even now trying his thug tactics.

"What's your name?" Jason asked.

The Skav didn't answer; he just stared and grimaced and like a caged animal he snarled at his captors.

Trevor held out his hand and offered Jason an envelope. "This was found on him, it's addressed to you."

Jason opened the envelope and removed the contents. He was stunned by the photograph he held.

"No it can't be," he said to no one, he couldn't take his eyes from the photo, his naked wife wore a contorted mask of pain and Reginald Smith was on top of her grinning as he fucked his beautiful wife.

"I took dat photo," Sharpy said and grinned in spite of his hopeless position.

"Where is she?" Jason asked, he could feel the tendrils of

shock taking over his already fragile mind.

"She's dead, we fucked her to death," Sharpy answered, the confused faces of those around them changing to horror as the realisation of what had happened dawned on them.

"She made a good whore," Sharpy said, goading Jason, hoping for a quick death.

Jason drew his pistol and stepped closer to the Skavite gang boss, he pointed the gun at the man's groin and pulled the trigger.

Sharpy fell to his knees and began squealing like a stuck pig, his private parts a bloodied mess. Everyone took a step backwards as Jason looked down at the Skav that had ordered the rape of his beautiful Jacky, he let him bleed, crying out in pain for his broken penis, he then lifted the gun to the man's forehead and pulled the trigger once more.

The Skav fell dead to the marble floor, his blood running down the gaps in the ornate slabs; Jason emptied the clip into the man's corpse and screamed in his anger and the pain of a broken heart which was etched all over his face for his comrades to see.

Jason's followers looked to each other for guidance but none dared to approach their leader, Jason appeared to lose all his senses and stared wildly about him, his grief stricken eyes wide and glazed.

At last, he fell to his knees and wept, he sobbed uncontrollably, his shoulders shaking violently as he convulsed in his anguish.

Chapter 24

Mr Jones stood in the road with his henchmen standing behind him as the exodus from Kalverstone began. At first they trickled out a few at a time, and then the escaping Skavs flooded out as it became apparent that the city had been lost.

"We lost the city," the Skavites lamented as they fled from death at the hands of the People's Army and some of the Skavs did look visibly distressed at the outcome but most tried not to show concern, the respect from their peers meaning more than the outcome of the war.

Vehicles were directed into the fields just outside the city, as the camp increased in size rapidly.

One Skav opened the window of the vehicle he drove. "What's up?" he asked Mr Jones.

"You're with me now," Mr Jones stated in his business like tone. "Tell me how many men did they have?" he asked.

"Fucking thousands, tens of fucking thousands," the Skav lied and then drove into the field. In truth the youth hadn't seen any fighting and the facts were that the Skavite horde still outnumbered the People's Army. Although the People's Army had captured the ammunition, they could probably mount a decent counter offensive if they did it immediately.

Skavs began to contact each other, talking on their cellphones and soon most had got the news of where the Skavs were regrouping and under whose leadership.

By the time the tri-eclipse had passed, the Skavs had

regrouped and twenty thousand lost souls gathered around Gavin Jones' camp. They ate and drank and everything had been requisitioned from shops and houses in the locality. They laughed, joked and even killed one another as the inevitable fights broke out.

Mr Jones sat upon the bonnet of a vehicle and brushed grass from his jacket, he watched as a family was dragged from their farmhouse onto their own field. The farmer was tied to the field's wooden gate and his wrists were slit. Then his wife, son and daughter were relieved of their clothes and raped, the farmer was forced to watch as he died, slowly bleeding out.

"We gonna fuck till we leave!" an ugly and skinny Skav laughed in the farmers face as he sobbed aloud.

Mr Jones's phone rang as he was considering stopping the atrocity that unfolded before his eyes; he looked down as though he only just realised it was there and took the phone from his pocket.

"Hello," he said.

"Jonesy!" Farrell screamed at him.

"Mr Farrell, Sir," Mr Jones was guarded and cautious.

"Little birds tell me you and your allies lost Kalverstone!" Farrell sounded enraged and Jones knew that Farrell was at his most dangerous.

"I ain't lost nothing, it was that prick Sharpy!" Gavin Jones said and his courage increased with his anger, he didn't like being blamed for something that wasn't his fault. He told Farrell the facts as he saw them, which was easy to do at the distance. "That man commands authority but he ain't clever enough to command."

"That's maybe how it is," Farrell conceded, his voice sounded calmer to Jones as he paused to collect himself. "What's the situation like?"

"Sharpy started a civil war between the gangs, our numbers were hammered and half are dead as far as I can tell." Gavin

Jones tried to explain.

"I've been informed," Farrell interrupted. "Listen, Jones, Sharpy's dead, it happened earlier, you take control and retake Kalverstone and do it tonight. Now!"

Mr Jones looked around at his people; they had become silent as they slowly edged forward to gather around him, listening to half the conversation. Mr Jones quickly switched the phone's loud speaker on and used the situation to his advantage.

"The men won't go back in there," he said.

"Don't tell me what the men will and won't do!" Farrell blasted, bellowing and not realising so many of Mr Jones' men could hear him clearly.

"I won't do it," Mr Jones said calmly, listening to Farrell's breathing.

At that point Farrell got angry and more of the Skavs fell silent and strained to hear what was being said. "You get that group of inbred northern mother fuckers back into the city and kill that ponce de Silva!"

The Skavs around Jones looked past annoyed and on to angry. They took the insult from the man they had all considered to be almost a god as a personal slur.

"I won't do it, they deserve more than the death that you offer them they deserve at least a chance of survival." Mr Jones argued.

"They'll get whatever death I prescribe for em, you ungrateful bastard!" Farrell yelled, unbeknown to him how badly he'd fallen to Gavin Jones' quick thinking.

"Well I guess this conversation's over then!" Mr Jones cancelled the call and felt extremely pleased with himself; he had trapped his former boss into a string of comments that made him look like a hero in front of his newly formed army.

Reginald Smith stood close to Mr Jones; he could feel the mood of disappointment in the camp as the news spread to its fringes. He jumped onto the bonnet of the vehicle next to the one Mr Jones sat on.

"Jonesy, Jonesy!" Reginald began to chant.

Within a matter of seconds the entire camp took up the chant. Gavin Jones turned to Reginald and acknowledged his thinking with a quick bob of his head. *'That's official then, they follow me now,'* he thought as Reginald smiled back at him, still chanting.

Sunlight streamed down upon fields around Eldersfield. Thousands of tents covered the ground and thousands of people went about their business. Those tents were used as housing for the escaping politicians and their aides and the camp was a hub of activity as the people worked in and around the marquees that had been set up to house the retreating government.

Thousands of the retreating police force had also made it thus far and they camped with the few hundred military personnel that had remained loyal to the elected rulers of Albion.

Supplies, mainly foodstuffs and other essentials vital for the camp's survival had been organised for daily delivery. A few miles to the south and just within sight was a much larger camp, that one was a refugee camp, full of the citizens that had evacuated Capital City. The government tried to help them as much as it could, but there was only so much they could do, the people were mainly left to fend for themselves.

The largest marquee in the Government Encampment was located at the very centre and it housed the Cabinet, where the Minsters of the government held its council of war.

Peter Dickinson sat on an ornately carved wooden chair against the back wall of the huge tent in which hundreds of politicians were shouting and arguing with each other. Members of the House of Representatives had been called into session and for once, every member had turned up, along with their entourages of aides. The Speaker of the House smashed his gavel repeatedly on its wooden block but the sound of it was lost beneath the sounds of chaos as he called for order.

The opposition parties called for the Prime Minister's resignation, whilst the government called into play the ancient by-laws of times of warfare, no votes could be held until a time of peace. The politicking continued for hours without any firm resolutions.

Colonel Dempsey stood near the entrance of the marquee, watching the politicians bicker amongst themselves. With him were two of his Majors, his second in command Major Stevenson and the recently promoted Major Dawkins.

"We should have gone north with the King's men," Major Stevenson said, just loud enough for the other officers to hear him.

"Is it too late, do you think?" the Colonel asked. "What do you think Dawkins?"

"I don't have thoughts on matters of politics Sir," Dawkins answered unable to see the funny side of the situation, he found the whole scene disturbing.

"Lighten up Dawkins," Colonel Dempsey laughed.

Dawkins didn't answer; he stared at the chaos unfolding on the floor of the tent and wondered how anyone could make out what was going on.

The well dressed ladies and gentlemen certainly knew how to argue their point, as no one wanted to concede any argument and more than a few personal insults were bantered back and forth.

The newly promoted Commissioner Kingsley stood at Peter Dickinson's right hand side, he turned to the Prime Minister, his eyes pleaded for peace.

Peter Dickinson had also had enough of the pointless bickering that was getting them nowhere; he moved his head slightly, shaking it in a gesture that might have been a nod. The Prime Minister moved his massive bulk and stood up slowly, he got to his feet by himself and he refused the help of one of his aides, waving the young man away as he came close.

Seeing the Prime Minister stand was enough to silence some of the voices, enough so that the speaker of the house could be heard calling for silence, his hammering of the gavel no longer went unnoticed. Peter Dickinson raised his right hand, waving it palm downwards in a motion signalling for silence.

"That's better. We are at war with more than one enemy. We are surrounded by those that would end us totally and forever." The Prime Minister looked around the silenced crowd. "We, the political privileged are all that stands between democratic choice and chaotic feudalism that would consume the land of Albion," he paused and dared any to respond. "Ladies and gentlemen," he continued, calm but serious. "We neither have the time, nor the luxury to argue about the finer points of past, present and future. Your seats will remain as they are and there will be no more wrangling on a personal level. We need decisive and unanimous action and we need it today without further delay," he waved the army officers forward, and as they moved, he sat back down.

The three officers walked forward through the crowd of politicians and felt many eyes boring into them. This was their battlefield and they let the military be aware of the fact. When they reached the Prime Minister the three officers turned to look out at the faces of the politicians, Major Stevenson again wished that he had gone north with the King's own.

Colonel Dempsey cleared his throat. "Esteemed Members of the Chamber, I stand before you at the request of our leader. As you all know we have lost the capital of Albion, its population starves and suffers and the disenfranchised are scattered throughout the land." he paused for a second, letting his words play in the minds of his audience. "But I have graver news to tell you."

"What could be worse than losing Capital City and our seat of power?" a politician heckled from the floor. With that comment, a murmuring began to spread through the marquee and the Speaker was forced to shout for order and sweat ran down his brow.

"Our scouts have reported a large Skavite horde headed directly for our position here at Eldersfield," Colonel Dempsey said and the murmurs silenced at his words. For perhaps the first time in its history, the assembly was completely silent; the members looked to one another in shocked disbelief.

"What to do?" one lady sounded panicked.

"All is not lost," Dawkins bellowed as he stepped up to join the Colonel, he faced the crowd before him and stared until they became quiet again.

"Well, go on Major, do you have something to say?" the Prime Minister asked from behind the other two officers.

"We can fight," the Major said loudly. "I stand here watching men without honour argue over the scraps of a broken nation. I say to you ladies and gentlemen, reclaim your honour and put down this scum rebellion." he finished speaking almost as a poet putting passion into verse.

The assembly were silent for a moment and then shouting erupted once more as the insults from the army officer hit home, Dawkins looked to his Colonel.

"Don't worry Dawkins, you only said what I was thinking myself," Colonel Dempsey said to the Major, '*Courage indeed*,' he thought as he tried to block out the sounds of furious voices.

Kieron, the nineteen year old Skav, that had saved Douglass Farrell's life from the police sniper whilst he crossed the bridge that spanned one of the many canals of Capital City, looked behind him as he marched away from the smoke stained skies. The city burned in places, the flames and chaos raged unchecked and civil order had broken down to be replaced by all the chaos that the Skavite horde had to offer.

"You, you're Kieron ain't ya?" Farrell asked. He had walked

up from Kieron's blind side to catch him off guard.

Kieron turned to look up at the large Skav leader. "Wassup Mr Farrell Sir?" he managed to reply without appearing to be frightened.

Farrell was flanked by two burly men, both well known hard men from Albion's underground criminal world and both more than willing to kill or be killed for the man they served.

Albion's criminal crime boss stepped up close to Kieron and put an arm around his shoulder, dwarfing him. "I owe you thanks," Farrell said as he looked back to the south, following Kieron's stare.

"Nah man, soz hard pig bastard had to die," Kieron cast his eyes down to look at the ground as he kicked at a tuft of grass.

"The power is going to run out at some point, Albion would die without its infrastructure and it is starting to fail," Farrell said. He did not acknowledge the respect given to him. "Tomorrow we need to move north and attack the government; we need control of Albion so I can impose my rule." Farrell watched the smoke pluming above them, black ugly clouds darkening the day.

"Them pencil pushin turds gonna die then?" Kieron asked, his confidence soaring as Farrell had taken him into his confidence, made him privy to his plans. '*He must trust me*,' Keiron thought and his respect for the top man of all Albion grew more.

"One of my commanders died in the struggle for Capital City," Farrell's mouth twitched at the corners as he looked to the skyline of the ruined capital, he watched as tiny flames rose from within a tall structure, its roof gave way and the tiny flames seemed to lick the sky.

"I guess there's nobody there to put out the fires," Kieron said, looking at the same burning masonry. He could feel his excitement mounting and he fantasised that he was getting promoted.

"I want you to take his place; you've got more than five

thousand of my men. Take them north and make haste, lead them against the government." Farrell was pleased with the youth, not least for saving him from the sniper's bite.

"Where they at?" Kieron asked.

"Eldersfield, it'll take you a day to march the distance by foot," Farrell said.

"Surely we ain't peggin it, its miles away," Kieron griped.

"Stop ya bitchin, come see me in the morning," Farrell said. He smiled at the young Skav, who was now the proud leader of men.

"Thank you Mr Farrell… Douglass," Kieron dared call his boss by his first name and Farrell grunted, then he turned and walked off laughing. Keiron asked himself. *'Why shouldn't I call him Douglass?' 'I saved his life didn't I?'*

Chapter 25

Skav vehicles sped south past Kalverstone heading towards Ramby, the intention was to thread between the Midland's two major cities, heading down the country's major roads towards the capital. The sun had risen just above the horizon and the Skavite horde, led by Gavin Jones, moved away from the People's Army. Reginald Smith, or Smithy as the only surviving child of old Ma Smith had come to be known, was driving the lead vehicle in the convoy of criminals. The force followed Mr Jones one hundred percent and offered him their allegiance after the revelations of the morning before. Mr Jones had split his new army into twenty groups, each with its own commander who was the only one told the time and place of the rendezvous. Mr Jones split his forces for the sake of speed; he needed to make haste in escaping Jason de Silva and his revenging army. Jones didn't like the risks involved, but he knew he had no choice if he wanted to get the bulk of his army moved from the Midlands to fight another day.

Over two hundred vehicles raced past Ramby in the first convoy. They travelled down Albion's major highway and must have looked a frightful sight with over a thousand Skavs pointing guns at any vehicle that was about so early in the morning. Most of the vehicles simply pulled over to let the danger pass them by, a few fools tried to race ahead and their vehicles became target practice for the Skavites near the front of the convoy. Gangster rap music blasted from the vehicles and any conversation was a struggle above the noise. Most Skavs sang along to their music as they headed south, towards rather than away from the war.

An hour past Ramby and the convoy led by Gavin Jones approached a major settlement and the convoy slowed as it neared the service station that served the large town. Mr Jones turned his radio off. “Get ready lads,” he said over his shoulder, not sure whether the station was guarded or not and he did not take chances.

As the lead vehicle entered the service station they could see people running in all directions, none of them were armed and all of them were in a state of panic. The vehicles passed the restaurant and the motel, and drove directly into the fuel cell bays of the garage forecourt.

“Spread the word, get the fuel cells powered up and get gone, I want no fucking about,” Mr Jones ordered, speed was still the essence of his plan’s fruition.

Eight cell bays stood empty and a young, freckled youth sat at the operation booth. Smithy pulled his vehicle into bay one and seven other vehicles pulled in around him. Gavin Jones stepped out of his vehicle’s passenger side and walked steadily and purposefully into the operation booth. The shop was filled with all manner of snacks and soft drinks. The young lad had hidden himself behind his counter, his fear was apparent; he held his face in his hands. Mr Jones leaned over the counter as dozens of his men ransacked the shop, emptying it of everything useful or otherwise. “It’s this simple, operate the charge points on the forecourt, help to get us moving and I’ll let you live,” he cocked his gun as he finished his sentence.

The young man nervously looked up from behind his hands, his tear stained face making him look dirty.

Mr Jones pointed his gun at the youth, resting its barrel on his forehead. “Up ya get, ya brainless bastard.”

“Please don’t hurt me,” the youth stammered, a wet patch stained his trousers as he pissed himself.

"Up you get," Mr Jones motioned with his gun, and pulled it away, it was clear that he'd made his point.

The youth got to his feet slowly, not daring to move too fast and gingerly he stretched out his hand to press eight green buttons, the word 'Charge' was written on all of them.

Mr Jones smiled and pulled the pistol back level with his temple. "Now that's real sociable of ya!" he said and turned around and walked back to the door. "Don't make me come back in here," he added as he opened the glass panelled door.

"Ye ye yes Sir," the spotty youth stammered.

Vehicles filled the service station queuing system, waiting their turn for the free top up and the Skavites ran amok. Mr Jones watched as his men beat innocent people and ran through the businesses and buildings, to steal anything that wasn't nailed down. He watched one scene as he walked back to his vehicle; one of his men repeatedly stabbed a father that shielded his daughters from the Skav's advances. Surprisingly, something was sickened inside of him as the man's wife was slapped away when she tried to save her husband, his mind doubting his righteous disposition for the first time.

"Must be getting old," he told himself, as he climbed back into his seat.

"What?" Smithy asked, as he heard Mr Jones mumbling.

"Nothing, move the vehicle, I want to get going as soon as possible," he said, shutting the vehicle's door. Every available space on the vehicles was crammed full. Every scrap of food and drink had been taken from the services, their cells were powered to full and the vehicles were ready to roll once more. The whole process had taken less than half an hour, the vehicles' fuel cells whined as they lined up along the exit slip road. Mr Jones opened his door and climbed out as the vehicle's fuel cells strained against the power of the brakes.

"Let's have it!" he yelled and got back into his seat and closed the door as Smithy disengaged the brakes. The vehicle took off like a rocket. Gavin looked over his shoulder, staring back at the deserted station, *'Is this how it's going to be, like a ghost town wherever we go?'* once more doubt blossomed in his mind, *'It's too late to change sides now, Mr Jones.'* in his mind he knew now it was all about survival and he smiled but it was without any trace of humour, he was trapped.

"It was so much easier when we were in it for the gold," he said and looked at Smithy in a vain hope for intellectual conversation.

"I like it dis way boss, all da chaos innit," Reginald said and he floored the accelerator and the rest of the vehicles followed suit.

The Skav that had killed the man that protected his family looked in the mirror as he cleaned his blade and then slid the knife back into its sheath. He stood in front of the urinal and unzipped his flies. As he started to urinate he heard the vehicles' whine alter pitch as the cells were engaged and they began to move off. He heard the whine alter again as the cells pushed against the brakes.

He'd only half finished when he ran out of the toilet; his tracksuit bottoms were wet around his groin. He ran past a large group of people, some were bleeding and others were holding torn clothes about them and he burst through the doors onto the warm tarmac. He was greeted by the sight of his colleagues driving away down the highway.

"Ah fuck!" he said and quickly scanned the service station for a vehicle to steal.

Suddenly the doors burst open behind him, the crowd of unhappy people had followed him out. He whirled around and growled, baring his teeth. "Stay back ya mother fuckers," he snarled.

They ignored him and approached him slowly.

"Show some fucking respect!" he snapped, trying to control the situation.

The crowd surrounded the Skav, the bruised wife of the murdered husband came to the front, holding a carving knife that a member of the kitchen staff had just handed to her.

Flight came to mind too late, the citizens had blocked off his escape route. He drew his knife and thrust it at the people but he was quickly grabbed from behind. He screamed insults as the mob pulled him down and he thrashed uselessly until he was pinned to the tarmac by the weight of hands. Then he squealed in pain as his own knife slowly entered him, piercing his abdomen. The murdered husband's wife smiled, revelling in the murderer's agony.

Philip Robinson sat on his horse at the head of his cavalry. Dave Hilbert, his Bannerman sat beside him with the stallion flag unfurled. The long line of horsemen and women had camped the night at the very fringes of Kalverstone just south of the old city before the countryside made way for the outskirts. They had watched the far off explosions and heard the muffled blasts, but were too far away to get to the action. Now they had broken camp and skirted around the government held half of the city. They made good time and did not want to meet the government forces they had no desire at this time to fight, especially as the horses would probably scatter and bolt with the sounds from the hover jets engines. They had found that out the previous day when one of the government flying machines flew low over them.

They had broken camp early and decided to enter the city. Messages had arrived in the night proclaiming the victory of the People's Army but that didn't mean there was no work to be done, so Philip ordered the advance. The sun had only been up an hour when the front of the column turned toward the city's centre, the suburbs up ahead had been plundered and ravaged as the city's infrastructure had collapsed. Philip's cavalry entered from the east of the city and they bunched together as they formed up eight abreast to fill the four lanes of empty road.

Philip's Bannerman and Ethan's friend that had fought so bravely at the battle of Mount Aamor sat at Philip's side holding his flag proudly.

"The weather's warming up," Dave said, not really caring either way.

"Yeah man, the season's definitely changed," Philip agreed. "Tell me, what are you going to do when this is all over?" Philip asked.

"Let's hope it don't end too quickly," Dave said.

"Why by the five moons would you say that?" Philip asked, shocked at his attitude.

"Well I'm liking the adventure and also, I love killing Skavs," Dave answered solemnly.

"I suppose everything that's bad has its good points," Philip ceded, seeing Dave's point of view.

"Pros and cons," Dave agreed.

"Ain't you worried you might die?" Philip asked him, wondering if this mad man had any fear.

"Well I ain't a religious man, but if I were I would say I'd rather have my honour intact and go to hell than be a coward and reside in heaven," Dave smiled at his own comment, pleased with his answer.

"Let's hope you don't have to find out any time soon," Philip said and turned to the man who had fast become a close friend.

The cavalry crested a humped bridge, a railway running beneath its raised span and all of a sudden vehicles raced down the main road toward Philip and his corps.

The lead vehicles slammed their brakes on when they saw the masses of horse ahead carrying flags at the fore, one of which they recognised as the Dragon flag of Jason de Silva's People's Army. Blue smoke filled the air above the road as the mass of the vehicles had to stop in a short distance.

"Skavite bastards," Philip yelled, as the cars began to shunt each other, blocking the road ahead.

The People's Army drew their weapons, mainly swords and long daggers, spears and lances but a few had hand guns also.

"We gonna have to attack on foot," he said to his Bannerman. "Dismount!" he stood in his stirrups as he yelled out his order to his men.

Up the road not fifty metres ahead of them, their enemy began clambering out of their vehicles, some were a little dazed and obviously suffered from the collisions and all of them were caught off guard, surprised at the appearance of cavalry. Philip waited for a few seconds whilst his people ran up the line of march. Philip raised his right hand, holding his long sword aloft. He looked about him at his massing corps and his eyes rested on Dave Hilbert, "Charge!" he yelled and sprang forward just inches ahead of the rest of his army.

Philip thought of his Bannerman and wondered if he was going to enjoy the slaughter, the Skavs had no chance, they were badly disorganised and grossly outnumbered.

Some of the Skavs drew hand guns and fired into the charging mass of flesh. Some tried to run, their lust for the fight gone once they realised that they would lose. Some unfortunates stood no chance, trapped in their vehicles and unable to open the doors because of the other vehicles from their column had crashed in to them.

Then Philip's men reached the foot of the bridge and the first Skavs, they swarmed around them and it only took moments as they were disarmed and unceremoniously put to the sword. Soon the bridge became slick with blood and every Skav was dead. Only those right at the rear of the convoy managed to escape.

Philip jumped over the bonnet of a vehicle to slash a Skav diagonally across the chest, he fell away squealing as another jumped up on the next vehicle's roof, the Skav levelled his pistol at Philip's head. Philip looked at his death, unable to move as his life threatened to flash before his eyes and then his own flag came from behind and above him, its metal tipped flag pole pierced the Skav in his chest. The Skav's shot went harmlessly into the air, lost above the heads of Philip's corps, as Dave pushed forward. The flagpole entered the Skav's right lung and he coughed up blood, spraying the air with his death. He grabbed the flag with bloody hands as he fell to his knees but he was unable to fall because Dave was holding him up.

Philip turned to look at his Bannerman and saw a Skav jump at him from his unprotected flank. Dave was completely oblivious to the Skav's presence and Philip drew his hand gun and he killed the Skav with a wild and lucky shot, he had no time to aim as the Skav raised his arm which held his long blade. Philip had returned the favour, saving Dave's life and in that instant they had entwined their souls in brotherhood and friendship till the ending of their days.

Then the Skavs were trying to escape as the People's Army swamped the bridge. Skavs were brought to their knees and suffered the greatest of indignities; their lives were taken in the name of justice. Around them, Philip's men were going berserk; hacking at the Skavs that fell to their knees in surrender, one Skav had his ear bitten off by one of the cavalrymen. Another was blinded, his eyes were plucked from his skull and he made a grisly sight as he screamed and felt his way as Philip's people teased him with the points of their blades.

Philip looked at Dave, who looked at the flag, its white and black was infected by the blood of the Skav it had killed.

"Leave it there, never wash it out," Philip ordered his Bannerman and Dave looked back at him, a question in his eyes. "To remind us of this war, lest we forget," Philip said, thinking of the generations to come after they had long gone.

Dave nodded and they both stood and looked. The Skavs that hadn't got away were all but dead, finished off at the point of the sword as the blood thirsty orgy came to an end.

Jason sat on the ornate wooden chair in the Town Hall's conference room; the room was filled with the People's Army's commanders and their lackeys. Men and women shouted orders, the recipients of which ran off to complete their tasks. Thousands of the city's townsfolk that had lay hidden came to the Town Hall, they brought gifts and provisions for their liberators and some joined the ranks of Jason's army, coerced by Captains that Jason didn't know.

As all that was going on, Jason sat high in his chair, not speaking a word as he overlooked the comings and goings. The morning had all but ticked by, working towards the day's zenith. Jason hadn't slept, he just sat there in the chair thinking of Jacky and grieving at her broken life. He sat and looked as spent as his tears and he thought about the revenge he would have and the beautiful smile his Jacky used to wear.

'*I need to bury my wife*,' the thought occurred to him.

Something had changed within him, there was a definite shift of sanity as his mind had snapped with the pressures of his loss. He was no longer the man that he had been before; he had stepped over the thin line that separated the sane from the insane.

Ethan and the Robinson brothers and Jimmy, Jonas and Teddy approached him, to stand before their leader. None dared to speak, they feared that he was unstable but none of them wanted to know for sure if their friend was crazy, it would break their hearts and ruin their plans.

"Well?" Jason spoke nonchalantly and he remained slumped in his chair.

Randell cleared his throat, relieved that Jason wanted to communicate. "The remnants of the Skavite horde regrouped north of the city, they burnt a village to the ground and wiped out the people," he said, not knowing if he did the right thing by informing Jason where his wife's tormentor may have fled to.

"Have you found my wife yet?" Jason asked, straightening

in his seat. "I mean her corpse," he added, looking forlorn and lost, darkness ringed his tired eyes.

"We haven't but we know who has it," as Ethan spoke, he looked directly to Jason's eyes and he prayed to every god that Jason wouldn't go berserk, but he knew his leader had a right to know.

"Who has her?" Jason asked, his eyes narrowed and his lips thinned as he leaned forward almost out of his chair.

"We checked the city's street cameras," Teddy stepped up to Ethan's side to defend, if necessary, the man he pretended to hate. "Up at the station, they never revoked my security clearance, so I still get access to certain facilities. It was Reginald Smith; he loaded a body bag into the storage compartment of a vehicle the day before we took the city. He took off with the local gang boss, a man called Mr Jones, notorious around these parts even before the troubles began. I would think that it would have been him that gave the orders to attack your house and start the troubles at Mount Aamor."

Ethan nodded, turning from Teddy back to Jason. "They escaped the city ahead of our advance," he said.

"We attack them, now, this instant!" Jason rose from his seat shouting. Everyone in the hall turned to look, but none dared to say a word.

None but Philip, who pushed his way through the crowd in front of Jason's temporary throne. "They've already gone, running south. They split up into small groups, we ran into one of them as we entered the city."

Philip's brothers surrounded him joyfully, only Dominic stayed out of the hugs because his upper torso and left arm were rigid in his cast.

"What the fuck happened to you?" Philip laughed, and in that instant the atmosphere changed.

"I'll tell ya later," Dominic said, wincing with pain, as he tried not to move too quickly.

"Clear the hall, clear the city! We head south and give chase. I want every Skav dead by day's end!" Jason yelled and stepped away from the chair. His commanders moved aside to create a path for him to walk down. Ethan, Jimmy and Randell screamed orders as they followed him. Philip turned to Trevor and Dominic. "What's wrong with Jay?"

"It's Jacky," Dominic sounded sad, his gaze followed Jason's back as he left the hall. "They raped, tortured and hung her," Trevor said, wiping a tear from his face as he remembered Jason's lovely wife.

Chapter 26

After a brief rest and under the cover of night, five thousand Skavs marched as quietly as they could. They approached the city of Eldersfield which was bathed in the light of the moon Serene. The Skavs were jumpy in part because the surreal glow almost tricked the eyes into seeing shadows everywhere, even against the city's far off buildings and in part because their drugs were wearing off and withdrawal symptoms were jangling nerves. They could see a few guards doing their rounds; tiny little figures in the distance but other than that, the camps of the government forces looked at peace.

A large refugee camp lay to their west, they had skirted around the camp, because it was not what they were after. Their target was the government whose forces had been thinly spread throughout the south of Albion, thanks in part to Gerard Fontaine, who had ordered the forces to be divided at Douglass Farrell's request.

'*Divide and be conquered*,' Kieron thought. His confidence was high; he knew the enemy hadn't spotted them.

Kieron had ordered complete silence from his men; they kept his command close to their hearts, which pounded with the thoughts of the combat to come. They crept within the last half mile of the camp. Amazingly the camps sentries still hadn't noticed them. The camp was vast, it housed all the politicians and their aides and followers, here was all of the workers from the government offices that had been burnt to a cinder. There were thousands of them, pencil pushers and office juniors still attempting to run the nation. Apart from the government workers, there were also a few hundred military personnel and a few thousand police constables that had made it to Eldersfield.

The Skavite forces hoped the element of surprise would win the battle for them as they crept closer and closer, the grass making the barest rustle under hand and foot. They crawled within a quarter of a mile; the sentries at that distance could easily be made out walking the route that edged the camp's perimeter.

Two of the sentries paused, as they saw the grass swaying in a windless night. They peered into the luminous night that surrounded the advancing Skavs and they all froze still on their hands and knees, with hearts threatened to burst from their chests as the adrenalin and withdrawal made pulses race.

"Alarm, alarm!" the two sentries yelled as they identified the movement in the tall grass.

Bullets fizzed over Kieron's head as the sentries opened fire and the trace of the bullets left lines of light in his vision.

"Yaahhhhh!" Kieron stood, already at the run even before he reached his full height.

Battle cries and screams split the peace of the night, the senses for a moment confused, as along the Skavite lines, men stood and charged up the gentle slope towards the camp. More gun fire penetrated the night as gun fire from both sides erupted. Chaos ensued as half dressed people panicked, woken from their slumber they raced around screaming, not knowing what to do.

Less than a hundred metres separated the Skavite forces from the low stone wall that edged the politician's camp. Two heavy machine guns that overlooked the slope and protected the approach were brought into play as soldiers made it to their posts. They opened fire into the ranks of the charging Skavs five metres to Kieron's left. One of his men seemed to burst apart as his flesh disintegrated under the high calibre rounds. His men fell all around him as he dived face first into the dirt. The direction of the anti personnel weapon changing as it swept overhead and again Kieron stood at the run and sprinting to the wall, he leapt straight over it. A soldier jumped at him, silhouetted by the camp's lights that had come alive. Kieron shot the man dressed in khaki and he grunted but came on with his knife raised above him. Kieron shot two more times before the soldier's forward momentum ceased and the soldier finally gave up and slumped to the ground, succumbing to his wounds.

High commissioner Kingsley lay awake in his bed, reading reports from his Inspectors. Thousands had made it to Eldersfield and even more had made it out of the city to retreat to other towns and camps.

"Alarm, alarm!" the muffled shout went up somewhere off to the south. Then gun fire sounded from that edge of the camp before he could stand. He pulled his boots on and took a look at himself in his tall mirror. His patterned pyjamas were hardly the clothes for a fight. '*They could have given me time to dress*,' he thought and pulled his coat from the back of the chair that stood next to his bed. He pushed his arms into the coat sleeves and it covered most of what he wore, at least to his knees. He retrieved his hand gun and his heavy cane from the wooden chest at the foot of his bed. "That'll have to do," he said to his reflection as he took another look in the mirror.

Kingsley stepped through the tent flaps and into the night and he joined the chaos that moments earlier had been a camp in slumber. All about him men and women ran in their nightclothes, the police officers in that part of the camp began to group around him as he emerged from his tent.

"Right lads!" he yelled, as more and more of his men joined his group, carrying whatever weapons they could get their hands on. "Let's get into this fight!" he pointed his cane off to the southern edges of the camp.

Commissioner Kingsley turned to look into the night, down the hill which sloped just enough for him to see the battle unfolding. Along the bottom of the camp, the low stone wall had been breached, the soldiers on sentry duty had been overrun and in the distance, the men fighting looked like toys in a dream, a horrible nightmare as the Skav forces pushed into the camp. The low ranking government officials that had been placed at that edge of the camp had panicked and they fled into the camp, falling into tents, they pressed for the gaps between the canvas and they tripped over the ropes that held them fast.

Kingsley began to march towards the nearest part of the fight, perhaps a thousand metres away but for some reason he looked south west and he witnessed a crazy scene, politicians, councillors and their aides had charged the far right of the attacking force to catch them completely off guard and they pushed them back over the wall.

The closer Kingsley got to the fighting, the more chaotic it became. Tents fell in as people scrambled to get up the hill, fearful of the combat taking place behind them. On and on Kingsley ran and the numbers of his force grew as they charged towards the stone wall. Then, without any notice they were in the thick of it, the sounds of combat became actual combat.

All around him civilians were being executed and the government personnel were struggling to defend themselves against the highly motivated enemy force that pressed ever forward. The surprise night attack had penetrated deep into the camp, tents blazed as braziers were knocked over, sparks and burning red hot ashes sprayed canvas and other flammable materials to spread the fires further.

“Fucking bastards!” Kingsley yelled, and he whipped the nearest Skav with his cane and then shot him in the face at point blank range.

Constables slammed into the Skavs and tried to halt their advance, the small army contingent led by Major Dawkins hammered at the Skavite left flank at the same time. The disorganised rabble stood no chance against their military discipline. The initial retaliation from the government forces halted the Skavite advance, but the battle hung by a thread, the numbers were almost even, their determination the same. Then without warning, the tide of the battle turned as thousands of government clerks and officials waded into the fray, the fleeing non-combatants turned and found the courage to lend weight to that of the police and military.

A man wearing nothing more than a knee length night gown, which was stretched about his waist, appeared at the commissioner's side; he was barefoot and armed with nothing more than a pen. In the same instant a burly and heavily muscled Skav carrying a huge long sword jumped at him, Kingsley held his cane above him to ward off the blow, but it was knocked out of his hand as he fell over and the Skav stepped up, determined to end Kingsley's life with a stroke of his sword.

Commissioner Kingsley stared his doom in the face and as the Skav raised his sword above his head and was ready to strike, the the little fat man dressed for bed and writing by candlelight, jumped beneath the raised arms of the attacker and buried his pen deep up into the flesh under his chin. The surprised Skav staggered back, shocked as the office worker withdrew his ballpoint and stabbed him again in his shoulder. He dropped his sword and tried to flee, but the grimacing clerk had other ideas, he jumped up onto the back of the Skav, wrapped his free arm around the criminal's neck and finally buried his pen in the Skavs temple. The Skav hit the floor at the side of the commissioner, the look of surprise was still in his eyes as the clerk withdrew his weapon and disappeared into the fighting. Kingsley could hardly sit upright for laughing; he placed his hands on his knees and roared insanely. *'The pen truly is mightier than the sword,'* he thought to himself, glad that the metaphor proved to be true on this night.

"There's fucking thousands of em!" a Skav yelled in Kieron's face as they fought on up the slight gradient. Black smoke darkened the night as the tents caught fire with the sparks that blew on the otherwise pleasant breeze. Kieron swung his sword and cut off the head of a constable with its sharpened edge. He looked to his left and right and saw that both flanks were being pushed back as his battle line was met, his enemy were proving themselves. '*Maybe if we can hold a united front we can still win through*,' he thought as he stepped backwards to edge back down the slope. As he stepped, he looked for his next victim but suddenly the man who'd shouted at him fell screaming and holding his face. Then dismay overtook him as he saw soldiers fighting and killing his men.

It was at that point that Kieron realised the battle was lost, he spun on his heels as a military officer swung at him with the butt of his rifle.

Kieron ducked beneath the crude blow and sprinted down the hill into the safety of the smoke filled night.

"Bastard Skav!" Major Dawkins yelled after the retreating Skavite commander.

Dawkins could just make Kieron out among his fellow Skavs fleeing for their lives, he was the one that turned around to make rude gestures as he ran.

Serene disappeared as daylight announced its return with a steadily increasing brightness on the horizon. Serene's luminescent properties were no match for the power of the sun and at last, like the Skavs, Serene conceded defeat and retreated. The camp was alive with activity after the night's battle; the government counted its dead and tended to its wounded. Under armed guard, the captive Skavs were put to work, burying the dead and cleaning the ground of broken and burnt equipment.

Peter Dickinson and the Cabinet stood with their military commanders at the top of the hill to survey the damage. "Have you got a body count yet?" Peter Dickinson, the fat Prime

Minister asked as he wafted the smell of burnt flesh from his nostrils.

"Not yet, but it's probably thousands on both sides," an aide replied.

"Would you look at that?" Kingsley pointed south, shading his eyes against the sun as he looked into the distance.

To the south, the refugee camp that housed tens of thousands of the displaced citizens of Capital City was on the move. Its population spread out in two directions, east and west and the ground almost seemed to shift in the distance.

"Me thinks they can smell the dead!" Commissioner Kingsley leaned forward on the walking stick he'd acquired to replace his broken cane.

"Or maybe the shit coming up from the south," Dawkins thought out loud.

Major Stevenson stood with his hands clasped behind his back in his usual stance, half at ease and half at attention, he stood next to his Colonel "Maybe a tactical withdrawal would be the thing, another fight like that and we'll break," he said confidently.

Peter Dickinson turned to the Colonel, who nodded his agreement to the Major's statement.

"Where are all the troops?" the Prime Minister asked, as he threw his hands in the air, his mood changed and he became angry.

"They're spread throughout Albion, protecting the towns and cities against the Skav hordes," the Colonel said and he frowned as he remembered where the orders came from.

At the same time the Prime Minister flushed scarlet as he too remembered who gave the order to divide their forces. "Surely your trained soldiers can beat off a few raggedy criminals?" he suggested, thinking of Gerald Fontaine.

"A few yes, but there's tens of thousands of the bastards," Colonel Dempsey kept his calm.

Peter Dickinson seemed to slump, drained of all enthusiasm for the fight. He turned to his military commander. "What do you suggest?" he asked.

"If we stay here we're dead! We have a large military base at Edmondsville; a large force is stationed there. Its fifty miles away, near the sea. If we make our way there we can pick up any troops as we go. There are a few villages and small towns along the route," the Colonel looked hopeful, his contingency plan was the only course for survival.

"We should go north before we head east, to give the refugees space to manoeuvre," Stevenson suggested.

The powerful men assembled nodded in agreement. After all, their sole purpose for being in the job was to serve the people that had elected them.

Chapter 27

Farrell watched angrily as his advance force limped back into camp, a few at a time. He stood waiting for his newly elected commander but none of the faces belonged to Kieron, the man that had saved his life.

How many returned he couldn't tell, but it was less than two thousand and most sported injuries of some description. Every one of his returning Skavs were bone weary almost to the point of passing out with exhaustion.

"Five thousand men!" Farrell ranted as he paced in front of his gang bosses that stood sensibly out of reach. "I sent five thousand bastards at em!"

No one dared speak, lest he vent his anger on them personally. 'An angry Farrell was a murderous Farrell', was the saying amongst his men.

"Put the word out, I want Kieron's head on a plate!" Farrell didn't turn to face any of his men; he just spoke the words as calmly as he could. He'd made his decision. "I owe him fuck all," he said to himself.

A phone started to ring in the pocket of one of his commanders' jackets and Farrell turned to glare at the guilty coat until its owner, a tall dark haired fellow with black teeth and a face that looked like a rat, removed the phone from his pocket.

He flicked the phone open, "Wassup?" he answered the call and tried not to look at Farrell who now stared at him. He began to sweat as his lord and master kept an unwavering gaze on him.

"Well?" Farrell spoke loudly, asking the man what the phone call was about and he only needed half a reason to kill the ugly gang boss.

'Rat Face's dark hair was getting damp as sweat ran down his scalp. He knew the position he was in, he closed his phone and tried to smile as he put it in his pocket. "Tis dem government, they're leavin my lord," the man bowed, happy for the distraction.

Farrell's eyes widened at the news. "Are you certain?"

"Yessir! Homie undercover Skavs, ya get me blud?" the gang boss replied, almost begging to be believed.

"How reliable is this spy?" Farrell took a step towards the man, silently demanding answers.

"Undercover Skavs my lord, them's hench nuff said," the ugly man pleaded.

Sometimes Farrell had trouble deciphering the Skav language, but this time, the meaning was clear, the source was reliable.

"Right then, get your bastards up and marching, we're havin' the fuckers!" Farrell bellowed, he pondered for a moment as he watched his men run off to do his bidding. '*Why would they move from a dug in position?*'

The gang boss that had received the news stepped forward. "Sir," he said, becoming brave as he approached Farrell. "Them government peeps is hurtin, they banged up innit," he showed a double row of broken and blackened teeth as he grinned, he knew he wouldn't die today by Farrell's hand.

Farrell breathed deeply. "We've got 'em boys, they're on the run!" Farrell's shout echoed across the valley, thousands of heads turned and they cheered and shook their weapons in the air to display their approval.

Kieron feared for his life, Farrell's wrath would be boundless with the loss of his men; he led ninety one of his soldiers west, travelling parallel with a large group of refugees as thousands of citizenry tried to escape the conflict. They picked their way through the forest using an old animal trail and after half an hour they came upon a road that cut through the forest.

As far as the eye could see in both directions the refugees from the camp of Eldersfield had turned north and they used the road as they trudged wearily away from the fighting.

The Skavs stood at the side of the road, and it didn't go unnoticed that all eyes stared at them, one small group of Skavs who stood for a short time transfixed by the sight of people uncountable in number. Children cried in the hands of their mothers, none laughed and all the time they walked past, looking at some of Albion's tormentors, at some of the men that had caused so much distress.

"Bastards!" a man's voice yelled from the sea of faces which were as grim as their feet were tired.

"Come on bredrin, at em!" Kieron ordered quickly, yelling as he ran at the thick line of potential enemies.

They reached the line and the refugees, desperate to get out of the way, parted as they panicked and Kieron, a pistol in each hand led his men through their line.

Kieron stood on the opposite side of the road, daring any to follow them as his men slipped into the undergrowth; he watched the people as he backed into the wood and the line of refugees closed tight behind his men.

He was the last one to gain the cover of the trees and he followed his men, escaping from the road was the best thing they could have done, as the grumbling crowds began to turn from fear to anger at the sight of their aggressors.

They jogged on, tired from their fight and a night with no sleep, they were becoming desperate, some of them close to showing actual tears,

Kieron ran past his small band of fleeing men, little more than a troop of bandits.

"Rest soon lads aiight? We'll put a mile tween us and dem peasantry," he smiled, trying to hide his own emotions that mirrored those of his men.

After a quarter of an hour jogging away from the road and the pursuit that never came, Kieron slowed to a walk. He held his arm up, his hand made a fist as he smelled fires and cooking. The smells of breakfast filled his nostrils; the sounds of voices filled his ears, thousands of voices were barely a whisper because their camp was still some way off.

"Quiet lads," Kieron whispered, mouthing the words over his shoulder.

They crouched down, thick ferns and long forest grasses hid their position. Kieron looked at the man next to him, using his fingers he pointed to his eyes then to his Skav follower and finally to the sounds ahead of them.

"Hey?" the Skav said, confused. He looked at the man he'd followed away from the battle at Eldersfield and wondered what the hell he meant.

"Check it out bruv," Kieron whispered through gritted teeth he tried not to make too much noise but he was rapidly realising that the men that he led were either stupid or their brains had been fried from all the drugs they'd used or perhaps both.

"Oh, ok. Laterz," the Skav stood, and took off at a run.

"Do it peaceful like, don't let 'em see ya," Kieron dared raise his voice, making sure the man understood his mission.

"Yeah, I ain't stupid!" the Skav yelled as he disappeared into the forest.

"Yes you fucking are." Keiron whispered to himself and sighed.

No more than a few murmurs were spoken as Kieron turned back. He looked at his men, they had become little more than refugees themselves, waiting quietly and glad for the rest.

It wasn't long before the grasses rustled as Kieron's scout returned at an easy pace, with a broad grin that gave everybody hope.

"Howz it goin?" Kieron asked, wondering about the scout's

happy return.

"Homies blud," the man said, looking over his shoulder, "bout half mile."

"What, out here? Datz sic dat is" Kieron said as his small tired force jogged past him. "Wait..." he said, but too late, they had gone past. He caught them up and, jogged to the front, he needed to show that he was the leader, he did not want to be left behind and he wanted to have a look at the friendly force before he committed his men and made the introductions.

Seven minutes at a tired walking pace brought them to the edge of the forest, before them, the fields dropped gradually away to the west and the wide open plains of Eldersfield looked inviting. The plush green landscape looked heavenly in the spring sunshine, with the occasional cloud that skittered overhead the only thing to ruin the effect as it cast its shadow.

About two hundred yards away, a complex of buildings sat on the slope and around the complex, arranged in untidy rows, sat thousands of vehicles. Skavite yobs sat about them or lounged in the grass, warming in the sun, thousands of them laughing and eating breakfast.

An old woman dressed in a nun's greys swung from a post, her eyes were wide and her tongue lolled as flies buzzed around her swinging corpse.

"Dis is minging! They're dis close to me fighting and they're no help, propa minging," Kieron broke cover and walked down the hill towards the massive Skavite camp.

Kieron looked behind him to make sure his men were following him, they were, they had no other options, all other avenues had been exhausted. Along the hillside, men started to stand when they noticed Kieron and his men approaching. Their black tracksuits were a stark contrast against the greenery around them, they pointed up the hill and shouted the alarm.

Their ranks opened up as a middle aged man walked to the front, he looked out of place amongst the Skavite horde that drew their weapons to threaten the newcomers.

Kieron didn't recognise any of the Skavs in front of him. He tried to smile as he got closer to them but he stopped twenty metres away. He faced the horde with his tiny force; the threat of death was very real as the Skavite horde jeered his arrival.

The little man raised his hands to command silence and the mob quietened immediately and they seemed to obey this normal looking man without question. *'That's strange,'* Kieron thought as the man stepped forward, flanked by a group of muscular Skavs armed to the teeth with all manner of weaponry.

"I'm Mr Jones," the little man in the suit said. "Who are you?" he asked Kieron.

"Kieron, my names Kieron," he replied.

This time his men stayed rooted to the spot, the two men met in the middle and Kieron offered Mr Jones his hand and Mr Jones took it.

"Survivors?" Mr Jones asked as the two men released each other from their iron grip.

"Why d'you not come blud?" Kieron neither smiled nor grimaced as he asked the question he couldn't wait to ask, his curiosity got the better of him.

"Not my fight," Mr Jones answered; shocked that Kieron would be so forward.

"But we all bredrin," Kieron said, looking almost threatening.

Mr Jones was impressed by Kieron's bravery in the face of impossible odds. "You've got some fucking bottle lad, ain't yer?"

"I'm pissed off, I had five thousand bredrin last night," Kieron answered honestly, he could not see the point in hiding obvious facts.

"Well then, you'll join me, I'll let you keep the lads you've got now and any others that wish to join you," Mr Jones didn't give Kieron any options, he turned away knowing his horde had grown a little, Kieron had no future but death if he returned to Farrell.

"We all roll behind Farrell, or so I thought?" Kieron wanted to take this usurper by the throat, but he knew if he returned to Farrell's army it would mean his death.

"Join us or fuck off and back into the woods ya go," Mr Jones turned back to face Kieron and his men. His conceited air made him appear like a snob, he turned back and the smile never left his face as he strode off towards the largest building, followed closely by his guards.

Kieron was soon surrounded by his small group of men, all talking at the same time. "Aiight, aiight," he shouted them to silence, as those facing them began to disperse.

"Safe blud, we'll join ya outfit," Kieron said to Mr Jones' back as his men looked at him.

Kieron's men cheered him and rushed past him to be handed food by their new friends. They were greeted warmly, in stark contrast to the threatening behaviour displayed just moments before. Kieron left his men to introduce themselves and he followed Mr Jones at a respectful distance into the compound. He followed the unimpressive man that had somehow gained control of a large following of Skavs.

Following Mr Jones under the archway wasn't easy as people purposefully got in his way, daring him to fight with stares and shoulder barges. Eventually they left him alone to walk into the courtyard beneath the archway. Nuns ran all over their own compound, rushing with breakfasts and cups full of all types of beverages.

Some Skavs chased the old ladies as they were forced to do their bidding, the Skavs hit and slapped the poor old dears who were trying their best to stay alive.

Mr Jones entered a doorway and his men followed him in. Kieron made his way toward the doorway, accidentally colliding with a Skav who fell backwards and it was only when she had landed on her behind that Keiron realised that there were female Skavs in the compound too. Before Kieron could apologise he felt her fury as she leapt to her feet cursing him. He chose to ignore her for the most part and stared her down, sucking through his teeth in a display of disrespect as he passed her by.

He followed Mr Jones and his guard into the building and he heard screams of terror echoing through the building's halls and down the corridors as some unfortunate was being tortured. They went then down a short corridor and into a large dining hall where they stopped and sat around a long oak table.

"Come, sit with us," Mr Jones didn't look up as he broke bread to dip into a goblet of red wine.

Kieron worked his way around the table and he sat directly opposite his new leader.

"Dis's a convent," Kieron said, stating the obvious.

The man next to him laughed. "There ain't no virgins here, 'cept maybe da old hags," they laughed as yet another scream sounded in a distant room.

Mr Jones clicked his fingers and a nun raced over to the table. "Coffee, black coffee," he ordered.

The nun raced away, Keiron saw her face and it was a mass of cuts and bruises.

"Tell me Kieron, what's the state of the Capital City, who's in control?" Mr Jones looked at Kieron and the nun returned with his drink.

"Farrell won the battle for the capital," Kieron answered. He looked down the table at another nun who served Jones's guard.

One of the Skavite leaders had put his hand up the nun's greys and lifted it from the floor as he massaged her crotch. She had just placed a flagon of red wine in front of the Skav but now she blushed to match its colour. She was in her middle years and the ageing nun had never been touched before. Now her face reddened as she stood with her legs apart. She moaned as though in agony, her hands were palm down on the table before her and tears streamed down her face as she tried not to react to the ecstasy that her body was feeling.

"Ya like it don't ya chick?" the Skav said as the nun moaned again. Her ability to block out her feelings failed her.

"Argh, no," she whispered as she came.

Laughing the Skav removed his hand and the nun turned and slapped the Skav across the face. Everyone that was sat around the table fell about laughing. Kieron laughed and was tempted to grab the nun; he was aroused by his new comrade's antics. '*Maybe laterz*,' he thought.

"How many answered Farrell's call to arms?" Mr Jones said when he had controlled his laughter.

"Tens of thousands came but thousands died in da fighting for control of Capital City," Kieron answered, he looked at the nun, she was more handsome than pretty, she wailed and sobbed as she leaned against the wooden table.

"If you like her, I'll save her for you," Mr Jones said and he nodded to one of his men who swung his legs free of the table.

"Yeah, good," Kieron replied, his erection stiffened momentarily as the Skav dragged his new toy away into another room.

"What's the fuel and food situation like?" Mr Jones asked.

Kieron began to feel like he was being interrogated but he didn't mind, if the roles were reversed he would be acting the same.

"The city burns propa, nothing left and no one to put out the fires," Kieron said.

"So Farrell's left the city then?" Mr Jones asked, raising a questioning eyebrow.

Kieron thought for a moment that he might be betraying his former boss and the question of guilt crossed his mind momentarily but he didn't care, Mr Jones seemed more than reasonable and the thought of the nun he was about to defile made him smile.

"By the five moons he has! Buildings are burning unchecked and the smell of burning flesh is everywhere, the city's all banged up and there's no one left in it to rule," Kieron answered. He looked at Mr Jones in the eye as he told the truth willingly. "What's ya plan, why are you here?" he asked.

"De Silva and his People's Army are chasing us," Reginald Smith said, leaning over the table to smile at the newcomer.

"So you want to give him a bigger target than the one he's got," Kieron said and looked from Mr Jones to the Smith boy.

"That's right then we'll break off to the west." Mr Jones was surprised and looked at Kieron in a new light. "You're not as daft as ya look are ya?"

Nuns surrounded the table; they had been herded in by some of the female Skavs. Food was placed before them and Mr Jones was served by the pretty one with the venomous tongue that had cursed Kieron earlier. Mr Jones saw Kieron looking at her behind as she worked. Now that he realised that there were women in the camp, they were easier to spot and there were more than he had first thought.

"You like our Sharon?" Mr Jones asked, happy for the information he had gleaned from Kieron. "Then she's a gift to ya, she's yours."

Sharon froze and turned slowly.

"I belong to no one, ya got me?" she shouted and spat in Kieron's food.

Kieron stood quickly and grabbed her by the face before she had time to react. "Yeah? You're my wife now!" he yelled at her and his free hand made a fist and slammed into her solar plexus.

"I'll take my leave of ya now," he said, looking at the man who had carted away the nun.

"In dat door, she in one dem rooms mate," the Skav said, pointing to the door he'd escorted the nun through. Keiron nodded and dragged his new wife behind him.

Douglass Farrell sat in the passenger seat of his vehicle, he was frustrated as it crawled along at walking pace and behind him his entire army marched and grumbled, but not too loud for fear of being heard.

"When we win this war, the first thing I'm going to do is get the energy flowing again," Farrell was annoyed at the slow progress of his army because of the energy shortage that had arisen especially where the fighting was taking place and with no one to operate the power matrix, the energy ran dry.

Albion had certainly entered dark times; the essential personnel had been murdered or were on the move with the displaced citizenry. The services required by the nation couldn't continue and as a result the fabric that was civilisation had begun to unravel.

They were only three miles from the government held town of Eldersfield, the other five men in the vehicle with Farrell were considered to be the highest ranking Skavs in Albion, and all of them commanded a large force.

Up ahead, a team of energy bike riders came into view. The bikes had been adapted for all terrain and sent forward to scout out the government positions. Farrell opened his door and the driver killed the power which was the signal to the rest of the army that it was time to rest. Farrell's favourites joined him and climbed out of the vehicle to stand in the middle of the highway. They remained silent, sensing Farrell's mood at the inertia of his forces; he needed fully charged vehicles and lots of them. He looked at his tired Skavite forces and wondered if they would have a fight left in them. He turned back and moments later the four energy bikes were powering down their fuel cells as they pulled in.

"Mr Farrell Sir," the scout leader saluted, his feet rested on the ground either side of the heavy two wheeled machine for balance. "The city of Eldersfield is completely deserted," he said, his voice coming from his blacked out visor.

"Any sign of our lost troops and their leader?" Farrell asked.

"No Sir, but there are thousands of burnt corpses all over the battle field, they've been piled up too. The huge refugee camp is gone, the large one we been hearing about, tracks lead off in all directions with all fearing your coming," the rider bowed in his seat, a difficult task and his head almost touched his handlebars.

"That'll be all, get five minutes rest," Farrell said and smiled, he was pleased with the creeping compliments of the rider, if not the news he heard.

"Thank you my lord," the scout's leader replied and he and his men stood the bikes onto their stands and left them where they were to save energy.

Farrell watched them as they dismounted and sauntered off to sit on the grass verge not too far from their rides.

"I like him, reliable he his," Farrell smiled, turning back to his main gang bosses. "Well lads, we got 'em on the run," he said, '*All of us should've come*,' he thought, regretting his decision to send Kieron on his own.

One of his men pulled his phone out of his pocket and its ringing brought Farrell out of his train of thought. Farrell looked around at the man as he answered it.

"Howz it hanging?" the man asked and then there was a short pause. "Tis for you Doug," the man held out the phone to Farrell.

"Put it on loud speaker," Farrell wondered who it might be, obviously someone that knew he could be with this gang boss. He looked at the sun rising. '*Probably Gavin Jones*,' he thought.

"Eze on blud," the man said after pressing a button on the side of his cellphone.

"Douglass, it's me!" Mr Jones sounded cheerful on the other end of the phone, wherever he was.

"Mr Jones, ya rat bastard," Farrell said calmly, and then smiled.

"Where are ya Douglass?" Mr Jones asked, the fun had gone from his voice and he took on a businesslike tone.

"What's it to you Jones?" Farrell answered sharply.

"We're at the convent on the Eldersfield plains," Mr Jones said and that piece of information caused a ripple of excitement in those within earshot.

"Ok, and what, you wanna come rejoin the fold? Come on down Gavin, we can talk about the many insults you have hurled at your master," Farrell said and looked around at his men. He was confident that Mr Jones would want to make his peace and rejoin his army.

"Here, I got someone for you to talk to," Mr Jones said, there was no pause for thought at Farrell's question, it was as if Mr Jones had planned the conversation.

"Farrell, fuck you ya fat twat," the voice said and then laughed, mocking him, and then many other voices joined in, laughing at the other end of the connection.

"Kieron, is that you? You're dead, ya hear me? You're all dead!" Farrell snarled as he grabbed the phone, but it was too late to shout threats because the phone's connection had been cut.

Chapter 28

Jason de Silva stood on the service station forecourt looking out over the highway at the thousands of refugees walking away from the war, they fled the stench of death and burning that saturated Capital City and they headed north.

"We're going to take the last of their power supply," Jimmy said to Jason, wondering if he would really drain the place of energy.

"Fill 'em up, use it all, take notes. They'll get their gold later," Jason hadn't smiled since he'd found out that Jacky no longer walked upon Albion and although the tears had dried up, the nature of her horrific death seemed to drive him on relentlessly.

"Jason, even if we drain the last of their power, we'll only have enough in the fuel cells to get us home." Jimmy reasoned.

"They're down that road, perhaps ten miles at the most!" Jason shouted unexpectedly and his throat croaked with the effort.

"Jay, with all these people on the road the vehicles are going nowhere fast," Randell butted in to state the obvious which Jason failed to see as his emotions churned.

"Yeah, we'd be better off walking," Trevor agreed with his brother and at the same time he tried to make Jason see sense.

"Then that's what we'll do, walk," Jason said. He looked over at the lines of Philip's horsemen that had overtaken them and it seemed that every time Jason looked there were more of them. They moved along riding four abreast and they stretched back as far as the eye could see, travelling on country lanes that paralleled the highway.

Jason looked at his commanders and the People's Army; their vehicles blocked the south bound carriageways of the highway and held up twenty thousand of his men.

"Jimmy, get power in these fuel cells, the rest of you order the men to disembark, we're going to march the rest of the way," Jason ordered, just as his phone began to ring.

Jason searched for the phone, fumbling in his pocket and he took a few seconds to answer the call. "Hello," he said and accidentally activated the speaker option so everyone could hear.

"Dis is Reggie Smith, ya get me pics de Silva?" Smithy mocked him.

"Where's my wife's body?" Jason asked calmly.

"I got her wid me, she's in da vehicle," Smithy replied.

"And where might you be?" Jason asked, using all the will power he had to remain calm, he couldn't afford to get emotional in any way neither to get angry nor to break down; he couldn't give his wife's murderer and rapist that satisfaction.

"We bout ten miles south of ya, I fink. We gave Jacky propa sendin off," then the phone line went dead.

Jason threw his phone across the service station, he ran to the horsemen, not looking to see if his commanders were following, his anger finally got the better of him.

He didn't take long to reach Philip's corps and he reached up and grabbed at the nearest horseman, the rider's horse danced away and lifted Jason off his feet for a moment. The whole line of march was disrupted as Jason pulled the startled rider from his saddle and unceremoniously dumped the man on the ground. Horsemen struggled with their mounts as the riderless horse skittered about and the rider next to the empty horse grabbed its reins just in time and stopped it prancing and knocking Jason over.

Jason grabbed the pommel of the saddle, put his foot in the

stirrup and mounted in one quick motion. In a flash he settled himself in the saddle, took the reins from the waiting horseman and was off, kicking the horse to action. The horse needed no further encouragement, it was already spooked and it shot forward at the gallop. Jason looked like a fish out of water in the saddle, his legs were slack whilst he tried to hold on and guide the horse with the reins. Jason nearly fell from the panicked horse and he leaned forward to steady himself, he grabbed hold of the horse's mane and held on grimly as the horse shot past the cavalry near the head of the line of march.

Philip and Dave were riding side by side, chatting about the simple pleasures of riding in the sun; they were both taken aback when Jason shot past them at the gallop.

"Fuck me, what's he doing?" Philip shouted to those around him as he spurred his horse forward.

Jason only half succeeded in leaning into the horse, he bobbed around in the saddle gripping desperately at the reins. He managed to look over his shoulder he saw the thousands of horsemen chasing him, as Philip's corps tried to catch him up. Jason smiled as he steadied himself, thinking how they must have looked to any bystanders, thousands of horsemen chasing one lone rider.

He managed to gain control and slowed the horse a little by pulling back on the reins as he entered a lane that ran parallel to the highway. The horse's gait changed to a canter as Jason got the hang of the animal, but his body was battered and sore, he was not used to the ancient form of travel.

Philip slowed his own mount into a canter, pulling up at Jason's side and grinning at his leader as his troops bunched up behind them. Philip tried not to look annoyed, the thrill of the gallop and the chase making this easy, as the adrenalin gave him a rush.

"What the fuck?" Philip began, catching his breath.

"Not a word!" Jason yelled over the sounds of thousands

of tramping hooves. "Jacky's murderers are over those hills, I intend to have their heads on pikes by day's end!" the face of a maniac was where Jason's used to be.

"We're with you all the way, just don't kill the horses," Philip yelled back at him.

They slowed to a trot; Jason finally gained control of his mount. Neither of them said another word and behind them thousands of horsemen and women reorganised themselves cursing. Dave eventually sorted out his standard, his annoyance apparent as everyone, including Jason, received an irate glare.

They broke into a routine of trot, walk, trot to save the horses legs and prevent any injuries, and as the afternoon wore on, they came at last to the bottom of the gentle slopes they'd first seen earlier in the day.

"How many men have you got?" Jason asked.

"Don't know, they just keep coming, everyone with a horse wants to be part of the cavalry, apparently!" Philip answered as they halted the horses and dismounted.

"Let's have an hour to let the rear catch up and have a rest," Jason said to Phil.

"And after that?" Philip asked.

"The plains of Eldersfield lie beyond these hills and the city is beyond the plains. We're going to catch my wife's killers. Besides its what we're here for, killing Skavs," Jason looked back across the expanses they had crossed in such a short period of time, miles behind them he could just make out the lines of infantry, their tiny flags and banners flapping in the wind.

Creeping lower in the sky the sun was beginning to set, Douglass Farrell and forty thousand Skavs reached the convent of Eldersfield. The place was deserted but for a lone nun, her bloated and fly-blown corpse hung at the end of a rope from a nearby tree. All that remained of the nun's complex was cinders and scorched brick.

"Where the fuck are they?" Farrell fumed as he paced at the side of the vehicle.

"Pass me the phone, any phone!" Farrell yelled, killing something his main priority.

One of his leaders stepped forward and offered him his cell phone. "Here my lord," the Skav gang boss smiled.

No thanks were given as Farrell took the phone and he dialled Jones's number and listened, but there was no ringing tone.

'Why would he goad me like that?' Farrell thought, his anger boiling. 'What could he possibly have to gain?'

Farrell gave the phone back to its owner, he rubbed his temples and wondered what to do, the beginnings of a headache thumped beneath his fingers. He looked around at his barbarian pack as they filed past him and he realised he'd made a terrible mistake.

"You all follow me without question?" he asked himself, thinking out loud.

"Yes my lord mans respectin innit bruv," a muscular Skav said, the puckered scar ran down his face and creased when his mouth moved.

"Let's make camp and bed down for the night, there's not a lot we can do tonight," Farrell calmed down. '*If I'm to lead this nation I can't keep getting angry*,' he thought, doing a little soul searching, anger was the only emotion he normally allowed himself.

"Sir, we aint got nuffin, our forced march," one of Farrell's commanders told him.

Farrell held up his hand to quiet the man. "Send out foragers, see what we can find, we'll have to live off the land tonight," he said.

"And in the morning?" another one of his commanders dared to ask.

"In the morning, we'll see what tomorrow brings hey!" Farrell said and smiled.

Putting up tents in the warm spring evening was pleasant work, the warmth of the sunlight turned to the cool luminosity that emanated from Serene's surface. The shades of light danced pleasantly across the hillsides as the sun was setting to the west and Philip's men prepared to settle down for the night too.

The tiny pop up tents each rider carried was enough for warmth if combined with a sleeping bag, thousands of them were spread out across the hillside and fires blossomed to force back the eerie luminescence.

As the sun finally set, twenty thousand horses were tethered and sentries were posted at the edges of the camp. Twenty thousand small domed tents looked like giant mushrooms as the light of the night hit their tops.

Jason, Philip and Dave settled down at a camp fire as the moons rose up in opposition to the day in their eternal fight for dominance of the night sky.

"You're well equipped," Jason said as he looked about the camp, the horsemen cooked and the horses ate grain.

"This is Jimmy's handiwork," Philip said and pulled his saddle bags open to take out his dry rations. "But it won't last long; he could only give us food to last a week before we left Kalverstone."

"He's a clever one that Jimmy, finding that warehouse with the camping stuff," Dave said, he looked out over the camp too and he stood to remove his jacket. "It's going to be a warm night tonight."

"Yes, I think…" Jason began.

"Alarm, alarm!" guards from the hilltop began shouting.

Panting, a man came to a stop at their fire; he addressed Philip and Jason, unsure of the correct protocol, "Skavs my lord, off road on energy bikes."

Philip jumped up, not waiting for further explanation; Jason and Dave were right behind him. They raced for their horses which weren't that far away and luckily, still had their saddles on their backs, the man detailed to remove them had been busy until that point.

They mounted quickly and spurred their horses up the slope toward the guards that were sounding the alarm; Jason struggled for balance he was still not used to riding or the pain in his groin.

Four Skav riders crested the ridge above the camp, and then their fuel cells lit up their progress as they disappeared back down from whence they came.

Jason struggled to keep up as twenty horsemen joined their small party with weapons drawn as they crested the hill. The sounds of the fuel cells whined in the valley below and they rode down into the dark valley hidden from the moons glow in the early night, the terrain and the darkness made the ride a terrifyingly dangerous gallop.

Jason clung to the horse's neck and a sharp jolt nearly threw him from his saddle as they reached the bottom of the hill and immediately raced upwards again.

It seemed only seconds passed until they were reining in their horses, they paused at the top of the next rise and the horses stamped and danced, they still wanted to gallop.

"Over there!" one of the riders yelled, as he spotted the bright lights of the fuel cells as they came into view over the next rise.

Racing off again headlong down the opposite slope, over the next rise and into a small valley they gave chase. They moved uphill again until they crested the hill, it was the last one before the plains of Eldersfield which now lay before them. The plains stretched away to the south of them and were a vast expanse of open grasslands. Sprawled across the plains was a vast horde of Skavites at ease, their camp fires blazed for miles around, making a patchwork in the moons glow and it seemed to Jason that all the hordes of hell had come to rest, to laze on the ground before him.

The energy bikes could just be made out as they disappeared

into the camp and hundreds of Skavs stood yelling insults at them as they sat upon their mounts, mesmerized at the size of the camp and the sheer numbers gathered against them.

Philip rode slowly down the slope, walking his horse until he was within a few hundred feet of the edge of the Skavite encampment. "I see you e'er the sun rises, death, death to you Skav bastards!" he yelled, his voice resonating as it was carried on the wind and out across the plain. Thousands of Skavs stood, rising to the challenge, and a few shots were fired in Philip's direction.

Philip quickly turned his mount and rode back up the slope to Jason and the others. Without saying a word they turned as one and rode full tilt to gallop back into the shadowed shallow valleys towards their own camp less than a mile away. More riders had left the camp to chase after them and they joined the rear of their group as they rode back in silence and, upon reaching their own camp, they quickly dismounted and returned to the warmth of their camp fires.

"Spread the word, get some rest, we attack at dawn." Philip ordered the men who had gathered around them.

Like a wave the news spread out across the camp. Not many would sleep that night, a combination of excitement and fear would infect most minds on the eve of battle.

Jason sat down by his camp fire and settled down. He picked up a nearby blanket and wrapped it around himself.

Philip strode off into the night shouting orders about sentries and weapons being at the ready. Dave joined Jason at the fire and without saying a word he took a clay pipe from inside his jacket, prepared it and lit it with a piece of burning kindling from the fire.

"Night's turning chilly," Jason said, without looking up as he stared into the fire.

"Yup," Dave agreed, drawing smoke from his pipe, as he watched the flames dance above the fire.

Chapter 29

"Jason, Jason."

Jason opened his eyes, the moon had gone from the night sky and daylight had started to warm his body and he looked up at Philip who was shaking him gently awake.

"What time is it?" Jason sat up and drew the blanket about him the camp fire was black and cold.

"Dawn's about to break, I've had your horse saddled," Philip offered Jason his hand.

Jason accepted his help. "I didn't know it had been unsaddled," he said, as he was pulled off the dew wet grass.

"Yeah, I had some of the lads do it," Philip said grinning with excitement. "Are we doing this then?"

"Let's get it over with, shall we," Jason said, showing no emotion on his blank face. "The Smith boy, he's mine," he felt compelled to say it but knew it would be impossible to single Reginald out.

"The whole army kinda knows that," Philip turned and walked away and was passed by a man leading Jason his horse.

Jason mounted the animal and wheeled it about slowly, his saddle sore body still aching from yesterday's ride and he was trying to get a fix on things as his horse stopped. Jason looked down to see Dave looking up at him, the Bannerman held the horse's bridle in one hand and a cup of coffee in the other.

"Here, coffee," Dave offered Jason the tin mug that had a dark liquid swirling around in it.

Jason took a sip, it wasn't hot, just warm enough and he drained the mug and threw it back. "Thanks," Jason said, as he felt the liquid warm his insides.

He thought of the battle to come as the Bannerman mounted his own horse, of the revenge he would bring down upon his enemies and of his dead wife, her broken body yet to be reclaimed.

'*Everything happens for a reason*,' he kept telling himself and turned the horse with the reins. He spotted Philip in amongst a group of green clad horsemen. All around the camp men and women were mounting their horses, grim faces told of the battle to come, they knew that many of them would never see another daybreak after this one and the thought of blood and death infected their hearts and minds.

Jason walked his horse up to Philip's and just as he was about to talk, Philip stood up in his stirrups.

"Let's have at em!" Philip bellowed his eyes wide with excitement. Then he wheeled his horse about as the cheer went up and the battle cries filled the air and felt like thunder. Off and up they spurred their steeds and like a mighty tsunami they crested the first ridge to crash down the opposite ridge without a care for their own person.

Jason screamed a battle cry and rent forth his emotion. His shout was not even heard by himself over the sounds of so many thundering hooves. He looked to Philip who faced front and was smiling, then he looked to his left at the grimacing faces and hands that held weapons aloft, shaking them at an unseen enemy hidden by the terrain.

They rode over another hilltop and for a brief moment the plains of Eldersfield came into view and they caught a glimpse of the vast enemy that awaited them. Down again before the final slope, the People's Army slowed its pace as it ascended the last hill. Then all along the final crest, for more than a mile, the People's Army, Philip's Cavalry corps crested the ridge as one to show themselves to their foe. They moved out onto the top of the slope that dropped away onto the plains of Eldersfield.

More than a mile away a vast horde of Skavite bastards awaited them with their black banners and flags flapping in the wind that whipped across the open plains. Then the sun finally broke and its rays splashed the plains with heavenly rays of light.

It was a contradiction that wasn't lost to Jason, heavenly light playing across something so darkly evil.

The Skavite horde stood in silence as the full extent of the People's Army showed itself in all its glory. Both armies faced off and for a brief time nobody spoke. The only sounds were those that the horses made and that of the flags snapping as the wind increased.

A quarter of an hour passed and still both armies faced off in silence. Finally Philip, Jason and Dave edged their horses forward, the Bannerman's flag rising and falling in the breeze.

Jason and Philip looked at each other, they both waited for the other to speak. Philip looked over his shoulder, to his waiting army that looked to him and awaited their orders. Philip wheeled his horse around and rode off up the line of his men. He looked into their eyes and saluted them silently, hand held high. He rode the entire length of his cavalry line before returning to Dave and Jason, who had also turned to face the waiting riders.

"It's time to get this show on the road," Philip said to Jason. He turned his horse and stood in his stirrups.

"I may die this day!" Philip began, his voice echoing in the valley. "But I would rather ride down there and face my demons than turn back now," again he paused, his last syllable trailing off. "For I would rather reside in hell for all eternity with my honour intact, than live in heaven's delight as a coward!" he finished, a bit of spittle flying from his mouth.

The army couldn't contain its silence any longer, they cheered and yelled battle cries in their leader's honour and hurled insults at their enemy. The Skavite horde yelled back in direct competition to the People's Army's hullabaloo.

Then Jason yelled his now famous battle cry. "For our children, our honour and the blood of our ancestors!" and the three leaders of men wheeled their horses about.

The People's Army erupted yet more at the unexpected shout of encouragement. They yelled until their lungs were empty, then they started their advance and the twenty thousand moved forward. The flags unfurled, the weapons were drawn and down upon the plain they charged to the field that would run red with blood.

They gained speed all at once as the horses seemed to miss their trot and passed it over for the canter and all around him Jason felt and heard the People's Army. Its charge was present in his mind like a mighty heart beating. Then like a wave it hit the valley floor and the grass seemed to pulse before them like ripples on a pond. They soon covered half the distance to the Skavite lines and Jason had time to look at Philip, who had edged slightly ahead. He held his sword out ahead of himself with the tip pointing forward. Jason felt more than heard Philip's screaming command. "Charge!" He could also feel his contorted features as adrenalin coursed through his veins.

It seemed that until then the riders had been holding something back, but now their steeds needed no prompting as they all leapt to the gallop together. Jason looked forward and could see the faces of his enemy, every Skav with a gun seemed to fire at the same time and the riders to either side of him tumbled, but whether they or their mounts had been shot he couldn't tell.

On they rode into the hail of lead, the charge of the mighty less than a heart's beat away. They had closed to within a few seconds of the largest gathering of criminals ever to stand upon the land and Jason looked at the faces of his terrified enemies, their faces seemed frozen in time. It was a photograph in his memory of a frightened enemy that he would carry with him till the end of his days.

The fear that his enemies obviously felt gave him heart and hope, then all fleeting thoughts left him and only the face of his wife remained. He knew tens of thousands of battle cries were being screamed to the heavens in that instant, but he only heard one, his own, as all the others joined to rush like the blast of a gale.

"Jacky!" Jason yelled his torment.

More riders fell as the guns continued to fire then Jason's mind captured another image, the image of a youth who threw his gun to the floor as his nose exploded with the pressure of his scream. The lad just stood there and panicked, yelling as he looked into Jason's eyes, his tears mingling with his blood.

Then the world seemed to slow down around him as his life flashed before him. The hooves of the horses seemed to take an age for each beat as they lifted and stamped. The screaming faces of their riders seemed frozen with angry battle yells as they brought their weapons high and their eyes bulged as they looked down into the panicked faces of the Skavs whose lines pushed forward in a futile attempt to hold the horses at bay. The faces of the Skavs, in contrast, were a mask of tears as they faced the realisation of their own deaths.

Then they were in the thick of it. The two armies came together, the Skavite horde tried not to yield under the weight and sheer power of the horses. Within seconds thousands died, trampled under hoof or smashed by swinging sword and stabbing spear. Not for a thousand years had Albion seen such a sight, even the long lived trees had forgotten how futile it was for infantry to stand out in the open against such a charge. Bodies were thrown up into the air to bounce off the fronts and flanks of the horses. Skulls were split and backs were broken by the horses' hooves as the cavalry pressed ever forward.

In places, the Skavs managed to turn the charge aside as they clumped together as the charge streaked past and they struck out at the riders or their mounts to stab and slash at them or hit out with their hammers.

Jason swung his sword down to his side but at the same time did not dare to slow the horse's progress lest he fall prey to the Skavite weapons. Off to his right Jason saw the largest man he'd ever seen, he stood atop the roof of a vehicle yelling frantically at the Skavs around him. The man looked up into Jason's eyes as he passed and he stopped yelling, his mouth made the shape "de Silva" but the the sound was lost in the tumult and the giant gave Jason a look of devilish defiance. Jason watched the man as a rider pulled up to the vehicle's side and stabbed him with a spear. The spear remained in the man's side as the rider was shot by the Skavs who surrounded and protected the vehicle. Then his horse seemed to jolt forward and Jason turned his head towards his front. They were in open ground and thousands of the Skavs who had been at the back were fleeing for their lives. Philip appeared at Jason's side smiling and spurring his horse at the fleeing men and women.

"No mercy, no mercy! No quarter asked, none given!" Philip screamed as he brought his long sword down to cut a youth's head clean off. Riding on, Philip swung his sword high and brought it down once more as he aimed for the back of a Skav's neck. He missed the neck and hit the back of the skull instead. The Skav fell and took the sword with him. Philip had to let go as his blade was stuck fast in the Skav's bone and he could not drag the dead weight.

Jason was definitely up for the game as he rode on smiling too. '*It's like polo but with a bladed mallet*,' he thought.

More than half of the cavalry had made it through the Skav lines unscathed on that first charge and they revelled in the bloody slaughter as the fleeing and defenceless Skavs were cut to pieces. Twice while he rode, Jason thought the sport too cruel but both times Jacky's smiling beauty came to mind to strengthen his sword arm and his resolve.

The cavalry charge stopped short of a forest, close to some smoking ruins, some Skavs escaped after they had run half a mile from their starting point, their fear helped their flight.

Philip's corps wheeled about and turned around to face the back of what was left of the Skavite horde. Approximately seven thousand Skavs were regrouping around a vehicle.

Jason sat and looked at the battle field as the People's Army gathered about him, readying for another charge. He was mesmerized by the bodies and carnage their charge had left in its wake. Thousands of Skavs that had sustained heavy injuries crawled or moaned. '*Like the hordes of tortured souls writhing in the pit of despair*,' he thought as Philip and Dave joined him one either side.

They sat for a moment in silence, watching as dying men from both sides stood and fell back down again. Horses kicked out as they struggled for purchase and breath, and they too would die from their injuries. Thousands of maimed humans dragged themselves away, some still trying to fight their nearest foe.

"Like a bowl full of maggots, look how they wriggle!" Dave said.

"You're sick, proper sick." Philip cursed his Bannerman, who still smiled but said nothing.

"Well we can't charge through all those corpses, the horses will slip and fall," Jason said, looking at Philip. "They'll break their necks."

"And ours," Philip agreed, nodding. He looked back across the plains. "There's no need though look, they're making a run for it."

The Skavs that remained began to split apart as the different factions and groups made a run for it. Still a few thousand huddled around the vehicle, the one with the giant of a man standing on its roof.

"Who's that man?" Jason asked, pointing at the Skavite

leader.

"You mean the man standing on top of the vehicle, with that broken spear shaft sticking out of his side? I was wondering that myself," Philip followed Jason's stare.

"That's Douglass Farrell, the leader of Albion's underworld and the Skavite movement, he's Albion's most wanted," Dave smiled wryly. "He's mine."

Philip stood in his stirrups once again. "Let's cut 'em down, kill 'em all, no prisoners, no survivors, no mercy!" he shouted, swinging his head from left to right.

The People's Army seemed not to tire of death and all of them as one spurred their horses forward. Jason found himself surrounded by blood thirsty riders. '*There's not enough to go around,*' he thought as he charged and joined once more in the race for death, shaking his sword in the space above his head.

"Get 'em together, pull 'em in," Farrell stood on his vehicle's roof, the sharp end of a barbed spear was still stuck in the side of his abdomen. He was yelling orders like the angry manager of a death match on the wrong end of a thrashing. To look at him you would think there was nothing wrong with him but in truth he knew he was going to die but the hefty cocktail of narcotics he'd taken that morning would have a chance of resurrecting long lost ancestry and he felt invincible.

"Mr Farrell my lord," one of Farrell's guards looked at him, pleading. "Give me a white flag, let me end this, we ain't gonna win."

Douglass Farrell reached around his side and grabbed the shaft of the spear that protruded from his abdomen. He yanked the weapon from its bloody purchase, sending gouts of blood and lumps of flesh thudding to the vehicle's roof with a sickening, wet sound. No drug could hide the pain he felt, not even his special mixture and he looked to the sky to focus on a cloud that hung overhead and with his arms outstretched he bellowed a mighty roar that burst forth from his soul.

All faces turned to look at their master, his last few thousand faithful watched as the mighty Skav leaned forward and rammed the broken spear through the neck of the guard that dared to suggest he surrender.

"We die today, we die well today!" Farrell yelled, as his dead servant fell away from him, the spear's broken shaft hit the ground and forced its point through to spray the air with blood. What was left of his army cheered, they knew they had lost the fight and the war.

The People's Army rode down the cowards that fled when the second charge skirted the battle field. Those that stood with Farrell watched as their comrades were slaughtered by the thousands of mounted riders, the People's Army rode around the battle field and all thoughts of escape evaporated. They were trapped and facing a certain death, which in the face of it, those that remained seemed for the most part to accept.

"Courage lads, we'll all get fucked out of our faces on the other side, there'll be parties in our honour, hey?" Farrell laughed at his own folly; he had thought that he had a chance at the throne in the first place.

Jason de Silva looked at the centre of what was the Skavite horde. '*Not many left*,' was his first thought and '*Fuck this*,' was his second.

He dismounted and allowed his to horse roam. Less than half a mile away two thousand Skavs waited to die.

"Come on lads, lets fuck 'em up!" he yelled.

Stepping up to the edge of the mass of dead and dying, he had to plan his movements so as not to stand on anyone alive and although the dead and dying looked like a carpet from far off, close up there were still plenty of clear spaces. Then he was passed by his own soldiers, some of whom didn't seem to care where their feet fell. As they walked they trod on and over the bodies. Jason watched as one dismounted rider paused at the side of a dying Skav, he leaned over and stabbed the youth through the throat to put him out of his misery as he groaned and writhed.

"Fuck it," he said to himself, as more of his men joined him.

There was no charge now, no glorious end to the hard won fight, the foot padding cavalry simply closed in, surrounding the Skavs completely. There was no shout for mercy, no white flag waving frantically in the Skavite centre; they waited for their fate, already knowing the outcome. They brandished their weapons wanting to make good account of themselves in the end.

More than ten thousand dismounted riders joined Jason; they closed to within a few yards of the Skavite horde which had been reduced to nothing more than a Skav huddle. Jason stepped forward and swung his sword at the tightly packed enemy, he hacked and slashed at them and he was joined by his men who thrust and chopped at them too.

Farrell's Skavs were outnumbered; they were completely surrounded and they fought like cornered beasts. The battle raged around Farrell who screamed orders at his men, but they started to die quickly, their swords no match for the spears and lances that stabbed at them. Some of the Skavs were dragged out of the press kicking and screaming and they were passed backwards to be beaten slowly to death by their captors who used them for sport and revenge.

It took less than half an hour and the People's Army eventually hacked its way into the centre, the soldiers at the front covered red with Skavite blood and gore, Jason was amongst them.

Surrounding the vehicle were Farrell's elite guards, their ammo had been spent ages since and they fought with hammers, daggers and other hand held weapons. They were all vicious, hard men, impossible to grapple with. The last of the Skavite horde was less than one hundred strong and gave good account of themselves in their final stand, slashing and hammering at the People's Army. But in the end they too succumbed to the might that was the People's Army, the sheer weight of numbers telling as one by one, Farrell's guard were hacked at. Limbs were lopped off, chests were opened up, heads crushed with eyeballs hanging from a cord. Carnage and blood lust reigned until only Farrell remained.

Farrell took two claw hammers from his belt. "Bastards!" he shouted and grimaced as he defiantly waved the hammers at the thousands that surrounded him chanting for his head.

Dave stepped forward, carrying his standard and he thrust up with its metal tipped shaft and stabbed Farrell in the side of his thigh. Dave withdrew his improvised weapon and Farrell sank onto one knee, thundering his hammers on the metal roof of the vehicle in anger. Dave thrust forward again with the metal tipped pole, pushing until the metal disappeared into his flesh, the blood stained black and white material entered the flesh of his upper groin and through the shaft, Dave felt his enemy's hip bone as it cracked.

Again Farrell bellowed angrily and he hit down with his hammer to smash the wooden shaft that had maimed him.

"Bastards!" he yelled again as he struggled but failed to stand. Farrell fell forward, trying to escape the pain from his broken pelvis; he rolled onto his side and fell from the vehicle into the crowd that had gathered around him. He hit the ground and rolled onto his back and the men of the People's Army jeered and laughed.

Dave forced his way through the men who stamped at Farrell, he pushed them away from the monster, and he actually seemed to be guarding the gangland crime lord. Dave pulled the last man off of Farrell, the knife he gripped dripped blood red he had stabbed Farrell several times. Farrell gasped for breath and looked up at the sky, its blue expanse dotted here and there with wisps of white cloud. He looked at the man who now bent over him. '*The man with the flag*,' he thought and smiled as the man screamed something in his ear.

Farrell watched as his nemesis produced a set of hand cutters from his pocket and lifted his large hand, Farrell felt faint with the blood loss from the injuries he had already received and he watched detached, as though it was happening to someone else, someone a long way off. He was numb and cold, facing his death as the man with the flag cut off the first of his fingers.

"Well I guess I didn't need that," Farrell laughed, as that pain joined that of his other various wounds.

The riders moved back from Dave to form a quiet circle and they watched as their comrade tortured the underworld kingpin. Jason looked to Dave's hands as he worked, he noticed for the first time that he missed his little fingers.

Farrell grimaced and gritted his teeth as, one by one, the madman with the wide eyes cut off all his fingers and thumbs. He hadn't the strength or the will to look at his fingerless hands, he refused to look as the sky turned from blue to black, and he closed his eyes and no longer felt the pain of life.

Jason looked on as Dave's berserker rage finally ebbed away; Philip's Bannerman stepped away from Farrell's corpse, his breathing heavy and laboured. Then Dave turned away from the fingerless Farrell and walked past Jason but he paused. "Revenge is a great motivator," then he continued walking and the crowd opened up for him.

Dave didn't know it but he was not the only one that imagined what would happen to Farrell next. There were more men than he realised that were missing fingers or loved ones and the image that played in his mind as he walked his solitary way across the plain was similar to others that were being played in heads across the battlefield.

Farrell stood looking at his hands; he looked pale, translucent but his fingers and thumbs were intact and he wiggled them. The sounds of the world seemed muted, the figures of the People's Army slow in their movements, and they seemed not to notice him at all. The world seemed to ebb in phases, from solid to liquid and back again.

"You can't stay here," a voice said.

Farrell turned around and saw a little old man as pale as he was. He sat upon Farrell's vehicle and his white full length robes almost covered his sandals. He held a long white staff which appeared to be oak and it had a single leaf growing from its end.

"Who are you?" Farrell asked.

"Who am I? Says the fractured soul," and the old man jumped from the vehicle. "Why, I'm your guide, they send me for the special cases."

"Where am I going?" Farrell asked and feared the answer.

"You'll see!" the old man said and he pointed his staff at the ground at Farrell's feet.

Mumbling something inaudible, the old man seemed to disappear, fading away with the world and Farrell entered a dark realm, a fiery realm full of despair.

Dave smiled at the imagined fate of the man that had stolen his fingers when they were both little more than boys. If Farrell had not been treated so leniently by the justice system then, would he have become the relentless and ruthless bastard that he did or would punishment have sorted him out whilst he was young enough to learn from the error of his ways?

Dave no longer cared.

Perched on their vehicles, they had watched the battle from afar, transfixed by what they had just witnessed. The small group was silent for awhile.

Mr Jones was the first to speak. "That was slaughter, Farrell's lot didn't do a deal after all." he said, he looked at his men, then brought the binoculars he held back up to his face.

"Farrell's banged up blud, soz hard propa," Kieron said, and yanked the chain that was attached to Sharon's collar.

"Dem horses sic man, homies hench on horseback," Smithy was shaken and fearful of Jason de Silva's wrath for the first time.

Jones sighed and once again wished for someone that would speak properly rather than the constant stream of Skav slang. He understood it but it grated on his nerves.

"We gotta get the fuck outta here," one of Mr Jones gang bosses suggested.

They turned, to follow the man's finger. A huge column of men marched toward them from the north, the flags of the People's Army fluttering along its length.

"Come on then, let's fuck off. The plan stays the same, nothing has changed," Gavin Jones jumped from the bonnet of his Vehicle.

He was joined by the others, none of them wanted to hang around.

Chapter 30

Finding and mounting their horses took a while, some had bolted, the sounds and stresses of combat had been too much. Philip had lost thousands of horses and men from his corps, more than a hundred were left without a mount, some of the animals had to be put down because of injuries they had sustained.

Jason was extremely saddle sore and was more than happy to donate his horse to a healthy rider.

Jason sat alone and looked down from the hillside at the death they had wrought, when Lindsey strolled up. She was looking down at her feet and she sat down in front of him but didn't dare to look into Jason's eyes.

"No camera, pen or paper?" Jason was the first to speak. He did not look at Lindsey but was more than aware of her presence.

"No," Lindsey's response was short.

"When did you get here?" Jason asked. He leaned to his side and propped himself up on his elbow to look at Lindsey.

Lindsey's dress fluttered in the wind and she held it to her sides with her hands, modestly not wanting to show off her legs. "We were here for the charge," she said tentatively, nervous as she came with her metaphorical cap in hand.

"Did you get Philip's speech?" Jason asked. "Inspirational it was, very moving," he spoke calmly, devoid of any emotion after the battle, his mind was blank and he was happy for it to be so for a while.

"Jay, I've come to apologize," Lindsey turned to Jason, her lip quivered.

"Go on," his eyebrows rose in concern, Lindsey seemed genuinely distressed.

"I called you a murderer," she whispered so none of the riders that rested on the hillside could hear.

"Well, I guess I am. We all are that rode in that charge." he said and smiled, he thought of the slaughter of so many Skavs.

"Yes, but you had good reason, I heard what those bastards have done to the convent of Eldersfield," she wept then, uncontrollably sobbing as she thought what must have happened to the nuns and all the girls in their care.

Jason sat up and pulled her close, a tear rolled down his own cheek.

"It burnt to the ground and where the fuck are all those young girls?" she wasn't quiet any more, she blurted the words out as she cried. "Then there's your wife Jacky."

"Where's your news crew?" Jason asked her gently.

Lindsey calmed herself slightly. "On top of this hill, they're packing up all the gear," she sounded like a wounded child and she wiped her eyes, dark streaks had already stained her cheeks.

Jason released Lindsey slowly, and then pulled her to her feet. "Tell them not to pack up just yet, look, we've got company," Jason pointed across the valley at a line of army all terrain vehicles heading in their direction; they flew the flag of Albion.

The government forces stopped short of the battlefield, the People's Army began to stand, more than a thousand mounted their horses and formed a line ready to charge, they awaited orders.

Breaking from the government convoy was a single small four seater vehicle which had a white flag attached to its roof.

Philip and Dave joined Jason's side. Dave had recovered his flag, it was half stained red with Farrell's blood but he had obtained a new pole.

"Looks like they want to talk," Philip said as he looked from the approaching vehicle to Jason.

"Well let's have a chat then. Dave, go tell the men to stand down," Jason ordered.

Dave ran off, shouting Jason's orders.

Jason and Philip, side by side, walked down the hill towards the vehicle that stopped a short distance from the bottom of the hill. Commissioner Kingsley and three other men stepped from the vehicle; they wore tentative smiles as they faced the leader of the People's Army.

"What are you so happy about?" Jason stopped ten metres away from the government men.

"You've just killed our enemy, that's why we're so pleased," the commissioner said.

"Have you come to arrest me?" Jason asked mocking the commissioner and the threat he'd made after the battle of mount Aamor.

Commissioner Kingsley removed the handcuffs from his belt and threw them at Jason's feet. "When you're ready de Silva, put those on," Kingsley quipped back, enjoying the banter.

"I don't think I'm quite ready for that just yet. Tell me gentlemen, why are you here?" Jason asked, looking up from the metal at his feet.

"Jason de Silva, Colonel John Blithe Dempsey, leader of the government forces," Kingsley stood back after introducing the two leaders.

"Colonel, what can I do for you?" Jason asked, as he folded his arms and faced the older man.

"We were attacked a few days ago by some of Farrell's army; we beat them back and forced them to retreat. One of my men ran off with the retreating men, he was disguised as one of them and was supposed to infiltrate Farrell's army," Colonel Dempsey looked about him at the tens of thousands of corpses that littered the battle field. "But by chance and luckily for him, the group he ran off with have joined another group of Skavs, under the leadership of a Mr Jones."

"Yeah that's some of those men we encountered trying to escape Kalverstone." Philip said and looked to Jason for confirmation.

Jason went a little pale as he realised that Reginald Smith was definitely still alive and running free.

"Those Skavs are the ones that destroyed the convent, they have hundreds of nuns and their students," Colonel Dempsey became angry as he spoke. "They are calling them the naked nunnery."

"So you have a man on the inside?" Jason asked, picturing the Smith boy as he smiled.

"He's short and skinny and limps real well. He's a soldier in my army and has volunteered for this duty, he has informed me that Mr Jones and his army, with more than ten thousand in their force are headed south west," Dempsey paused and waited for a response.

Jason stared off into space, no longer making eye contact with the men in front of him. "We've been played!" he said thinking out loud.

"So it would seem," one of the other men answered, the name on his uniform announced him as a Major Dawkins.

"Well it's time for us to go," the Colonel said as he climbed back into the vehicle.

The other two men joined him, waiting for Commissioner Kingsley who was still facing the two commanders from the People's Army.

"I'm sorry about Jacky, we heard from Dempsey's spy. Smithy brags about nothing else apparently," Kingsley climbed back into the vehicle; they wasted no time in driving back to the waiting convoy, the fuel cells at their rear lit up as they prepared to move off.

Jason returned from his trance and looked at Philip.

"We need to rest Jay, you'll kill the horses if you push 'em too hard," Philip advised, he knew what Jason was about to ask.

"Of course, you're right," Jason turned and walked back up the hill to the waiting horsemen.

Philip kept in step with Jason, thinking his leader had every intention of giving chase. "We're going to bury our dead Jason!" he said, telling Jason what he needed to know, but not what he wanted to hear.

As Philip finished speaking, a patrol rode into the camp and came to find their leaders. Philip looked up, waving the riders over, grateful for the distraction.

"Mr Robinson, Sir," the lead rider spoke, bowing his head as he did so.

"Your report?" Philip asked.

"The other corps have arrived my lord," as the rider finished speaking, as if on cue, twenty thousand pairs of feet could be heard stamping towards them as they marched. At that distance, the sound was muffled by the terrain of the hillside, but unmistakable all the same.

It was ten minutes before the head of the foot sore corps marched into camp, led by a line of three vehicles. In the lead vehicle Ethan sat grinning like a Skav who'd smoked too many drugs.

They pulled up at the side of Jason and Ethan jumped from the vehicle. "Fuck me, we heard already!" Ethan sounded excited. "That must have been a marvellous sight to behold."

"Lindsey's got it all on tape," Jason told him. "She's up on top of the hill," Jason pointed up toward where she and her colleagues had set up camp.

Jonas appeared from the line of march as the corps fragmented to find itself space on the open plains. "It is good fight yes?" the giant leader of the islanders asked smiling.

"What have you got in the lorries Jonas?" Philip asked.

"Food," Jonas replied.

Randell and Trevor rushed over to hug their brother. Philip was overwhelmed by his brothers behaviour, "You're all right," they laughed.

Jason watched, listening to the conversations as Teddy Williams came next, he was greeted by Philip and ignored by Ethan, '*You can't like everyone*,' Jason thought.

"Gentlemen, I'm tired, I'm going for some rest and hopefully some sleep," Jason made his apologies, he hadn't slept in days and although he still needed to sate his appetite for revenge for the death of his wife, he knew that he needed to lie down. Even though he had been assured that "Revenge is a great motivator," he also knew that if he didn't get rest, he wouldn't have the energy to carry on.

"Of course my lord," they said together. They watched as he walked up the hill, the spring sunshine on his back.

Jason wandered off and although the hour was still early and the sun nowhere near the horizon, the events of the day had sapped what little energy he had left. Eventually he found himself wandering into the little camp that Lindsey and her crew had set up. They had erected four large tents behind one of the ridges, apart from the rider's corps and their camp. Lindsey and her crew stopped what they were doing to watch Jason as he walked into the nearest tent without saying a word. Jason ignored their stares and went over to the first cot inside the tent and lay down on it, he did not even take off his boots.

"Are you ok?" Lindsey asked as she lifted a tent flap, the light from the sun silhouetted her slim figure. She was concerned with Jason's silence.

"I will be," he replied, staring at the tents roof and focusing on nothing. He was glad to be away from the clamour of the army for a brief time and his eyes drifted closed.

Jason's eyes opened to darkness, someone at some point had placed a blanket over him. That someone lay cuddled up to his side. The warmth and the press of Lindsey's body aroused him.

He blushed in the darkness and luckily Lindsey didn't stir, not even an involuntary twitch as he removed himself from the small cot they shared. He lifted the blankets and stole a look, he needed to see if she was clothed.

'Thank god,' he thought, she was fully clothed and he gently lowered the blanket over her, '*Just for the comfort of the thing*,' Jason was relieved, although he no longer had a spouse to share his world, he still considered himself wed and didn't wish to defile the memory of his wife.

He stepped into the night and Jason realised it was early because there was no light to speak of. Thick dark clouds filled the sky and cancelled out the glow from the moons that crossed the night. There was no light on the horizon to the east and although some of his army still moved about, most lay in tents or out in the open at their slumber.

Jason climbed up and over the ridge and his nose filled with the scent of burnt flesh. Large tracts of grass across the plains of Eldersfield had been dug up and open furnaces were set in the long shallow pits. The dead had been put to the flame after being stripped of anything useful.

"Fuck me, they've been busy," Jason said to the night air.

"So they have my lord," a voice answered from the darkness.

"Who's that?" Jason asked calmly, recognising the voice he couldn't put a face to in this light.

"It is me, my lord," and Jonathan Spalding emerged from the darkness.

"Ah, hello, you're that rich accountant," Jason rubbed his face, he was still half asleep and he looked at the long black jacket the man wore. "I see you're with Teddy Williams' Black Jackets then," Jason said, struggling to remember the man's name.

"Jonathan Spalding, my lord," the man said, sensing Jason's lapse in memory.

"I'm glad to see you still alive where so many are not," Jason said, happy to speak to someone familiar.

"Thank you my lord and the same to yourself," Jonathan replied.

"What are you doing up so late?" Jason asked.

"Guard duty," Jonathan replied.

"Every time I see you you're guarding something," Jason smiled at the man's misfortune.

"It's my turn," Jonathan replied.

Before either man could say more, the noise of an engine could be heard heading into camp, they both turned toward the noise as a vehicle headed their way and caused them to shield their eyes because they were dazzled by its headlamps.

The vehicle pulled up at their side and the window lowered, Jimmy was smiling at the two of them, "Watchya matey," the middle aged man said in greeting.

"What are you doing here? I thought you were heading back to Ramby?" Jason was puzzled; he knew Jimmy would need a good reason to travel against his orders.

"We intercepted a convoy of Recharges, ten of 'em heading north. They were stuck in the same traffic that we were. It was kinda funny, we were trying to catch 'em and they were trying to get away and all of us never exceeded five miles an hour. It was Jacob and some of his youngsters that took the initiative, they ran them down on foot," Jimmy still smiled with the humour of it all.

"Where are the vehicles then?" Jason asked, his excitement began to build, they might be able to chase down his enemy after all. "How much power is there in the Recharges' energy banks?" he asked.

"Well, the vehicles are two miles up the road where we left em, I wasn't exactly sure where you were, so we followed the tracks the army left until we saw the lights of the camp fires. As to the energy capacity, the Recharges' energy banks were all full," Jimmy leaned over his driver to point back over to the east. "I'll radio the convoy and tell them to meet us over there; the highway is about a mile that way."

Jason looked off to the east, looking for the first tell tale signs of daybreak, but as yet no light showed. "What time is it?" he asked.

"Jimmy looked to the vehicle's dashboard, as Jonathan looked at his watch. "Five o'clock," they both said at the same time.

"Get them up, get 'em up!" he ordered. "Alarm, alarm!" he walked around the camp, and bodies began rolling from their sleep and then jumping as the alarm was raised by a thousand shouting voices.

Chapter 31

Fifty miles south west of the plains of Eldersfield, Gavin Jones and his Skavite horde were resting in a small picturesque village by the name of Shepswood. The villagers had fled as the huge convoy approached and the Skavs entered the outskirts of their settlement. All but one of Shepswood's inhabitants had escaped by foot or vehicle into the nearby woodland. The one that remained was an elderly gentleman who refused to leave the home of his birth.

"I've lived here for eighty five years, ain't letting you bastards scare me off now!" he yelled and shook his fist at the Skavs as they approached his thatched cottage.

Although the Skavs mocked the little old man, they left him alone mainly because he had nothing they wanted, but also because of the man's courage, something that even the Skavs at times respected.

Kieron's jaw shook a little and sweat poured from his brow, he shivered uncontrollably although the evening spring air was particularly warm. He sat on the edge of the bed in his drug induced fever, he watched as Sharon and his middle aged nun writhed on the bed, clasped in the throes of passion in each other's arms.

"Drugs can do that," he heard himself saying, remembering the drugs he'd forced the nun to take.

He'd indulged and watched for most of the night but now he grew bored, he stepped from the bed and pulled his trousers on. Without even a backwards glance, Kieron walked from the room, opening the door onto the balcony of the mansion he and his men had occupied.

Five young Skavs leaned over the balcony looking at a scene of chaos below them. The large space below them was filled with Skavite revellers, their minds were bent by the narcotics and alcohol that Gavin Jones had provided for them. A few of the convent's students were part of the entertainment; they were dragged from one to another to be used continually by the hungry mob and the collective sexual appetite that knew no bounds.

One of the young Skavs turned from the scene below; he stood away from the balcony and faced Kieron, the muscles of his upper body twitched involuntarily.

The young Skav looked past his gang boss. "Is that off limits, boss?" he nodded into the room.

"Help yourself bredrin," Kieron said, he smiled distractedly as he tried to focus on the chandelier as it bobbed and danced in his mind.

The young Skav ran into the room, followed closely by the other four. "Safe, don't mind if I do!" one Skav yelled their thanks. They cheered as the nun cried out in ecstasy of her orgasm as the door closed behind them.

Kieron leaned on the balcony where his comrades had leaned; he watched the chaos for a while, the scene below him reminded him of a postcard like the ones you bought from the resorts next to the beach, only the scene he watched was moving.

Then the doors from the hall burst open and he turned to see Gavin Jones enter the room, followed by the young Skav Reginald Smith. "Get ready lads, we're moving out as soon as we can!" Smithy yelled and the giant bodyguard Henry loomed behind him.

'*Fuck me I'm knackered*,' Kieron thought as he re entered his room but his thoughts and mind quickly snapped back to reality.

"Fucking hell blad, what ya gone and done dat for?" he asked his five men.

The men looked at him as they held his skinny wife; her limbs were bent at awkward angles and her face was a mask of pleasure as they fucked her.

"Sorry boss," one of them said, but it was clear that he did not mean the sentiment.

"Get ya clothes on, we're movin out!" he grabbed his own shirt. "Dat was a perfectly good nun dat was," he said more wistful than angry. He looked at the naked nun for a second; the blood around her naked body still ran from the open wounds as one of the Skavs fucked her corpse. "Get ya fucking clothes on!" he yelled at his men, who were still bent on fucking his slave girl wife.

Kieron left the room, pulling his shirt over his head as he went. He turned to look back into the room, his hand on the door. "Hurry up then ya fucks!" he shouted and slammed the door shut. He felt aggrieved at losing his nun but at the same time felt a little aroused by the scene on the bed, he quickly shut the thoughts of rejoining the group out of his mind.

'Time for business, not pleasure,' he thought.

Keiron walked across the landing and down the stairs, he was one of the last remaining in the building, most of the Skavs had already left. He watched as his men were kicked awake or dragged out by their friends, in too much of a stupor to awaken. Then he walked out of the front door and in front of him stood Mr Jones and his henchmen. They looked out onto the streets with their backs to him. He followed their stares and leaned against the thick wooden frame of the outside structure. Vehicles were moving off in groups to speed up as they approached the main highway, their fuel cells blazing the trail for the next group to follow.

"What's going on boss?" Kieron asked, as another group of vehicles drove by, leaving the rural settlement.

"We're leaving Albion, we're going down to Port St Richards, we have two thousand vehicles spread out all over this town, get you and yours out as soon as possible!" Gavin Jones had to yell over the sounds of activity that tried to drown out his voice as more vehicles fuel cells whined and his Skav army stamped by.

"There's a large garrison of government troops holed up in an ancient fortress that overlooks the town's harbour, I'd estimate around two thousand full time soldiers," Gavin Jones looked at Kieron, trying to gauge his reaction.

"When do we attack?" Kieron asked enthusiastically. He did not want Reginald Smith to see any weakness that he might unintentionally display.

'*Not a coward then,*' Jones thought.

"We don't, they've agreed to give us safe passage to the port. They're even providing a large liner to take us out to sea. All we have to do is leave without attacking the town," Gavin smiled at Kieron's puzzled expression.

"Why would they agree to this?" Kieron said, fearing possible deceit.

"They stayed for the same reason that they don't want trouble, the town's population consists entirely of their families and it's a large town," Gavin Jones told him, more than happy to explain the reasons to one of his gang bosses.

"They got a militia as well, them's well armed bastards could be fuckers if there's trouble," Smithy turned away and walked down the path to the waiting vehicles.

They followed Smithy, they all wanted to flee Albion and free themselves from a war that, in truth, they and especially Reginald Smith had started and had no way of finishing to their satisfaction. Mr Jones jumped into the waiting vehicle and as he shut the door, the window opened. "I'll meet you at the docks," he said to Kieron, as his vehicle sped away, followed by twenty others.

Skavs and the females that had become hangers on were

piling into vehicles, grabbing seats wherever they could. One pulled up at Kieron's side and the door opened.

"Aiight bruv?" the driver asked with a grin.

Kieron didn't recognise any of the lads in the vehicle but he got in anyway as he saw others in his gang climbing into other vehicles. There was banging and muffled cries for help coming from the storage compartments underneath the seats.

"Don't worry blad, we got some o dem convent slags," the driver of the vehicle nodded, smiling as he engaged the power, the fuel cells burst into life as they sped off.

"Yeah, none o dem chicks is tight any more," another in the back yelled loud enough so the girls might hear him. They all laughed as the kicking increased for a few seconds as those that were trapped protested as the vehicle left town.

Long lines of men queued to climb into the vehicles. Teddy Williams' Black Jackets made one queue and parallel to their line was a corps dressed in red coats and jumpers, anything they could find that fit.

Jason watched them, surrounded by his corps commanders.

"Whose corps is that?" Jason asked.

"They mine," Randell blushed, a little embarrassed. "Some of my men suggested a uniform, they felt outdone by Philip's greens, I couldn't see how it could do any harm, especially when the idea was widely accepted with the men."

"Randells red coats," Ethan said as he watched the different shades of reds, they didn't match exactly, but they sure did look splendid. "We're turning into a proper army, we've got green cavalry and black and red infantry." he added still smiling.

"Is it really a good idea though?" Jason looked at Ethan. "I can't see how it can do much good."

"Quite the opposite, morale will go through the roof, give 'em pride and an identity and it's always useful to see your troops on the battlefield from afar," Ethan corrected Jason, still happy that his thoughts mattered.

"What do you want me to do?" Philip asked, holding the reins of his horse.

"Go back to Ramby," Ethan answered. "We're going to be travelling fast."

"Your lads won a great victory yesterday, and at such a huge expense of life, let the other corps have their glory, you deserve a rest now." Jason encouraged the leader of the green coats because he could sense Philip's disappointment.

"By your command my lord," Philip said and tried to hide his disappointment, but failed. His straight lipped expression gave away his feelings. "Try to come back alive and well all of you," he said as he mounted his horse. He looked down at them and nodded before he turned his trusted steed and walked it back towards his waiting riders.

"Go look after Dominic," Trevor said quietly, watching his brother's retreating back.

"Right let's get this show on the road," Jason brought them all back to the task at hand. "Rejoin your corps. Ethan, you're with me in the lead vehicle," Jason ordered.

"Yes Sir," they all agreed and marched off towards their men.

"Randell's red coats?" Jason frowned at Ethan, when the others were out of ear shot.

"Why not give 'em a name? Pride breeds courage and belief in one's abilities," Ethan replied.

"I suppose you're right, shall we get going then," Jason walked ahead of his advisor who fell in just behind him, they walked down the hill to join the convoy, leaving the hillside.

Mr Jones looked down at the port town, while behind him his Skavite horde lined the road, the fuel cells of their vehicles whined gently with the power plates disengaged as they idled. The town was less than a mile away, it sat in a huge geological feature that could have been an extinct volcano or the crater of an ancient impact sight, either way the grass covered bank fell away gently on all sides except for the seaward side. At the very bottom of the crater, the town of Port St Richards spread up towards them to occupy the banks as each layer of the town stood higher than the last.

In the centre of the built up area there was a small hillock of solid rock and upon that was built the town's impressive fort. Its twenty metre walls rose up above the town's lower half and formed the main feature. Its walls were lined by the garrison's soldiers who sported the white flag granted by the town's commander.

"Thank fuck they're giving us free passage," Kieron said, he stood next to Mr Jones scratching his face.

"It's hardly surprising though is it?" Mr Jones asked, a smirk appearing at the corner of his mouth. "From here, at this distance, a sniper could have a merry old time and with today's modern warfare the fort could be taken out."

"Ya know what boss, ya talk weird, ya get me bruv?" Smithy said.

"You watch your tongue or I'll have it removed," Mr Jones joined in with the pointless banter.

"What now boss?" Kieron asked, he looked back at the army as they powered down the vehicles and got out to stretch their legs.

"Well now," Mr Jones began, then thought for a moment and turned to two of his gang bosses. "You two take a hundred vehicles each, one north and the other south on the coast road and make me a road block, destroy the vehicles if you have to," the two men nodded then turned and walked back toward their gangs, shouting out orders as they went. "The rest of the vehicles I want burned out where they stand," Jones ordered.

"My vehicle?" one gang boss protested.

"It can't swim blud," Kieron said to him to the amusement of the Skavs within earshot.

When the laughter died down, Mr Jones turned to his gang bosses. "The People's Army is on the move and headed for us, we need to get on the boats down there and out to sea," he said, gauging their reaction as their expressions became grim.

"How d'you know dat guv?" a short wily young gang boss asked. "If ya dunna mind me asking."

"I've a spy in the People's Army, they're less than two hours drive away," Mr Jones, his smile gone, was deadly serious.

"Ya got an undercover Skav in the People's Army?" Smithy asked, also became serious, he was a little upset at not being party to such information.

"Yes. He infiltrated their ranks when we fought at Kalverstone," Mr Jones replied, proud of the covert placement.

The news spread quickly amongst the Skavite horde, the gang bosses ran amongst their men yelling orders. Two lines of vehicles quickly passed them and entered the town to drive both north and south along the coast road. At the rear of their convoy, vehicles had their tyres slashed and were set ablaze; it didn't take long before thousands of Skavs stood at the crater's rim, looking down at the waiting boats and their liberty.

"Shall we gentlemen?" Mr Jones said, walking off towards the harbour.

"Look there, smoke, on the horizon!" Ethan pointed out as he looked over Jason's shoulder from the rear seat of the vehicle.

The convoy heading south west was huge, one of the largest that had ever taken to Albion's roads. Its passengers, the People's Army, were bent on destruction and were only ten miles from the quarry.

"That's got to be that large port town," Jason said, gauging the position of the plumes of smoke.

"Port St Richards," Horace said, breaking his usual silence.

"They're trying to escape to sea," Ethan sounded quiet but his voice was tinged with urgency.

They entered a tiny village, the main road was dotted on either side by the houses that spread over a square mile, a gathering of people were surging in the road, apparently having no care that the convoy had to stop. Jason had Horace stopped the vehicle near the edge of the crowd, the whining lessened as the line of vehicles followed suit and powered down their fuel cells.

The first thing Jason noticed was the noise, "Skav slag, Skav slag!" the yelling was directed towards a young naked lass, she would have perhaps been beautiful but for the cuts, bruises and grazes that covered her slim figure.

Teddy Williams appeared with fifty of his Black Jackets and they made a firing line but didn't threaten the crowd. Then Jason noticed the five naked youths that swung from tree limbs at the side of the road, they had soiled themselves as the knot tightened at the back of the neck which was common in a slow hanging.

Jason watched as the crowd, who were mainly men, grabbed the young woman. A man grabbed her long blonde hair and yanked it hard. The lass went limp in their arms and Jason caught her eye. "Help me," she mouthed as the man grabbing her hair began to cut the blonde locks from her scalp, not caring if he cut her pale skin.

Jason climbed from his vehicle and watched with sick amusement as a post was driven into the ground. Its thick top had been whittled down to a point. Jason watched as the now bald girl was punched in the mouth and the crowd cheered. She looked at Jason again as he watched. "Help me, please" she mouthed again, as two large weights were attached to her legs. A large man grabbed her cheeks. "This is what happens to witches and bitches," he snarled, then he spat in her face.

The crowd had grown, more of the People's Army gathered to watch the ancient ritual of witch on a stick. The young lass screamed as she was hoisted up and blood sprayed from her broken mouth with the noise. They carried her above them, two men carried the heavy weights that she was attached to and together, they walked over to the post.

She held her face in her hands as the village elder, wearing the chains of mayorship, grabbed her bottom and spread her cheeks wide as she was lowered down and the sharpened pole entered her anus.

She screamed letting go of her face to grab at her arse as she tried to reach the pole which slipped in an inch as she struggled. The crowd cheered with delight as they let go of their prey and only held hands up to steady her if she started to overbalance.

Jason nodded but shouted at the crowd. "Now get out of the fucking road, we've got Skavs to kill!" he walked back to his vehicle and knew the Skav female would be dead by the morning.

More than nine thousand Skavs stood at the dockside; they milled about waiting to board the flotilla of ships. The largest of the ships was the 'Elven Maiden', a sleek cruise liner. The Captain and crew had been conned by the commander of the fort. They had taken the job to vehicle refugees and it was too late to cast off once they realised exactly what they had been paid to do, the Skavs were already on their decks sporting weapons and threatening the crew.

Mr Jones walked up the metal stairs to the ships nerve centre; he was followed by his huge guard Henry and twenty other guards. The ship's bridge was the highest room on the liner, with windows of toughened glass on all sides so that you could look at the entire deck. Mr Jones lifted the door's heavy iron bar and entered the bridge.

"Hello Captain," Mr Jones said as he walked onto the bridge, eyeing up the ship's wheel.

"Mr Jones I presume?" the Captain asked.

There were five members of the Captain's crew on the bridge, their uniforms were impressively clean, and the white almost glowed.

"Captain Faine, thank you for volunteering your ship," Mr Jones looked out of the window as his Skavs boarded the ship, dragging their hundreds of hostages with them, some still wore the nun's greys albeit bloodied and torn.

"No need to thank us," the Captain looked ahead and wondered what his fate might be.

Smaller boats began to draw up to the docks as both men watched, they were mainly fishing boats, their crews had volunteered to take the Skavite horde as far away from their loved ones as possible. It didn't take long before some of those were crammed with Skavs and headed out of the port and away from the dock to sit waiting in the open sea with their hulls laying low in the water.

Kieron climbed onto the bridge and also looked out towards the port town. He could just make out Smithy who had been ordered to supervise the mass embarkation of the Skavite retreat. Everything seemed to be going to plan, the uneasy truce of the town's occupying force relaxed their trigger fingers as more and more of the Skavite horde boarded the ships to leave Albion's shores.

An hour passed and they continued to board the ships with many of the sea going craft waiting just out to sea, their decks already full. The sun had long passed its zenith but still blazed. The liner was more than half full, when one of the soldiers from the fort leaned out over the crenelations above the gatehouse, he was an officer by the look of his uniform and he began yelling at the Skavs who loitered at the dockside.

Smithy stood before the gates, out in the open, gesturing rudely up at the officer. "Fuck you ya bastard, mine ya hear, they mine," he dared the officer to do something, anything.

Skavs began drawing their weapons as the soldiers stood to on the castle walls, most of the Skavs that had guns dived behind any cover they could find and there was instant tension between the two forces.

"I said release the sisters and the children in their care or we will open fire!" the young officer had watched as some of the naked nuns had been dragged onto the ships. His resolve had finally collapsed in his disgust for the crimes which were being perpetrated before him and his revulsion overcame his orders.

Two hundred females of varying ages, dressed in rags or nothing but a collar around the neck were being led towards the cruise liner. The Skavs leading them hurried them along as the argument between Smithy and the officer began. They were soon at the side of the liner and being forced up the gangplank into a life of sexual slavery.

Smithy started to back away from the castle's wall, the clicking of cocking weaponry sounded all around and before him. The men leading the hostages toward the ship yanked on the leads, choking women that didn't complain, already resigned to their worthless fate. They paused at the gangplanks as the government soldiers on the walls levelled their rifles at the Skavs on the docks.

"Get 'em on board," Smithy yelled.

"Stay your hands," the officer yelled in direct contradiction to his opposite number.

Smithy dived behind some crates and pulled his weapon free of its holster. "Get 'em on the fucking boat!" yelling his order, he turned and aimed his revolver at the young officer and fired four times.

By the time the fourth shot was fired all hell had broken loose, both sides fired and bullets ricocheted off the walls and the old cobbled stone quay. The young officer had dived behind cover and the slaves almost ran onto the liner in fear for their lives. As half of the hostages made it onto the liner the other half struggled for balance as the liner began pulling away from the docks.

The liner creaked for a moment, straining on its thick

mooring ropes, and then they snapped as the liner powered away from the dock. The nuns and girls still on the gangplanks fell into the water.

"Fuck!" Smithy yelled as he realised that he was trapped and all around him the bullets fell like deadly rain and so did his Skavs. Small arms fire exploded from the deck of the liner, its tall decks almost level with the height of the fort's lowest walls.

An artillery piece had been pointed at the liner the entire time and now its crew rushed to fire it. They loaded its shell into its huge barrel and a rocket propelled grenade, fired from the deck of the liner in a lucky shot hit the cannon and enveloped its crew in a fiery death just before the cannon exploded and destroyed part of the ancient fort's wall as its ordnance blew up.

There was a brief respite to the firing and Smithy took advantage of the lull and jumped up to run away from the fort as fast as he could. He was joined by every Skav on the dock that still breathed. There were three thousand of them and they began to die as the bullets began to rain down on them from the fort once more. Then Smithy was in amongst the buildings and the relative safety of the town. *'Thank fuck for that,'* he thought, panting and he turned to watch the liner as it moved away from the docks and turned towards the open ocean.

"We need to get out of this town!" he yelled at the Skavs who clustered around him.

"We destroyed all the vehicles," one skinny and dirty young Skav said with panic written in his eyes.

Reginald Smith looked around him; he wracked his mind for an escape route as the ridge at the top of the crater filled with people.

"No!" Smithy screamed, as Jason de Silva stood half a mile away and stared straight into his eyes. He looked wild with rage; the People's Army about him were dressed in red and their dragon flags flapped in the wind blowing in from the sea.

"This way lads, fall back this way!" Smithy yelled, fleeing

south from both de Silva and the fort.

They fled, tightly packed, through the narrow cobbled streets. Small shuttered windows slammed open above them as the town's militia began shooting from the windows and rooftops above them. The Skavs didn't have chance to return fire as they ran for their lives. Many dropped their weapons in pure panic, knowing their end was at hand.

Then they were out of the town and Smithy ran at the head of his fleeing force that dwindled by the heart beat as they were shot and killed by their pursuers.

"C'mon lads!" he panted, drained of energy as he ran up the south road to head away from the town and out of the crater. Smithy looked over his shoulder, nearly a thousand Skavs ran with him and the rest fought in the town or ran north up the coast road, fleeing for their lives. The Skavs that fought in the town were being cut to pieces, caught in a horrible cross fire of the town's soldiers, militia and People's Army as they all lent a hand in the death of his fellows.

He looked left and the banners of the People's Army fluttered as the People's Army ran parallel with him. de Silva came closer as the ridge line ran towards the road. Smithy felt his heart beating faster as he turned from the road near the top of the hill.

"Bastard!" he heard de Silva yelling.

Then they crested the hill, and ran along the cliff's edge, a line of young men and women blocked his way. They couldn't be older than eighteen but there were thousands of them. Their leader was a tall, well muscled youth and he was grinning with delight. He drew his sword and charged and his force followed him, screaming their battle cries.

Then they were all around them, his Skavs fought for their lives but they were outnumbered and Smithy still looked for any possible escape route.

Suddenly, the pain he felt surprised him and the sword point that burst out of the front of his thigh as he looked down surprised him more. He stood shocked as the metal grated on the bone and the holder of the blade twisted it slightly to cause maximum hurt.

"Where's my wife?" Jason de Silva yelled from behind him, his breath was warm against his ear and Smithy was surprised again at the detail he experienced.

"She's dead," he heard himself answering.

"I know she's dead, I saw the pictures," de Silva yelled and he stabbed Smithy in the lower back, to one side of his spine with the dagger that he held in his free hand.

Jason de Silva withdrew the dagger and the sword from his flesh at the same time and Smithy dropped to his knees screaming in agony. Hands grabbed at him and pinned him to the ground. He felt his trousers being pulled down around his ankles. A warm hand pulled at his penis and he looked down at the rough hand and followed its arm up into the face of Jason de Silva. The leader of the People's Army smiled at him as he showed him the sharp dagger, then Smithy watched as de Silva cut his penis slowly, howling like a madman. Smithy watched in a dazed shock as blood, his blood, spurted from where his penis had been. Then de Silva stood, covered in his blood and he flung the dismembered lump of flesh over the cliff into the waiting sea and de Silva's people let him go.

"I guess you won't be raping anybody else then," de Silva said and smiled. He looked almost friendly, even as he stepped forward to push his knife slowly into Smithy's belly.

It was Jason's turn to imagine the fate of his nemesis, as Dave the Bannerman had done at the end of the battle on the Plains and he stared into the distance and willed Smithy's spirit to stand at the side of him.

'*Not a good day*,' Smithy thought, as he stood and looked out to sea.

A little old man appeared at his side, he looked pale and almost see-through, his clothes were white and he sported a ridiculously long white beard.

"You, fractured soul, you can't stay here," the old timer said.

"Fuck you," Reginald Smith replied and a tunnel of water rose up from the depths below, its black and crusted foam enveloped the dead Skav as it dissolved his spirit and dragged his soul down to the darkest of waters.

Jason stood at the edge of the cliff, looking out at the flotilla of ships that headed out to sea; the liner's horn gave long mournful blasts as the remaining Skavs were flung off the cliff to their waiting death below.

"What now my lord, do we give chase?" Randell asked, appearing at Jason's side.

"What with? They got all the boats." Ethan pointed out to Randell as he appeared at the opposite side of Jason. He had Skavite blood staining his clothes.

"What is it that drives us, why is human nature so cruel?" Jason asked the sea, as those around him stopped, seemingly listening for the sea to answer back.

"Mankind is long overdue its next evolutionary change, let's see if we can tame the beast within and bring about that change," Jason shouted.

And as if in answer, lightning flashed out to sea, and huge waves crashed against the cliffs. Unbeknown to Jason de Silva and his people, his call had been heard.

Lightning Source UK Ltd.
Milton Keynes UK
UKOW031502291011

181148UK00002B/4/P